"A bright tapestry of love and life . . .
in Mrs. Keyes' most important novel."
—*Boston Herald*

BRENT WINSLOW: A pioneer who heard the call of
adventure, he forged a Southern empire for himself and his family.

MARY WINSLOW: Devoted to Brent and with courage to match his own, she followed him to the
new land where fortunes could be made.

LAVINIA WINSLOW: Their beautiful daughter, she
dared not defy tradition even though she loved
her husband's cousin.

CLAUDE VILLAC: Lavinia's husband, his constancy
had won her hand in marriage, but he would
never win her heart.

FLEEX PRIMEAUX: A wild rogue, he loved Lavinia
in his own way and brought tragedy to the lives
of those who loved him.

Over one and a half million copies of BLUE CAMEL-
LIA have been sold worldwide to fans of the remarkable Frances Parkinson Keyes. A distinguished
author whose novels sell in the millions, she has
written such critical and popular successes as *The
River Road, Came a Cavalier, Joy Street,* and *Dinner at Antoine's*—all of them national best sellers.

BLUE CAMELLIA was originally published
by Julian Messner, Inc.

Books by Frances Parkinson Keyes

Fiction

All That Glitters*
Also the Hills
Blue Camellia*
Came a Cavalier*
The Career of David Noble
Crescent Carnival*
Dinner at Antoine's*
Fielding's Folly
The Great Tradition*
Honor Bright
Joy Street*
Lady Blanche Farm
The Old Gray Homestead
Parts Unknown
Queen Anne's Lace
The River Road
The Safe Bridge
Senator Marlowe's Daughter

Nonfiction

Along a Little Way
Capital Kaleidoscope
The Grace of Guadalupe
Letters from a Senator's Wife
Silver Seas and Golden Cities
The Sublime Shepherdess: The Life of St. Bernadette of Lourdes
Written in Heaven: The Life of the Little Flower of Lisieux

Poetry

The Happy Wanderer

Juvenile

Once on Esplanade

*Published by POCKET BOOKS

Rose

Frances Parkinson Keyes

Blue
Camellia

PUBLISHED BY POCKET BOOKS NEW YORK

BLUE CAMELLIA

Julian Messner edition published 1957

POCKET BOOK edition published January, 1975

*Plan of farm and plan of
maisonette by Thomas O. Nehrbass.*

**This POCKET BOOK edition includes every word contained
in the original, higher-priced edition. It is printed from
brand-new plates made from completely reset, clear, easy-to-
read type. POCKET BOOK editions are published by POCKET
BOOKS, a division of Simon & Schuster, Inc., 630 Fifth
Avenue, New York, N.Y. 10020. Trademarks registered
in the United States and other countries.**

Standard Book Number: 671-78756-X.
Library of Congress Catalog Card Number: 57-5083.
Front cover illustration by Bob Berran.

Printed in the U.S.A.

To
Mary Alice Fontenot
whose suggestion that I should visit a rice mill
and
whose subsequent helpfulness, hospitality,
confidence and affection
sowed the seed which resulted in
Blue Camellia

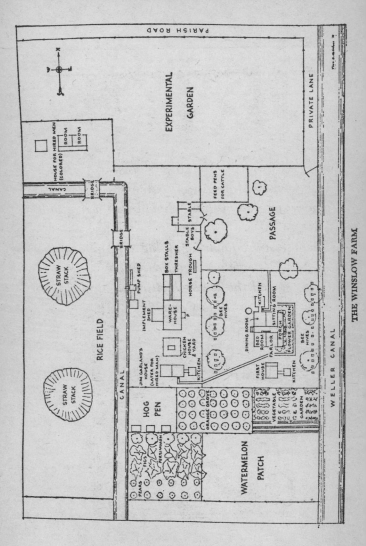

THE WINSLOW FARM

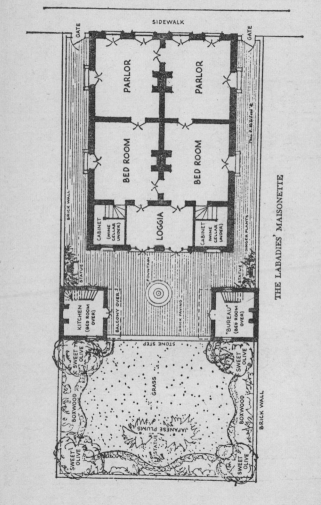

THE LABADIES' MAISONETTE

PROLOGUE

"The Piece in the Paper"

MARCH, 1886

The snow, which had fallen quietly at first, was now pelting against the windowpanes, driven by a wicked wind; the storm was rapidly assuming the proportions of a blizzard. Mary Winslow replenished the kitchen stove, and then bent over the woodbox a second time, filling her arms with a supply for the airtight in the bedroom. As she straightened up again, she surveyed the woodbox with growing concern; it was already more than half empty and she would have to make another trip to the woodshed in the very near future. It was bitterly cold there, and the snow drifted in through the ill-patched roof and around the sills of the ill-fitting doors; it had done so, even in the morning, before the wind had risen; now it would be coming in great gusts. However, it was not the cold and the snow and the wind that caused her concern; she was strong and healthy and young, she could take the weather as it came. But Brent, her husband, whom she loved with all her heart and soul, had been critically ill with pneumonia; and though their doctor had told her that the sick man was practically out of danger now, he had added cautiously, "That is, if he doesn't catch cold again. You'll have to keep the house at an even temperature, or he may have a chill. And that could be disastrous, at this stage."

So far, Mary had kept Brent's room at an even temperature, though some of her beloved plants had frozen in the kitchen; but she did not know how much longer she could do so, especially in such weather. The woodshed had been chockablock in the autumn; but its contents were disappearing fast and this was only March. Even with a normal spring, there might well be two more months of cold weather. And nothing so far pointed to a normal spring,

9

this untimely blizzard least of all. Besides, wood was hard to come by; she had supplemented their stock as well as she could with corncobs, but those did not go far or last long in such weather, and coal was prohibitively expensive.

She had pressed her lips together hard and shaken her head as she stood looking down at the half-empty wood-box and realizing what it meant. But her head was high again, and she was smiling cheerfully when she went into the bedroom with her load. Brent was well covered up, she was relieved to see that; while he had been delirious, he had threshed around and thrown off the bedclothes faster than she could keep them tucked in. Now that the fever had left him, he was quieter, and though he sometimes protested at the number of blankets Mary piled on him, he did not actively prevent her from keeping them drawn up to his chin. Moreover, since he had been permitted to have his pillows arranged in any way that suited him, his complaints had been less vehement. There were two of them under his head now, very white against his tumbled dark hair and bristly beard. He looked gratefully up at his wife and returned her smile rather ruefully.

"I hate to see you toting a great armful of wood like that, Mary, just to keep me comfortable. But it won't be long now before I'll be doing the toting and you can stay abed and rest, if you're a mind to."

"You know I'd never have a mind to unless I was sick, and I don't expect to be sick."

"No, you leave that to me."

"I didn't mean it that way, Brent."

"I know you didn't. Just the same, you're getting tuckered out, or you would be, if it was any woman but you. How you've stood it all this while, doing your work and mine, too, and nursing me at the same time. . . ."

"It's only what any woman would do, under the circumstances."

"Maybe you think so. I know better. And I know you're getting tuckered out. Or else you're worrying about something. What is it, Mary?"

Without replying, she opened the door of the airtight, raked the fire expertly and began to put the wood, which she had previously laid on the floor beside it, over the still radiant fire, a stick at a time. When she closed the door, the fresh fuel was already burning briskly. She dusted off her hands and then, crossing to the washstand, poured a little water into the basin from the smaller pitcher and

10

scrubbed them thoroughly. After that, she turned to the neat array of bottles, glasses and spoons that stood on the dresser, flanked by two small pots of begonias, and began to measure out medicine.

"What would you do to me if I said I wouldn't take that unless you'd answer my question?" Brent asked teasingly.

"I'd say that until now I'd always supposed I'd married a sensible man, not a peevish child."

He laughed and accepted the glass she handed him. "All right, you win. But you really don't need to answer. Because I know you are worrying. Only I'm not sure what about. Is it because I'm not getting well fast enough to suit you? Or because you think Lavinia's getting spoiled at her grandmother's? Or what?"

I suppose I'll have to tell him about the wood, Mary said to herself. *I'd lie to him and say it was Lavinia I was worrying about, which of course it isn't—she isn't getting spoiled. She might be with my folks, but not with his. And he'd know right away I was lying, just as he knew I was worrying about something. If I could just keep him from worrying a few days longer—the doctor said in another week.* . . . She took the empty glass from him. "I'm going to set this in the kitchen sink with scalding water in it," she said. "Then I'll come back and stay with you a while, if you'd like to have me. There isn't anything else I need to do right now. But I wish you weren't so bound and determined to talk about this, that and the other thing—it's liable to start you coughing again. Why don't you let me read to you for a while? Carl Rivers brought the mail this morning, before the storm got so bad. You were having a nice nap right then, so I didn't bring it into the bedroom. It was just the paper and a seed catalog and an advertisement for patent medicine, anyway. It doesn't look as if we needed to be thinking of seeds right off, and Dr. Nelson doesn't hold with patent medicines. But there might be something in the paper. . . ."

She picked it up and glanced through the brief items of local and national news. None of them seemed likely to interest an invalid. Then her eyes fell on a startling announcement.

LAND BUYERS!

— From The —

NORTH.

a

WEST. n EAST.

d

SOUTH.

Will receive prompt attention by doing
their business with

W. W. DUSON & BRO.

REAL ESTATE AND COLLECTION

AGENT.

I have many fine tracts of improved and unimproved
lands in the parishes of St. Landry, Lafayette and Vermil-
ion. All these lands

ARE THE RICHEST

in this section and will produce abundant yields.

All visitors coming to this region will be shown the
surrounding country

FREE OF CHARGE

Underneath this announcement, which was set in bold-
face, was an article in smaller print. Mary read on with increasing absorption.

The southwest portion of Louisiana is a region of
undulating prairies traversed by heavily wooded
streams called bayous. The soil is productive and fertile and is especially well adapted to stock raising, the

herbage on the prairies being excellent for fattening the herds of cattle which roam at will through the land, winter and summer, without shelter. The soil is clay loam, and bears fine crops of corn, cotton, rice, oats, cane, sweet and Irish potatoes and hay, while fruits of every species common to the United States and tropical climates can easily be grown. The bayous or streams are bordered with fine timber, principally oak, pine, cypress, hickory, gum and ash. In plain view from the car windows of the passing trains of the Southern Pacific Railroad is an orange grove which attracts considerable attention from strangers passing through the country by rail.

The climate is mild, healthful and salubrious. Work is possible in the open fields twelve months in the year. The rainfall is always abundant and droughts unknown and there are few failures of crops from any source. Diseases caused by cold weather and sudden changes are rare and in many districts unknown.

In fine, Southwest Louisiana has everything the immigrant can ask for, who seeks a comfortable home where his labor will prove profitable to him—cheap lands, a fertile soil, a healthy climate, large and profitable crops.

"I guess there *was* something in the paper," Brent remarked, puzzled by his wife's long and preoccupied silence. "Mind letting me in on the news?"

"It isn't news, exactly. But—well, just listen to this!" Slowly and carefully, she read aloud to him the passages which had so amazed her. "It's funny, isn't it, that there should be an ad and a story like that in one of our papers?" she said, when she had reached the end. "Louisiana —why, that must be nearly a thousand miles away! Whoever'd be interested, around here, in Louisiana land or house lots?"

"The man who put that ad in the paper must have thought someone would be. Ads cost money."

Brent made the remark objectively, as if stating an undeniable fact which was, nevertheless, no concern of his. Mary was not sure whether he had found the piece in the paper tedious or whether he was getting tired. The sound made by the wind had now risen to a howl and the snow, driven against the windowpanes, was packed so high and hard against them that the room was growing dark, though it was not yet four o'clock. Mary rose, lighted the kerosene lamp that stood at the farther end of the dresser, moved the little begonia plants, so that they would not get overheated, beyond the medicines, and put more wood on the fire.

"I guess I'd better light the lamp in the kitchen, too, and have another look at the cookstove."

"All right, but don't stay out there long, will you?"

"Just long enough to do what I said and see to your broth."

"We won't have any chickens left, if you keep on feeding me broth, Mary. Then what'll we do for eggs?"

"I've used mostly the old roosters so far."

"And we ought to be selling more milk."

"Who's worrying now? You haven't drunk enough for me to see any difference in what we've sold."

"Then you haven't had enough yourself!"

"Brent, will you stop taking on so? You seem to have forgotten that Lavinia's getting all her milk at her grandmother's! That makes a big difference, I can tell you. She's the heavy drinker."

"Well, a little girl eight years old ought to drink a lot of milk."

Mary went out into the kitchen and Brent lay still, conscientiously refraining from moving the bedclothes, and thinking about his wife and child, but mostly about his wife. Lavinia, who had been named for his mother—a disbeliever in nicknames—was a sturdy little girl, whose flaxen hair was already long and thick enough to make two sizable braids, whose big blue eyes looked trustfully and contentedly out on a pleasant and comfortable world, and whose plump person, rosy cheeks and abundant vitality all bespoke her thriving condition. He had no reason to worry about her and he did not. Moreover, being as honest with himself as he was with others, he admitted that he had not really missed her very much during her absence, which had been indicated by his illness. He loved his daughter, of course; however, he loved his wife even more, and he had enjoyed being completely alone with her again, after eight years when Lavinia had always been with them and when much of that time she had logically laid claim to the major part of her mother's attention. But he had not enjoyed being dependent on Mary. It was the man's prerogative to care for his wife, not to lie helpless when she ministered to him, as if he had been her child instead of her husband. . . .

Mary came into the room and sat down again in the

rocker, but she did not resume her reading. The one kerosene lamp did not give enough light for that and usually, at dusk, she busied herself with knitting during the brief periods when she sat still. This time, however, she did not even pick up her work bag, but clasped her hands together loosely in her lap.

"Tired, aren't you, Mary?"

"No, I keep telling you I'm not. But it's almost time to go out to the barn. Matter of fact I think I ought to go early. The storm's getting worse every minute and the drifts are bound to be bad. I'll have to shovel my way through some of them."

Brent did not answer. Most of all, he resented the fact that Mary was doing the outside chores. Housework, of course, was a normal occupation for a woman and Mary had always made light of it, saying that cooking and cleaning, washing and sewing for three persons was so easy that she could have done it with one hand tied behind her. Brent had not objected, either, when she took over the poultry yard because she "did not have enough to keep her busy," although she spent more time "fussing" over her flower garden than any other women he knew. But the livestock was something else again. He was alternately humiliated and enraged by the consciousness that she was milking the cows and bedding down the horses. It did no good for Mary to remind him she had read that in many parts of the world women did all the milking, or to ask him whether he had forgotten that her father raised horses and that she herself had never been happier than when she was making the rounds of the stables with him. Brent's rather curt reply had been that whatever they did elsewhere, women did not milk the cows in Monroe, Illinois, and no matter what her father had done and was doing, her husband always had done and always would do something quite different, and liked her to keep out of the barns. At least, this had been his reply when the matter was first discussed. They had long since ceased to discuss it, because he realized, as well as she did, that she would have to take over the barn work during his illness, whether he wanted her to or not. Their nearest neighbor—with the exception of Mary's people, who, though close to them had their hands full—lived three miles away, and had all he could do on his own farm.

Brent was thankful that at least she had not been obliged to bother with the bees. They were hibernating, in their well-protected hives, covered with burlap and located

15

where they would be sheltered from the north wind, in the angle between the henhouse and the barn. Brent loved his bees and never permitted them to starve to death in the fall, as some of his neighbors did, to save feeding them through the long cold winter months. He saw to it that they had plenty of honey left for themselves before he wrapped them up and left them to their long sleep. Then, in the spring, he released them with joy and spent long happy hours straddling the hives and watching the bees at their work. There was mutual understanding and affection between them and him; they never stung him and when they swarmed around him they seemed to make him one with them. But in Mary's case it was different. She had to tie a knitted fascinator around her head, even in the warmest weather, when she went near the hives, because the bees got in her hair and stung her. They stung her hands and ankles, too, if she did not watch out. Nothing she did and nothing Brent did could change this antagonism, which was mutual. If his illness had come in the summer, Mary would have suffered terribly, because of the bees.

Brent turned slightly on his pillows, still without disarranging the bedclothes, and looked at his wife searchingly. She had said that she was not tired, and he knew she was very strong; if she had not been, she never could have carried, so long and so steadily, the load with which she had been burdened. But even if the gleam from the oil lamp was not bright enough to read by, it was still bright enough for him to see that she was much thinner than she had been; while the glow from the airtight—now red hot —reflected in her face, did not deceive him as to her own color; she was much paler, too. Normally, there was a strong resemblance between Mary and Lavinia, though the little girl was so much fairer and plumper. It did not trouble Brent because Mary's hair was no longer flaxen, but a soft brown, or that her cheeks were no longer the color of ripe apples, but of wild roses, or that her arms and hands were slender instead of chubby; those changes had begun in adolescence and he had seen them take place, for he and Mary had been childhood friends and youthful sweethearts; the gradual transformation had made her more, rather than less, beautiful in his sight. He was proud, too, of her careful grooming and trim figure. She had never "let herself go," like so many farmers' wives, who left their hair in curlpapers, discarded their corsets and went sloppily around their household tasks or sat slumped in

16

their rockers; she had always been neat and pleasing to look at from top to toe, moving with easy swiftness and sitting erect at the head of his table. But this new thinness, this new pallor, had nothing to do with natural changes or orderly habits; they came from overwork and they were intensified by anxiety. If he had been doing his job, if he had kept well, Mary would not have been overworked or anxious.

"I guess I'd better be getting under way," she said, rising from her chair with a slowness which still further betrayed her fatigue. "Is there anything I can do for you before I go."

"It's a long time since I've read anything myself. I've a notion I'd like to look at the paper for a while. You might hand it to me and set the lamp a little nearer."

"I'll move the medicine bottles out of the way and bring in the lamp from the kitchen. That'll help some. But promise you won't keep on trying to read if it tires you."

"I promise, Mary."

"And you must let me put that old wool jersey on you if you're going to get uncovered."

"All right. Mind you bundle yourself up, too."

She made the indicated arrangements for his well-being and bent over to kiss his forehead. He lifted his weak arms and held her tight for a moment while neither spoke. Then she went out to the kitchen and he could hear her moving about, putting more wood on the fire, shifting the position of the teakettle and the soup kettle on the stove, stamping her feet into her rubber boots, taking the snow shovel from its corner. Then the kitchen door slammed behind her, and the only sounds came from the wind and the snow and the timbers of the house, creaking in the cold.

It was not much of a house. If it had been, it would not have creaked so, even in a storm as bad as this one. When he and Mary were married, Brent had expected that within a few years they would be able to have a better one; instead, they had not even been able to keep this one in proper shape. Outside, it had once been painted yellow and, with bright green blinds, it had been cheerful and cozy looking. But the yellow paint was mostly peeled off now, leaving the clapboards a dingy gray; and in winter, when the double windows were put on, the blinds had to come off; so, after a while, Brent had stopped putting them back again every spring, because there was so much else to do at that time of year, what with the plowing and planting and the new calves and pigs and the chickens and the bees. The house had no front piazza, just a small side porch toward the rear, leading into the kitchen; and though Mary tried hard to keep this small porch neat, it was inevitably cluttered with the utensils for which there was no space anywhere else. The side door, leading from the porch to the kitchen, was the one by which they habitually went in and out; indeed, the front door, which led into a small, narrow passageway, was so seldom used that when a comparative stranger came there seeking admittance, it was hard to unlock, and stuck when Mary tried to open it. The parlor door was apt to stick, too, because the parlor was hardly ever used, either; it would have been one more room to heat, and there was no way of heating the passage; for a large part of the year it was so cold you could see your breath in it. The dining room was not used much, either, though that could get some heat from the kitchen; it really did not need an airtight, except in the very worst weather. But then, Brent and Mary and Lavinia did not need the dining room. They lived, moved, breathed and had their being in the kitchen and the two bedrooms off it, both small, but one slightly larger than the other. There was running cold water in the kitchen sink, so Mary did not have to draw it from a well, as many neighboring women did; but there were no other conveniences. Hot water for bathing and washing clothes and dishes was heated in the teakettle and in the reservoir at the back of the stove. The wooden washtubs stood on the side porch, except on Mondays, when they were brought into the kitchen, and the hat-shaped tin bathtub stood behind them, except on Saturdays in the wintertime and Wednesdays and Saturdays in the summertime, when this was brought into the kitchen, too. There was also a small painted tin foot tub, with a tall tin pitcher to match, in the larger bedroom, where they complemented the china pitcher and bowl and mugs on the washstand; Mary customarily used this foot tub and pitcher to provide supplementary baths for herself and for Lavinia, who had no complements to her small washstand equipment. During Brent's illness, Mary had also used the tin foot tub for his bath water; it was heavier and harder to lift than the china washbasin, but it was less likely to break; and the toilet set, decorated with a floral pattern, had been one of their wedding presents. She would have felt very badly if it had become incomplete through breakage and she had then

18

been obliged to substitute a plain white bowl for the flowered one.

Mary's people were more prosperous than Brent's and they had given her a number of nice things when the young couple were married: a plentiful supply of household linen, table china, including a set in the moss rose pattern for best, some thin, pointed teaspoons that were made of solid silver, besides plenty of good silver plate, including even a tea set, the rosewood furniture upholstered in horsehair for the parlor, and of course kitchen pots and pans and mixing bowls. They had offered to do more. They had some furniture in their attic, which the first Garlands, who pioneered on the Illinois prairie, had brought with them from New England in covered wagons: a big tester bed with carved posts, a secretary with little slides that pulled out of hiding when you wanted to set candles on them, a gate-leg table adjustable to several sizes, a highboy with brass knobs, a tall clock with a brass face. Brent and Mary were welcome to all these, her parents said. But Brent had declined to accept them, partly—though he did not say so—because, of course, nobody used old things like that any more, though he could understand why the Garlands clung to them out of sentiment; and partly—this he did say—because he wanted to buy some of the household gear himself, not to feel beholden to his wife's folks for everything. So he had purchased golden oak for the dining room and the nuptial chamber and, a year later, a painted crib for Lavinia and, a few years later still, a bedroom set for her, too. He had also bought pictures to go with the furniture: "A Yard of Roses" for Mary, "A Yard of Pansies" for Lavinia, because they both loved flowers so; and two Currier and Ives prints, showing farm scenes, one in summer and one in winter, because farm life was what he liked himself, though these prints both so greatly idealized the farm life which Brent himself knew that he hardly recognized it as depicted here. He had been very proud of everything when he bought it, and Mary had given every indication of being pleased with it, too. She had never said since then that she was not, either, and Brent could not imagine, if Mary was satisfied, why he should have taken such a dislike to their furniture and their pictures. But as he lay in the bed with the plain high headboard and the equally plain footboard, not quite so high, and glanced from his paper to the washstand with its flowered toilet set and the dresser with its blurred mirror, he felt that they were hid-

19

eous and wished that he need never look at either of them again.

Telling himself resolutely that this was only because he had been imprisoned with them too long, he tried to think about his outbuildings, his stock and his land, instead of his house and its contents; but the thought of these proved no more cheering. Not that they were any worse than those of his neighbors, with a few unusually prosperous exceptions; but one of his sheds had collapsed in a previous storm, because the roof was not strong enough to stand the weight of the snow, and the barn was crowded in consequence. The herd comprised only grade cattle, low grade at that. The land needed more artificial fertilizer than he could afford, and a hard shower of hail, as untimely as the present blizzard, had flattened his oats the previous year, just as they were ready to harvest, making his crop a total loss. He was a farmer by tradition, upbringing and experience, and it had never occurred to him that he might be anything else. It did not occur to him now. But for the first time he began to wonder whether it would be possible to farm under different conditions, in a milder climate, and to try a different kind of produce.

Well, it would do no good to lie there brooding. He picked up the paper, which Mary had put within easy reach, and, after looking at the local news, which he found dull, as she had thought he would, turned to the piece which had caused her such astonishment. It was easier for him to digest this, reading it to himself, than when she had read it aloud to him. But the effort tired him, as Mary had foreseen that it would and, even with the two lamps, it hurt his eyes. So finally he laid the paper down beside him. But he did not stop thinking about what he had read. There were a few books in the parlor, among them the geographies that he and Mary had studied from in school; he was sorely tempted to go and get them and see what they said about Louisiana. But he knew he was not strong enough to walk so far, that he might collapse on the way; also that it would be a poor return for Mary's steadfastness if he took a risk that might bring on a relapse which, besides what it would mean for him, would mean more hard work and anxiety for her.

It seemed a long time before he heard the kitchen door slam again and felt the momentary draft of cold air which, try as she might, Mary could not keep out of the bedroom when one of the outside doors was opened. She called to him cheerfully: nothing was wrong in the barn;

the reason she had not come back sooner was because the drifts were so bad; she had had to shovel and shovel. But she was sure the stock was not suffering any. He noticed she did not mention the poultry and he could not help wondering about the henhouse until she added, of her own accord, that she had brought some of the chickens into the shed and that if the storm kept up, or it grew any colder, she would bring them into the kitchen. She would be in to fix his fire and bring him his broth right away.

"I suppose you'll have to fix the fire, or it'll go out. But couldn't the broth wait? I want to talk to you about something."

"No, it's time you had some nourishment and afterward you ought to go to sleep."

"I shan't go to sleep, Mary, until I've told you what I have on my mind."

She realized that he was in earnest and did not make the mistake of insisting. When she had mended the two fires and given him his medicine again, she started to pick up her knitting, before sitting down in the rocker beside him. He held up a deterring hand.

"Just a minute, Mary. I want you should go into the parlor and see if you can find my old geography book—or yours."

"Have you any preference? I know just where to lay my hands on both."

"All right then, bring both. They might say something different."

"About what?"

"About Louisiana. I want you to read me what both of them have to say about Louisiana."

"Why, Brent?"

"I can tell you why better after you've finished reading to me."

She looked at him in a puzzled way and hesitated, as if she were on the point of asking another question. But she did not actually voice it and, after a moment, she disappeared into the cold parlor and presently returned with two battered old books under her arm.

"Do you care which I read from first?"

"Well, suppose you begin with mine. It's a little older. Yours might be more up to date."

"Yes, all of three years!"

She laughed and opened the smaller of the two dilapidated books, holding it close to the dresser, so that she could get as much light as possible from the oil lamp.

"Louisiana isn't listed by itself in the Table of Contents," she said. "But there's a section devoted to '*The Southern States*.'"

"Well, read me that."

Mary turned the pages until she came to a print, entitled "A Crevasse," which graphically depicted a floating palace proceeding at full steam down a swollen river, cluttered with derelict houses and bordered by washed-out banks, where a few men seemed to be struggling to no avail amidst driftwood and the stark limbs of trees. "'*Seven of the Southern States, Arkansas and Tennessee —Lesson I*,'" she read.

"'*1. The map following this lesson represents seven of the Southern States, with Arkansas and Tennessee.*

'*Arkansas and Tennessee are Western States.*

'*2. The Southern States occupy the southeastern part of the United States, and, with the exception of West Virginia, lie along the coast of the Atlantic Ocean and Gulf of Mexico.*

'*3. South of Virginia, much of the country is low and level and in many places sandy, or marshy.*

'*Many of the sandy districts are covered with forests of pitch-pine, and are called pine-barrens. The marshy lands are chiefly near the coast and along the rivers. They are valuable for raising rice.*

'*4. The rivers of this section sometimes rise higher than the neighboring land. Banks of earth, called* levees, *are thrown up along the sides of the Mississippi River, in Louisiana, to prevent that great stream from overflowing the country.*

'*The river, however, sometimes breaks through the levee, doing immense damage. Such a break is called a* crevasse. *The engraving is a representation of one.*

'*5. Cotton is the most important product of the Southern States.*

'*Indian corn is raised in great quantities in all of them.*

'*6. Labor in the Southern States is performed, in a great measure, by Negroes, who form a large portion of the population.*'"

She stopped and looked toward Brent. "Are you interested?" she inquired.

"Very much. '*Labor is performed, in a great measure, by Negroes,*' that's what you said, isn't it, Mary?"

"That's what the book said. Do you want me to go on?"

"Yes, please."

"Lesson II—North Carolina, South Carolina and Georgia are especially rice growing states.

'South Carolina produces more rice than any other state.

'The Palmetto tree grows abundantly in this state.' . . . There's a picture of a palmetto tree—I mean a picture that belongs in the book—and someone has pasted a picture of a little girl in beside it."

"I did. I remember doing it. I thought the picture looked something like you and I thought the palmetto tree looked better with that other picture beside it. I never thought I'd care much for the palmetto trees. But I wonder why South Carolina produces more rice than any other state?"

"The geography doesn't say. It says that Georgia produces more sweet potatoes than any other state and it doesn't say why that is, either. Then it goes on to say that Florida has many unhealthy marshes and that in Louisiana sugar cane is raised. That's practically all it says about the southern states. Do you want me to read what it says about the western states?"

"Tennessee and Arkansas? No, I don't care about those. Let's see what your geography says about Louisiana."

Mary laid down one book and picked up another. "This one groups the states differently," she said. "There's a section called *'Nature of South Atlantic and Gulf States . . . North Carolina has no large cities,'*" she reported, reading at random. . . . *"'In the mountains of Georgia are the richest gold mines east of the Rocky Mountains. . . . Florida contains no large cities. . . . In the northern part of Alabama are quarries of fine marble. . . . Texas has no large cities. . . . Austin, capital of the state, is a small town situated on the middle course of the Colorado River, Galveston is the principal commercial city of Texas. It is situated on a fine bay. . . . New Orleans is the only large city of Louisiana. . . .'"*

"Well, we seem to have come to a large city at last. But actually I don't care so much about those. What else does the book have to say about the nature of those states you're roaming around in?"

"'These sections include the warmest parts of the United States. The winter is mild in all of them. The soil is generally fertile. The higher lands produce cotton, corn and sweet potatoes. The lowlands produce rice, tobacco, Sea Island cotton and, on the Gulf Coast, sugar cane.

23

Note—South Carolina produces more rice than all the other states taken together.' "

"It's coming right along, isn't it? When I studied geography it produced more rice than any other state. By the time you took up the subject, it produced more than all the others put together."

For a few monments, he appeared to be pondering this mysterious progress. Then he looked up with a smile.

"Is that all?"

"It's about all I can seem to find that I think would interest you."

"Well, I guess it's enough. Sounds pretty good, doesn't it? Mild climate—fertile soil—plenty of willing labor. How'd you like to go south, Mary?"

"How would . . . Brent, what are you talking about?"

"I'm talking about moving to Louisiana. I don't know about you, but I've had all I want to take of blizzards and pneumonia and working night and day just to make both ends meet. I've had enough of seeing *you* work night and day, getting more and more peaked and pale while you're doing it. I've had enough of seeing you worry about things you won't talk about, for fear they'll worry *me* when I'm not strong enough to stand them. As soon as I'm on my feet, I'm starting for Louisiana to have a look at some of the land advertised in this paper."

He picked up the paper, which was still lying beside him on the bed, and handed it to her. He had already folded it in such a way that the notice which had attracted her attention and astonished her so, earlier in the afternoon, came immediately into view.

"You said you wondered who'd be interested in an advertisement about Louisiana, way up here in Illinois," he said. "Well, I'll tell you: *I'm* interested. And I hope you won't start telling me this is just a notion I've taken because I'm sick and weak. I may be weak, but I'm not delirious. I've got all my senses about me. And I hope you won't start telling me we can't afford the trip, let alone the land; we've got a little in the savings bank, thanks to you, and when we've sold this place and the stock on it, we'll have more. I wouldn't even stop at borrowing something, for once, if I had to, though you know I don't hold with making a practice of getting into debt. And I hope you won't start saying this is our home, that we can't leave it just on a whim. It's *been* our home, but we won't be leaving it for a whim, we'll be leaving it for a better one. I'm

24

just as sure as I'm lying here that we'll improve our lot and our child's lot by doing so."

He spoke with an earnestness that was rapidly mounting to vehemence. Mary had stood staring at him in growing amazement while he talked, but she had not tried to interrupt him and now, as he paused for breath, she did not cry out in protest. She still stood looking at him speechlessly, but tenderness and trust were mingled with the astonishment in her gaze, and suddenly she dropped on her knees beside his bed and took his hands in hers.

"I'm not going to start telling you anything," she said, "except that since you know what you want to do, I'll help, every way I can."

PART ONE

Jonathan Fant

CHAPTER I

Life was sometimes puzzling to Lavinia Winslow, but it was never dull, and she could remember when it had begun to seem both more bewildering and more exciting. It was the spring after her father had been so sick, and she had made her grandmother and grandfather Winslow a long visit.

She did not enjoy visiting them as much as she enjoyed visiting her mother's parents, grandfather and grandmother Garland. Grandfather Garland raised horses and was in and out of the stables and pastures all the time that he was not out riding and driving and going to auctions and harness races. He took Lavinia with him wherever she wanted to go, which was everywhere he went; and he was a very jolly man, always joking about something, and when he did this, he seemed to laugh all over and not just in his throat. He was a heavy man, not fleshy but thickset, and his laugh was hearty enough to shake all of his stocky frame. His cheeks were very red and Lavinia had heard it explained that this was not because he was a drinking man, but because he was unusually husky and spent so much time out of doors; and though his face itself was clean shaven, his ruddy cheeks and firm chin were encircled by a short stiff growth of dark whiskers, which somehow added almost as much to the joviality of his appearance as his snapping black eyes. He wore high boots and heavy, serviceable clothing, and almost always carried a long tasseled whip in his hand, though Lavinia had never seen him use it.

Grandmother Garland did not laugh and joke as much as her husband, but it was plain to Lavinia that she enjoyed having him do so; her face, which was always smiling anyway, brightened still more whenever he came into the sunny room where she sat. She was a cripple, confined to a wheel chair, but apparently she did not mind this at all; she seemed very happy and she made everyone around her happy—her husband and her unmarried daughter Sally and her only grandchild, that is to say, Lavinia herself. This was all she did, except a little needlework, which hardly counted; but it never occurred to Lavinia that grandmother Garland, who made everyone so happy, was not a useful woman, until she heard her grandmother Winslow say so, in the course of that long visit.

"You couldn't ask for better housekeepers than Mary and Sally," grandmother Winslow said to a caller, referring to Lavinia's mother and aunt. "But if you asked for my opinion, it's because they both found out, before they were knee high to grasshoppers, that if *they* didn't do the work nobody would and they just naturally didn't take to going hungry and dirty. Sarah Garland's never so much as lifted her little finger, since I can remember."

The caller had not asked for grandmother Winslow's opinion and, to Lavinia's intense joy, she now came to the defense of grandmother Garland. "The poor woman couldn't could she?" inquired the caller. "Crippled as she is with rheumatism and suffering a lot, most likely."

"She wasn't crippled when she married James Garland," retorted grandmother Winslow, who was the only person who did not refer to Lavinia's maternal grandfather as Jim. "She was out going to dances, here, there and everywhere."

"Well, wouldn't that make it all the harder for her to sit idle later on?"

"I don't see that it follows. I think she likes to sit idle and let someone else do her work for her. If you ask me, I don't think she ever tried to exert herself, except for her own amusement. She's not a God-fearing woman, either, any more than her husband's a God-fearing man."

Apparently it was because grandfather and grandmother Garland were not God fearing that Lavinia had been sent to stay with grandfather and grandmother Winslow while her father was so sick. She did not quite understand why people were supposed to fear God, when they were also admonished to love Him; this was one of the many things that was puzzling to her; she herself had never been in the least afraid of anyone she loved. But it was quite true that the Garlands did not go to church every Sunday, much less twice every Sunday and to Wednesday evening prayer meeting besides, like the elder Winslows, and they did not lay much stress on Sunday school, either. But grandmother Garland had her Bible on her lap quite as often as she had her fine needlework, and she read aloud from it to Lavinia—exciting stories about David and Daniel, beautiful stories about Ruth and Mary; Lavinia learned a great deal more about them from her than she did from her other grandmother, and this increased her puzzlement over the charge about the lack of God-fearing qualities. However, she went dutifully to church and to Sunday school and to day school, too, all through the course of that long visit which she did not enjoy very much, and finally it came to an end and she went home.

Her father was up and about now, part of every day, and helped her mother with the chores more and more all the time; but he tired very quickly and went to lie down in the middle of the morning and again in the middle of the afternoon, besides going to bed very early at night—so early that he generally was not drowsy yet and did not even try to go to sleep, but instead lay and talked to Lavinia's mother, who sat beside him and sewed. Lavinia was put to bed early herself and she was not always drowsy, either; so she could not help overhearing, through the open door between their rooms.

"Of course, I won't do anything rash, Mary. I'll go down and have a look at the lay of the land before I start selling off here. I know what I want to do all right. All the same, I know I mustn't just shut my eyes and jump."

"That's the sensible way of looking at it, Brent. And of course you won't try to take a journey like that until you've got your strength back."

"Well, I don't know. Sometimes I think it might help to get my strength back if I could feel I'd made a start. But I'd hate to leave you with all the work to do while I was gone."

"You mustn't let that stop you. I didn't mind doing it before. And it'll be easier when the weather's warmer."

"As soon as the weather's warmer, we'll have to begin thinking about spring plowing and planting. You couldn't do that."

"I'm sure we could find someone who'd help."

"We didn't, before. . . . Of course, we *could* try to sell right away—house, land, stock, everything—and you and Lavinia could go and stay with my folks while I was away."

"I'm sure they wouldn't approve of such a hasty action,

Brent. When it comes to that, I'm not sure *I* would. But I'm not going back on my word. I'll do whatever you think best. Only . . . if you decide to sell and not to plant, couldn't I go and stay with my family while you're away, instead of yours?"

"You know Father and Mother wouldn't approve of that, either. And it would make a lot of extra work for Sally."

"No it wouldn't. I'd help with the work. It would really be easier for her. She wouldn't be so tied down. She could get out once in a while. It troubles me sometimes, Brent, to think that Sally's never had a chance."

"A chance?"

"Yes—a chance to marry. I've been so happy with you, Brent, that I want Sally to have the same kind of happiness—married happiness."

Lavinia did not hear any more after that; either her parents lowered their voices, or she really was drowsy by that time; anyway, it did not seem to matter just then. But afterward, she kept thinking about what she had heard; she was sorry to learn that Aunt Sally had never had a chance to be happy, for she was fond of Aunt Sally; and she was surprised, too, for Aunt Sally had always seemed ready for fun, like grandfather Garland, whom she resembled much more than she did grandmother Garland. She was rosy cheeked and chubby and loved a good joke; she laughed all over, too. Lavinia thought that her father and mother must really be mistaken about Aunt Sally, so she did not worry long about that; but she was more concerned over the rest of their conversation and, the next day, when she came home from school, she began questioning her mother, who was in the kitchen, ironing, and who held up a warning finger and said, "Sh-h-h," very softly. The door leading into the main bedroom was closed, and Lavinia realized that her father must be taking a nap. She spoke very softly, too.

"Mother, is Father going away?"

"Perhaps. . . . What made you think he might be?"

"I heard you and him talking about it last night, after I had gone to bed. I didn't try to listen. I just happened to hear."

"It's all right, darling. Father and I would have told you about it presently, anyway. Only nothing's settled yet. We thought it might puzzle you, if we talked to you about it while everything is so uncertain. And perhaps it would be

30

better not to tell anyone else what you overheard, or thought you overheard, just yet, either, because other people might be puzzled, too."

Lavinia nodded. She did not want to admit that she *had* been puzzled, but she was pleased at being permitted to share a family secret which would puzzle outsiders.

"If Father does go, he won't stay away from us long, will he?"

"No, just a short while—only long enough to find out about making a new home for us."

"Isn't this our home?"

"Yes, but Father thinks perhaps we could have a better one, somewhere else."

"Where else?"

"In Louisiana."

"Where's that?"

"It's in the South, where the weather's warm and pleasant all the year round and the ground's very fertile—that is, very good for crops. I'll show you a map, if you'd like to have me, and read you what our geography books says about Louisiana."

Lavinia nodded again, a little more doubtfully this time. She was getting more and more puzzled, but she was still more averse to saying so than she had been before. She had never looked at a map close to and she was a little ashamed to confess it, for there was a big tattered one on the wall of the schoolroom, to which she had seen the teacher pointing with a long stick when the latter was giving geography lessons to the boys and girls older than Lavinia; but none of her own classmates studied anything except reading, writing and arithmetic. Her anxiety drove her on to other questions, without waiting to have these causes of bewilderment explained.

"Would Father sell our house before he got us another one, better?"

"He might. That isn't decided, either, darling."

"But then we wouldn't have any place to live, unless—"

She did not want to say, "unless we went to stay with grandfather and grandmother Winslow." She did not want her mother to know that she had not been happy there during that long visit. And she did not suppose, if her other grandparents did not approve of it, that there would be any chance of going to stay with grandfather and grandmother Garland, with whom she could be so happy; she had learned that the approval or disapproval of grandfather and grandmother Winslow carried great weight. She turned her head away, because she thought her lips were beginning to tremble a little, and she did not want her mother to see that, or the tears that were spilling over from her eyes, no matter how hard she tried to wink them back. . . .

Her mother folded the garment she had been ironing and placed it on the wooden clothes rack where the neatly folded sheets and pillowcases and towels already hung. Then she replaced on the stove the iron she had been using and tested another, by moistening her forefinger and putting it quickly against the bottom part of the iron. The iron hissed, as it could be expected to do if it were hot enough to use. But Lavinia's mother did not seem to think it was. She replaced that on the stove, too, and came over to the chair where Lavinia was sitting and put her arms around her little daughter.

"I don't think Father will sell our home until he has a better one for us," she said. "But if he does, we're going to stay with grandfather and grandmother Garland. While you were at school this morning and Father was resting, I went to see my mother and talked all this over with her. I've always found, Lavinia, that it helps to talk things over with my mother—most people do. So she knows about our plans, too. And everything's settled, at least about our visit. Let's go and tell Father together, shall we? I think he must be awake by now."

When the warm weather finally came, Brent Winslow went to Louisiana and Lavinia and her mother went to stay with grandfather and grandmother Garland. But their house was not sold yet; it was only loaned to a young man named Jonathan Fant, who had said he did not mind keeping house for himself, and who had agreed to plow and plant and look after the stock while Father was gone, if he could have a job for the rest of the summer and a chance to buy the place, in case Father should decide they could have a better home in Louisiana than in Illinois.

CHAPTER II

Nobody seemed to know much about Jonathan Fant at first, and grandmother Winslow did not hesitate to refer to him openly as a tramp and to hint, less openly, that he might be an escaped convict. He simply came to the house one day on foot and rang the front doorbell, the one that was hardly ever used. Lavinia went to answer it, because Brent and Mary were both out at the time, and she was near by, having stolen into the parlor and found the old geographies. She was trying to locate Louisiana on the map when the doorbell rang. Jonathan Fant smiled at her in a nice way and asked if her father and mother were at home. When she said well, they were out doing the chores, he seemed surprised and said, "What, both of them?" So Lavinia explained that Father had been sick and that, though he was better, Mother was still helping him, and Jonathan Fant said, "Perhaps I could help, too. I'm looking for work." Then he went off to find them and by-and-by all three returned together and Lavinia discovered that Jonathan Fant was going to stay for supper. Next it was decided that, as it was so late, he had better spend the night, and Mary said she would fix a shakedown for him in the parlor, because there was no other place. When they went in there, the old geographies were lying on the floor, because Lavinia had not had a chance to pick them up, and she admitted she had been looking for Louisiana and asked Jonathan Fant if he knew anything about maps. He said well, he ought to, and the next thing they were all sitting in the parlor together, just as cozily as if it had been the kitchen and Jonathan Fant was showing Lavinia how to find Louisiana.

When he had located the map of the "South Atlantic and Gulf States" and read aloud from the accompanying text, he laughed and turned back the pages until he came to one which had only a few sentences, completely unintelligible to Lavinia, and underneath these some numbers and a strange word: COPYRIGHT. She read these aloud, as Jonathan Fant pointed them out to her.

"1-8-6-7," she said. "What does that mean, Mr. Fant?"

"It means this geography's almost twenty years old—nineteen, to be exact," he said.

"It's the one I had when I was in school," Lavinia's mother explained. "The only other one we have is the geography Brent used, and he was three years ahead of me in school. So that's older still."

"I see. Well, we ought to be able to find a newer one somewhere. Perhaps a schoolmate of Lavinia's—one of the older boys or girls—would lend a geography book to her, over Sunday. But meanwhile, I can tell you that there's been quite a change in those sections during the last twenty years. This book doesn't say much about South

33

Carolina, except that it's a rice-growing state, but Charleston's a fair-sized city—around fifty thousand. And I wouldn't call Austin a 'small town' exactly, though it isn't coming along as fast as some of the other places in Texas, like Houston, for instance, that isn't even mentioned here."

"I'm not so much interested in large cities as I am in a mild climate and generally fertile soil. Those conditions haven't changed, have they?"

"No, those haven't changed. Not in South Carolina anyway. I've lived there most of my life."

"You *have!* Then perhaps you can explain why it produced more rice than any other state for a long time, and why now it produces more than all the others put together."

It was Brent who had spoken both times, and he sounded very much interested. Jonathan Fant laughed.

"I'm afraid I can't, especially because I don't believe it does, any more. But I can tell you how rice happened to be grown there in the first place, if you'd care to have me. It's a rather interesting story."

"Yes, please tell us."

Lavinia had spoken at the same time with Brent and Mary. Jonathan Fant closed the old geography and leaned back comfortably in his chair. "About two hundred years ago, a ship going from Madagascar to England was blown off its course by a bad storm—do you know where Madagascar is, Lavinia?"

"No, I never heard of it."

She had the impression that her father and mother had never heard of it, either, though this time they did not speak at the same moment she did. Jonathan Fant reopened the geography and leafed through it until he came to the map of Africa; then he pointed out the island of Madagascar lying alongside its coast. Next he found another map, showing the two hemispheres, and traced the course that a ship might take in going from Madagascar to England. Lavinia looked on in fascination.

"It's a long way, isn't it?" she said at last. "Lots of things could happen if you were going such a long way."

"Yes. Lots of things could happen. Lots of things did happen. And finally, the ship was so badly damaged that the captain had to make land in Charleston. Charleston's a very important city and it has a very fine port. Don't let any old geography book give you the idea that it isn't and hasn't."

He turned the pages again and showed her Charleston on the map they had looked at first.

"And what happened then?" Lavinia asked breathlessly. She had not understood all the words he used, but she had understood enough to know that there had been trouble, bad trouble.

"Why, the storm blew over, the way storms always do in the end, and the ship was repaired and went on its way. But before he left, the captain gave the colonial governor a small package of rough rice. The governor had this seed planted and pretty soon there was enough rice grown to supply not only South Carolina but all the neighboring colonies. Presently, it provided the wherewithal for a thriving export trade, too."

"And all this prosperity was just an accident, in the beginning?"

This was Brent speaking again. Jonathan Fant answered rather slowly.

"I suppose you could call it an accident. Or maybe not. You know,

'There is a tide in the affairs of men,
Which, taken at the flood, leads on to fortune;
Omitted, all the voyage of their life
Is bound in shallows and in miseries.' "

Mary looked up quickly. "Is that from Shakespeare?" she asked.

"Yes. *Julius Caesar.*"

Mary and Brent both seemed to be thinking intently. Then Brent said, "That's what I believe. That's what I've been trying to tell my family. But they're hard to convince." And Mary said, "I'm not. Because I believe something else. I believe that sometimes, when we can't see our way very well along some unfamiliar path, God leads us on until it's bright and clear again."

"Yes, that's possible, too."

Again there was a deep silence in the parlor. By-and-by Mary asked another question that seemed to have no connection with what she had said before. "When Brent asked you if you could tell him why South Carolina led all the other states in the production of rice, you said you couldn't, because it didn't any more. But since then, you've said that this small parcel of rice the captain gave his friend the governor soon supplied enough not only for

35

that colony, but for all the neighboring colonies. What happened?"

"You've heard of the War Between the States, haven't you, Mrs. Winslow? And the Reconstruction period?"

Something had made a difference in Jonathan Fant's voice. Up until then, it had sounded as if there were a laugh behind it somewhere, all the time, even though he had actually laughed only once or twice. Now there was no hint of a laugh anywhere. His voice was stern and it was sad, too.

"The War Between the States?" Mary repeated.

"Oh, excuse me. The little skirmish called the Civil War, north of the Mason and Dixon Line. But I believe the term 'Reconstruction' is used in all parts of the country."

"I've heard about them, of course," Mary said rather hastily. "But they didn't happen to touch our family very closely and there wasn't any fighting around here."

"They touched us plenty close in South Carolina and in lots of other places, too. Some people in those places have been finding it mighty hard, since the war, whatever you call it, to believe in the beneficent hand of God, Mrs. Winslow. I might mention Louisiana among those places, since you seem to be so interested in that state. There was quite a lot of rice grown there, too, not so much for export, but for plantation and local use, especially down on the Delta and along Bayou Lafourche. Also, sugar, cotton, corn, sweet potatoes and tobacco. Some on the highlands and some on the lowlands, some farther north and some farther south, but all in Dixie Land."

"There was a piece in our hometown paper—" Mary began. But Jonathan Fant interrupted her and now he was laughing again, though not in the same way he had before.

"What, one of the Dusons' broadsheets? They're sending those out by the thousands, mostly to the Middle West. I reckon they can't get much of anyone in Louisiana to listen to them."

"Who are the Dusons? Do you know them? Why won't anyone in Louisiana listen to them?"

Brent and Mary were both talking at once again, and they sounded not only interested but excited. Jonathan Fant shrugged his shoulders.

"Yes, I know the Dusons. I've spent quite a little time in Louisiana myself, first and last. I wander about a good deal."

"Tell us about it! Tell us about *them*."

36

"All right. The Dusons are a couple of mighty smart promoters. Their father was a Scotsman—or rather, a Canadian, who sided with the French element instead of the English, in some kind of a revolt against the Crown. I don't know just what it was all about, but he had to flee for his life, and he also decided it might be the better part of valor—not just Scotch economy—to lop off his last name, which was McNaughton, and call himself by his middle name, that is to say, Duson. He must have been plenty scared, for he wasn't satisfied with fleeing to New England; he fled as far south as he could get without falling into the Gulf of Mexico and, eventually, he settled in Breaux Bridge."

"Breaux Bridge?"

"Yes, that's a village in Southwest Louisiana. . . . Then he died, leaving a widow and several children—among them, C. C. and W. W., as they're always called. These two boys were the mainstay of the family and I must say they did a good job. They herded cattle and worked in sawmills, moving from one small settlement to another, but all in the same locality, and eventually they opened a store in Plaquemine Brulee—another little village. Finally, they went into the real estate business in still another small place—there aren't anything but small settlements around there. This place where they went into real estate is called Rayne now. It used to be called Poupeville. At least, Poupeville was a little farther south, maybe a mile or so; but when the Southern Pacific got its right of way, and the leading citizens found out that the railroad would by-pass Poupeville, they up and moved every building there by ox team."

"So the village of Rayne *is* on the main line?"

"Yes. It's had regular train service for three or four years now. And it's been well laid out. I don't know why the Dusons weren't satisfied to stay there—they were doing well by that time. But they've got a bee in their bonnet about dividing the parish where Rayne is, St. Landry—"

"The parish?"

"That's what counties are called in Louisiana, parishes. I suppose that's all they were, in the beginning. Anyhow, the term stuck. . . . Well, as I was saying, the Dusons got a bee in their bonnet about dividing St. Landry Parish in two, and founding a town in the new one that would be the parish seat. One of the brothers, I'm not sure which, made some kind of a crude sign, labeled THIS IS THE SITE OF THE NEW COURTHOUSE, and stuck it in a crawfish hole.

Now he's bought up a weekly paper that has just started publication in Rayne and is arranging to move the plant over to this imaginary parish seat of his. Next, he started sending out advertisements, in that and other weeklies, telling everyone about the wonderful future of this undeveloped prairie, that has just a few shacks on it and some low-grade cattle and stunted wild ponies roaming over it. I don't know who he thinks would believe him."

"I believe him," Brent announced surprisingly. "What's more, I'm going down to have a look at that undeveloped prairie for myself. I think something could be raised on it. And I'm going to make a point of meeting those Dusons. Men who've done what you said they've done already aren't just smart speculators. They're farseeing pioneers. Moving a whole settlement by ox team to get it on a railroad! . . . You're more than welcome here, Mr. Fant, and I've enjoyed talking to you. What's more, you've given me a lot of new ideas and a lot of information that'll be helpful to me and I'm sure you can give me a lot more. But it's getting late for a workingman to be up. Unless you can think of something more my wife and I could do to make you comfortable, we'll bid you good night."

CHAPTER III

Lavinia was not sure, afterward, how much of that evening's conversation she actually remembered, without prompting, and how much of it she thought she remembered because it was recalled so often by her father and mother and repeated, in substance, by them to her grandfather and grandmother Winslow and her grandfather and grandmother Garland. But the purport of it all was very vivid, and not nearly as perplexing to her as many of the things that were said and done before and after.

For instance, there were all the questions grandmother Winslow had asked and all the comments she had made when she heard about Jonathan Fant's unannounced arrival, unrecommended presence and prolonged conversation with her son and daughter-in-law. Why did he need to look for work in Monroe? A man who could spout Shakespeare, as if it were as natural as breathing, ought to be able to get a teacher's position almost anywhere; unless he had some kind of a criminal past, he would not be going from house to house, asking if anyone needed a hired man. Of course, his people must have been Secessionists, since he had talked about the War Between the States instead of the Civil War, and since he made those harsh allusions to the just policy of Reconstruction. But she would say this: whoever and whatever he was, he evidently had shed enough light on that piece in the paper so that Brent would give up the idea of going off on a wild-goose chase in search of something better than what he had already, which ought to be good enough for any sensible man. Of course, she knew Brent was pretty sick when he read that paper; but she had never heard before that pneumonia affected the brain as well as the body, at least after there was no more fever—was Mary sure he was over his queer spells when he read that piece? Anyway, she never, in all her born days, had known of anything so downright crazy as wanting to give up a good farm and go off to some God-forsaken place at the other end of the world because of an advertisement in a newspaper. Folks with their wits about them knew that advertisements were just a pack of lies— you had only to look at the claims of patent medicines! And now this Fant fellow came right out and said the pretended paradise was nothing but a barren prairie!

Brent Winslow was not present when his mother stormed away in this vein at his wife, but Lavinia was, and she watched closely and listened carefully while Mary answered in her mild way. Jonathan Fant had not told them much about himself, she admitted freely; but after all, there had not been much time yet. He had started right in, the morning after his arrival, helping with the chores; and he was good help, he did not just have book learning. She agreed that he was obviously a southerner— indeed, he had told them that much himself—and a southerner who, for some reason, had decided to leave the South; but she did not believe it was a criminal reason. If he did not volunteer more information about himself within the next few days, and they all continued to like him and Brent continued to be satisfied with his work, Brent would ask him a few questions; but they were going to wait and see if he did not tell them more of his own accord. As far as his having said anything that would make Brent change his mind about going to Louisiana, Mother Winslow might as well give up that idea right away; Brent was more than ever determined to start out and look over the lay of the land there, as soon as he knew he would be leaving the farm in good hands. He thought already, and Mary agreed with him, that those hands might very well be Jonathan Fant's.

After she had said this, she rose quietly and told Lavinia they must be going home; it was time to get Father's supper and, though she left without any appearance of haste, it was impossible for grandmother Winslow to argue with her any more.

When the same story about Jonathan Fant's appearance in their midst had been told grandmother Garland, also in Lavinia's presence, the pleasant old lady was inclined to agree with her daughter. "Of course, you shouldn't make decisions hastily," she said, folding up her fine needlework, "except when you find you can make them instinctively. Perhaps this is one of those times." Mary said that was just the way she and Brent felt, and it was very evident to the little girl that her mother was pleased because grandmother Garland felt the same way. Then grandmother Garland suggested that they should all come over to dinner on Sunday, and by "all" of course she meant to include Jonathan Fant.

Lavinia thought there had never been a pleasanter gathering in the sunny room where grandmother Garland sat in her wheel chair most of the time and that the old lady had never looked prettier. She had put on her best lace cap, the one that was almost as fine as a cobweb and trimmed with pink ribbons—she always wore pretty caps, but this was the prettiest of all, one that gave her a winged look, from the way it was set on her soft white hair. She had on her best dress, too—a pink cashmere. She had several cashmere dresses, none of them in "old lady colors" which she said she despised; but this was made in the most becoming way of all, with a deep fichu of the same lace as the cap. Aunt Sally also wore her best dress—a challis with little bunches of bright flowers scattered all over a pale blue ground. Lavinia was glad that she and her mother were dressed up, too, though their best was never as pleasing to her as grandmother Garland's and Aunt Sally's—a plaid wool for her, a brown grenadine for her mother. And of course, since it was Sunday and they had all been to church, the men had on the neat black suits that they never wore at any other time. At least, grandfather Garland and her father did. Jonathan Fant had on a gray suit that looked a lot more comfortable than theirs, but it was a very nice suit, too; and he wore it as if he were used to wearing his best clothes most of the time, which was another mysterious thing because, after all, the other hired men Lavinia had seen looked rather ill at ease in their best clothes.

For the first time, Lavinia noticed that Jonathan Fant was very good looking. Up to then, she had only noticed that he had crinkles around his eyes when he laughed and that he was taller and slimmer than any of the other men she knew and did not handle himself in the same way. He could sit still for a long while without being uneasy, but when he did move, it was with a sort of effortless speed that made her uncertain where she was going to see him next. Now she discovered that his eyes were unusual, too —neither blue nor brown, but green in some lights and almost yellow in others, shielded with very long lashes, and sleepy looking part of the time because his eyelids drooped over them, but sparkling when he opened them wide. She thought the way he wore his hair—long over a very white brow—strangely becoming and next she noticed that he had beautiful hands. It was the first time it had occurred to her that hands could be beautiful. The ring he wore was beautiful, too, though it had no colored stones in it, only some queer carvings that meant nothing to Lavinia.

Dinner was very good, all sorts of fixin's to go with the baked chicken, and ice cream as well as pie for dessert. Sally had got out the best tablecloth and the best china, so everything looked as nice as it tasted. But that was not the only reason the occasion was such a success. Jonathan Fant made it a success. It turned out that he knew a lot about horses and he talked with grandfather Garland about them. He also knew a lot about the Bible and he talked with grandmother Garland about that. And he talked with Sally about a little of everything, including himself, so no one had to ask him any questions. It turned out that his mother had come from a place in Louisiana called St. Martinville, and that she had met his father, who came from Charleston, at a party in New Orleans, where she was visiting relatives and he had gone on business. It had been a case of love at first sight.

"Such things do happen sometimes, you know," he said gaily, addressing the company at large. And then he had looked across the table at Sally, who had blushed deeply and sprung up, saying she must go and get some more ice cream, and Jonathan Fant had sprung up, too, saying he would help her.

They were gone quite a few minutes, and after they came back to the dining room, and everyone had more ice cream, nobody said anything about getting up and clearing

41

the table or doing the dishes. While they sat there peacefully, Jonathan Fant told them all more and more about himself. He still went to visit his mother's people every now and then—in fact, he had been there fairly recently. And how far was St. Martinville from Rayne, where those Dusons lived, Brent wanted to know. Oh, only about thirty miles as the crow flies. Of course, a man can't fly, and the roads don't amount to much, but news travels with the crows. *(There!* Lavinia said to herself triumphantly. *Tomorrow, Mother will tell grandmother Winslow exactly how Jonathan Fant happens to know so much about Louisiana!)* His people did not have their plantations any longer; they had held onto them during the war, but lost them soon afterward. His grandfather and grandmother Arcenaux were still living; they kept urging him to come to St. Martinville and make his home with them, but nothing would induce him to. There was practically no land connected with the house where they lived now, and he liked land—that is, good land, like this up here in Illinois, not overcultivated land like that in South Carolina, or land that might be good for something someday, like that the Dusons were talking about. *(Mother won't tell grandmother Winslow he said that,* Lavinia told herself; *he meant the land in the advertisement.)* Besides, the Arcenaux were very old now and lived entirely in the past. They sat in the parlor, with the shutters closed, facing a picture of the plantation they had lost, which they kept draped in black. They hardly ever even went out on the gallery, much less in the yard any more, though the yard was pretty, even if it was small. The only time his grandmother Arcenaux bothered to pick flowers was when she wanted to put them on the family tomb. She still did go regularly to the cemetery. . . .

"What kind of flowers does she have in her yard?" Mary interrupted to ask.

"Why, all kinds! Paper-white narcissi in January, day lilies and iris in the spring, chrysanthemums for All Saints', camellias from October to April, roses all the year round—"

"Roses all the year round! Camellias from October to April!" Mary echoed unbelievingly.

"Well, of course, if there's a bad drought, you don't get roses in midsummer. And I'm not sure she has the earliest and latest varieties of camellias any more, because she's neglected everything so, or the rarest kinds, because she can't afford them. But aside from that—"

"What kinds does she have? What colors?"

"Why, all the ordinary kinds—Alba Plena, dead white; Governor Mouton, named for a neighbor of ours, red and white; Colette, that another neighbor brought home from France, red and white, too, but darker than the Governor Mouton; Colonial Lady, variegated. There are almost all colors—except blue, of course."

"Mary's crazy about flowers," Sally broke in. "To hear her talk, you'd think she'd rather have camellias than diamonds—not that she's ever seen one. She'd probably be disappointed if she did—unless it was blue."

"No I wouldn't. I've read about them and I know. They're simply beautiful and—"

"You interrupted Mr. Fant, Mary. The rest of us were interested in everything he was saying, not just the part about the flowers."

There really wasn't much more to say about the Arcenaux, Jonathan Fant went on. As he'd already remarked, most of the time they just sat and looked at a picture of a house, draped in black. When they did talk, it was about life "before the war"; the war had been over more than twenty years now, but they still talked as if Grant and Lee had met at Appomattox Courthouse just the day before yesterday. It was the same in South Carolina. Not that he was surprised because Carolinians—or Louisianians, either, for that matter—found the war hard to forget. His father's people had gone through even more than his mother's people—their plantation had been destroyed and nearly every male member of the family had been killed or maimed for life. The women had mostly grieved to death or starved to death—or perhaps they had died from a mixture of too much sorrow and too little food. He didn't know. Anyhow, very few of them had had the stamina to survive. His mother wasn't one of them. He had been brought up in Charleston by a great-uncle and great-aunt who had not lost quite as much as the rest of the family, thought they had had to scrimp and save, too. By scrimping and saving, they had managed to send him to the University of Virginia—that was where all the Fants had gone, in better days. Virginia was coming back to normal faster than the states farther south and there was less bitterness there—or, if it were there, it was less apparent. There was actually a Yankee—a Bostonian—at the head of the Greek Department at the University, and he and his wife—a gay, pretty New Yorker—were living in James Monroe's old house and were very well liked. They entertained quite lavishly—made a practice of never having the table set for less than six, even if no one had been specifically invited to dinner, and guests were always dropping in, glad to do so. He had done it several times himself. On the whole, he had enjoyed life at the University. He had never been much good at mathematics or science, but he learned languages easily and he loved to read. Of course, French came to him quite naturally, as that was what they mostly talked in St. Martinville still and, as a matter of fact, so did a good many people in Charleston, where the descendants of the French Huguenots were so numerous. He read French and English classics with equal enjoyment and facility and he was grateful to the University for giving him a better understanding and appreciation of both. He supposed he could have stayed on in Virginia, but again it was a question of land and he didn't own any there and he had no money to buy any then. He didn't want to read all the time, only in the evenings when he'd been outdoors all day. So he had gone back to South Carolina and had got a job as overseer on the plantation that had once belonged to some distant kinsfolk and which had escaped the general destruction. He had often gone to visit there when he was a youngster.

"What do they raise there?" Brent wanted to know.

"Just the usual things—rice, cotton, corn, oats. More and more corn and oats all the time. Rice isn't the money crop any more and there aren't enough good cotton pickers."

"You're as bad as Mary, Brent. Flowers are all she wants to hear about and crops are all you want to hear about. The rest of us want to hear about everything," Sally said breathlessly. "Do you like the people who own the plantation, Mr. Fant? Are they nice people?"

Well, they were rich Yankees and they had paid well, Jonathan Fant replied, with his crinkly smile. They were not as well received as the Yankees he had met in Virginia; but he really thought that was partly because they took no stock in the old superstition, so prevalent among Carolinians, that it was fatal for an Anglo-Saxon to breathe the night air on a rice plantation in the lowlands from the end of May until the first of November. These Yankees stayed right on where they were, instead of bothering to move away a few miles to a belt of pine woods, or to the nearest mountains, which were fairly close, too. Of course, such bucking of general opinion made them unpopular.

"Did any of them die?" Brent inquired.

No, and of course that made them all the more unpopular, Jonathan said, laughing; and they had other habits which annoyed the natives. But, in his opinion, they were all right in their way. Only of course working on someone else's land was not like working on land of your own. So he had saved the money he made working on this plantation and he had also come into a small inheritance. The great-aunt and uncle who had brought him up had died and, as they were childless, they had made him their heir. They had practically no money left, but they still had their house and its contents; so he had sold the house and most of the things in it—to other rich Yankees. He would never have supposed these possessions would have brought in so much. The sale hadn't meant wealth for him, to be sure, but it had meant independence. He had no ties of any kind, he was free to go anywhere he chose. . . .

"But how did you happen to choose Monroe?" Lavinia burst out. Jonathan Fant had told them so much by then, she didn't see why he should mind telling them that, too.

"Well, you see—" he began. Then he glanced away from Sally, at whom he had been gazing steadily most of the time he was talking, and looked at grandmother Garland instead. She answered for him.

"I've been corresponding with Mme Arcenaux of St. Martinville, Louisiana, over the years," she said quietly. "Her daughter Arthemise—Mr. Fant's mother—and I met at Saratoga Springs, when we were both brides—it was a great place for honeymooners from both North and South in those days, especially honeymooners who were interested in horses, as well as each other. We never met afterward; but we wrote each other frequently, until we were both too busy with our babies for much letter writing. But when Arthemise and her husband both died, so tragically, during the war, I wrote a letter of condolence to Mme Arcenaux. In answering, she said it would mean a great deal to her if I would continue the correspondence—with her. I meant to, but somehow I didn't very long; it seemed to be harder and harder for me to find the time to write." It was like grandmother Garland to put it this way: to say that it was harder and harder for her "to find the time," instead of saying that her painful rheumatism made any activity harder and harder. "But after Brent began to ask questions about Louisiana and to talk about going there, I naturally tried to think what I might do to help," she went on, "and I remembered Mme Arcenaux. So I wrote to her, apologizing and explaining the situation at the same time. I didn't feel too sure she'd accept my apology—after all, it was she who'd made a friendly overture that I hadn't seemed to appreciate. But she wrote back right away, saying she was delighted to hear from me, and there was a special reason for that, too: her only grandson Jonathan Fant was visiting her and he was very restless. He didn't want to stay in the South and he felt he'd like to have a look at the Middle West. She thought our problem might be the solution of his. Then, of course, I wrote again and, to make a long story a little shorter, here Jonathan is and I'm sure I'm speaking for everyone when I say that he's very, very welcome!"

She looked around the table, smiling at them all. There was a moment of startled silence. Then Jonathan Fant shifted his gaze again, this time toward Brent Winslow.

"The Old South is dead," he said, speaking in that sad, stern way, with no laughter behind it, which had disturbed Lavinia once before. "Believe me, I know."

"May be," Brent answered evenly. "But the New South isn't. I'm as sure of that as you are of the other."

That evening another long conversation took place in her parents' parlor, but Lavinia did not hear it. She was tired when they reached home after the big Sunday dinner and all the visiting that had followed it, and she was willing to go to bed early; there had been enough surprises already that day, as far as she was concerned: Jonathan Fant hadn't come to their house by accident—he had come on purpose! And grandmother Garland had known about him all the time! And grandmother Winslow was going to be furious! And Aunt Sally—well, something had happened to Aunt Sally the minute she looked at Jonathan Fant! Lavinia wasn't sure just what it was, but somehow she knew that was the most exciting thing of all!

The next evening, when she came home from school, Mary told her it had been decided that Father could start for Louisiana right away, because Jonathan Fant was going to look after the farm while he was gone and that, meanwhile, she and Mother were going to stay with grandfather and grandmother Garland.

CHAPTER IV

Nothing very exciting happened while Brent was gone. He did not write often and, when he did, the letters began "Dear Folks," and ended "Aff.," and were rather impersonal. He failed to say much about what he was doing and seeing. "Train trip pretty tiring, but New Orleans worth it. Never expected to like a city, but this one is different. Will tell you more about it when I get home." . . . "Climate everything I hoped for and more. I don't see why almost anything shouldn't grow here. Have stayed overnight at St. Martinville with the Arcenaux, who were very kind; but they live entirely in the tragic past, like Jonathan told us; and, as I told *him*, I'm looking to the future. So I got more out of staying at the Plaqucmine Brulee you heard about—now called Church Point—with the Daigles, who keep a store and are part Canadian, part Indian by descent; at the 'Cove' near Rayne with the Gossens, German immigrants who homesteaded there when things were really rough—wild hogs and longhorn cattle kept getting in their way—and who have now built a lake for irrigation and are raising rice; and with Mr. Jean Castex, a French carpenter in Mermentau—quite a variety! They are all prospering, so I don't see why I can't, too. Am encouraged by general conditions. The prairie isn't barren, it's just uncultivated. And Mary will be crazy about the wild flowers —banks and banks of sweet-smelling violets and masses of bridal wreath and quantities of blue flag, which is similar to what she raises and calls iris; but in Louisiana it doesn't require any cultivation, so she won't have to wait until she can plant a garden to have flowers. To my way of thinking, the violets and the flag and the bridal wreath are as pretty as anything Mrs. Arcenaux has, though perhaps it isn't fair to say this, as her camellias have stopped blooming now. But she is going to give Mary slips—not only of the kinds Jonathan has told us about, but others, too. I wrote down the names so I could be sure to tell you about them. There is one called Opelousas Pink, and another called Wax Leaf and another called Elegans, all short stemmed and floated in bowls when they are brought into the house; then there is one called Dixie that has long stems and is put in tall vases just like roses."

The letter about the flowers was the longest one Brent

wrote and the one that gave Mary the most pleasure. There was another one, very short, in fact only one sentence long: "Have met the Dusons, they are both grand fellows and are trying hard to get action from the railroad," and Mary said that Brent must have thought this was terribly important, or he would not have spent money on postage just to say that. But nearly every letter ended like the first one, "Will tell you more about this when I get home," and Lavinia began to feel that her father would have so much to say when he got home that he would never be through talking.

She was very contented with grandfather and grandmother Garland, especially after she was through school for the year and could be outdoors nearly all the time. In fact, she was not at all sorry to have left home, where there were no horses, except those actually needed for farm work, because she was never so happy as when she was out romping and riding. Two or three times a week she went with her mother and Sally when they drove over to "straighten things out" for Jonathan Fant, to leave the clean clothes they had washed and mended for him and the delicious food they had cooked for him. He always seemed glad to see them, and made no objections to their tidying processes; but he never failed to assure them that he was making out all right. Lavinia saw no reason why he should not; he spent a good deal of time at the other house anyway.

He handled the stock and the bees well, and it was plain that he not only loved the land; he knew what to do with it. He plowed and planted more of it than Brent had ever done and talked about further development of the pastures. He also doubled the little flower garden in size, rearranging to better advantage such perennials as iris, peonies and moss roses, and adding other varieties to the annuals like sweet peas and nasturtiums and zinnias which had, hitherto, been almost its limit. He explained that he did this mostly because he liked the names of these other flowers; sweet William, Johnny-jump-up, candytuft, baby's-breath, bleeding heart, marigolds, mignonette, heliotrope; and he said he was sorry he could not add camellias, especially blue camellias, as that really would have made a difference. But that was just one of the jokes that went with his crinkly smile; he had wrought a great change and he and everyone else knew this. However, the greatest difference was in the house. He asked Mary if she would mind if he moved some of his books into the parlor, and when she said no, except that there was only that one small bookcase, he answered that he could build some additional ones very easily. He did this, putting them all around the room, and filling them with more books than Lavinia had ever seen in her life; they came in big boxes, by express, from Charleston. Then he said he had a few family pictures he would like to put around, too, if no one had any objections; they also came by express and proved to be very pretty pictures. The parlor did not look like the same room when he had installed these belongings of his, and he kept it open all the time. He sat there and read every evening, when he was not over at the Garlands' house, and sometimes he played the piano for a while. Lavinia had never heard a man play the piano before; she had supposed they never did. She knew that some families had one and that little girls began to take music lessons, when they were ten or eleven, and learned pieces, so they could play for company by-and-by or for the family when it gathered together on Sunday evening to sing hymns. But Jonathan Fant sat down at the antiquated instrument he had installed in the parlor, which was not cold or musty any more, and played all kinds of music. He said he thought he could teach her, too, if she would like to learn, and she said she would, very much. So, though she was only going on nine, she began to take music lessons with Jonathan Fant. Then he told her he thought he could teach her French, too, and presently she was having French lessons. She did not mind taking lessons in vacation, because he made them so interesting.

One day, when her mother and Sally went up to the attic in the Garlands' house to put the winter clothes away in moth balls for the summer, after they had been thoroughly aired, Lavinia asked if she couldn't help, and then Jonathan Fant asked if he couldn't help, too—with the heavy carrying and lifting and all that. But after they had climbed the steep attic stairs and had all arrived, a little breathless, he stood staring at the old four-poster and the old secretary and the rest of the old things that had been stowed away there.

"What perfectly wonderful furniture!" he exclaimed, continuing to stare at it instead of starting to move trunks out from under the eaves. "Why on earth don't you use it in—"

Lavinia had thought he had started to say, "instead of what you do use." But he checked himself and Sally and Mary both looked at him inquiringly.

"Father and Mother offered to give it to me when I
49

married," Mary said. "But you see, it's very old—Father's people brought it with them when they came to Illinois from New England. So—"

"Very old! I should think it was! Old and beautiful enough to be very valuable. Those early cabinetmakers certainly knew their craft in the North as well as the South, though I hate to admit it. Well . . . when you move to Louisiana you'd better send for it—the way I sent for my pictures and books and piano."

"Of course, it isn't certain yet that we're moving to Louisiana," Mary said, looking attentively first at Jonathan Fant and then at the furniture.

"No, of course not. But you might keep it in mind, in case you do . . . unless you'd rather have the furniture that's in your house and let me use this."

Nothing more was said just then, either about moving furniture or going to Louisiana and, in the excitement of her father's return which occurred a few days later, Lavinia forgot all about the furniture for the time being, though later she remembered it.

Brent walked in on them, entirely without notice, just as they were sitting down to supper one stifling hot evening in August. They sprang up from the table with one accord except, of course, for grandmother Garland, who had to sit quietly in her wheel chair. But it was easy to see, from the look on her face, that she was almost as happy to have him home again as Mary, who threw her arms around his neck and kissed him, over and over again, in front of everyone, and as Lavinia, who jumped up and down with glee and tried to get close enough to hug him, too. He hugged and kissed his wife, just as heartily as she was hugging and kissing him, and then he freed himself and tossed Lavinia up and down two or three times, getting near his mother-in-law's chair as he did so. Somewhere along the way, he gave Sally a rather casual peck on the cheek; but there was nothing casual in the way he bent over grandmother Garland. When he straightened up again and began shaking hands with grandfather Garland and Jonathan Fant, he cleared his throat once or twice before he said much.

"My train was late; I was afraid you'd be finished and that I'd have to go hungry," he remarked at last, glancing around the laden table. "But it looks as if there were still something left for the tired traveler."

"We don't have supper as early as we used to, because of Mr. Fant's bath," Lavinia informed him, pleased to be in a position to explain.

"Well, I sure am glad he took one tonight," Brent said, drawing up a chair that stood against the wall and making room for himself beside Mother.

"He takes one very night. He puts on all clean clothes, too," Lavinia explained further.

Brent laughed and helped himself to the beef stew. Sally had hastened to set an extra place, and Mary was busily filling a cup with coffee and supplying biscuits and butter and pickles and jelly.

"Now that your father's home again, he'll be the one to decide what time to leave the fields," Jonathan Fant reminded Lavinia. "I've been staying out as long as I could see to work. That makes a difference, you know."

He said it in his usual pleasant way, yet it seemed to Lavinia he was suggesting that her father might like to knock off work earlier than he did and this did not seem to her quite fair. For the first time, she was disturbed instead of delighted by something Jonathan Fant had said. To be sure, her father did not take a bath every night, but he did work long, hard hours, and they had been accustomed to waiting for him, in the summer time. She wanted to explain some more, but so many grown-up people wanted to talk to her father and there were so many things he wanted to say himself that she didn't have a chance.

"You're looking like a different man, Brent. That's a good healthy tan you've got and I believe you've put on weight."

"Well, it'd take some doing not to get tanned in the kind of sunshine they have down where I've been. And I've gained ten pounds. I weighed myself in the depot the day I left and again tonight when I got home, so I know. I guess it's partly what I've been eating. I've got some ideas about food to pass on to you, Mary—not that this isn't a mighty fine stew. But wait until you eat a stew made out of crawfish!"

"Is it really all just wild prairie where you went?"

"No. There are patches of land under cultivation. And there could be a lot more—there will be."

"You wrote that you met the Dusons and that you liked them, but you never told us whether they got their railroad through where they wanted to."

"You bet they did. Not that it was easy for them. . . . You remember about Rayne—the place that had its name changed from Poupeville and that was

51

moved from one location to another by ox team? Jonathan told us—"

"Yes, yes! What happened next?"

"Well, while some of its leading citizens and those of near-by Prairie Hayes were discussing which of the two places would be better for the new parish seat, C. C. Duson got busy. He was general manager, by that time, of the Southwestern Louisiana Land Company, with headquarters at Opelousas."

"What a funny name!"

"It's an Indian name," Brent explained. He seemed perfectly willing to talk now, as if he were trying to make up for all the things he had not said in his letters. "Opelousas was the Confederate capital of Louisiana for a little while during the war, though it was a small city then and still is. It's about forty miles from Rayne. C. C. persuaded Alphonse Levy, the president of the company, that they ought to buy a tract of land still farther west—about six miles from Rayne. They got the whole tract for eighty dollars —one hundred and seventy acres or more—that's less than fifty cents an acre, isn't it? And they made definite plans for laying out a city on it. Told just how wide all the avenues and streets would be—good and wide, too—just how they should be named and numbered. And they decided to call this model place Parkerson, after some other prominent citizen. Then, after they thought everything was under control, including the right of way, the Southern Pacific refused to place a station and agent in this new 'city' unless the Dusons would guarantee the agent's salary and various expenses for six months. But C. C. got around the bosses. He brought some pressure to bear on the ground that the station at Estherwood—"

"Estherwood?"

"Yes, that's another near-by place. Another story, too. Let me get on with this one first, will you? It's about all I can do to tell one at a time, particularly as I'm trying to get something to eat, too."

Brent reached for some more stew, while Mary refilled his cup and went to the oven for the few biscuits which still remained in the pan. "As I was saying," Brent continued, "Duson hinted that the railroad didn't have a clear title to the ground the Estherwood station was on; and one dark night it was surreptitiously moved by flatcar from its original location to a new one—right by the model city that still existed only on paper. A mile or so west of there was a spur track that had been laid when the railroad was being built—one crew coming from the west and the other from the east. The crew from Orange, Texas was in the charge of a genial Irishman, named Pat Crowley, and his men, who liked him a lot—he had risen from section hand to roadmaster—generally referred to it as the Crowley Switch. It didn't take much argument to persuade them—and him—to move this spur slightly to the east and the job wasn't done surreptitiously this time. On the contrary, there was quite a celebration—a bottle of champagne was broken across the track and as the fizz water went bubbling into the ground, the crew christened their handiwork the 'Crowley Switch' in honor of their boss. What's more, the city that the switch connected with the main line was named Crowley, instead of Parkerson."

"That's just the opposite of the story Jonathan told us about Poupeville, isn't it? Remember? The people moved it by oxcart so it would get on the railroad and now it's Rayne. That's right, isn't it, Jonathan?"

"Yes—or so I've always understood. That time, Mohammed went to the mountain. This time, the mountain went to Mohammed. I reckon no one but the Dusons could have managed to pull off a coup like that."

The reference to Mohammed and the mountain was somewhat puzzling to most of Jonathan's hearers and particularly so to Lavinia. On the other hand, it was clear to all that when the Dusons set out to do something, they accomplished their purpose.

"So Crowley is really a city already?" Mary exclaimed.

Brent grinned. "Well, there's a depot—of sorts. And I understand that a blacksmith shop, a livery stable and a company store are going up pretty soon."

"Brent, you couldn't call that a city, even in fun! Why on earth weren't the Dusons satisfied to stay in Rayne, where they were doing so well? Did you ever find out?"

"Not for sure, There are two or three stories about that, too. One is that they went to Mermentau. . . . Look, couldn't I just have some pie and—"

"Oh, please, Father! Please tell us what happened when they went to Mermentau. Then we won't ask you any more questions."

"All right, but remember you promised. It had to do with money. Some have it that they decided to fish, after going there on business, and then discovered they didn't have enough money along to buy the necessary tackle. They took it for granted they could get this on credit, but the store wouldn't let them have it. Another story is that

53

they did confine themselves to business, but that when they tried to buy land on the waterfront, the prices were out of all reason. So instead, they bought that tract I told you about—at forty-five cents an acre! I believe they knew what they were doing. Just the same, Mermentau, right on a river like it is, would have made a good port. Crowley's twelve miles from that stream and almost as far from Bayou Queue de Tortue."

"What's a bayou, Father?"

"Look here, you promised. This time, I really am all through teaching you geography or current history or whatever you choose to call it. Please pass the pie!"

It was so late before they finished supper that, without much discussion it was decided Brent should spend the night at the Garlands' and that the next day he and Mary would move back into their own house and Jonathan Fant would move out. There was no discussion at all as to where this move would take him. Everyone knew.

Nevertheless, after Brent and Mary went to bed, Lavinia, who was occupying a trundle in the same room, realized that Jonathan Fant was again the topic of conversation.

"I didn't like to say this at supper, Mary. But I didn't know where I'd find you, and I stopped by our house first on my way from the depot. I'd hardly have known it."

"Yes, Jonathan has made a good many improvements."

"I suppose they are improvements. But it doesn't seem like my house—of course, I mean our house—any more. Why, the parlor—"

"But don't you think it's pleasant that way, darling, and —and livable? We never had much use out of the parlor before. Now it's used all the time. And all those books and pictures and then the piano. . . . Do you know, Brent, I think Lavinia's got quite a good deal of musical talent. Jonathan's giving her lessons and. . . . If we go to Louisiana will there be anyone who can give her music lessons? And French lessons?"

"*If* we go to Louisiana! Why, it was all settled, before I went away, that we were going! My trip was just to look over the lay of the land."

"Yes, I know. But since then—"

"You told me you'd be glad to go. You said that whatever I wanted was what you wanted, too. You don't mean to tell me that you've been influenced by this tramp, so that you've changed your mind?"

"He's not a tramp! He's the son of one of Mother's oldest friends! He's a kind, cultured gentleman!"

"Mary, I don't like the way you're talking."

"I can't help it. I think you're being very unfair. The changes Jonathan made *are* improvements. And he hasn't made anywhere nearly as many as he might have. He says all that furniture up in the attic is very beautiful—very valuable. He doesn't see why we don't use it instead of—"

"Instead of the furniture I bought you for a wedding present?" He had forgotten momentarily that he himself had taken a dislike to it when he was sick—the first time he had looked at it long and steadily enough to recognize its ugliness. It suddenly seemed beautiful to him again.

"Well, we might as well give the old furniture to Sally for *her* wedding present," Mary said. "Of course, Father and Mother wanted me to have it, but if we're never going to use it—"

"Mary, this is the first time I've heard that you wanted to use it."

"I didn't appreciate it before. But I do now. And I think Sally'd better have it. Because I'm sure she and Jonathan are in love."

"What!"

"It was love at first sight. Jonathan said so himself."

"Well, of course if that's the way things are. . . ." Brent did not finish the sentence, and when he went on, the rising anger was gone from his voice. "How could Sally leave your mother?" he asked thoughtfully but not resentfully.

"She couldn't. They'd live right here, for the present."

"And our house would be empty?"

"I suppose so, for the present anyway. Jonathan could go back and forth between the two places—after all, it's what he's been doing while you've been gone. He says it's just a step—he nearly always walks instead of taking a team, the way we have." She rushed on and Lavinia thought that perhaps this was because it sounded as if she were intimating that Jonathan Fant was a better walker than her parents, though she had not really meant it that way. "Jonathan could still stay here and help Father with the horses. He knows a lot about horses. Father would be glad to have him. He thinks a good deal of Jonathan."

"Well, of course if that's the way things are—" Brent said again and left his sentence unfinished. It was Mary who went back to what he had said before.

"You know it wasn't I who suggested leaving our home,

Brent. It was you. And you didn't seem to mind. You said we'd have a better one. I thought you didn't care what happened to that one. I didn't think you'd mine if it were changed or empty."

"No, I don't mind," Brent said slowly. "That is, I don't mind much. But I think maybe the sooner we get started for Louisiana. . . ."

They did not get started right away, however, after all. Brent was very much excited when the news came through that a separate parish, called Acadia, had been formed from the southwest portion of St. Landry in accordance with the Dusons' schemes; also, that Crowley was to be the new parish seat, likewise in accordance with their schemes; and that the plant of their newspaper, the *Signal*, had been moved there from Rayne. It was easy to see that he was itching to be off; but he agreed it was only fair he should stay in Illinois until the crops were all in, since Jonathan Fant had worked so hard to do well with them, alone, up to then. Jonathan had taken all of his things out of the younger Winslows' parlor immediately, and had apologized for not doing so before Brent's return; of course he would have, he said, if he had only known when Brent was coming. His books and pictures and piano were now in the Garlands' parlor, which was a good deal larger than the Winslows', and looked very well there. Both grandfather and grandmother Garland seemed to be pleased to have these additions to their belongings and, as for Sally, she was delighted with them and with Mary's offer to give her the old furniture stored in the attic. In fact, Sally seemed to be delighted with everything these days, and though she had always been rosy and merry and chubby, she was now rosier and merrier and chubbier than ever. It turned out to be quite true that she was planning to marry Jonathan, and Brent realized that she would want to have her sister present at the wedding, besides really needing her sister's help to get ready for it, especially as grandmother Garland was getting frailer and frailer all the time. She had never been one to refer to her crippled condition if she could help it, but finally she spoke to Brent about it.

"I do hope I'm going to live to see Jonathan and Sally safely married, Brent."

"Why, of course you are! You're going to live for years! Whatever put the idea that you weren't into your head?"

"I didn't say I wasn't," grandmother Garland answered, still smiling.

"But you said—"

"Well, what makes you think I was talking about my miserable body? I might have been talking about something else."

"You don't think Jonathan Fant would go back on Sally, do you? Why, no man could do a thing like that to a girl like Sally! And she worships the ground he walks on."

"Yes, she does. And no—no, I don't think he'll go back on her—once they're married. I think he'll make her a good, faithful husband. But he's been a rover for a long time, Brent. It's hard to change the habits of years. He's talking now about returning to South Carolina before the wedding. It seems there are some matters there he wants to wind up, and some more things he wants to have sent here."

"That sounds reasonable. But why doesn't he marry Sally first and take her along? It would make a fine wedding trip for her."

"I thought of that myself, Brent, and I thought of suggesting it. But I refrained. There are lots of things a woman thinks of that she's wiser not to mention to a man. I've learned that. But Sally hasn't, I'm sorry to say. She *did* suggest it and Jonathan didn't think well of the suggestion. He says he'd rather be married after Christmas."

"*After Christmas!* Why then I couldn't get started back to Louisiana until sometime next year!"

"Well, early next year. Would you mind waiting that long?"

"Yes, I would. Once I've decided on a move, I want to make it."

He did not change his mind about this, but Jonathan Fant did not change his mind, either. As soon as the crops were in, he left for South Carolina, with rather vague references as to just when he would return. Sally went ahead with the preparations for her marriage, and everyone talked about the wedding that was to take place soon after Christmas, with Lavinia for flower girl and all the neighbors invited in for a big supper. But Sally did not look as rosy or seem so merry as before he went away, and she grew thinner, and grandmother Garland kept looking frailer and frailer and growing more and more helpless. And every time they saw grandmother Winslow she sniffed when she asked if they had heard when Jonathan Fant was coming back, and Lavinia knew that meant she did not believe he intended to, ever. Lavinia began to be afraid she was right.

He wrote very nice letters, not only to Sally but also to grandfather and grandmother Garland and to Lavinia herself. He likewise sent them all very nice Christmas presents; but he still did not say when he was coming back. And, early in January, grandmother Garland died one night in her sleep, so quietly that not even her husband knew she was dead until morning.

They wired Jonathan Fant and he arrived in time for the funeral, much to grandmother Winslow's discomfiture. He was kind and helpful to everyone and sympathetic with everyone. He seemed to understand that it comforted Sally to cry on his shoulder and have him stroke her bright hair while she did so; that it was an effort for Mary to make the funeral arrangements and that she could turn only to Brent for support; and that grandfather Garland did not want to talk at all, as he sat hour after hour staring straight ahead of him, his massive frame shaking, as it always had, but not with laughter any more. They all realized that Jonathan was grieving, too, not only because grandmother Garland had died, but because he had not seen her again before her death; the affection and admiration he had felt for her were unquestionable. At the services, he sat with the family, beside Lavinia; he held her hand and every now and then he unobtrusively gave her a clean handkerchief. And in that awful, vacant period, after they had returned from the cemetery and the house was in order again and there was nothing to do and everyone was wishing that there were, he went into the parlor and played soft, beautiful music that gradually brought solace. Then, the next morning, the wheel chair, which had confronted them all with its appalling emptiness, was gone. None of them ever saw it again, and they all knew Jonathan Fant had quietly disposed of it in some way that would hurt them least and they were all very grateful to him.

There was only one thing he did not do which all of them, consciously or unconsciously, were waiting for him to do: he did not say anything more about marrying Sally.

It was Mary who finally spoke to him on the subject. Possibly she had never heard her mother say that there were many things of which a woman thought, but which she knew it was wiser not to mention to a man; or possibly, like Sally, she had not learned the wisdom of this saying, even though she had heard it fairly often. She was at the Garlands' house a great deal, going through her mother's belongings: giving away some of the clothing to the needy, sorting old letters and souvenirs, checking precious items of linen and china and silver, to make sure nothing was missing and that everyone would receive a just inheritance. Rightly, she had reasoned that it would be less painful to do all this immediately than to allow a certain period to elapse and then return to the task, reviving the poignancy of the loss which time had begun to temper mercifully. Sally could not see it that way; she shut herself up in her room and cried, and sometimes Mary sent Lavinia to stay with her, telling her to keep very quiet but adding that often, when people were unhappy, it helped them to have someone they were fond of near at hand, even if that person did not speak at all. So Lavinia tiptoed in and out of Sally's room. Sally did not always notice when the little girl stole in, because she herself was lying on her bed, with face muffled in the pillows while she cried; and Mary did not always notice when the little girl stole out, because she herself was preoccupied looking at old valentines or counting old teaspoons.

The day that Mary spoke to Jonathan about Sally was one of the times she did not notice that Lavinia had come back into the room where she was working. She was sitting at a desk, very busy with the contents of its pigeonholes and, though she did see Jonathan, that was because he came and stood so close beside her and because his footsteps had made a slight sound as he came across the floor, so that she had looked up to see what this was. But she had her back to the door and Lavinia had paused near the threshold, not wanting to interrupt when she saw that her mother and Jonathan Fant apparently had something important to say to each other, and not wanting to startle them, either, by making a noise.

"Will it bother you if I sit down for a few minutes?" Jonathan asked Mary.

"No. I'm at a good stopping place and I've been wanting to talk to you anyway."

"That's good. Because I've been wanting to talk to you."

"Shall I begin or will you?"

"I'd rather you began. It might help with what I have to say."

"All right. It's this, Jonathan. I know you've hesitated to —to do much love-making, so soon after Mother's death. I know you've been careful to show respect to her memory and to consider our feelings—Sally's feelings. But I honestly believe it would be a comfort to her if—"

"I have infinite respect for your mother's memory. But it wasn't on that account I've refrained from making love to Sally. It wasn't on account of Sally's feelings, either. It was on account of my own."

"But this loss can't be such a deep personal grief for you as it is for the rest of us."

"No. I wasn't referring to a deep personal grief. I was referring to an entirely different kind of feeling."

"I don't know what you mean, Jonathan."

"Don't you, Mary?"

"No. If I did, I wouldn't ask you."

"And you are asking me?"

"Yes."

"All right then. Remember I didn't tell you until you did. I'm not in love with Sally. I'm in love with you."

Mary sprang up, scattering the papers she still had on her lap as she did so.

"How dare you—" she began. But she could not say any more, for Jonathan took hold of her shoulders and pressed down on them, not roughly, but hard enough to force her back into her chair. Then he continued to stand over her, preventing her escape.

"Remember I didn't tell you until you asked me to," he repeated compellingly. "So don't ask me how I dare, and go on to remind me that an honorable man doesn't tell a married woman—especially a woman with a child—that he's in love with her. I was attracted to Sally, superficially, when I first saw her. She's a very pretty girl, in her way— comely might be a better word for it. I didn't dream she'd take my casual compliments seriously or that anyone else would. I didn't realize her complete lack of sophistication. And evidently I underestimated my own powers of attraction—for her. At all events, the first thing that I knew she was assuming that we were engaged."

"*Assuming!*"

"Yes. That's what I said and that's what I meant—assuming. I never asked her, in so many words, to marry me."

"Perhaps not in so many words. But you must have given her to understand—"

"She *mis*understood. I don't think your mother did. I think she guessed. At least, I think she guessed I wasn't anywhere nearly as much in love with Sally as Sally was with me. I don't think she guessed I was in love with you. I hope not."

"You *hope* not! That's a pretty mild way of saying it! She would have died if she'd thought—"

"Well, she did die, didn't she, Mary?"

For a moment, heavy silence hung over the room. Then Jonathan spoke again, less harshly.

"That wasn't fair. I don't think she died of grief, or shame, or anything of the sort. I think she died of perfectly natural causes and I think she died with her mind at rest. I think she knew I'd left because I didn't feel too sure then whether or not I could go through with this marriage. I think she wasn't certain I was coming back—until just before the end. Then I wrote her that I *was* coming back. You'll probably find the letter before long. I think it comforted her, that she died happier because of it. I think she'd been worrying about Sally before she got it—about Sally's hurt pride at being jilted."

"A lot more than hurt pride is involved and you know it."

"Oh, yes, I know it. I wasn't going to put that too plainly, either. But you've asked me again to say something I wouldn't have said otherwise. She was worrying about Sally's unrequited desire, about her need for fulfillment through physical union, about her thwarted maternal instincts."

"Jonathan Fant, will you stop!"

"In just a minute. I'm ready now to go through with this marriage, if Sally will stop crying long enough to make the necessary preparations for a suitable ceremony. But I'm not ready to go through with it under false pretenses. I want Sally to come to her senses first. I want her to admit that, though I'm proposing marriage now, I never did before, and I want it understood that I'm not being cajoled or coerced into this by her urgency or her tears. I'm doing it because it seems the most sensible possible arrangement under all the circumstances. I can't expect you to get rid of Brent, either by fair means or foul. In fact, I'm not sure I want you to. He's a pretty decent sort. I can't expect you to leave your child who, by the way, is a very nice child, with some intelligence; she may be a little on the prim side, but if she has the right kind of a suitor, he'll take care of that when the times comes. I can't expect you to stay at home and have a surreptitious affair with me; it would hurt your conscience terribly and whether you believe it or not, it would hurt mine a little, too. Besides, I think you're pretty fond of Brent and, that being the case, you wouldn't put much warmth into an affair with another man. You see I've thought over all these phases of the situation and decided that they're all either impractical or undesirable or both. But I'd like to be a member of your family and see as much of you as I can within the reasonable bounds of decency. And don't make a mistake. I think Sally's an attractive girl and I think she'll make a good wife. I'll do my best to be a good husband and make our marriage a success. But if it fails, I don't want you to tell me afterward that this was all my fault. Because, no matter how hard I try, it probably won't be as much of a success as it would have been if I'd fallen in love with Sally instead of you."

It was getting dark when Mary and Lavinia started home. Lavinia thought that her mother was crying, but she was not sure, because she could not see very well in the dim light; besides, Mary was walking very rapidly, as if she wanted to leave the Garlands' house behind her as fast as she could and reach her own as soon as she could. Lavinia was more puzzled than she had ever been, despite all the other bewilderments of the past few months. She did not understand at all what Jonathan Fant meant by saying he was in love with her mother instead of Aunt Sally and evidently her mother did not, either, or she would not be crying about it; she was not only puzzled, she was grieved. Lavinia longed to comfort her, but she could not do that without letting her mother know what she had overheard and something told her that she should not do that, though this "something" was another source of bewilderment. Moreover, her mother kept walking faster and faster.

Darkness had completely closed in when Mary and Lavinia reached home. Brent had finished his chores and was sitting at the kitchen table reading his paper. There was no sign of supper, and Lavinia was afraid her father might be rather cross about this; he was still inclined to be resentful over late meals. However, he did not say a single word about supper. When Mary opened the door, he jumped up and rushed toward her and Lavinia, waving his paper excitedly.

"Listen to this!" he exclaimed. And then, before either of the others could say a word, he began to read:

"CROWLEY, LA.—LANDS! LANDS AND

LOTS FOR SALE. AUCTION SALE WILL TAKE PLACE FEB. 10, 1887—OF TOWN LOTS IN CROWLEY, AND 150,000 ACRES OF GOOD LANDS SITUATED IN ACADIA, ST. LANDRY, LAFAYETTE AND CALCASIEU PARISHES. SOUTHWESTERN LOUISIANA LAND COMPANY, OPELOUSAS, LA. OR W. W. DUSON, GENERAL MANAGER, RAYNE, ACADIA PARISH, LA."

He flung the paper down on the table and looked at his wife, his normally firm mouth quivering.

"I know that's less than two weeks off," he said excitedly. "But I've got to go. This is my big chance—*our* big chance. Don't tell me you can't get ready to go, too. You've *got* to get ready. This time, you and Lavinia have got to come with me."

"Yes, Brent, I know we have," Mary answered.

The night before they left their old home, to go forth seeking their new one, Brent walked through the yard to the outbuildings a second time, after the chores were done, and he let Lavinia go with him, though it was later than she usually stayed up. He walked past the henhouse without even stopping, and he did not linger in the barn, though he did stop briefly in front of each stall. But when he came to the beehives, on his way back to the house, he stayed and stayed, looking down at them. The hives were all still snugly wrapped in their winter coverings, so he could not watch his bees at work, as he was in the habit of doing during the summer. But Lavinia knew that he was longing to do so, and that he was going to feel sorry a long, long time, because he had not been able to say good-by to them. He had not bothered to say good-by to the chickens, and he had not minded saying good-by to the cows and horses; but this was different. The chickens did not count at all and the horses and cows were only animals, but the bees were people, as far as he was concerned. Lavinia's heart began to hurt her, as she stood there beside him, watching him while he looked steadfastly and silently at the well-covered hives, and a choked feeling came into her throat.

But when he finally did speak to her, all he said was, "Come, Lavinia, we mustn't stay out here all night, losing our sleep. We've got to be up before dawn or we won't catch the local that makes connections with the excursion train from Chicago. Besides, it's terribly cold. It's going to be nice and warm in Louisiana. And you'll have a fine time riding on the cars."

PART TWO

The Dusons

CHAPTER V

It was terribly crowded on the excursion train and no one was in good humor any more. At first there had been hearty greetings, cordial self-introductions, long conversations about past experiences and future plans, exchanges of lunch box contents, card games, community singing, even impromptu prayer meetings. Now everyone knew everyone else's name and as much of any person's background and prospects as that person chose to tell. The lunch boxes were empty, and the untidy remains of their contents littered the red plush seats and the uncarpeted floors, which were not only grease stained, but rank with stale tobacco juice. Even the water cooler at one end of the car was empty, and the communal glass beneath it, which had been filled and refilled countless times, was clouded with grime. Thirsty children clamored in vain for drinks, hurling themselves against their helpless and desperate parents; equally thirsty men tried to extract a few more drops from the flasks, already drained, they had carried about their persons, some with a swagger, some with stealth. Only the women who, being respectable, would never have touched liquor except in private, for medicinal purposes, made no effort to cool their parched throats; they recognized the futility of this, some patiently, some petulantly, some with voices which had become harsh and hoarse with complaint and cinders. They were more uncomfortable than either their husbands or their offspring, for travel imposed greater hardships on them. They could not brush and comb their long hair properly; they could not release themselves from their whalebone corsets; they could not even wash very much. Some of them carried bottles of cologne water with them, and dabbled this on their handkerchiefs, using them to wipe off the worst of the grime from their hands and faces; but the supply of cologne water was giving out, too, and the handkerchiefs were all soiled by this time. The neat, dark dresses, made with tight basques and bustles, in which they had started out, were spotted and disordered; besides, they were made of thick materials and were now far too heavy. It had been bitterly cold when the excursionists from Chicago and St. Louis had left home; now the weather was as balmy as May in the Middle West, and only the passengers from Mobile or some equally southern point, who had joined the other travelers in New Orleans, were more comfortably clad. The children, who kept rushing up and down the aisle, shouting at each other, were streaming with perspiration; the men mopped their faces and told each other, without abashment, that they were sweating like steers; the women tried to find clean corners on their misused handkerchiefs, with which they could surreptitiously wipe away the worst of the moisture that gathered around their high, tight collars and dripped from under the heavy hair on the temples. When the windows were opened, clouds of cinders blew in, and two or three persons got these in their eyes, thereby adding actual pain and disability to their already great discomfort; when the windows were closed, the atmosphere was malodorous as well as stifling.

If they had only been able to believe that the end was in sight, the midwestern excursionists would not have found these various trials so unbearable. They had boasted, at the beginning, that they were pioneers, that of course they expected privations and hardships; but somehow they had all visualized these as arising in connection with the new homes they would triumphantly establish, and not with the process of reaching them. They had been prepared to put up with primitive shelter, at least temporarily, and to experiment with making unfamiliar land productive; they had overlooked the crowding, the confusion, the disorder, the dirt that would precede their arrival in the promised land.

When the whistle of the engine first began to blow, they took little notice of it, because there was so much noise in the car already; but as the blowing became more and more insistent, the men grew curious and some of the women alarmed. Brent caught hold of a brakeman who was hurrying through the car and detained him almost forcibly.

"What's the matter? Are we in danger?"

"No, we ain't, but must be some damfool cow is. The

engineer's trying to frighten her off the track, but she just keeps runnin' along in front of the train. Looks like we might have to stop, so I can get out and chase her away."

"Stop! But we're running late already!"

The first protest came in a chorus. It was quickly renewed in various forms from various directions.

"We were promised we'd get there in time for the auction!" . . . "Three o'clock sharp it begins, and if I know anything about that man Duson, when he says three o'clock that's what he means." . . . "Well, even if we don't stop, we'll never get there on time if we have to chase a cow all the way from here to Crowley. We haven't got to Rayne yet, have we?" . . . "Can't the engineer slow down, without stopping, just for a minute? Then you could get off in front, drive her away and swing back on again at the rear."

The last was in the form of an appeal to the harassed brakeman. He nodded and broke away.

"I'll talk to the engineer and see what we can do."

The heavy door banged after him. Even the shouting children were momentarily quiet, as the train began to slow down, and the sounds of escaping steam and a ringing bell echoed through the car, mingling with the persistent whistle and a new noise—the indignant mooing of an outraged brindle cow. The children crowded to the windows in time to see her heading toward the surrounding prairie land, her tail and hind legs still registering protest. Then the bell ringing and the whistling stopped, and the train slowly began to gather momentum again.

"All there is in this Godforsaken country is Creole cows like that one and crawfish chimneys," the brakeman remarked scornfully. "Why anyone should think they wants to buy land around here, or anyone should think they could sell it, sure beats me."

"Well, some of us have come a long way with the certainty that we did want to buy, and we sure wouldn't have done it if we hadn't been certain Duson would sell it to us."

Brent had not aggressively or even consciously assumed the role of spokesman for the entire group. But they now spontaneously accepted him as such.

"That's right, Winslow." . . . "There's goin' to be buyin' and sellin' both today and both worth the money put into 'em." . . . "What does a brakeman know about the country anyway? Only what he sees out of a car window!"

"And I'm telling you that's more than enough for me," muttered the brakeman, slamming the front door of the car after him.

The incident of the refractory cow, instead of adding to the general gloom, somehow relieved it. Several men gathered around Brent and began to discuss their immediate plans with renewed enthusiasm. Mary called Lavinia and started fixing her hair, first brushing it smoothly away from its central part and then replaiting her long fair braids, determined that in this respect, at least, her little daughter should look neat. Several other mothers immediately followed suit, exchanging half-helpless, half-joking comments on the essential untidiness of children as they did so. While they were still thus industriously and pleasantly engaged, the train slackened speed again, and again there was the sound of escaping steam, this time to the accompaniment of screeching brakes. Then the brakeman flung open one door and the conductor the other, simultaneously shouting, "Crowley! Crowley!" and the stampede to leave the car began.

Brent was well to the forefront of the crowd, with Mary and Lavinia beside him; but Lavinia suddenly remembered that, in her haste, she had left her doll behind, and started elbowing her way back to get it. Mary, unwilling to be parted from her, waited a minute and then went back, too. By the time they caught up with Brent, nearly all their traveling companions were on the platform of the depot, where a babel of voices rose above the mingled sounds of creaking vehicles, plunging or floundering horses and near-by hammering.

"Take your bags, sir? Hack right here! This way to the Crowley House! Only hotel in town, so far."

"Only *hotel!* Only building, I'd say!"

"They're going up fast though. . . . Watch out for that mud, ma'am. Liable to go down deep, once you step off the platform."

"Told you this was no place for a woman to come, Martha."

"If Mary Winslow can come with her husband, I guess I can come with mine, Abner Barnes, 'specially as we don't have a young one to lug along. . . . Where is that auction, boy?"

"Ain't started yet. Going to be right in front of the Crowley House. Take your bag? Hack right here."

There had been a general rush toward the first hack and as many as possible of those who had missed it now elbowed their way along and piled into the second one. But a few persons, instead of pushing and plunging, either milled around aimlessly or stood motionless but observant, evidently preferring to take stock of their general surroundings before examining any of these individually. In like measure, a few scathing comments about "snow diggers" and others, exceptionally strange, shrill, amazed or vehement, penetrated the general hubbub or rose above it.

"J'ai peur que ces Américains nous dérangent beaucoup. Pire que cela. Ils vont—"

"Tais toi! Tu es trop grossier! Ils nous écoutent."

"Lord! Sounds as if we done come too far from Kansas and fell plumb off the bottom of the United States!" exclaimed the woman addressed by her husband as Martha, staring hard at the strangers.

"Those must be some of the Cajuns we heard tell about," Abner rejoined. "They don't look any too friendly, but maybe they're waiting for us to make up to them. Howdy, folks!"

One of the Cajuns walked away, muttering something unintelligible, but evidently insulting, for his companion called after him, voicing a sharp rebuke, and then, shrugging his shoulders, turned toward the Kansans with the grudging salutation, *"Comment sais."*

"I ain't sayin' nothin' more. I'm just a plain American from Kansas. Come on, Ma. Pick up your skirts!"

"We walkin'?"

"Hacks have gone. No other way to get where we're goin', that I know of."

"Then I ain't walkin' nor wearin' petticoats again until we get some sidewalks. I ain't used to this mud."

"I told you not to come."

"I guess we do have to walk," Brent said, turning to Mary. He had set down the two heavy bags he had been carrying, but now he picked them up again. "There were two hacks here a few minutes ago, but they seem to have disappeared. There's only that one wagon, on the other side of the road, and evidently it isn't a public conveyance —anyway, there isn't anyone in it. You don't mind going to the Crowley House on foot, do you?"

"Of course not. We'll be able to see things better, walking."

She was carrying a bag herself and Lavinia was clinging to her free hand. But, in spite of her weariness, her voice suddenly sounded eager and cheerful and she was abreast of him close to the edge of the platform. Suddenly he caught hold of her and jerked her back. The horse hitched to the wagon across the street had begun to rear and neigh; men were yelling, women screaming. The tumult, which had died down momentarily, had risen again with redoubled force.

"Look out for that horse!"

"Don't snatch at his bridle, you damn fool! Give him room!"

"Runaway horse! Clear the street!"

"He sho' can't run fast, no, nor neither far in this gumbo mud," a man, standing near the Winslows, with his arm around the shoulders of a stocky, shockheaded boy, remarked dryly.

"No, no. He'll be under control in a minute." Another man, who had just come toward them, spoke with a complete calm that was contagious. He was taller and slimmer than most of the others in the crowd and noticeably neater. Except for a small mustache, he was clean shaven, and the firm outline of his smooth chin, his fresh color, broad brow and high cheekbones all served to make him outstanding in a group, for the most part, bearded, swarthy and thick-set. The glasses he was wearing did not obscure the keenness of his blue eyes and, after a swift glance at the Winslows, he came closer still. "Good evening, folks," he said genially. "Glad to see you. Sorry I couldn't reach this side of the platform sooner, but there was a jam the first few minutes after the train got in. I overheard you say you thought perhaps you'd better walk. Don't think of it. The hacks will be here again right away and so will my surrey, which got pressed into service, too. We have to keep sending vehicles back and forth, because there's still such a scarcity, but there'll be only a short delay, I assure you. . . . Let me introduce myself. Duson's the name—W. W. Duson." He held out his hand and looked at Brent more closely still. "We've met before, haven't we?"

"Yes, but I didn't expect you to remember," said Brent, taking the proffered hand and finding the grip warm and firm. "I was here last spring for a while, just looking around, and I saw you once then. Winslow's the name— Brent Winslow."

"Of course, of course! At the Gossens', wasn't it? Yes, I thought so. And I recall telling myself afterward, 'That's just the sort of a man we need around here.' Glad to welcome you back. Come for the auction, have you?"

"I read about it in the paper," Brent said, "And I thought—"

"To be sure, to be sure! Shows I was right, the way I sized you up the first time. And now you've brought your family with you?"

"Yes. This is my wife," Brent said, turning toward Mary. "And our little daughter Lavinia."

"How are you, madam?" Mr. Duson inquired, somewhat more formally. "How are you, Lavinia? Delighted to see you both. I hope you had a pleasant journey?"

"Well—" Mary began a little doubtfully. Then she brightened, for no explicable reason except that it did not seem fitting to tell this pleasant stranger, who was greeting them so cordially, that the journey had not been pleasant at all, that it had been tedious and trying. "We're very happy to be here," she added hastily.

"And well you may be, well you may be," Mr. Duson assued her with heartiness. "This is going to be an experience you'll never forget. Not many people have the chance to be in at the birth of a town."

"That's true, they don't," remarked the man who had said that no horse could run far or fast in such mud, and who now volunteered the information that his name was Ursin Villac, and the further information that the stocky, shockheaded boy accompanying him was his son Claude. He had a decided accent, and Brent concluded that he must be another Cajun, but he was not unintelligible, like the first one they had seen, and he was speaking less dryly and more cheerfully now: he felt the auction should be a pretty good show—in fact, that was why he had brought Claude along, to see the fun. He had left five more young ones at home and all those who were old enough to talk had teased to come along, too; but one boy at a time was enough for a man to manage alone; it was different with a woman: she didn't mind having two tugging at her skirts, one in her arms and one under her apron, all together. The shockheaded boy, whose introduction had precipitated these remarks and who had been solemnly and silently staring at Lavinia, now grinned and, with a mumbled greeting, held out a stick of candy, part of which he had already munched away. Lavinia smiled back and accepted the offering with expressions of great appreciation. All in all, Duson's good will, like his calmness, was apparently contagious. He now went on, in a still more lively vein than that in which he had spoken before.

"We haven't got around to street improvements yet, but

that will come—yes, that will come. And we already have the best near-by farming and stock-raising land in the world. Good grass, good water, good timber and good health overflow."

"Looks like somethin' overflowed, for true," Villac remarked with a grin, nodding at the morass before them. "Never saw so much gumbo mud an' water in all my life, me."

"That's what it takes to make that good grass I was telling you about. Wintertime puts plenty of sweet water in the ground. Gives us year-round pasturage. You won't have to keep your cows and horses in the barn six months of the year, like you do in Illinois."

"I never come from Illinois, me. You must know that, yes, just hearin' me talk. I'm from Breaux Bridge, me, same like you."

"Breaux Bridge, eh? Strange we never met before."

"We been livin' in Lacombe, lately, the whole family, us. My wife's people, them, come from there. Now my brudder-in-law make up his mind they all oughta move to Slidell. Me, I don't fancy no livin' in Slidell an' I tell him so. I gotta speak w'at's in my mind, me. Slidell got a brick-yard. Slidell got shipyards, Slidell got a railroad. When you livin' in Slidell, you ain't livin' in the country, no, you livin' in the city, like it was Nawlins. I don't want to live in no city, me. So I tell my wife, her, I got relations, too, named Primeaux, that's homesteadin' out here an' mebbe we could homestead out here ourselves with my relations, 'stead of hers."

"I hope you do, I hope you do. You're welcome, Mr. Villac, most welcome. I want to see folks coming here from all parts of Louisiana. But Mr. Brent Winslow here from—"

"From Illinois. I know what you were talking about. We're lucky if we get by keeping our stock under cover no more than six months."

"You see, Mr. Villac, you see. And what about you, Mr.—?" He turned, questioningly, to another bystander.

"The name's Glenny, Daniel J. Glenny, from Harris County, Texas."

"Glad to know you, Mr. Glenny. You came for the auction, too, I presume?"

"Well, you might say I came to look things over around here. Investigate business opportunities. I'm no 'snow digger' any more than Villac here. But I saw an ad in my home town paper, just like Winslow here did. The ad sure made out there were plenty of them here."

"And so there are, so there are, plenty of them," Mr. Duson hasten to assure his hearers. "Now I guess this little lady's tired standing here while we go on talking, and I haven't begun to tell you the half of what I wanted to. The hacks aren't back yet, but here comes my surrey, with my good friend Elisha Andrus driving it, one of the best drivers and one of the best fiddlers, too, that you'll find in a month of Sundays. He'll play for you to dance any time you say the word. But that's neither here nor there right now. Why don't you let me drive you all down to the Crowley House?"

While he was speaking, a covered conveyance, with a lean, sandy-haired man in the driver's seat, had approached the platform and drawn up beside it. Although Mr. Duson had referred to it as a surrey, it was not only much larger than any vehicle, so designated, that the Winslows had ever seen, but was constructed on entirely different lines. It contained three broad seats, the two at the rear facing each other. Obviously, it provided plenty of room for the entire group, with space to spare.

"Why, that's very kind of you," Mary said gratefully, acknowledging the polite salutation of Elisha Andrus. "Perhaps there'd be time for Lavinia to take a bath before the auction," she added. "You see, we have been on the train rather a long while and—"

For the first time, Mr. Duson looked slightly dubious. "There must be some kind of a washtub available," he said. "Naturally, we haven't had time yet to install—"

"Oh, I realize that! A washtub would do finely!"

"Plenty of opportunities," Mr. Duson reiterated, turning to Mr. Glenny, after they had all climbed into his surrey and the horse had begun to flounder through the mud in the direction of the hotel. "You've already seen the depot. Good-looking building, isn't it? Used to be at Estherwood. The section gang loaded it on flatcars and carted it over, so it would be here in time for the auction. Besides that and the hotel, we've got a livery stable, a blacksmith's shop and store. We've got a schoolhouse going up, too."

"Can we see it from here?" Mary inquired with interest.

"No, it's down the road a piece. It hasn't progressed very far yet. We figured the first thing we needed was the hotel."

"And where that is?" Villac inquired.

"Why, right there ahead of you! Of course, it isn't finished yet, but they can put you up for the night all right. There'll be hammering going on as soon as daylight comes, but that's going on everywhere and anyhow you won't want to spend all your time sleeping."

He pointed proudly toward the skeletal form of a frame building which rose before them in the midst of the treeless bog through which they were floundering.

Mary pressed her lips tightly together and Brent, after glancing quickly at her, turned to meet the quizzical gaze of Ursin Villac. Glenny laughed, not very heartily.

"So that's the Crowley House, eh?" he said with scorn. "After reading that ad of yours in the paper, I thought you really had something here. But I see you was just stringing us poor suckers along. All you've got is a vast prairie land and a wild dream."

"You're wrong there, Mr. Glenny, dead wrong," Duson said earnestly. He brushed aside the scathing references to suckers as unworthy of notice and went on, "What we've got here is opportunity. Course it takes a good businessman to see that, but the fellows who bought lots here yesterday all realized it."

"You were selling lots yesterday? Before the auction?" Brent inquired. He felt that Duson had contrived to turn the tables on Glenny. The unmistakable inference was that, if the Texan could not grasp the obvious opportunities, he was the one lacking in acumen, and Brent could not keep a faint note of anxiety from tingeing his tone.

"Couldn't hold the crowd back. Meant to, honest I did, but I couldn't. Sold ninety-nine town lots and some farmland for a total of nine thousand five hundred dollars. Had a large crowd the day before that, too, and there'll be one just as large tomorrow. That'll give you an idea of the way we're growing." Mr. Duson lowered his voice, though there was no other vehicle near by, and the hammering which he intimated would prove effective as an alarm clock, the following morning, was equally effective in preventing the sound of speech from carrying now. "Crowley's going to be the parish seat of Acadia, the new parish we've just created," he said importantly. "That's what we call counties down here, ma'am, in case you didn't know."

"Yes, I happen to. A—an acquaintance told us that," Mary murmured, speaking at the same time as Brent, who gave the information less hesitantly.

"Well then, you know that the term 'parish,' the way I used it, has no connection with a church any more. And

74

yes, sirree, Crowley's going to be the Acadia Parish seat. We've got it all fixed."

"Fixed?" Mary inquired, more boldly.

"Yes, sirree," Mr. Duson said again. "We're going to give them the land for the site and the money to put up the courthouse."

Mary wanted to ask to whom "we" and "they" referred, but she was afraid the question might be indiscreet and, in any case, she was so engulfed with fatigue that even the simplest question was becoming an effort. The Crowley House had looked fairly near when it had first been identified as such to her and Mr. Duson's other passengers, but progress toward it was almost unbelievably slow. Mr. Glenny now made a further skeptical remark.

"A deal like that will run into money. Building's high these days."

"That's so. But we figure five thousand will do it. Anyway, that's what we're willing to give if they'll locate the courthouse here. This town's all set to be the commercial center of the new parish. It ought to be the political center, too. . . . Well, here we are and I can hear the band beginning to tune up and see that the barbecue's most ready. Complimentary, of course. You're all the guests of the Southwestern Louisiana Land Company today. Come on and get something hot and hearty inside you before the auction starts."

"If we could just go to our room for a few minutes first—" Mary said hopefully.

"To be sure, to be sure. Come right in, ma'am. We'll see what Dominic can do for you."

He climbed nimbly down over the wheel, his feet, encased in heavy boots, sinking far into the mud as he did so. Then he held out his arms and swung first Lavinia and then Mary clear of the mire and onto the wooden steps of the Crowley House. Brent, Villac and Glenny, all laden with bags, scrambled after them, followed by Claude. The opening at the head of the steps still lacked a door and the interior, jammed with a milling crowd, was plainly visible. It consisted of one vast room, unplastered and unpainted, so that the rough studs and beams were all in full view; an immense counter, running across one end of it, served as a bar and was doing a lively business. The roulette wheel and the chuck-a-luck cage, which stood near by, were also well patronized; but no one resembling a room clerk seemed to be stationed anywhere; in fact, no one appeared to be standing still or remaining quiet. However, Duson, after glancing quickly around, singled out a man who was starting for the bar, in company with two boon companions and, catching him by the shoulder, swung him around, not roughly or brusquely, but in the same easy, effortless way in which he appeared to do everything.

"Mr. and Mrs. Winslow of Illinois want accommodations for themselves and their little girl, Dominic," he said. "Mr. Glenny and Mr. Villac and Mr. Villac's little boy will be needing some, too. Mr. Glenny and Mr. Villac have been strangers to each other until today but we're all going to be friends now and I presume they won't mind sharing a room."

The stocky individual thus addressed, whose hair was liberally plastered with bear's grease and whose soiled pink shirt sleeves protruded from a fancy vest, appeared to take the suggestion as a huge joke. "Accommodations?" he echoed, with a loud guffaw. "Something like what they'd get at the St. Charles, down in New Orleans, I presume? We've got all the men who've come in here bunking together, on one side of a partition upstairs, and most of the women and kids on another." He squirmed slightly, for Duson's grasp on his shoulder had tightened, and he took a second look at Mary. "Well, there are one or two little cubbyholes boarded off," he admitted. "If you'll come with me, ma'am. . . . Of course, the rest of you can follow along if you want to," he remarked, as if in afterthought. "I suppose you've got to put your bags down somewhere before you start for the auction."

He led the way up a flight of rickety stairs and turned to the left, where something which had once presumably served as a sheet hung in front of an otherwise open doorway. Raising this dingy drapery, he disclosed a bed covered with a quilt of doubtful cleanliness, one straight-backed chair in an extremely battered condition, and an unpainted pine table surmounted by a chipped bowl and pitcher. Lavinia, who had scampered ahead of the others, was the first to peep inside. She swung around and faced her parents incredulously.

"Is this our new home?" she inquired. "The one Father said would be better than the other that we had before?"

CHAPTER VI

There was no note of mournfulness in her incredulity, but it was obvious that her implicit confidence in the wisdom of their ways had been subjected to a severe strain. Brent and Mary spoke almost simultaneously in attempted reassurance, which sounded inadequate not only to them, but to the other interested bystanders.

"This isn't our home, darling. This is just a place where we're going to stay for a few days while we're *choosing* our new home. And that *will* be better than the one we had before. You wait and see!"

"Why don't you and your mother both lie down and take a nice long nap? Then when you wake up I'll come and tell you I've found our new home!"

"But I'm hungry! And Mr. Duson said there was going to be a barbecue! And what about that auction? I've never been to an auction and I thought we'd come here on purpose to go to one."

Mr. Duson stepped forward. "That's right, sugar, so you have, so you have," he agreed. "You just wash your hands and face, like your marmer wants you to, and give her time to catch her breath and your daddy a chance to set down those heavy bags he's been toting. Then you all come on downstairs again and find me. I'll be outside, but I'll be watching for you. I've been on the lookout for a little girl like you for quite some time and I'm going to see you get all of that barbecue you can eat. You can have your nap and your bath afterward. I won't forget about that washtub, either. . . . Come on, Glenny. Come on, Villac. I'll show you where you're going to bunk."

The white pitcher was only half full, and there was no slop jar into which water could be emptied, after one of them had washed, so their ablutions were, necessarily, limited. Neither Brent nor Mary found very much to say—to Lavinia or to each other. Brent was more than ever impatient to get started. Mary was so tired that she would have been thankful enough to lie down, uninviting as the dingy bed appeared; she had long since passed the point of hunger and if she could have just stretched out quietly for a little while, and then washed herself all over and put on clean underclothes, that would have fulfilled her wants for the time being. The band was now playing loudly, and she could hear babies crying and children screaming and men shouting to each other above the sound of the instruments; it seemed to her as if she could not stand any more turmoil, after the days and nights of it she had had on the train. Never in her life had she wanted so much to be alone, to collect her confused thoughts and to draw on her inner reserves of tranquillity and strength. But Brent was already in the doorway and Lavinia was tugging at her hand. She could not let them guess how exhausted she was or lag behind, alone, when they wanted to press forward together. She quickened her footsteps to keep pace with theirs, and presently they had clattered down the rickety stairs and woven their way through the big beamed room, with the crowded bar, toward the outside of the Crowley House.

Mr. Duson, with Mr. Glenny, Mr. Villac and Claude beside him, was watching for them, as he had promised he would be.

"A barbecue I promised you and a barbecue you shall have," W. W. beamed. "Duson delivers, you know. Besides, my old friend Austin has had his boys everlastingly at it the whole livelong night, and if anybody in this wide world knows how to barbecue a beef, it's Austin. That's why I got him to come over here all the way from Opelousas." He broke off to let his eyes twinkle down at Lavinia, who was regarding him with the solemn appraisal of childhood for strange adult phenomena. "And as for you, young lady," he continued, "as for you, guess what we've got just prezackly for nobody else but you. You can't guess? Well, I'll tell you, lemonade. Real, simon-pure, trade-mark blown in the bottle lemonade made from lemons and with white sugar in it, none of your plantation granulated yellow stuff." They had reached the barbecue pit and refreshment stand by the time he finished, so he turned to one of the helpers and commanded: "Give this young lady some lemonade for a starter, and don't be stingy. Fill it up for her."

The attendant took a stoneware mug and from a wooden cask ladled the lemonade into it with a gourd dipper. Meanwhile, the presiding genius of the place, obviously the Austin to whom Duson had referred, was slicing loaves of crusty, cylindrical French bread lengthwise, spearing chunks of meat out of a washbasin at his elbow, and drenching the thick slices liberally with a reddish sauce from another basin. He was a huge man, whose enveloping bar apron had long since ceased to be white and whose titanic derby hat had an upcurling brim that complemented the sweep of his magnificent ox-horn mustaches. The silk-covered, ruffle-edged sleeve garters that spanned his thick biceps had clasps almost as showy as the oversized colored links that held his detachable cuffs, and a heavy gold ring, set with black onyx, adorned one of his fingers which, for all their thickness, were surprisingly deft. As he worked, he talked.

"Three more bobbycue coming up, them," he boomed at Mr. Duson, swabbing sauce on his meat with a small rag mop. "Tender like a young girl's kiss, I guarantee you, me."

"Ugh! Tough as a whore's heart, I'd say!" one of the bystanders remarked scathingly.

"It is sort of tough and the sauce burns my mouth," Lavinia said, chewing vigorously. Then she added, with interest, "What is a whore?"

"Hush, darling! You mustn't criticize and you mustn't ask so many questions," Mary whispered hurriedly. The observation about hardness of heart had been followed by an outburst of raucous laughter on the part of other bystanders and she hoped Lavinia's question would pass unnoticed; instead, it evoked other remarks similar to the first, and some vigorously defending the seasoning which *"les Américains"* did not know how to appreciate and asserting that no one could "sauce up" a barbecue like Austin. Partly because she feared that Lavinia might have hurt his feelings, and partly because she was genuinely interested, Mary asked the chef a question herself.

"Why do you have two fires?" she inquired.

"If you cook the meat on the flame, him, he get burn' black an' full wit' soot, yes," Austin replied, with no indication of having taken offense and without once pausing in his labor of making and passing out split sections of crusty French bread with their filling of meat and savory sauce. "So you got to have one fi' like yonnuh, fo' to burn the oak wood to coals, an' the coals, them, you got to shovel in the odder pit, yes, fo' cook the meat slow, slow, slow. You want a good bobbycue, you can't cook him fas', no, I tell you frankly, me." He rolled a knowing eye upward at the sheet iron loosely laid over timber to provide shelter above the pit and the fire. "She goin' rain sho', sho', biffo this day finish, him, yes," he prophesied, spearing another piece of meat from the handy washbasin and offering it to Mr. Glenny, who accepted it with alacrity, but who, meanwhile, resumed his protests that nothing was settled, as far as he was concerned, that he had just come to look things over.

"And as I told *you* before, Mr. Glenny, that's the kind of fellow we want down here—the man who comes with his eyes wide open and doesn't miss the opportunities we have to offer," Mr. Duson said emphatically. "Like Austin, for instance. He's the best cook in all Southwest Louisiana, and he's going to leave Opelousas, where he is now, and set up the first restaurant in Crowley."

"Mebbe if I listen to that gol'-tongued Duson man, me, I got to do like he say, yes," Austin chuckled, preening his mustache. "Onliest trouble is, my wife an' seven kids got to eat, them, an' it takes a steady job, not no prospects, no, to feed them. So I just come today, me, for to help my friend Duson, an' w'at he do? I tell you frankly, me' w'at he do, him. He keep sayin' I got to quit my good job in Opelous' an' set up rest'rong in Crowley, on some crawfish chimbley."

"Well, you want to be your own boss sometime, don't you, Austin? You don't want to work for another fellow all your life. You want to watch for opportunities like this one and make the most of them. . . . And speaking of opportunities," he went on, turning toward the others, "it looks as if the auction was about to begin. That's my brother C. C.—'Curley' we mostly call him—going up on the stand right now."

They looked in the direction he indicated and saw that a man, with a gavel in his hand, had stopped with one foot already on the steps leading to the block, to speak with someone, apparently a friend, who had detained him. As he stood there, engaged in earnest conversation which gradually became more and more animated, the newcomers had a chance to get a good look at him. There was a close resemblance between the two brothers, but "C. C." was more heavily built, more ruddy of complexion and even more jovial of manner than "W. W."; the absence of glasses added still further to the general openness of his countenance. He brought his exchange of remarks with his friend to a conclusion by giving the latter a hearty slap on the shoulder, accompanied by an equally hearty laugh; and, having continued his interrupted ascent, he immediately addressed the gathering as a whole.

"Here we are, ladies and gentlemen," he announced in a ringing voice. "It is three o'clock on February 10th, and you are standing in the heart of Crowley, Louisiana, the city with a future."

"Let's move over there, friends," W. W. admonished the little group that was with him. "You want to get a good pick of the farmland and lots, and to do that you'll need to be nearer. There aren't many seats, but we'll see that Mrs. Winslow gets one anyway. I'm sure the rest of you won't mind standing."

"Don't mind the mud, that's only a temporary inconvenience," the auctioneer was assuring his hearers, as they walked in his direction. "Our city is well laid out. This avenue on which you stand will be the principal thoroughfare. It's a hundred and fifteen feet wide. That square to the north is for the courthouse and we'll have business firms up and down both sides of the avenue and an expanse of grassy parkway in the middle." He stopped talking long enough to gesticulate in the general direction of the beautification he was describing and, as if mesmerized, his audience gazed toward the section of the street which bore so little resemblance to the boulevard of his vision. "All the roadways running north and south will be avenues. They are good and wide and we will designate them by the letters of the alphabet. The streets will run east and west and will be numbered. We are in the midst of planting four thousand shade trees."

"I'd like to see at least two or three of 'em, let alone two thousand," someone near the front growled audibly, while the man beside him guffawed loudly.

"You'll see all *four thousand* before the year's out," the auctioneer retorted. "What's more, Crowley will be the seat of the new Acadia Parish government by then."

"That ain't what I hear," someone in the second row shouted.

"Well, if there isn't my good friend Will Hockaday from Prairie Hayes!" exclaimed C. C. "That's all right, Will, we forgive you your doubts, and what's more, we'll sell you a lot, so you can live in the new parish seat."

"I'm giving ten thousand dollars to get that courthouse in Prairie Hayes," Hockaday responded vehemently. "You sure don't think the police jury's going to pass that up?"

"Not unless it's surer of getting something better, but we'll see to that when the time comes. . . . Now look around you, folks, and see the vast prairie that surrounds you. Practically no swamp or wasteland, ample timber bordering all the streams, fertile soil, ideal for almost any kind of crops, unsurpassed for rice. You can grow that all over this prairie, acres and acres of it. The natural rainfall will keep it watered."

"Here's some of that natural rainfall right now," Hockaday shouted back scornfully.

It was all too true. A slight drizzle had begun to fall a few moments earlier, but had been optimistically disregarded. Now the drops were growing larger and coming down faster. Several persons left their places and hurriedly sought the shelter of the Crowley House. Others looked around vainly for something with which to protect themselves. Only the auctioneer and his brother appeared to be entirely unperturbed.

"Don't mind the rain, folks," C. C. said with undiminished cheerfulness. "It's only a passing shower. Don't leave when we're just about to put up the first lots that go on sale today, right here to the west of us. Terms are one-half cash and the rest in twelve months, without interest. Not only that, but if you buy one lot, we give you a second one. Two lots for the price of one. Here we go: Lot 14, Block 64. Faces fifty feet on Avenue C and is a hundred and eighty feet deep. Buy it and we throw in Lot 12 in Block 173, north of the courthouse site; the first is a good place for your business location and the second is a residential lot. Come on now! Check your little maps, boys, and note the location of these two lots. What am I bid for Lot 14, Block 64?"

"Two dollars," ventured someone in the rear, rather uncertainly.

"Two dollars is bid for Lot 14, Block 64. Do I hear another bid? What about another bid, gentlemen?" There was quite a pause, but no one made another bid. "Two dollars once, two dollars twice, two dollars three times. Lot 14, Block 64 goes for two dollars and we throw in with it Lot 12 in Block 173. That's a good buy, my friend. What's your name?"

"R. M. Andrus."

"Just hand over a dollar to my brother, will you, Mr. Andrus? We'll be counting on you for another before next February. . . . Now here's another good buy, Lot 4 in Block 45, near the Levy Park—a swell place to build a home and raise a family. The kids will always have a place to play. The lot that goes with it free is Number 8 in Block 163."

"That's pretty far out," called a man who was studying his map. "Think Crowley's ever going to grow that much?"

"Remember that's being thrown in with the other. When you get something for nothing you can't kick about where it is. Besides, if you should want to add some farmland later on, the two would go good together."

"All right, five dollars."

"Someone here bids five dollars. Do I hear another bid?"

"Ten dollars!" someone else called out.

"Ten dollars is bid. Folks, I tell you this is a good lot—right near the park."

There was a chorus of derisive laughter. "The park! Which park?" several men called out simultaneously.

"The one right down this next street. Sure there's going to be a park—in fact, there's going to be four of them. Do I hear a better bid?"

"Twenty-five dollars," piped up a young man who had not spoken before.

"Well, we're getting some spirit here at last," the auctioneer said encouragingly. "Twenty-five is bid. Do I hear more? Twenty-five once—"

"Twenty-six!"

"Twenty-six once, twenty-six twice—"

"Twenty-seven!" the young man called out.

"Good for you! Twenty-seven once, twenty-seven twice, twenty-seven three times and the lot goes to this young boy. What's your name, son?"

"John S. Egan, sir."

"Why, you're too young to buy a lot in your own name! You can't be of age yet!"

"I know, but my father Mike Egan is here and he'll sign for me. I've got the money."

"All right, young fellow, you've got yourself two good lots. My brother here will fix up your papers. Now we come to Lot 19. What am I bid for this fine large lot right in the center of our fair city?"

"Ten dollars," Brent said suddenly.

"We have a bid of ten dollars for Lot 19. Seems a shame to sell it by itself, when there's another just as large right beside it. How about bidding on both together, Mr. —?"

"Winslow. All right, I'll bid on both. Twenty dollars."

"Twenty-five!" shouted the man who had so forcefully expressed doubt about the attractive layout of the city.

"Thirty!" Brent called quickly.

For the first time, the bidding became really brisk. There were no longer only two contenders for the coveted property, which was described as being more and more desirable the longer C. C. offered it for sale; four aspirants for the title had now entered the field. Far from putting Brent off, this seemed only to spur him on. Mary, looking at him in speechless astonishment, heard him go from one higher figure to another with such rapidity and such apparent recklessness that she was breathless with mounting apprehension and excitement. They did not have forty dollars to spare, she was sure of that. Much less fifty—sixty —seventy.

"Brent!" she whispered, putting her hand on his arm and rising from the rough bench Duson had found for her. Apparently, her husband neither saw her nor heard her.

"Seventy-five!" he cried belligerently.

Mary was conscious of an astonished gasp from someone near by, and of some indistinct mutterings farther off. But the men who had been bidding against Brent were silent as C. C. resumed his accustomed chant.

"Seventy-five once, seventy-five twice, seventy-five three times for Lots 19 and 20, the finest in the residential part of this city and the highest priced for any so far. We throw in Lot 23, a good business location. We don't usually throw in such sites, but then we don't get many fellows like Mr. Winslow here, either. Fix him up there, Will."

W. W., who was already briskly preparing the papers, looked over at Brent with a bright smile. "Half now and the rest in a year?" he inquired agreeably. "Remember that's all right with us. Your word is good."

"Thanks, but I've got the money. I'd rather pay cash."

"Well, just as you say, just as you say, of course. The Christian name's Brent, isn't it?"

"It's *my* Christian name. Put that on the lot that's going to be a business site. I want the other two put in my wife's name—Mary Garland Winslow."

"Brent, you can't—you shouldn't—we mustn't—"

"Please, Mary . . . it's going to be all right, I promise you. . . . Thanks, Mr. Duson. That 'fixes' us doesn't it?"

"Right as rain. And congratulations, Mr. Winslow. I see I wasn't mistaken. I had you sized up from the beginning as a man who recognized opportunity when he saw it. Also, congratulations to you, ma'am. I look to see the day you'll have the most elegant residence in this city, with fine well-shaded grounds all around it, too."

The bidding went steadily on for another hour or more, but there was not a second sudden spurt of excitement, like the one Brent had started, and Mary was still too

84

dazed to grasp the details of what was going on. Finally she realized the auction was over. C. C. Duson had come down from the block and joined his brother; they were both busy congratulating the new landowners and telling them what remarkable bargains they had secured. Other men and women were merely drifting past, and every now and then she caught some random remark. "Well, I may have got fleeced, but it can't be much worse than Kansas. The drought there last summer plumb broke me. I don't mind mud and water for a change, if I can get enough rain for my crops during the growing season." . . . "Course your crop may be washed away, but that's no worse than seeing it blow away." . . . "I'm going north to sell my wheatland, but I'll be back here next week to get some of this riceland. I've had enough ice and snow. I'm going to sit on my front porch and rock nine months of the year."

Eventually, Ursin Villac reappeared, with Claude in tow, and asked the Winslows to join them for supper. He was sorry, he said, if they had got the idea that not any of the Cajuns were pleased to have "*Américains*" coming into that territory. Some did feel this way; but it was because they did not know any better. What was more, he had not cared much for the barbecue sauce himself—it was *trop salé*—too salt. He was so obviously eager to make up for any discourtesy on the part of his fellow countrymen that Mary did not need any prompting from Brent to accept the invitation, much as she longed to be alone with her husband, in order that he might privately explain the extraordinary happenings of the afternoon. So again, they ate unfamiliar food in the midst of noise and confusion; then they thanked Villac for his hospitality and, after declining to have a try at chuck-a-luck, went upstairs. By this time, Lavinia was too tired and drowsy to ask any more questions. She undressed quickly without any help or urging, and climbed into bed, tightly clutching the doll she had almost lost two or three times that day. She forgot to say her prayers and, for once, Mary did not remind her. Within a few minutes, the child was sound asleep. But Mary made no move to undress or even to sit down. She confronted Brent, not accusingly, but resolutely.

"Brent, I told you I was willing to do anything you thought best, to go anywhere you wanted to go. But I don't understand what you think best, I don't know where you want to go. We can't go back to Illinois, to sell our farm, the way that Mr. Jarvis is going back to Missouri. Our farm's sold already—to Jonathan Fant."

"That's right."

"And you bought two lots here in Crowley today—"

"Three."

"Three. Yes, I forgot about that third one that was thrown in when you bought two. I'm grateful to you for putting those in my name—don't think I'm not. I know it was a generous gesture. But they're just lots. They're just —bogs. There can't be any houses on them for—weeks, maybe months."

"No, I guess there can't. But—"

"And we can't stay here in this—in this hotel. Not that I'd mind if there were just you and I. I'd put up with anything. But we can't keep a child here, in this filthy place, filled with roisterers and rough characters. Suppose she got sick. Suppose—"

"You haven't lost faith in me, have you, Mary? You haven't stopped believing that I really did come here to find us a better home than we'd had before?" Brent asked, interrupting in his turn. He had taken hold of her shoulders and was looking straight into her eyes. She drew a deep breath, but she met the searching gaze squarely and unflinchingly.

"No," she said. "I haven't lost faith in you. But I want you to tell me now, so that I can tell Lavinia when she wakes up in the morning."

"All right. I will tell you now. I didn't think the time had come to tell you before, but I guess it has today."

He sat down on the edge of the bed and drew her down beside him. "When I came south last spring, I bought some land, about five miles from here," he said. "Around two hundred acres."

"You bought two hundred acres when you came down here in the spring!" she echoed. "Why, how could you, without any money? We didn't sell our farm until after you came back, and it took all we had in the savings bank to pay your traveling expenses that first time!"

"I know. But I did have some money besides that. Your father gave me some—loaned me some, rather. He said he knew I'd pay it back when I got around to it, and it didn't matter when that was. He said he'd never miss it. This was money he'd made unexpectedly on some harness races at the County Fair. I guess he makes quite a bit, off and on, that way, though he doesn't say much about it. He told me we both had the gambling instinct, even though we don't

86

gamble on the same things, and that we ought to stand or fall together, because we were kindred spirits. He laughed all the time he was talking. You know how he was, Mary —I mean, before your mother died."

"Yes," Mary said in a dazed way. She was not speaking firmly any more. "Yes, I know how he was. . . . So you bought two hundred acres of land last spring with gambling money and never told me."

"There's nothing dishonest about the way your father got the money or the way I took it, Mary. Don't act as if there was."

"I didn't mean to act as if there was. But—"

"And the reason I didn't tell you wasn't because I wanted to hide something I was ashamed of. It was because I wanted to give you a surprise when we did come together—to have you find out we didn't need to start from scratch, that I'd made a beginning for us already. The land I bought had already been homesteaded and it has a house on it—a one-room house made of split logs. And it has a mud chimney. We can have open fires— you've always said you wanted a fireplace. It's about eighteen feet square, so we won't be crowded in it and we can keep clean in it. Of course, it'll be just a makeshift, but it'll do until we can have something better. There's plenty of water available and there's a well pump in the yard. There's been one vegetable garden on the place and we can start another one right away. We'll be getting stuff out of it before the ground's even begun to thaw in Illinois, and the same goes for your flower garden. There's lots of game in the woods and marshes. We can keep cows and pigs and chickens again and have a driving team right away. I can buy those and a yoke of oxen. I've still got enough ready money for all that, even if I did spend more than I expected today. You know Jonathan Fant paid cash for our farm and that he didn't haggle over terms. As a matter of fact, he more than gave me my money's worth."

"Yes, I know," Mary said again. "But those lots—"

"Those lots I bought today don't count to me—not in terms of a home. I hope they don't to you, either. I only bought them to sell again—for ten times what I paid for them, or more. It's the farmland that's going to give us that home I talked to you about. Inside of a few years you can have any kind of a house you want. But when it comes to a place for it, I hope it'll be out where I'm taking you tomorrow. Because that's where I want us to live."

CHAPTER VII

As Mr. Duson had predicted, the encompassing sounds of hammering proved an effective alarm clock the next morning. By seven o'clock the Winslows and most of their fellow immigrants had foregathered in the main room of the Crowley House for a hearty breakfast of grits, pork sausage, baking powder biscuit and coffee and, while they were still eating, "W. W." came in to bid them all good morning and asked if there were anything he could do to be helpful.

"I make a practice of driving anyone who's interested out to look over the land around here," he said genially. "Surrey's at the door right now. Any customers?"

"I suppose you mean just prospects, don't you?" Brent inquired, emptying his cup and looking up.

"I said anyone who's interested and that's what I meant," Mr. Duson replied emphatically. "Applies to you, doesn't it?"

"Yes. But, as I'm sure you know, I own some property that's been homesteaded already, besides those three lots I bought yesterday. I'm not in the market for any more land. But my wife's anxious to see the farm, and we were wondering what the best way would be to get there. When I was here last spring, I did most of my traveling on horseback, after I left the railroad—the people I stayed with were always kind enough to lend me a mount. But this time—"

"This time, the best way for you to travel is right along with me," Mr. Duson assured him. "You may think you're not in the market for any more land, but there's another small parcel, right alongside of what you've bought already, that isn't worth much in itself, but that would add a lot to the value of yours, eventually. However, that isn't the point. Point is, I was looking forward to taking you and Mrs. Winslow and this little girl I'd been looking for so long out for a nice ride this morning. If you're figuring on moving right away, we could stop at the store and tell Jac Frankel to send a barrel each of flour and sugar and anything else you need out by oxcart. Trunks and any other gear you checked could come at the same time. There's room in the surrey for your grips."

"Mebbe you could find a little place in the surrey, yes,

fo' me'n Claude, too?" inquired Ursin Villac. He had come downstairs a little later than the others and, seeing room to squeeze his son and himself in between Brent and another man, who, so far, had not disclosed his identity or, indeed, spoken to anyone, had seized the opportunity; then he had chatted volubly, if not always intelligibly, all the time he was stowing away immense quantities of food. Now he turned, addressing Mr. Duson. "My relations I tol' you about yesterday, named Primeaux, they homesteadin' right close by where Mr. Winslow an' his folks is movin' at. I find that out last night, me, an' I want to talk with my relations on account I might homestead out there, too. I gotta speak w'at's on my mind, so mebbe, if you could find a little room, yes, for me'n Claude—"

"Of course, we can make room for you, Mr. Villac," Mr. Duson responded with his usual enthusiasm. "Now, what about you, Mr. Glenny?" he inquired, going part way down the length of the table and stopping beside the gentleman from Texas, who had joined their group the day before. "Made up your mind yet whether to grasp the great opportunities we're offering?"

It appeared that Mr. Glenny had still come to no such decision, so the others set forth without him, first stopping at the depot to claim the Winslows' two trunks, and to tell the agent these would be called for later; then going on to the store where Brent, as suggested, bought flour, sugar, lard, dried meat, coffee, tea, candles and matches. As they jogged along, Mr. Duson, besides pointing out everything he thought might be of interest in the rather drab landscape, also spoke about practical matters. Some of the immigrants were clubbing together and hiring a freight car, he said, to bring down their household effects and farm implements—it had not taken them long to decide they wanted to settle permanently in the South; if anyone else was coming, or thinking of coming from Monroe, or near there, perhaps Mr. Winslow could make a deal which would be to his advantage. Unfortunately, Brent did not know of any such person; besides, he had sold his farm equipment with his farm and he did not have many household effects—just bedroom, dining room and parlor furniture, and he supposed that would come by freight, even if he could make no arrangements to share a car with anyone. Of course, of course, Mr. Duson assured him breezily, while they were fording a small stream and everyone else was clinging to the sides of the surrey for support; then, as to the farm equipment, Mr. Winslow could easily get whatever he needed at Rayne or at Opelousas—one day's shopping would take care of all that. Ursin Villac broke in at this point to say he was sure the Primeaux would be glad to lend whatever was most necessary along that line; any man would be glad to let a neighbor take a cart or a plow or such, for a day or so. Brent thanked him and said he would appreciate this very much, but that of course he would see about getting equipment of his own, right away. . . . What about farm animals, he wanted to know next. Well, there would be no difficulty about those, either, Mr. Duson and Ursin Villac hastened to tell him, speaking almost simultaneously; one settler would have a mule he could spare, another a cow, another a few hens; they would look around for a good yoke of oxen; and, as for the small Cajun ponies, running around half wild, probably all he would have to do would be to catch a couple, or more if he needed them. If someone came along and claimed them, Winslow could pay for them afterward; but the chances were they would never be missed.

"I can help catch them," Lavinia volunteered eagerly at this point.

"And I could help, if you couldn't do it alone," Claude announced proudly. He was again armed with a long stick of candy and, this time, he and Lavinia were taking turns at sucking it, without any formal offer or acceptance.

"Well, that's very kind of you, Claude," Brent said, smiling without condescension and looking at the young Cajun with more appreciation of the boy's friendliness than he had previously done. "As a matter of fact, Lavinia probably *could* go out and get a halter on a colt, if it was one of her grandfather's. Of course, it's different when it comes to these wild ponies. But she's got a way with horses. Hasn't she, Mary?"

"Yes," Mary answered with unwonted brevity. She had been silently gazing at the sky most of the morning, and Brent was beginning to wish that she would take more part in the conversation. There was nothing in her face to suggest discomfort or dissatisfaction, much less resentment or anxiety; but he could not help wondering if some of these sensations were not lurking behind her habitual self-control. It might be, of course, that she was merely focusing all her attention on what she was hearing and seeing and that, since so much information was being freely given, she had no questions to ask. Moreover, there was very little on which she could comment. The flat, dun-colored landscape was broken only occasionally by small clumps of trees; a few brindles—apparently more tranquil of disposition than the one which had demonstrated, the day before, that cowcatchers were essential on trains—were cropping grass which looked extremely unpromising from the viewpoint of nourishment; and a larger number of small, sturdy horses, presumably the "Cajun ponies" to which Mr. Duson had referred, were galloping about in a manner as aimless as it was spirited. Since leaving the vicinity of the Crowley House, the travelers had come upon only two or three forlorn shacks, which might easily have been vacant as well as isolated, for they betrayed little or no evidence of human habitation. The surrey had neither passed nor met any other vehicle and, in the course of its progress, had come upon only one or two riders, who had called out a greeting to Duson, looked at the strangers curiously but casually, and gone on their way. After all, there had not been much for Mary to say unless she had remarked that she never imagined any territory in the world could be so drab and dreary. Brent was having hard work to keep from saying so himself. When he had seen it before, the fresh verdure of spring had transfigured it; he should have waited until this seemingly barren countryside was again mantled with green and banked with iris. . . .

"What perfectly beautiful clouds!" Mary exclaimed suddenly, glancing back toward her companions as if she wished to be sure they were not missing a rare and lovely sight which she had been enjoying. "Just look at them—tier after tier of foaming white, against that deep blue! And in all kinds of shapes! You could imagine almost anything—mountains and buildings and figures of both human beings and animals! Can you see, Lavinia?"

"Why, yes! I see a lady with a big hat on and a waterfall in front of a palace. What do you see, Claude?"

Claude took a little longer to make up his mind, while he squinted at the clouds. "I think I see a big dog, lying with its head on its front feet," he said at length. "But it might be a lion."

"There now!" Mr. Duson remarked with satisfaction. "I've always said myself I didn't believe there was any place in the world where you could get such cloud effects as right here in Louisiana. Most usually though, I've had to call people's attention to them, the same way I have to call their attention to all our natural advantages. You're the first, Mrs. Winslow, to notice the cloud effects for yourself, and I'll take my Bible oath you'll be just as quick to see natural advantages. The same goes for these two children. I never saw smarter young ones in my life, or better behaved, for that matter. . . . Now, here's something else that might interest you all: right over yonder, where Bazinet still has a blacksmith shop, there used to be an Indian trading post. It was a favorite haunt of jayhawkers, too, during the war and for quite some time afterward."

"What's a jayhawker?" Lavinia inquired.

"A freebooting guerrilla."

"What's that?" Claude asked, with equal curiosity.

"A guerrilla's a soldier who doesn't belong to any regular regiment, just to some small independent band that makes surprise raids. Very often, such fighters attack settlements or people that aren't enemies, and rob them. When they do that they're called freebooting guerrillas or jayhawkers."

"Oh!" said Lavinia, with increasing interest, now slightly tinged with awe. "Are there any of them around here?"

"No, sugar, they've been gone a long while. It's too bad there isn't some kind of a store though, where the old trading post used to be. It would have come in handy for you folks. That's the beginning of your land right over there to the left, Mr. Winslow, beyond that split cypress fence. And if you look hard you can see your house a piece back."

They all gazed intently in the direction toward which Mr. Duson was pointing with his whip. At first, they could see nothing except a small dark cube, which stood out against the sky above the dun-colored grass, not far from the first clump of trees they had come across in a long time. But, as they continued to stare at it, they could make out a smaller cube beside it and, gradually, the two took on the character of buildings.

"Cypress slab," Mr. Duson informed Mary. "That's what most of the homesteaders around here used for their first houses. Got it from Lyon's Point, about ten miles from where we are now, and had it drawn onto their land by ox teams. Comes in mighty handy for building material. 'Course those slabs are just logs, split down the middle; they're not planed much of any; but they're sound and tight, when they're mortised right. Nearest sawmill we've got so far is down by Jeanerette, beyond New Iberia, and orders for boards are coming in so fast they have to work round the clock to fill 'em. But any time you and your husband decide you want more of a house than you've got here now, just say the word and I'll see you get service. Meanwhile, I think you're going to make out all right. You've got a kitchen—that's the smaller building—and a dogtrot between that and the larger one, so you'll be protected from the rain, going back and forth. You don't have to be protected from the cold, because there isn't any. And I took the liberty of telling Frankel to have a secondhand cookstove I've been advertising for sale for quite some time loaded on with the rest of your stuff. If you don't like it, you can send it right back where it came from—no obligation whatsoever. But I thought it might come in handy until you could get something better."

"Thank you," Mary said gratefully. "It was very kind of you—very kind and thoughtful, like everything else you've done."

"Well, now," Mr. Duson replied, "we all help each other out, best we can, around here, like I said before. Besides the secondhand stove, I've had them put on some posts and fence wire—enough for a small barn lot where you can keep a plow mule. The main fencing job will come later, of course. You'll find the Primeaux'll want to help, too. Their place isn't more than half a mile farther along. I figured on taking Mr. Villac and Claude over there, soon's I'd let you off. Then, on my way back, I'll stop in and see whether you can make out, right away, with what you've got here, or whether you want to stay at the Crowley House for a while longer. There's a good stick and mud chimney, and I stowed away a jug of water, in case your well pump doesn't work, and a few victuals underneath the front seat, enough for your noon meal, according to my reckoning. I'll have mine with the Primeaux and, like as not, some of them will be coming by this afternoon, too. They'll want to welcome you to God's country."

While he was talking, the surrey had gradually come nearer and nearer to the two small slab buildings, connected with a covered passageway. The small clump of trees, which they had noticed at the same time the houses came into sight, though actually not far from these, still appeared to bear no real connection with them; they stood out, as they had when they were merely dark cubes against a bright but distant horizon, unshaded, unadorned and unbeautiful in themselves, but with an almost defiant appearance of sturdiness and independence. As the surrey came to a stop, Brent climbed out of it and, walking a little stiffly after his rough ride, strode over to the doorway of the larger building and unfastened it.

The sun poured in through the wide opening, filling the long-closed room with warmth and light and patterning the hard-packed earthen floor with its radiance. In one corner stood a crude bedstead. The walls formed the headboard and one side; the footboard and the other side were made of hand-hewn planks. There was a mattress of sorts on the bed and, near by, a chair, also hand hewn, with a calfskin seat. Rough benches were ranged on either side of a corner chimney piece and, in the fireplace itself, hung several iron pots. In each of the remaning corners, there was a cupboard of sorts; otherwise the room was empty.

For a moment, Brent stood very still, looking carefully around him, but this was only to make sure everything was all right. There was no element of strangeness to him in the place; he had stayed there when he came to Louisiana alone, sleeping soundly on the mattress stuffed with Spanish moss, cooking what food he needed in the iron pots, hanging such clothes as he took off on the wooden pegs fastened to the inside of the door. He had been at peace with himself and the world then for the first time since his long illness, and confident of the future's promise in this land; now that he had Mary and Lavinia with him, he had a greater sense of responsibility and challenge; but he had no doubts and no fears about his ultimate success.

He turned and started back toward the surrey, already walking a little less stiffly. He had intended to lift his wife and daughter down over the wheel. But they had forestalled him by alighting without his help and were now coming forward to meet him. He put his arm around Mary's shoulders and gave Lavinia his free hand. Then the three went together, side by side, toward their new home.

CHAPTER VIII

The first thing he must do, Brent said, was to make sure the well pump was working all right; it was thoughtful of Mr. Duson to have supplied them with a jug of water, but that would not last long. The chances were that the leather, at least, would have to be replaced; if that was all, it would not present too many difficulties. But if one of the metal parts was corroded or cracked, beyond even temporary repair, they'd be mighty short of water until he could get a replacement. . . .

Brent had already set to work as he explained this. But optimistically he directed his first efforts to using the pump as it was; these resulted only in a discouraging wheeze from some recess deep within it. Next, having discovered in the dogtrot a rusty tin can, he filled this from a turbid rain puddle and tried to prime the pump by pouring the water into its slotted top with one hand, while frantically working the handle with the other. There was still not a sign of a trickle; and growling that it was a good thing he had brought along a couple of monkey wrenches, Brent pulled off his shirt and resigned himself to a task of complete dismemberment. At last, squatting on his heels amidst a welter of parts, he turned one of the pieces over and over between his right thumb and forefinger. Then he looked up at Mary, who had interrupted her own labors to bring him a cup of coffee, with a sigh of relief.

"It's just the suckling that's shot," he said, wiping the sweat from his forehead.

"The suckling?"

"Yes—a circle of leather with these two little weights riveted on. When the plunger is lifted, the leather flaps up and lets the water through; when the plunger comes down, the leather flaps shut and keeps the water from going back; so pretty soon, it starts running out of the spout. The old chair by the bed will provide all I need to fix up a temporary suckling. I'll just cut a circle out of the calfskin seat, soak it well and fasten these same weights to it. They'll last until we can get us a good store-bought one and sundown won't catch us without plenty of pump water in our kitchen."

While Brent was working on the pump, Mary had found a broom of sorts in one of the cupboards and she had swept out both houses, and with Lavinia's help, had carried the sorry mattress outdoors, where it would soak up sun. She took the benches out, too, dusted them off and arranged on one of them the "victuals" Mr. Duson had supplied. They were all glad to sit down and eat by the time their first labors were finished for they were rather tired and very hungry; the hearty picnic lunch revived them, besides satisfying their undemanding tastes. They had just finished this welcome meal when the oxcart, laden with their baggage and provisions, fencing materials and the secondhand cookstove, came jolting into sight. The driver—a squat Negro, who answered to the name of

Preacher, and whose feats of strength were as astonishing as the way the uppers of his heavy shoes had been slashed, so that his toes would burst through—assumed that he was expected to unload everything and help set up the stove; and, by the time this was done, the surrey had returned, with Mr. Duson as its only passenger, however.

"Well, I see you're not only getting along all right, but making out fine," he said, looking around him with a comprehensive and approving glance. The mattress had been taken in again and Mary had hastened to begin unpacking the huge Saratoga trunk she had inherited from her mother; so the bed was neatly made up and covered with a prettily patterned quilt. On Duson's arrival, she paused in the arrangement of towels and other household items on the cupboard shelves, which were now thoroughly cleaned and open to the air; but he could see how much she had accomplished already. She had even managed to get her sewing machine out of the second huge trunk, which had been bought to hold it and make it acceptable for checking, and it was now set up ready for use. She was sure the stove was going to draw wonderfully, she told him; but, even if it didn't, they would not need much supper, the lunch he had given them had been so filling. Not wholly satisfied with this cheerful assurance, he went out to the kitchen, but there, too, he found everything under control. Between them, Brent and the driver of the oxcart already had the stove up and a fire lighted; and when Preacher had been paid and given a list of necessities which he was to bring out the next day, if possible, the oxcart, now empty, went creaking off again, and Duson accepted an invitation to sit down and drink a cup of coffee before he started back to "town."

"I'll have to cut it short though," he told them, between sips from one of the tin cups Mary had found tucked away in the cupboard she was now allotting to linen. "My brother 'Curley' can handle today's real estate sales without my help all right—'course they won't be anything to compare with yesterday's, because no auction has been advertised. Just the same, I like to be around and keep an eye on how things are going. . . . Villac isn't going back with me tonight—matter of fact, it wouldn't surprise me any if he should come over here, later in the evening, if he and that cousin of his can ever get through visiting; but once a couple of Cajuns sit down to pass a good time together, there's no telling when they'll be through. By the way, it's settled already that he and Primeaux are going

96

into partnership, though, of course, Villac's got to collect
his family and bring them over from Lacombe before he
can really settle down. I don't know how many young
ones he's got, but it sure is a quiverful, as the Good Book
says. And Primeaux has another tribe, all wild as hawks.
He lost his wife a while back, and there's been no one to
look after them since then, not the way they should be
raised. It takes a woman to do that, as I don't need to tell
you. He's tickled to death with the idea of having Villac's
wife take over. Where on earth they'll all sleep, I don't
know—he's got a frame house already, the first one out
this way; but it's no hotel for size and that's about what he
needs. . . . Speaking of hotels, looks to me as if the one
in Crowley has lost some good customers," he concluded,
with a questioning look at Mary. "That is, if you really
think you can manage with what you've got here."

"Yes, I'm sure we can," she answered with a quiet conviction that sent a tremor of pride through Brent's consciousness. "That is, if you go on helping us."

"Anything I can do, anything at all," Mr. Duson assured her. "What was it you had in mind exactly, Mrs.
Winslow?"

Mary glanced at Brent, whom she had had no opportunity to consult, and caught the approving nod which indicated she was to go ahead with suggestions. "When
Brent was here last spring, he stayed with a Mr. Jean
Castex, a carpenter, in Mermentau," she said. "And I
thought—"

"Know him well, know him well," Mr. Duson answered
glibly. "Want I should get a message to him? See if he can
come here and do some work for you, or send someone, if
he can't come himself?"

"Yes, please. We need another bed, for Lavinia. Brent
thinks we can probably get a few planks from the Primeaux and that, with quilts over them, they'd be all right
as a shakedown for him; Lavinia and I could sleep in the
big bed for the present. But of course that would be just a
makeshift. And I want shelves in the kitchen for pots and
pans and some sort of a larder, besides more cupboard
space. Of course, Brent could fix all that up, if he had to.
But he's handier outdoors than indoors, and besides, of
course he'll want to get started right away on his planting."

"Of course, of course," Mr. Duson agreed. "He'll need
to begin plowing and harrowing right away, so that you
can get your vegetable garden going and your first crops

97

in. No hurry about the rice, you can't sow seed for that before May at the earliest. But the sooner, the better with everything else. I'll get a message to Castex right away and I know he'll do what he can for you. Just the same, I'm afraid he won't think putting up a few shelves and the like of that is really much of a job. What about a little porch? Most everyone has a porch, and I think Castex would show more interest in the work if you'd let him add one to your house right away. Naturally, I'll tell him you want some fencing done, too, as soon as you have stock, and some one-inch boards over that dirt floor would help a lot, even if they are rough sawed, especially if someone's going to sleep on it. There won't be any trouble getting enough of those. But I was hoping you were going to say you wanted him to start right in building you a better home. I told you all you needed to do was to say the word and I'd get you as much good lumber as you needed. If Primeaux can have a frame house—"

Again Mary looked at Brent and again she saw the signal that encouraged her to go ahead. "We will need the fences and the floorboards would help a lot," she said. "A porch would be pleasant, too. I believe we might have that. But I think my husband wants to wait and see how we do with our crops this year before we start to build a better home and, if he does, I'm satisfied to live in this house for the present. We've never had a chance to go out camping, like some of our friends, and this will be our camping trip, as well as our home." She looked around her, the pride of ownership and the pioneering spirit both ringing through her voice and revealed in her face. "It'll be very comfortable, when I get it settled," she went on. "You said one day's shopping, in Rayne or Opelousas, ought to be enough to get everything we need. So, as soon as we're sure what that is, we'll take a day off and have a nice outing. But meanwhile—"

"Meanwhile, I'll get that message to Castex," announced Mr. Duson, rising. "But I'll take the liberty of adding that, though you don't require much carpentry this year, you will next, and I'll see about getting some cypress sawed and saved for you right away. Because, of course, your crops are going to be tiptop. Can't fail, not if you tried to make 'em. Things grow practically by themselves, down here. . . . Well, I'll be back in a few days, just to keep in touch. Don't ever like to lose sight of friends, once I've made them—especially when I've found just the kind of little girl I've been looking for all my life." He chucked

Lavinia under the chin and shook hands, in turn, with Mary and Brent, his departure apparently imminent. But, with his foot already on the step of the surrey, he turned back. "About that small tract I spoke of," he said, "people around here never call it anything except the 'wet patch' and that's what it is—almost worthless in itself, like I told you, so it's a great bargain. And, along with what you've got already, it could come in mighty handy. Since you're not doing any building right away, you might like to put some of what you're saving on lumber into a little more land. Anyway, I'll drive you over to have a look at that tract next time I come out this way. No harm in just having a look. No obligation whatsoever."

When he had finally taken his leave, Brent and Mary exchanged glances and laughed. Then they kissed each other. As neither was habitually merry nor habitually demonstrative, Lavinia looked at them in some astonishment. But she laughed, too, without knowing quite why and then she sidled up to them, so that she could share in their embrace. They were all very happy.

Later in the afternoon, while they were resting after their day's work, they saw two boys coming toward them across the prairie. Each was leading an animal and each was carrying a basket. As they came a little nearer, the Winslows could see that one of the boys was Claude, that the animal he was leading was a cow and that the animal led by the boy they did not know was a mule. Because he was so completely loaded down, Claude could not wave a greeting, but presently he called one out.

"This is my cousin Fleex," he informed them. "His father, my Uncle Phares, sent us over. He thought you would need some milk for Lavinia and that you would want to start plowing soon as ever you could. So he is loaning you a cow and a mule. He thought you would like some eggs and some greens and some oranges, too."

"Oranges!" Lavinia exclaimed with astonished delight.

"Why, yes. Uncle Phares has got a real nice little grove."

"You mean you can go right out and pick them off the trees?"

"Why, yes," Claude said again. "You can come over tomorrow and pick some yourself, if you want to. There's plenty more besides what we've got with us. That's what we have in our baskets—the oranges and the eggs and the greens, I mean. Uncle Phares will be over tomorrow to

99

bring you some pullets and a rooster, and a sodbuster, so you won't be delayed with your plowing. He couldn't come tonight because he's too busy visiting with my father."

Brent and Mary laughed again, and again Lavinia laughed with them. They had gone forward to meet the boys, for, by this time, they already regarded Claude as a good companion, though it was only a little over twenty-four hours since they had seen him the first time; and they were quite prepared to welcome "Fleex" in the same role, though they were puzzled by his name, which they had not recognized as Felix up to this point. He lacked the inherent friendliness which made Claude's open countenance and genial expression so attractive, despite his unremarkable features; Fleex made no remarks on his own initiative and answered only in monosyllables when addressed; his hair was matted, his hands dirty and his outlandish clothing ragged. His coat had evidently been made from a blanket which was once bright colored, but now badly faded; and, though he was barefoot, a dingy shawl was wrapped around his head. Mary, remembering what Duson had said about Primeaux's loss, felt her heart go out in sympathy toward the motherless boy. His roving glance did not prevent her from seeing that he had exceptionally fine dark eyes, his infrequent and seemingly reluctant smile disclosed teeth almost startling white and his clumsy garments did not disguise the litheness of his figure or impede his quick movements; had he only been decently clean and properly clothed, he might have been quite handsome, in a hawklike way, and there was something undeniably intriguing about him. If Villac's wife were kindly and efficient, as Mary had every reason to believe after seeing Ursin and Claude, she was confident there would soon be a change for the better in this neglected lad's appearance and manner. Villac and Duson were both right; it took a woman to deal with a brood. She spoke to Felix kindly, asking how many brothers and sisters he had. Two sisters and one brother, he answered, without volunteering any information about their names or ages. It was Claude who gave this, along with some correlative data.

"Fleex is the oldest," he said. "Fifteen, two years older than me. Then there's Mezalee, just my age, and Marcelite, a year younger. Clement's only five—there were some that died in between. They're buried right here on the prairie—there's a little family graveyard back of the orange grove. Us, we're all alive. My mother's name is Anne and my sister Annette was called after her. Then there's Odile and Onezime and Odey and Olin."

"My, what a lot of names beginning with *O*!" Lavinia exclaimed.

"Yes, aren't there? I reckon Papa and *Maman* kind of got the habit and found it hard to stop. But we're going to get started on the *P*'s now. If the new baby's a girl, we'll name it Pauline. If it's a boy, we can name it Paul, so everything's all settled, either way."

It was not customary, in Monroe, to speak of new babies before their arrival and, indeed, little girls were not supposed to know where babies came from, though, if they were brought up on a farm, they usually had a pretty fair idea, by the time they were as old as Lavinia. Mary hastened to change the subject.

"Has the cow been milked yet this evening?" she inquired.

"No, ma'am, not yet. Would you like me to milk her for you? I'm a right good milker, me, for my age."

Mary thought it rather strange that Felix had not made this offer, since he was two years older than Claude and, since it was his father to whom the cow belonged; he must frequently have milked her before. But she accepted Claude's suggestion gratefully and asked both boys to stay for supper. Thanks to them, she could scramble some eggs and boil some greens and she already had the wherewithal for biscuits; they could have the oranges for dessert. . . . Quite obviously, Claude wanted to accept the invitation, but Felix, speaking on his own initiative for the first time, muttered something about having to get back. So Claude withdrew to do his milking and, while Mary began her preparations for the meal the boys were not going to share, Brent and Lavinia did their best to carry on a conversation with Felix. However, they were both tired and he had relapsed into sullen silence. The friendly effort was unsuccessful and they were relieved when Claude came in with the milk and said he supposed it was time to get going.

"It was kind of Phares Primeaux to send over the animals and the provisions and to promise he'd come over himself, as soon as he wasn't too busy visiting," Brent said. "But, to tell the truth, I don't take to his son Felix at all. I hope he won't have a bad influence on Claude, who's a fine little fellow."

"Why should he? Isn't it just as likely that Claude will have a good influence on him?"

"I don't know. I hope so," Brent answered. He did not sound especially hopeful, but Mary knew this was not because he was really doubtful, but because he was tired. It had been a crowded and an exciting day and Brent did not want to cram it any fuller with problems about other people. He wanted to close his consciousness to everyone, except his wife and child, and go gratefully to bed as soon as he had eaten; he did not even want to think of the work which they would begin together the next day. Without pressing him any further, Mary went on with her preparations for supper, though she could not dismiss the thought of the two boys from her own mind; and every now and then she glanced at Lavinia, who was in her thoughts, too, though why all these should have been intermingled, she did not understand. As a matter of fact, she did not try. She was slightly surprised that it was so, but she was not disturbed. She believed what she had said: that Claude would be a good influence on Felix, and while she had not added aloud that Lavinia should be a good influence on both, this now occurred to her.

PART THREE

Providence

FEBRUARY, 1887—DECEMBER, 1887

CHAPTER IX

The Winslows were all early risers by force of both habit and necessity, but they had not finished their breakfast the following morning when their first visitors arrived: Phares Primeaux was driving his cousin Ursin into Crowley, so that he could take the train to New Orleans, where he must change to another for Slidell, and they had allowed time for an exchange of greetings on the way. Claude had been left at the Primeaux' place; his father did not see any sense in just dragging the boy back and forth, and he meant to have all the rest of the family in tow when he returned, which he hoped would be within a week or so, though it might be longer. Before she started to pack, his wife would want time to think over the transfer; and though, in the end, she was sure to decide it was for the best—especially if Claude stayed behind—it might take her several days to reach this decision. Ursin would be glad to do any errands the Winslows would like to have him undertake in New Orleans. . . .

Primeaux had brought with him the promised pullets and rooster, as well as a few old hens "he would never miss"; he, too, would be glad to do errands, if there were anything the Winslows might have forgotten to put on Preacher's list. One thing was certain: he ought to make inquiries right away about a good yoke of oxen for sale, because that was something he did not have to spare and, of course, Winslow would be needing it straight off. The boys would be over a little later with the sodbuster, and if Winslow's plow needed sharpening they could take that to Bazinet's over at the old trading post, so there would be no delay about getting it done—they needn't go all the way into Crowley with it. Primeaux and Villac had figured that Winslow would want to start plowing the next day, and they thought he could, since a good north wind had sprung up, even though the ground was a little too damp, if he got busy with the sodbuster first—though no one but fools and strangers tried to predict weather thereabouts. Then, on the third day, he could disk and, the day after that, he could harrow. The boys would be glad to help, any way they could. Primeaux's own plowing was done already; so he could spare Fleex just as well as not. And Mezalee was handy in the house; it wouldn't do any harm at home if she let things go for a day or two and gave Mrs. Winslow a hand.

"But what about their school?" Mary asked conscientiously.

"Fleex never did take to book learnin', him; he ain't been near no school this here winter, no. An' it won't pay for Claude to start at the 'Island,' account Miss Millie, her, she be closin' down for summer March first."

"The Island?" the Winslows inquired in unison.

"Yes, sho'. Miss Millie calls it 'Island' account this schoolhouse stands on the onliest place, yes, w'at don't flood. She doin' a fine job, her, makin' the boys behave, without gettin' them wild bucks mad at her, no. Fleex was the onliest one she couldn't manage an' I gotta admit, me, that was his fault. Now she bearin' down, her, on the school board for glass windows an' separate seats an' desks. I guaarntee you, me, she gets them. Mebbe enough books, too."

"But even if your boys don't go, what about Mezalee?" Mary persisted.

"Mostly girl don't go to school around here," Primeaux told her. "In with all the rough boys, they couldn't. Fleex ain't the onliest one w'at's hard to handle, no, even if I gotta admit he's about the worst one, him, yes."

"Then how do the girls get educated?"

"They don't, not w'at you'd call educated, no. My *defint* wife, her, she taught Mezalee an' Marcelite some. Miss Millie loaned us a couple of schoolbooks through the summer an' the girls got so they could read pretty good. I bought slates for them, me, like w'at the boys had, an' Miss Millie, her, she showed my wife how she taught them to spell. She'd write words on the top of the slate, her, an' the boys would make copies until they got to the bottom. Then they'd lick their fingers, them, an' rub out the words an' start over again."

"I see," Mary said thoughtfully, looking at Lavinia.

104

"That way they got along fine, them. But now my wife's been taken—"

"I know. It's very sad. Perhaps I can do something for your little daughters. I hope I can, you've done so much for us already. And, of course, when Mrs. Villac comes—"

"She don't come unless I go get her," Ursin remarked with his customary dryness. "An' that train liable to leave Crowley while we are sittin' here, us, talkin' about how to educate young girls. So come, Phares, let's get goin' an' do the rest of our visitin' later, us."

They drove off, with hearty farewells all around, but leaving Mary somewhat disturbed over what she had learned about local methods of instructing the young. However, with her usual good sense, she reasoned that problems must be met one at a time and that others were far more pressing than that of schooling. Besides, Lavinia was so obviously bursting with good health and good spirits that her welfare and happiness were reassuring to the point of relegating anxiety about her, for whatever cause, to the background of her mother's consciousness. The little girl rushed outdoors to "help" her father, only to rush in again, a few minutes later, to "help" her mother; and, in the latter case at least, her handiness was more than a matter of good will. She dried the makeshift kitchen utensils that Mary washed; she straightened the quilts that had served her father for a shakedown; she carried clothing and linen from the Saratoga trunk to the cupboard for her mother to arrange. When the boys arrived with the sodbuster, she hailed them with excitement, which increased when she found they had brought five-year-old Clement with them; she had always wanted a little brother and she was going to pretend that now she had one. She gave the child the old alphabet blocks, which she had insisted on bringing from Illinois with her, to play with; and she chatted with him and Fleex and Claude as if she had known them all her life, eliciting a gratifying response even from Fleex, who was less taciturn with her than he had been the day before, though he still withdrew from Mary's friendly advances. Mezalee had not been able to come with the boys after all, because she had washing to do, as well as dinner to get; and eventually, Lavinia tried to persuade Mary to let her ride back to the Primeaux's place, so that she could meet the girls. She would not stay long, she promised, because she did not want to miss Preacher's return with the oxcart. But Brent protested; at this rate, she would have the boys driving back and forth all day. They

105

assured him they did not mind, that there was nothing else they really needed to do, but he was firm, and Mary realized that he did not want Lavinia to go off, unsupervised, with Fleex, that he was distrustful of the strange boy to an almost unwarrantable degree.

Momentarily, she was again disturbed by troubled thoughts and, again, she dismissed them quickly. Preacher returned sooner than had been expected and the contents of the laden oxcart required immediate attention. Then, before nightfall, Jean Castex arrived, spare, sprightly and full of well-vocalized enthusiasm over Brent's return. Duson had delivered his message with dispatch and Castex had brought tools and materials with him, ready to start work at dawn the next day. The questions of food and lodging in the meantime had not troubled him at all; he knew his good friend Primeaux would look after him; and, when Primeaux stopped by for a second time, on his way back from Crowley after seeing Ursin off on the train, he insisted that they must all come over to have supper and pass a good time. Sure, there was room; sure, there was lots to eat; he would not take no for an answer.

It was impossible to remain obdurate in the face of so much good will and, though Mary and Brent would much rather have gone to bed early again after a hard day's work, Lavinia was outspokenly delighted because she was going to meet Mezalee and Marcelite right away after all, and have a chance to see her "little brother" again that same day. The two Primeaux girls were, like their father, exuberantly friendly; and though Mary was secretly appalled at the haphazard way in which this kindly family was living, and the quality of their evening meal, she reproached herself for her critical attitude and mentally quoted the Biblical proverb about the dinner of herbs where love is. Even Fleex contributed his share to the general entertainment; it transpired that he had a violin and he played it quite willingly, displaying a natural talent that more than compensated for his lack of training. He was less successful in singing his own accompaniment, because his voice was changing, but his performance was a spirited one and, though the Winslows could not understand the words of *"Caïllette"* and *"Hier Après Midi,"* the verve with which he linked the verses together, by yelling, was exhilarating. When he switched to *"O Ma Petite Bergère,"* other members of the family joined in with the responses and, with the exception of Claude, who obligingly kept up a running translation in a whisper, they were all soon singing, lustily or pipingly, according to age. When Clement stopped piping and began to nod, Fleex switched again, this time to *"Fais Dodo, Colas, Mon Petit Frère,"* and the Winslows needed no translation to understand that he was singing a lullaby. His uncertain voice became soothing and tender and, presently, he laid the violin aside and gathered the little boy up in his arms. Clement stirred slightly and snuggled closer.

"I love you, Fleex," he murmured sleepily.

Fleex carried the little boy off to bed and the Winslows thought he must have gone to bed himself, for he did not return to the kitchen and no noise came from the direction in which he had disappeared. But, after they had started home, they heard the wail of the violin again and, above it, the cracked voice of Fleex, singing a wild, weird song.

CHAPTER X

In a relatively short time, the Winslows' life took on a well-ordered pattern. The extra shelves, the presses and the wood flooring in the little cypress slab house gave it added comfort and convenience; and the day's shopping trip to Opelousas provided the commodities which had not been obtainable nearer at hand, besides affording the family a pleasant outing. The well pump gave an ample supply, and was so close to the house that Mary did not greatly miss piped water in the kitchen; three sets of pails—large ones for Brent to carry, medium-sized ones for Mary, small ones for Lavinia—were kept handy, and whoever passed in or out filled or emptied them. Mary washed and rinsed their clothes and household linen in two tin tubs set on a bench in the dogtrot, and enjoyed the novelty of doing this out of doors; the drying was more of a problem, with the frequent spring rains, but she managed. The pullets gave them a plentiful supply of eggs and, once a week, they sacrificed an old hen for a feast of fricassee; otherwise, except for an occasional treat of fresh pork or game, they managed with the dried meat from "Frankie's." The turnip greens and other produce, still prodigally supplied by the Primeaux, were supplemented by their own vegetables, for all their garden stuff was coming up finely, as were the fields of oats and corn that Brent had planted. There had been quite a search for just the right yoke of oxen, but this had finally been found and, meanwhile, Sadie, the mule, had sufficed for every major farm need.

Besides the oxen, Brent had purchased a sow that was soon to farrow, a bull calf and six cows and these were effectively confined by the good fences and pens that Castex had built. For equipment, Brent had already secured a secondhand farm wagon from Rayne and had a new one on order. As Duson had predicted, it had required no cash outlay and very little effort to secure a couple of Cajun ponies. As a matter of fact, Fleex has not only caught them, but broken them, and had shown great skill in the matter. Praise of his prowess had brought to the boy's face the first responsive smile that Brent had ever succeeded in evoking. From then on, there was less strain between them, and Brent was willing to concede that there was some good in Fleex after all, adding that, of course, Mrs. Villac had done wonders in bringing this out, even in the short time since her arrival.

Anne Villac was a roly-poly little woman, with snapping black eyes, neglected teeth and an infectious laugh. Everything about her was round, not only her figure, but her face and features; and though she lacked the quiet and thoughtful determination which carried Mary so well through every crisis, and the even and patient disposition which made her so easy to live with, Anne had tremendous energy, abounding kindliness and a temper which burnt itself out as quickly as it flashed into flame. She always wore earrings, but she did not always wear shoes; she was apt to put these on rather late in the day, about the same time she combed her hair which, like that of all her children, was thick, black and either really unmanageable or so nearly so that they preferred to regard much attempt at management as hardly worth the effort. She did not scrub and scour, the way Mary did, nor did she worry about opening windows and doors to let fresh air and sunshine into the house; much less did she drag household equipment outdoors to air and sun it. But she swept vigorously, as she did everything else, and the shuttle of the long-silent loom was clicking again, hour after hour, and beautiful striped coverlets and towels, as well as homespun for all sorts of garments were reeling off it. Moreover, she ground corn for meal, rendered lard, made candles and soap from tallow and got thee meals a day on the table which, both as to amplitude and seasoning, far surpassed Mary's. Besides, there was always a coffeepot on the hob, which was not allowed to become empty or even cold, a stew or a gumbo simmering in an iron pot from which anyone could dip out a ladleful at will, and potatoes buried in the ashes overnight to bake against the morrow's need. Her own children were all merry, healthy and reasonably tidy, though they had never heard of daily baths until Lavinia mentioned them and recoiled from the idea with suspicion; her adopted brood soon became merrrier, healthier and tidier. All of them were a little afraid of her tongue when she was roused, and of the whippings she did not hesitate to administer when she thought these were indicated; but they loved her laugh, her quick caresses, her excellent cookery and her tireless and, apparently, effortless care. She, in turn, mothered them all alike and was prodigal in her love for them all.

The Villacs had arrived, bag and baggage, about a fortnight after the Winslows, and the children for the most part wonderfully congenial, were constantly going back and forth between the two places. Lavinia had her favorites, she confined to her mother, though she tried to be careful, as Mary told her she should be, not to betray this favoritism. It included Clement among the younger ones, because he was so exactly like the little brother she had always wanted, and Claude's sister Annette among the older ones. Not Claude himself, Mary inquired. Why, yes, Lavinia guessed so; she hadn't thought of Claude as a favorite though. She had sort of taken him for granted, because he had been around from the very beginning.

The Villacs and the Primeaux were the Winslows' only near neighbors, a scant half mile away across the prairie; but they had other visitors, all of whom proved friendly. One of these was Will Milton, a former captain of militia and now the first tax-collecting deputy sheriff of Acadia Parish, who drove all over it in his shiny buggy, behind two spirited bays Star and Fly. The scattered residents of the prairie never thought of "worrying themselves" by going into the new parish seat to pay their taxes, and Mr. Milton did not "worry them" by suggesting that they should. He enjoyed his drives, and frequently prolonged them for as much as six or seven days without going home at all, though his house in Crowley had been almost the first to go up there; he spent the night wherever he happened to be when darkness overtook him. When he reached the Winslows for the first time, they already had two beds, so he and Brent shared one of these and Mary and Lavinia the other. It was his last night out, he told them, and he kept the moneybags, filled with silver and

gold coins, close beside him and a pistol within reach—
not that he was looking for trouble, he explained, but you
never knew; there were still some marauders around. . . .
However, he seemed to take an immediate liking to his
hosts and soon came to feel implicit confidence in them;
for, on a subsequent visit, he told them that the next night,
in accordance with his custom at the end of a trip, he
would bolt all the doors of his home and pull down all the
window shades; then he would lay a thick silence pad,
about six feet square, on the floor of his room before he
opened the moneybags and poured out their contents, as
quietly as possible. Next, he would take pencil, notebook,
tax roll names and tax receipts and check the amount of
the collections against the names of those who had paid.
When everything tallied to the last penny, the money
would be returned to the bags, which would then be
stacked in a big roll-top desk that he could padlock as well
as lock; and when he finally went to bed, he would lean a
Winchester rifle against the desk and put his pistol under
his pillow. His wife could use the Winchester, if she had
to. . . .

"And don't you ever let anyone see you emptying out
all that gold and silver?" Lavinia asked breathlessly. She
thought this was the most exciting story she had ever
heard, much more thrilling than any fairy tale.

"No, sugar. Only my wife."

"*Wouldn't* you let anyone see you?"

"Well now, I don't know. Time might come when
there'd be so much money in this parish, I'd need someone
to help me count it, besides my wife. Are you good at
sums?"

"Yes," Lavinia said with pride.

Mr. Milton looked delighted. "That's fine. Keep me
posted on how you're coming along with your sums and
whether you learn to handle a rifle. That might be handy,
too. You'll have plenty of chances to keep me informed.
You see, I'll be in to visit your daddy pretty regularly."

Brent laughed then. He did not begrudge the tax money
he had paid William Milton. The immediate liking had
been mutual.

Another welcome visitor was Dr. Mouton, the kindly
physician whose practice was largely among the pioneers,
though nominally he lived in Rayne. The Winslows all
kept in the best of health throughout that first spring and
summer; but, if Dr. Mouton were called to anyone out
their way, he was apt to stop by just to make sure there

was nothing he could do for them at the same time, or, if he were not too much rushed, just for the sake of sociability. He could also tell stories and, though Lavinia did not think these were as exciting as the one about the money-bags, she enjoyed them. Once, Dr. Mouton told them, he was on his way at nightfall to see a patient who was desperately ill, and his mare shied when he came to a stream he had to cross; then he saw that the bridge was down. So he unhitched the mare, kicked her gently toward the stream and crossed it by clinging to her tail, meanwhile holding his satchel above the water with his free hand, while she swam across.

"And did the poor man you went to see get well?" Lavinia wanted to know.

"That he did, and a strong husky fellow he is to this day. I can't afford to have my patients die, Lavinia, of anything except a ripe old age. I'd lose my practice if I did. And then how would I pass the time? Just sitting in Rayne, eating frogs' legs? No, no, that wouldn't suit me at all."

"Is anyone sick out this way now?" Mary inquired, as the doctor finished his coffee and rose to leave.

"No, not what you'd call sick. But I knew Mrs. Villac must be near full term and I thought I might as well pass by. I couldn't have timed it better. I meant to tell you straight off, as soon as I got here, but somehow, we started on stories—"

"But this is a story, too! Do you mean to tell me it's all over—with no one there to help?"

"Lord, Mrs. Winslow, why should I need any more help than what her husband and cousin and all those young ones can give me? Many's the time I've done with less—and her, too. She'll be glad to see you feel like going over though—and maybe Lavinia would like to see the new baby."

"Oh, I would! Is it Paul or Pauline?" Lavinia asked.

The doctor looked puzzled for a moment, then laughed. "Pauline," he said. "So now, they've got four boys and three girls—a fine family. But maybe they ought to have another girl to even things up. Primeaux's children are coming along all right, too—I've even begun to have hopes of Fleex. It's unfortunate, of course, that they lost their own mother—one way you look at it. But she wasn't half the helpmate Anne Villac's proving herself to be. We can't look too closely into the ways of Providence. Keep that in mind, Lavinia."

111

"I'll try. But I don't know as I can, until I've seen the baby."

The visits to the baby and her mother took up so much time, during the next few days, that Lavinia and Mary missed another welcome caller, the most regular one of all —Anna Kutsch, who rode out over the prairies several times a week, delivering mail to the scattered pioneers. In spite of Dr. Mouton's casual reassurance, Mary was horrified that Anne had not had some capable and experienced woman with her at the time of her confinement, and insisted on taking over the care of mother and child, and supervising the performance of household tasks and of the younger children by Annette, Mezalee and Marcelite. Anne was properly grateful, but more for the good will than for the actual nursing.

"You ain't never had but one, *chère,*" she told Mary, "that why you make so much about it. I gotta admit, me, sometimes it go hard the first time; once you over that, it ain't no more than a bellyache, no, mebbe a bad one, mebbe a light one. Don't you worry none, no—you got lots to do by your house an' me'n Pauline is gettin' along fine, us, yes."

Mary remained unconvinced until she arrived one morning to find Mrs. Villac not only up and dressed, but standing by the stove stirring gumbo. "The young girls don' make it to suit that Ursin, him," she explained. "They ain't got the knack yet. But this here'll be ready soon— soon an' it's goin' to be good, yes. Sit down, *chère,* an' I'll fill a couple bowls, me, for you an' Lavinia."

"I'd be much happier if you'd go back to bed and let me finish the gumbo," Mary objected.

Anne Villac's eyes snapped. "An' w'at you know about gumbo, Madame Illinois?" she inquired shortly. "There, I didn' go for to hurt your feelings, me, no. Just the same, it's true. An' I ain't goin' back to bed. When I get finish' with this gumbo, me, I'm goin' to start a batch of shortbread. You kept everything so clean, I got no sweepin' to do, an' no washin', only the diapers. All I got to do, me, is set an' rock the baby the rest of this day."

Mary saw that it would be not only futile, but offensive for her to argue; so she left, taking Lavinia with her. The little girl was even more reluctant to go than her mother; she still called Clement her "little brother," but she had already begun to call Pauline her "little sister" and Clement had a formidable rival in her affections. She very seldom

112

sulked, but she did so now; she had been promised that she could hold Pauline, sometime that day; and they had left before Mrs. Villac would let her take the baby, who was sleeping peacefully, out of the packing box which served her as a cradle. Her resentment increased when she found she had missed Anna Kutsch, to whom she had taken a great liking. Unreasonably, she insisted perhaps this was the very time that Anna would have let her go along; then they might have flushed pheasants or scared prairie chickens or even have come suddenly upon a deer, the way Anna had once. Vainly, Mary pointed out that Lavinia could not accompany Anna until she had a horse of her own; when Anna had said she could go along "sometime," there had been nothing definite about this; it was just a pleasure she could look forward to, in the future, like so many others. But Lavinia refused to be placated; it was the same as holding the baby, she said perversely; she had been promised, and then she had been put off. . . .

"Stop acting like a baby yourself, Lavinia," Brent said, more sharply than was his habit. "Your mother's tired enough as it is, without having you plague her like this. . . . Mary, there's a letter from your father. I put it on the shelf in front of the clock."

They did not have a great deal of mail and they looked forward to Anna's visits, just as they did to Dr. Mouton's, for the enjoyment of her presence rather than for any service she rendered them. They had been on friendly, rather than intimate, terms with their neighbors in Monroe; and besides, those young farmers and their wives were too busy, trying to raise their families and wrest a living from the soil, to have much time or inclination for correspondence. Brent was an only child, and his father and mother had not approved of the move to Louisiana; one of the ways they showed their disapproval was by the infrequency of their letters. Sally's status as a bride was offered as a pretext for similar negligence; she was rapturously happy and her every thought, like her every act, was centered on her husband. Once in a while, she dashed off a few lines to say that she was more and more in love every day, that she had never imagined marriage could be a condition of such sustained and unalloyed rapture, and that she was forever discovering new aspects of perfection in Jonathan. Eventually, she wrote to say she believed she might be pregnant, and that the thought of bearing Jonathan's child filled her with unspeakable happiness and pride; a few weeks later,

113

she wrote again to say now she was sure, and that her cup of joy was brimming over.

It remained for her father to send the immigrants news of more general character. Jim Garland did his best, but it did not come naturally for him to express himself on paper, and Mary opened the envelope, which Brent had propped up in front of the clock, with no great anticipation of pleasurable interest. But because she *was* tired, she sat down in one of the rockers which had lately been added to their household equipment; and, after a time, Brent, coming back briefly to the house during a break in his work, realized that she had remained seated far longer than was her habit. He looked at her questioningly and then, struck by a certain strangeness in her expression, came over and put his hand on her shoulder.

"You haven't had bad news, have you, Mary?"

"No, not exactly. That is . . . Brent, Father wants to come and live with us."

"What?"

"He wants to come and live with us," Mary repeated, in a rather dull voice. "He's got it all planned. He says he can come for nothing in an immigrant car. All our furniture and all of his that he wants to bring with him would come in the same car. His livestock, too. One passenger is entitled to ride free in a car of that sort as a 'guard.' That's what he wants to do."

"But why—"

"He says he'd feel better if we had some real horses, not just these Cajun ponies we've told him about. He wants Lavinia to grow up a really fine horsewoman and he thinks you and I are too busy to see that she has the proper training for one. And it seems he has a few purebred cows now and he thinks we ought to be raising those, not making do with the range cattle we've described. He says he doesn't like to think of us living in a one-room house, either—he's got so he's brooding over it. He knows we can't afford anything better just yet, but he's prepared to help us pay for a better one—a better one and a bigger one, so that there would be room for him. That's what he *says*. But, Brent, I can't help being afraid—"

"Yes, Mary?"

"I can't help being afraid that he isn't happy. Not just because he misses Mother so much, but because Sally and Jonathan have made him feel—well, that he's in the way, that they want the place to themselves."

"But, good Lord, they've got two places!"

"Well then, that they want both places to themselves."

Briefly, Mary and Brent looked at each other in meaningful silence. Then Mary spoke with hesitation,

"I know you don't want to build until after the first crops are harvested. But if Father helped pay for the house—"

"I don't want that, either. I was grateful for the money that made it possible for me to get this place. But I said, from the beginning, it must be just a loan and I'd rather not borrow any more—much less take anything as a gift. I like your father, you know that, Mary. But I want this to be *our* house, yours and Lavinia's and mine. I wouldn't feel it was, if someone else's money went into it—*any*one else's money. I'd feel just the same, for instance, if it were my father who had written that letter instead of yours."

"On the other hand, you don't want Father to feel that he isn't welcome with either of his daughters, do you, Brent?"

"No, of course not. We must think of some way to manage."

Again, there was a short silence. It was Brent who broke it this time, speaking thoughtfully rather than hesitantly.

"Once, when Primeaux was over here, and he and I were standing outside talking, he said I'd always have a use for this house, even after we moved into a better one, because by-and-by, when I got to having hired hands, they'd need some place to bunk. He said he'd seen one place that had two cypress slap houses built on it, while it was being homesteaded, and they'd both come in handy after a while. Maybe your father'd take the money he thought of letting us have and build himself a house like this on our land—or a different kind, if he wanted to. That would be up to him. Then, later on, after we got our new one, he could move in with us or stay in his own, just as he preferred. My guess is he'd rather stay in his own, except for meals—naturally, he'd take those with us, his dinner anyway."

"Brent, I think you've had a wonderful idea. I think that's just what we ought to suggest."

"He'll want more shelter for his horses than any we've got for our animals, so far, too," Brent continued. "Not just a lean-to—a real stable, probably with quarters for a stableboy attached. No doubt he has one he'd like to bring with him, and some sort of arrangement could be made for him in the immigrant car, too. If your father wants to build a stable like that, too, with his money, I've no objection. The horses would still be his."

"I think we'd both better write him, don't you, Brent? You could give him your point of view and I'd give him mine. Of course, they'd be the same, really. But we'd express ourselves differently, and he'd get more the feeling that we'd really like to have him if you'd write, too."

"I guess he would. I'll find out, right away, how soon we could get the lumber he'd need, and how Castex is fixed for building time."

"Mr. Duson said whenever you needed cypress—"

"Yes, and I've been meaning to have a talk with him, anyway. . . . You remember that tract he kept harping on?"

"The wet patch? The one he said was worthless?"

"Worthless *by itself*. Not if it were part of our property. And Primeaux thinks it's much better suited for my rice crop than the place I was planning to sow. It's got a deep gully running through it, with well-wooded banks, with some ash on them—the hardest wood of all to get, as you know. A patch ought to be wet for rice and this one would provide better drainage than any I've got elsewhere. Drainage is mighty essential and I believe that tract might be a sound investment, just as Duson said. I'm planning to sow at least twenty acres with rice and, if I can get the best conditions for growing it by spending a little extra now, I ought to be able to make up for it later."

"Is there enough money left?"

"I think so—just about. If not, I know Duson will give me credit and I don't mind taking advantage of that."

He did not have to take advantage of it; a bargain Duson had promised, and a bargain the wet patch should be, he told Brent as soon as he was approached on the subject. Brent had taken title to it, plowed, disk-harrowed it and begun the slow and wearisome process of hand sowing, by the time the cypress slabs for the second house and the lumber for the stable had arrived, with Castex in their wake. By the time the new buildings were finished, the young plants had begun to show above the water on the low ground. There was a slight slope to the wet patch and, acting on Primeaux's advice, Brent had dug a crude reservoir on the higher part of it; this served as storage space for rain water and supplemented the supply that the gully provided for irrigation. Under these favorable conditions, the young plants were flourishing. They were coming up

116

slim and straight, jade green in color and very beautiful. Mary, who had viewed the sprouting corn and potatoes and the thrifty young cabbages, turnip greens, peas and beans with satisfaction, but with no sense of wonderment except in their early shooting forth and rapid growth, was awed by this beauty of the young rice. Nearly every afternoon, no matter how tired she was, she walked over to the edge of the wet patch and stood gazing at it, entranced, until the quick-fading dusk reminded her that she must return to the household duties of the night. And it was this tract of land, where the shoots, sturdier and sturdier now, were turning from jade to emerald green, to which she eagerly led her father the evening after his arrival.

"Isn't that the loveliest sight you ever saw?" she asked him. "The green rice—the red sunset—the pink clouds in the blue sky. . . ."

"You certainly have got an eye for color," he told her teasingly. "But yes—I'll admit it's pretty. I won't go so far as to say it's the prettiest thing I ever saw, but it *is* pretty. From what I hear, rice is a pretty chancy crop though. It requires a lot of water. What happens when there isn't enough rain?"

"I'm afraid there isn't a very good crop, either. But you see, people hereabouts trust in Providence that there will be. That's why they call this 'Providence' rice."

"I see. Well, it's a good thing to trust in Providence. But I believe the Almighty likes a little co-operation now and again. To my way of thinking, it wouldn't be a bad plan to try and figure out some way of getting artificial irrigation."

"Well, you and Brent must talk that over. I know he'd be glad of any suggestions."

"I'm not so sure. Brent's always struck me as a man who liked to figure things out for himself. And he doesn't do so badly at it, given time. Don't tell him what I said right away, Mary. See if he doesn't say it himself, before long."

It required considerable self-control for Mary to act on her father's advice, but she managed to do so, helped, not inconsiderably, by the fact that the early summer was one of abundant rainfall and that the Providence rice in the wet patch ripened without a setback, though not without constant care. Brent had bought the best Honduras seed he could obtain; but he had quickly learned that he must be on the lookout for the indigo and the red rice that could damage and even spoil his crop. He weeded it early and late, finding willing and efficient help from his father-in-law and Joshua, the stableboy Jim Garland had brought

117

with him from Illinois. Villac and Primeaux and their sons showed every disposition to be helpful too; however, they had their own crops to care for, and it was only occasionally that they could lend a hand. When Brent came in one night, dead tired, and wearily admitting that the red rice was getting ahead of him, Mary announced that the next day she was going into the field, too.

"You'll do nothing of the kind," Brent told her shortly. "It was bad enough having you do chores in Illinois, when I was a sick man. We're not in Illinois any longer and I'm not a sick man any more. I'm not going to have my wife out working in a rice field."

"Anne Villac is out working in their family field. She puts Pauline on her back and goes along with the men."

"All right. When you've got a baby to put on your back, you can go out and work like a common Cajun."

"Brent, it isn't like you to talk this way. It just shows how overworked you are."

"So you'll overwork, too, and then we'll both be talking this way and, presently, we'll quarrel."

It was Jim Garland who eased the mounting tension between them. From the beginning, his presence had been an advantage, as well as a pleasure, and he had fitted extremely well into the general picture. If he had any regrets over the drastic move he had made, he never said so; even the announcement that Sally had triumphantly produced a nine-pound boy, which she had named for him, elicited very little comment on his part; and he expressed no desire to see his new grandson or his younger daughter and her husband. Apparently, he considered the break with them definite, if not final, and neither Brent nor Mary felt it behooved them to question his attitude, expecially since he seemed so satisfied with the reception he had received in Louisiana and his mode of life there. His arrival, with two immigrant cars, instead of the usual one, had caused quite a sensation; he had come as a "guard" in the first, and Joshua in the second. The horses and cattle he brought with him had been of far higher quality than any so far introduced into the region; they were viewed with widespread admiration and envy. His modern farm machinery, better suited to the Midwest than the Deep South, caused less covetous feelings; and his easy geniality was disarming in a situation where an attitude of aloofness might well have made him enemies. Whereas Brent and Mary almost never went into town, he managed to do so frequently, driving a horse which was even more dashing

118

than Will Milton's pair and which was hitched to a sulky as light and elegant as Duson's surrey was capacious and serviceable. He was soon a familiar figure at Frankel's Store, at the Dusons' Land Office and at the bar of the Crowley House, and he quickly made friends in all three places. He did the necessary purchasing, swapped stories and gleaned items of neighborhood news. He was apt to stay in town for supper and, when he came back, he dropped in to tell Mary and Brent that the errands were all done, or that the Dusons were going to start laying out another town, or that it was rumored there was going to be a new lumber mill, nearer than Jeanerette. It was to offer such bits of information as these that he appeared when the argument about work in the wet patch had trailed off into uncomfortable silence; and, without appearing to notice that anything was amiss, he put down his bundles on the large center table that had been added to the household equipment, and drew up the chair whose original seat, now replaced, had been sacrificed for the first repairs on the pump.

"Mary wants to help with the rice weeding," Brent said suddenly. "I've told her it isn't to be thought of. I hope you'll tell her so, too."

"Well now," Jim Garland said easily, glancing from his son-in-law to his daughter. Then he drew his pipe from his pocket, filled and lighted it, before he spoke again. "*I* wouldn't have thought of it, I've got to admit that. I'm not surprised you didn't, either, Brent. But you've probably noticed before this how many things a woman can think of that would never enter a man's head."

"And much better if they didn't enter a woman's, either."

"Well now," Jim Garland said again. "I wouldn't go so far as to say that. When they get a feeling about something, I mean a strong feeling, once in a while there's a reason for it, even if we menfolks are pretty slow to find out what it is. Mary's got a strong feeling about that rice. You'll recall it was the very first thing she wanted me to see. Took me out there to look at it the day I got here, before I even had a chance to unpack my grips. Asked me if I didn't think it was the prettiest thing I'd ever looked at."

"She's welcome to look at it all she wants to."

"Yes, of course. But maybe she's thinking it wouldn't be so pretty to look at, come harvest time, if that red rice should get ahead of us. Maybe she's thinking it wouldn't be good for her, either. Then it wouldn't pay for that new home you're hankering after."

"You're not suggesting——"

"I'm not suggesting anything, Brent. You never asked me to and I know any man likes to make up his mind for himself. I've told Mary the same. But I suppose a woman likes to make up her mind for herself once in a while, too."

"Yes, she does, Father," Mary said quickly.

"Well, if you've made up your mind to hitch up your skirts and put on a pair of rubber boots and go out there in that muddy field, I don't suppose Brent can stop you, even if he is your husband, or that I can, even if I am your father. Watch out for snakes, that's all I can say. I wouldn't have believed there were as many snakes in the whole U.S.A. as there are in that one rice patch."

That settles it, Brent said to himself triumphantly. Mary had a deadly terror of snakes, which she had never been able to overcome, though she was not afraid of anything else in the world. When Lavinia had fearlessly killed one that had crawled out from under the new cistern and had showed it proudly to her mother, Mary had shuddered and screamed and run into the house, to shut off the sight. She had shuddered and shrunk away every time she had seen one anywhere else on the farm, alive or dead, and very often she had screamed, too. *The old man has settled it,* Brent repeated to himself; Mary had never been beyond the edges of the wet patch; she hadn't thought about having to kill snakes, too, if she went out to kill red rice.

Nothing more was said on the subject that night. But the next time Jim Garland came over from his house to find out what errands he could do in town, Mary asked if he would mind taking the buggy instead of the sulky, so she could go with him; there was some shopping she wanted to do personally. The shopping proved to consist of two pairs of rubber boots, one for herself and one for Lavinia.

CHAPTER XI

When the rice headed in September, it was as golden as it had once been green, waist high and of the same density as wheat. The omnipresent ricebirds had done some damage by milking the young grain before the dough stage, and a few "blue hens" had destroyed the plants in their nesting grounds; however, these were not more than ten feet square in any area, and there were few indigo weeds and little or no red rice in the entire wet patch. The hot, dry months which had succeeded the warm, wet spring had given the ground time to solidify; there were hardly any low pockets of standing water to hinder harvesting and reduce the yield per acre, for Brent had dug his drainage ditches early and they were adequate. The excellence and abundance of the crop were both unquestionable. When Mary gazed out over it now, at eventide, it was not only beauty of which she was conscious, despite her awareness that the landscape was more beautiful than ever. She was also conscious of its proud fecundity and of sorrow for those who had never intimately known seedtime and harvest time, because such persons blindly believed that visible signs of fertility were confined to the animal kingdom and could not realize, as she did, how greatly the good earth was vitalized by impregnation, how enriched throughout the period before production.

It had been decided, in family conclave and acting upon the advice of their more experienced neighbors, that, since the reaping would take at least three weeks, it must be started before all the rice was fully ripe; even so, some of it would be overripe before it was harvested. No effort was spared to prevent an unwelcome degree of maturity. The men breakfasted, hurriedly, in the darkness before dawn, in order to be out with their sickles by daybreak, and Mary and Lavinia carried midmorning coffee and their dinner to the field. The Winslows' rice had ripened a little earlier than the Villacs' and Primeaux' and there was more of it. Ursin and Phares had no wet patch and, moreover, they had planted some cotton, so that Anne would have it for weaving, and enough sugar cane to provide for family consumption; Brent had attempted neither of these crops, which were not ready for harvesting at the same time as the rice. This meant that the friendly Cajuns were all able to help at the beginning and end of the reaping and Anne sent over extra food by one of the girls, not only enough to supply her own menfolk and growing boys, but enough to supplement what Mary prepared. None of the reapers went hungry, but they often went thirsty. It was impossible to keep water cold enough to really slake their thirst and next to impossible to keep enough stone jugs in circulation, though even the younger children willingly helped the elder ones in carrying these vessels back and forth.

When the reaping was done, the rice was bundled, tied

121

with hemp twine and shocked in the field, with twelve bundles to a shock. It rose in golden rectangles above the golden stubble, awaiting the time when it would be dry enough to be hauled away for threshing. Jean Castex had built a wooden platform, raised on four-foot stilts above the ground, and near the house for easier supervision. This was where the threshing was done. The bundles of rice were put on the platform to be beaten by paddle-shaped hand flails; and, as the grains were broken away from the straw, this was discarded by being thrown on the ground. When the separation seemed more or less complete, the remaining stalks were swept to the center of the platform, and the straw, to which a few grains hung tenaciously, was beaten again. This process was repeated over and over; and finally, the rice was put into buckets and held high in the air before the buckets were overturned. As the grains fell in a golden shower to the platform, the wind blew away the chaff and the few remaining pieces of straw. Then the rice was sacked and covered with canvas while awaiting sale.

The wait was not a long one. News about the surprising excellence of Brent Winslow's rice crop had been quietly spread by word of mouth. Jean Castex had spread it, not only in Mermentau where he lived, but in every place where his skill in carpentry called him. Villac and Primeaux had spread it among their Cajun kith and kin, who were scattered all the way from Breaux Bridge to Lake Charles. Anna Kutsch had spread it on her mail route, Dr. Mouton on his medical rounds and Will Milton in the course of his tax collecting. The Dusons had spread it in Rayne and Opelousas and in the new settlements they were busily promoting. W. W. and C. C. were urging Brent to add a timber lot to his holdings; an unusually fine one was available at four dollars an acre—well, they could call it three. Now that the wet patch had turned out so well and Brent could depend on the money he earned from rice to pay for the new purchase, he shouldn't let such an opportunity go by. But quite aside from this perennial sentiment on the part of the Dusons, they liked Brent well enough to be sincerely disinterested. Jim Garland was disinterested, too. But he saw nothing amiss in admitting, without much urging, that his son-in-law had done a fine job for a man who had never attempted to raise rice before, and who had never even seen it raised, until he had come to Louisiana, only a year and a half earlier, on his first tour of inspection. When Jim's cronies at Frankel's Store and the Crowley House spoke to him about the rumors that were rampant, he did not deny their accuracy or even make light of them. He echoed and applauded them.

Presently, purchasers began to appear, at first individually, then two or three at a time and, eventually, in larger groups. Sometimes they bought only a single sack of rice for seed; some of them, as many as half a dozen. Most of them were comparative strangers to Brent and Mary, who had stayed so close to their land that they had made few acquaintances. But Jim Garland was hail-fellow-well-met with a surprising number of them, and when they left the Winslows with their bulging buggies or laden carts, it was with a feeling of good will all around. Lavinia had inherited much of her grandfather's ease in making friends; she was not essentially shy, like Mary, or essentially reserved, like Brent; and though none of them was aware of it, she was a tremendous asset in overcoming the impression made by her parents' diffidence. She organized games, introducing the ones she had learned in Illinois, but which were strange to her new acquaintances, and readily picking up the ones that were equally strange to her, like *monte échelle,* and *cache, cache, bien ma bague* which was fine for rainy days, because it could be played indoors. On pleasant days, the yard was full of youngsters tossing beanbags to one another, playing hopscotch, joining hands for London Bridge and ring-around-a-rosy. When Jim Garland bought a croquet set in Rayne and gave it to Lavinia for a birthday present, the Winslows' grounds became an undisputed center of attraction.

Meanwhile, Mary had surmounted her feelings that everything must be "just right" for company; she had learned to keep a coffeepot on the stove all the time. Moreover, though she still could not compete with Anne in flavoring her stews, these were adequate and abundant, and her bread and rolls surpassed any biscuit Anne could turn out, while her frosted cakes were a triumph. The men who came to buy rice and stayed to drink a cup of coffee or share a meal began to bring their wives and children with them, and to suggest visits from the Winslows in return. Outstanding among these invitations was one to attend a *boucherie* at the Primeaux–Villac farm.

Phares and Ursin already considered themselves—and were considered by others—as co-owners of the property; it was therefore fitting, as prospective co-hosts, that they should deliver this invitation jointly and in person, as soon as they decided from past rains and other natural signs that there was a real chill on the way. However, it had not actually set in yet and Fleex and Claude who, as usual, had accompanied their fathers, remained out on the porch with Lavinia while their elders went inside to drink coffee.

"What is a *boucherie?*" Lavinia inquired with interest.

"A hog killing," Claude told her, astonished at her ignorance. "Don't they have hog killings in Illinois?"

"Of course they have to butcher a pig, every once in a while, for food. But they don't make a party out of it. They feel sad about it—at least most people I know do. It's just one of those things that has to be done."

"We don't feel sad about it around here," Fleex said, with one of his rare laughs. "We all pass a good time at a *boucherie.* Me, I'm glad there's going to be a real big one at our farm this year—ours haven't amounted to much these last few years, because Marcelite and Mezalee haven't been old enough to take hold. But now that *Tante* is here, everything will be fine."

"What will she do?" Lavinia asked.

"She'll have a big, big kettle of gumbo cooking on one of the fires outdoors, because the pots in the chimney pieces will be full of rice to go in the gumbo and the stew, and the ovens will be full of biscuit," Claude said proudly. It was not often he took over from his cousin, and Lavinia had been looking at Fleex when she asked her question; but after all, it was Claude's mother they were discussing, and he felt that this time it was his turn to speak.

"*One* of the fires outdoors?" Lavinia echoed in astonishment. "How many are there going to be outdoors?"

"Four. Besides the fire for the gumbo, there'll be a couple to heat the water in the iron washpots that are used for the pig sticking, and one to give us the coals for the barbecue pit."

"What do you use the barbecue pit for?"

"To roast a shoat that's been killed two or three days before the *boucherie.* The barbecue'll be good this time—a lot better than the one they had the day of the auction. I remember you didn't like that much, but you'll like *Maman's.* And there'll be lots of other things to eat besides. The women who've loaned us extra washpots will bring big cakes, too. I hope your mother'll bring us a cake, whether she's got a washpot to spare or not. She makes wonderful cake."

"Yes, she does," said Lavinia with pride. "I know she'd

124

be glad to bring a cake. Only she might not know she was expected to. I'll tell her, to make sure."

"Maybe she'd bring us two," Claude went on enthusiastically. "There's no one can beat her at making cake. That's one sure thing." Suddenly his conscience smote him for having left his cousin so long out of the conversation and he strove to make amends. "And I've heard ain't no one around here can handle a knife as good as Fleex," he added. "Likely Isidore Lasseigne will do the butchering—you know who I mean, don't you? The father of that fat boy Polydore, that's always hanging around the Blakes' place. Isidore, he's a first-rate butcher. But I heard N'Onc say he was going to let Fleex do the pig sticking."

"You won't stick a knife into Polydore by mistake, will you, Fleex?" Lavinia inquired, jokingly. "He looks so much like a pig, you could, you know."

"That's right, I could," Fleex answered abruptly. Then he added, with growing vehemence, "But if I did, it wouldn't be by mistake. It would be on purpose."

He slid off the edge of the porch, where he had been sitting, dangling his legs and, without another word, strode rapidly through the yard and out of it, slamming the gate of the picket fence after him. Lavinia turned to Claude in troubled surprise.

"What's the matter?" she asked. "I was just joking. Did I say something that hurt his feelings?"

Claude looked down at his hands, obviously embarrassed. "No, I don't think you hurt his feelings exactly," he said hesitantly. "But Fleex hates Polydore Lasseigne."

"Well, that's nothing to get mad about. None of us likes him."

"No, but the rest of us don't hate him the way Fleex does—or for the same reason."

"What reason?"

"Well, like I said, Polydore is always hanging around the Blakes' place," Claude replied, with increasing confusion. He was embarrassed not only by the turn the conversation had taken, but also by the reluctance of a male adolescent, just beginning to grope his way toward the harsh realities of sex, to attempt an explanation of these to a little girl who was still happily unaware of such urgencies. "Fleex would hang around there, too, if he had the chance," Claude ended lamely.

"Why?"

"Because he likes Prudence Blake. And Prudence just laughs at him. She says he's only a kid. Polydore's fat, but

125

he's older. Prudence doesn't seem to mind having him hang around."

"I think Polydore Lasseigne is disgusting," Lavinia said decidedly. "And Marcelite says Prudence Blake is a sly, sneaky girl. Even Mezalee, who hardly ever calls anyone names, says she's silly. I don't see why Fleex should want to hang around her. Do you?"

"No-o-o," Claude answered. But he spoke with less finality than Lavinia expected and hoped for. However, before she could ask for further explanations, Phares and Ursin came out on the porch accompanied by her parents, and Claude rose with alacrity, as if he were not sorry to have the conversation come to an end.

"We goin' butcher two hogs, us, so we got to start the fires soon-soon in the mornin', by three-four o'clock," Phares was saying. "That way the water in the washpots will be boilin' plenty by daylight, when the *boucherie*'s ready to start. . . . *Bien*, we got to be goin' on to the Sonniers. We ain't invited them yet. *Bon soir,* all of you."

"Good night," the Winslows said in unison.

They stood on the porch watching their departing guests out of sight. When these were swallowed up in the early darkness, Lavinia spoke to her mother about the cake; had either Mr. Primeaux or Mr. Villac asked her to make one for the *boucherie?* No, Mary said, but of course she would be glad to.

"Claude said he hoped you would make two," Lavinia added. "He said he thought you made the best cake of anyone he knew." She had given her message faithfully, but her mind was not on her mother's superior cakemaking any longer. It was on Fleex's skill with a knife, on his hatred of Polydore Lasseigne and his unaccountable desire to hang around a silly, sly, sneaky girl like Prudence Blake.

When the great day came, Jim Garland was on hand to help start the fires; he would not have missed it for anything, he said: the air was like wine, the stars were still piercing the dark heavens with their bright points, a late moon hung like a golden melon just above the horizon, and when the flames began to leap and glow around the great iron kettles, the dun-colored prairie took on a radiance which no man in his senses would want to miss. Early as he was, the young Primeaux and Villacs were all scampering around in a state of great excitement, gathering up additional scraps of wood with which to feed the fires; and presently, other girls and boys from neighboring

126

farms were joining in their harum-scarum gleanings. The three Winslows arrived somewhat later than most of the visitors. Brent had teased Mary a little, saying she was missing part of the *boucherie* on purpose—she had always been squeamish about hog killing. She had tried to deny the charge, insisting that her tardiness was caused by the preparation of the gold and silver cake, on which she had lavished great care that morning, after whipping up one of lesser importance the evening before. But whatever her reason, it was nearly eight o'clock when she appeared with her husband and her daughter, carrying her cakes very carefully, and threaded her way through the yard which was already filled with people and with the oxcarts and buggies in which the majority of them had come, though a few had done so on horseback or on foot. The guests were laughing and joking together in French, and crowding around a wooden bench on which Phares and Isidore were just laying a kicking, squealing pig, one man grasping its hind legs and the other its forelegs. Marcelite, holding a china washbasin, and Fleex, holding a sharp, long-bladed knife, were standing beside the bench and, as the Winslows approached, Fleex cast a rapid glance in Lavinia's direction.

"You may hold the basin if you want to," he said. "Marcelite doesn't care one way or another and Mezalee would rather not. But be quick about it. We're all ready."

"If Lavinia doesn't want to, either, I'd be glad to," Prudence Blake called out boldly, wedging her way forward. "She's just a little girl, Fleex. She might drop the basin. It's always one of the older girls who holds that."

"I won't drop the basin," Lavinia retorted, seizing it from Marcelite's not unwilling hands and glaring at Prudence. "If Fleex thinks I'm old enough to hold it, I guess I am."

A cheer went up from some of the bystanders, a murmur of dissent from others. Lavinia had no idea what was being said or what was going to happen next, though she was quite sure the latter was something dreadful, and she wanted to shut her eyes, so that she would not see what it was; she was afraid she might scream or be sick if she did. But her successful defiance of Prudence gave her courage, and she stood as near to Fleex as she could, holding the china basin firmly and watching him closely. With zestful speed he flung himself on the hog and plunged the blade of his sharp knife into the right side of his victim's throat, driving it swiftly downward, then twisting it adroitly to the

127

left and turning the knife handle, after the blade had sunk home, so that its tip would move in the hog's chest at exactly the point where the big veins and arteries and heart came together. Again he glanced rapidly in Lavinia's direction and shot a question at her.

"Are you ready?"

"I guess so. What do I do?"

"Come closer and hold the basin so it will catch the blood. I'm going to pull out the knife."

She nodded and squatted down beside the bench. A curving stream of crimson followed the withdrawn blade and splashed into the basin. Prudence, who had remained as near as possible to the scene of action, let out a shriek.

"You're spilling it! The blood for the pudding will be wasted on the ground!"

"I'm not either spilling it!"

It was true. Lavinia had continued to hold the basin steadily; she had not shut her eyes, she had not screamed, she had not been sick. Fleex looked down at her with one of his rare, flashing smiles, and she knew she had earned his approval. But he had no time to tell her so now. The hog's struggles had become feebler; when they ceased altogether, Fleex, who was still holding his bloody knife, cut a slit in front of the big tendon in each of its hind legs. Then, after Phares and Isidore had pushed a length of broomstick through these slits and lashed a rope to the center of this, he laid the knife on the ground and helped the two men lift the dead hog and suspend it from the overhanging limb of a tree near one of the fires where a washpot was boiling. Lavinia still squatted on the ground beside the bench, steadily holding her brimming basin.

"You done fine," Anne said heartily, coming up beside her and taking the basin from her. "Fleex was right when he picked you to help. Now run around an' pleasure yourself, yes. Marcelite, you carry this into the kitchen, so I can start the blood puddin', soon as we done finish our coffee, us. Right now, we got to have something to warm us up good."

"Coffee'd hit the spot all right, but the chill's passing. Look at that rice stubble over yonder! The sun's chased the frost clean off it already."

"You're right, Isidore. I hope the sun don't get too bright though. We got a lot of meat has to cool out."

Fleex had retrieved his knife and been swallowed up in the crowd. But Claude had come forward with a mop to swab the suspended hog under his father's direction and afterward to scrape the carcass with a hoe blade, until all the bristles were gone and the skin was clean and pink. Until then, Lavinia had continued to stay near at hand, not wanting Claude to feel that she was interested in the proceedings only as long as Fleex was connected with them; but when Isidore began to disembowel the hog, the sensation of sickness, which, so far, she had managed to keep under control, threatened to overcome her, and she asked Claude if he were needed there any longer.

"Not really," he said. "I want to get the bladder for you, because you'll have fun with it, after it's blown up and tied to the end of a cane pole. And I'll have to fight for it, because all the other boys will be trying to get it, too."

"What will I do with it after you've given it to me?"

"Why . . . you'll chase the rest of the boys and girls and hit them with it if you catch them. Don't you want to?"

Lavinia did not want to, but again she tried to be fair: she had held the china basin at Fleex's suggestion, so she must accept the blown-up bladder at Claude's. But she was glad of the respite offered by a summons from the kitchen: her mother was going to help make the stew of fresh liver and rice which, with the barbecue and gumbo and cakes would make up the noon dinner; wouldn't she like to help, too, so she could learn how it was done? She would, indeed, and ran gratefully into the house, so she did not see any of the next activities in the yard, though the guests who came in and out of the kitchen, helping first in one place and then in the other, kept reporting progress: on the removal of the two "leaves," which must be tried out at once, for the preservation of the chops and the "tenderlines"; on the salting and stacking of the jowls and bacon sides and hams in a clean wooden barrel, where a little saltpeter was sprinkled in with the salt; and on the division of the entrails, part saved for *andouille* sausage, to be smoked later over fires of bagasse; and part turned inside out, scrubbed and made immediately into chit'lings. Each of the visiting families which had helped would have its share in these delicacies—the *morceau de voisin*—just as the Primeaux and Villacs would have a share in the products of *boucheries* which took place on other farms; so all this was a matter of vital interest to everyone but Lavinia, who was glad so much progress had been made in her absence—until she learned that, when the second hog was killed, Prudence Blake had held the china basin for the blood that was to go into the pudding.

Prudence had sidled up to Fleex and whispered something to him, Marcelite, coming in with a fresh supply for *andouille*, told Lavinia. He had stared at Prudence for a moment, and then he had grabbed her around the waist and whispered something in return and both had nodded and laughed. Marcelite thought they had struck some kind of a bargain—that Prudence had agreed to something Fleex wanted to do, if he would let her hold the basin, which was what she wanted to do. But of course Marcelite was just guessing. . . .

While Lavinia was trying to figure out what the bargain could have been, feeling very much puzzled and unaccountably hurt and not helping very much with the liver stew, Ursin had sawed the empty carcass of the first hog in half and cut the rib sections into chops, to be laid away in an earthenware crock with the newly tried out lard for *confit*; and while the second carcass was cooling off, a halt was called for dinner. Claude had been right; the barbecue this time was much better than it had been at the auction, for Anne's sauce was superb; the gumbo, the stew, the biscuits and the cakes were all delicious, too. Coffee was passed again and a bottle of brandy, freely circulated among the men, also found its way into the hands of some boys, Polydore's among them. The fat boy had not appeared early in the morning, while the hardest work was being done; but he had turned up in plenty of time for the feast and had managed to sit by Prudence while he wolfed it down.

In the pleasant pause following repletion, Isidore, who was as skilled in making *andouille* as he was in butchering, had begun to stuff sausage casings with a mixture of meat and fat and garlic, using a long, smooth stick and singing to himself as he did so. Presently the solo had become a chorus, with Fleex playing his violin and Drozemon Sonnier his accordion by way of accompaniment. Most of the songs were old favorites with which everyone had long been familiar: *"Mo' L'aime Toi, Chère"*—*"Pauvre Petite Mam'-zelle Zizi"*—*"Poulette Blanche."* But Jim Garland, who had drunk his full share of the brandy, caused quite a sensation by suddenly rising and bursting out in a ballad, new to everyone except his family, about some strange, mythical character of the North called Paul Bunyan, and insisting that everyone must join in the refrain. Brent and Mary and Lavinia knew the song, too, and soon all the others were imitating the words, even if they could not

130

pronounce them exactly and had no idea what they meant. Fleex and Drozemon quickly caught onto the air and played with even greater spirit than before, weaving their way in and out of the crowd as they did so, sometimes advancing and retreating together and sometimes separately; then they took turns, one playing while the other danced to "*Le Pommier Doux*" and "*Fli-Fla-Flou.*" Everyone danced, from the oldest crones to the youngest toddlers; the weariness of the morning's hard work, the lassitude that had followed the feast, were alike engulfed in gaiety. And then, so suddenly that no one knew how it had happened, Fleex and Polydore were fighting and Prudence, who, just the minute before, had been dancing with Fleex, was standing beside them screaming that Fleex was going to slit Polydore's throat, just as he had slit the shoat's. . . .

It was only a moment before the scream had become a general outcry, only a moment before the two furious boys, still struggling and panting and swearing, had been pulled apart by the strong men who instantly set upon them. But those moments had sufficed to show that Fleex had, indeed, held a knife in his hand, the same knife he had used twice already that day. It fell clattering to the ground as it was wrenched from him, and his father and his uncle hustled him off into the house, belaboring him, not only with blows, but with loud reproaches for the horrible disgrace he had brought upon them by quarreling with an invited guest, thus unforgivably breaking the laws of hospitality. Jim Garland did his best to smooth over the awkwardness of the pause that followed by starting another ballad, even louder and longer than the previous one, and Drozemon again picked up the air and played his accordion with all his might and main. But the spell of carefree lightheartedness was broken. Husbands and wives began to tell each other it was time they were getting home, and some even wandered over toward their carts and buggies without returning to the kitchen for their share of the spoils. Anne's appearance on the porch, reminding them of their due—and, tacitly, of their obligation to bid a courteous farewell to their hostess, whatever happened to disturb the peace—put an end to such slinking away; then presently Phares and Ursin came out of the house with Fleex between them, and walked over to the place where Isidore and Polydore were still standing apart, and apologies were offered and accepted—sullenly between the boys, good naturedly among the men. Hand-shaking followed, also with some differences in manner; and by now it was evident that the party was breaking up all around, proper amenities having been observed. Half a hog's head was pressed on the Lasseignes, ostensibly because of Isidore's major share in the day's work, but actually as a peace offering, for only four of the families present would get this particular *morceau de voisin* for making into cheese the following morning. The Sonniers, the Blakes and the Winslows were the other favored couples. Drozemon had helped, if not so much with the work, at least to pass a good time with his playing; the Blakes obviously felt they were entitled to be placated for the bad scare their daughter had received; as for the Winslows, they were the newest comers and the nearest neighbors, and that would have been enough to entitle them to special recognition, even if it had not been for Mary's two cakes and Jim Garland's ballads, though, as a matter of fact, they neither expected nor wanted a souvenir of the occasion.

Lavinia had long since ceased to chase her playmates with her homemade balloon when her mother called to her that they were starting home. But she came forward slowly, tapping the ground with it, obviously still unwilling to depart.

"I can't find Fleex to say good night to him," she objected, "and I haven't thanked him yet for letting me hold the basin."

"He's gone off," Claude volunteered. "I don't expect he'll be back again tonight."

"Gone off! Where?"

"I don't know. He does that lots of times, 'specially when he's mad about something. He was plenty mad tonight—mad enough to fight Polydore and then a lot madder because *Père* and *N'Onc* made him say he was sorry when he wasn't."

"What do you suppose made him mad at Polydore?"

"How do I know?"

"Do you think it had anything to do with what Fleex and Prudence whispered about?"

"I said, how do I know."

"Lavinia, we're waiting for you!" It was Brent who called this time from the farther side of the yard.

"He did try to stick a knife into Polydore, and it wasn't by mistake, either, like I said when I was joking," Lavinia remarked to Claude, still lingering.

"No, it wasn't. . . . Lavinia, you know I don't want you to

132

go, but it sounds to me like your folks think you ought to."

"All right then, if you're tired answering questions. . . ."

He had told the truth when he said he hated to see her go, and he was not tired answering questions, on general principles, but as a matter of fact, he was glad of an excuse not to do so this time. For he had reason to be very sure that when Prudence had whispered to Fleex, she had told him he could hang around that night, instead of Polydore, if he would let her hold the blood basin, and that the fight had been provoked because, somehow, Polydore had found this out.

CHAPTER XII

After the Primeaux–Villacs', several *boucheries* took place at other farms, near by as distances were reckoned on the prairie, and the newcomers were invited to most of them. Jim Garland accepted all such invitations; he had less difficulty in understanding the patois and making himself understood in English than his daughter and son-in-law; and his ballad singing became an established and welcome feature of the hog killings. But he was the only member of the family who really enjoyed them and, when they felt they could do so without giving offense, Mary and Brent begged off; as for Lavinia, nothing could persuade her to go to another.

The stack of dingy greenbacks which represented the profits of Brent's excellent rice crop, and which he was carefully salting away, continued to grow, and his chief interest lay, not in festive outings of any sort, but in what this might mean to his family. He and Mary counted it together, over and over again; and one day, in mid-December, he hitched up the Cajun ponies and drove off, without telling anyone where he was going or why. Lavinia, who loved to go driving, caught sight of him too late and ran back into the house, bitter disappointment clouding her normally cheerful little face.

"He might have waited for me," she said stormily. "It was mean of him to go off like that."

"You mustn't call your father mean, Lavinia," Mary said quickly. She was a little hurt herself, and because this was so, she tried all the harder to defend Brent to their

133

daughter. "Perhaps he's planning a surprise for us," she added, still speaking hastily, but more soothingly.

"What sort of a surprise?"

"Why, I don't know. But remember it's getting close to Christmas."

"It doesn't seem like Christmas," Lavinia said stubbornly. "There's no snow and no sleigh bells or anything like that."

"We didn't have holly or mistletoe in Illinois—only pictures of them. We couldn't afford to buy the real thing because, coming from such a distance, it was too expensive, and it was very scarce anyway. Here we can have all we want by just going out and gathering it."

"Well, holly and mistletoe don't make up for snow and sleigh bells," Lavinia persisted. "There won't be any Christmas parties, either, at school or at church—at least, only boys will go to Miss Millie's party at the schoolhouse on the 'Island,' if she has one, and there isn't any church —our kind. The Primeaux and the Villacs are going all the way to Rayne; that'll take up so much time that they can't come to our house or ask us to theirs. Claude says Miss Millie makes them go. She wakes up her own family at two o'clock and starts out with a lead wagon. All her pupils' families follow in their wagons—old people and children and everybody. Even the Bazinets, who live at the Indian trading post, are going."

"Now, Lavinia, you know you wouldn't like to get up at two o'clock in the morning and go jolting all the way to Rayne in the dark."

"I wouldn't mind if that would get me to *Réveillon*."

"*Réveillon?*"

"Yes. They have a big feed they call *Rèveillon* in Rayne after church, before they start home again, and all their relations come to it from everywhere. Claude says they have lots of fun, almost as much as when they go to First Communion in May, and then eat *pâte brisée* made with dewberries for breakfast. I don't suppose we'll have any fun. There's no place for us to go and we haven't any relations here except Grandpa. I don't suppose we'll even have a tree or presents or hang up our stockings or anything."

"Of course we will. Your grandfather was talking to me about all that just yesterday."

"He was?" Lavinia inquired, brightening.

"Yes. But you mustn't ask questions about it. It's very bad manners to ask too many questions around Christmastime. Remember that when your father gets home."

It was so late when Brent returned that Lavinia was fast asleep and Mary, though she had tried hard to keep awake, had gone to bed and was very drowsy herself. She had learned not to worry when her father was out late at night, because this was such a frequent occurrence that it had ceased to seem a matter of concern; and somehow, she had not worried about Brent, either, this time, though it was seldom he left the farm for long and had never done so before without some explanation. However, she probably would have forgotten all her good advice to Lavinia if she had not been so drowsy; and it was just as well that she was, for Brent had no intention of telling her that he had gone to Mermentau to see Jean Castex and ask him what it would cost to build a house—a real house, not a cypress slab cabin.

"How big a house you want?" Castex had asked cautiously.

"Four rooms downstairs and three upstairs. And a kitchen in an ell."

"Three *upstairs?*"

"Yes. We didn't have any upstairs rooms in our house at Monroe, like most of our neighbors—just an attic that had never been finished off. I know my wife's always wanted a house with upstairs bedrooms."

"It makes plenty more steps."

"Well, that's what she *wants.* And a front hall."

"You mean what they call a *salle* around here? Short for *salle à manger?* A big square room?"

"No, I mean a narrow corridor that you enter from the front door, instead of going straight into a bedroom or a *salle*—that way, anyone coming to your house is right in your face before you have a chance to stop him, if you'd rather. A hall like the kind I'm talking about gives a lot more privacy."

"We have that kind in Paris, too," Castex admitted. "But nobody builds houses with corridors in them, out on the prairie, not that I've ever seen."

"Well, I'm telling you that's what my wife wants. So that's what I want, too. And I want to figure on having a pump in the kitchen. That'll save her a lot of steps."

"I must tell you, me, the Abbott brothers got a new idea for a pump. They think, them—"

"I'd like to hear about that some other time. Right now, I want you to give me a price on that house, with the same kind of pump we're got already, only inside. I want good-sized rooms, plenty of cupboards and closet space,

135

too. And the best building materials you can get. I want this house to last."

Castex took a stubby pencil from his pocket, reached for a copy of the *Signal* that was lying on a near-by table, and began to do sums on the margin of the front page. "I reckon it would cost around a thousand," he said at length. "But you must remember, yes, that's no final estimate. It's just rough."

"All right. I'll accept your rough reckoning. How soon can you build it for me?"

"I don't know for sure. Sometime soon. Why you snow diggers always have to be in such a damn hurry?"

"I notice you Cajuns don't object because we hurry about paying our bills."

Ordinarily, such an exchange of epithets would not have been considered complimentary and would have been avoided among congenial acquaintances. In this case, it did not even fit, for Jean Castex was actually a Parisian by birth and not an Acadian, though he had become more and more colloquial in his speech. But he and Brent were such good friends by now that they could call each other anything they pleased. Castex grinned.

"You right, we don't. I'll build you a house as soon as I finish my work by the boardinghouse in Pointe-aux-Loups Springs. Maybe February, maybe March."

"You can't make it any sooner than that?"

"I tell you frankly, me, no, I can't."

"All right. Then will you build me a model of it?"

"What you mean, model?"

"I mean a little house, no bigger than a dollhouse— come to think of it, that would make a fine present for Lavinia, a dollhouse. But build it to scale. Along the same lines as the real house you're going to build when you get through at Pointe-aux-Loups. And give me your word you'll have that model finished before Christmas. I want to put it under our tree."

Probably Brent would not have succeeded in keeping his secret if he had not taken the wise precaution of sharing it with his father-in-law. Jim Garland, as usual, showed himself resourceful and enthusiastic. They must have the tree at his house, not theirs, he told Brent; he had wanted it that way all along, but, on the other hand, he had not wanted to horn in on their plans. His cabin had been built with two rooms, instead of one, besides the kitchen, partly to provide storage space for the extra furniture he had brought with him, until the Winslows could accommodate it, and partly because he had forestalled them in saying he wanted to live independently. When he had written about joining forces with them, it had not, for a moment, been his idea that they should be cooped up together all the time; and since he would probably occupy his quarters much longer than they would their present ones, he wanted space to turn around in. He was very handy about a house—a natural handiness which his wife's years of confinement to a wheel chair had served to develop—and he kept his cypress slab cabin as neat as a pin, cooked most of his own meals and pressed Joshua into service for washing up afterward, a task which the stableboy performed very aptly, with agreeable pauses during the course of which he himself ate. When Brent consulted his father-in-law, Garland immediately suggested that since Lavinia never went into the room that was still used for storage, the tree could be set up and trimmed there and moved later; if Brent though it would be safer, they could put a padlock on the door leading into the other room, the one where Garland slept and ate, and where they would have their Christmas party. Perhaps it would be just as well; you never knew, Mary might take a notion to go into the storage room, too, after the little house had been delivered. This was not just a case of planning a nice surprise for a little girl, as he had thought in the beginning; it was a case of planning a surprise for a grown woman, too. And grown women, as well as little girls, were apt to reveal undue curiosity at the wrong time, you might say to get downright nosy, even the best of them. . . .

Between them, the two men saw to almost everything. They went, turn and turn about, and as unobtrusively as possible, to see how Castex was progressing with his model, to suggest a change here, an improvement there; and finally, they went together, in the farm wagon, and brought it back from Mermentau with them, smuggling it, after dark, into the padlocked room. They had convinced Mary that she would have enough to do cooking the dinner, without bothering about anything else—well, of course if she wanted to make some wreaths, and pop and string some corn to go on the tree, that would be all right. Yes, she could make a silver star out of tinfoil, and some tinsel balls, if she wanted to; and if she needed to get into Crowley to do some private shopping, they would see that she got there, and they would put the presents she bought

137

or made under the tree or into the stockings. But aside from that, they were taking over. There was to be no arguing. . . .

She fell in, readily enough, with their plans, touched that they were intent both on saving her work and giving her pleasure. Fleex had brought her a wild turkey he had shot, and much of the day before Christmas went into the careful preparation for stuffing and roasting this fine bird and cooking its accompanying fixings. When evening came, Mary was glad that they were to go to her father's for supper, that she did not have to prepare that, too. As they walked across the yard, they could see tallow candles, encircled by homemade wreaths, tied with ribbons, shining in all the windows of his cabin, and there was a bigger wreath and a bigger ribbon on the door. Then, as Jim Garland flung this open, there stood the Christmas tree in all its glittering glory and, below it, with wrapped packages on either side, a little wooden house: a house that stood two stories high, a house with a porch and an ell, in short, the house, in miniature, that Mary had dreamed about and talked about for years. . . .

Lavinia rushed toward it with a shout of joy. She had seen pictures of dollhouses in catalogs, and two or three of her schoolmates in Monroe had been the proud possessors of something that dimly resembled the gaudy illustrations and glowing descriptions in these boastful brochures. But none of these had approached this paragon that she saw before her. She knelt down in front of it, her jubilant cries trailing off into a murmur of almost inexpressible delight. At last, she turned and looked, with shining eyes, at the three who stood behind her.

"Is this really and truly my dollhouse—my very own?" she asked in a voice hushed by awe.

Her father stepped forward, one arm linked in his father-in-law's and the other around his wife's waist. Somehow, his daughter was swept into this wholesale embrace. "Yes," he said, and his voice did not sound quite natural, either. "That's your house, honey. But tell your mother to take a good look at it, too. Because hers is going to be exactly like that, only bigger. Not just big enough for dolls. Big enough for real people. For us. Comes summer, we'll all be living in it together."

PART FOUR

Progress

CHAPTER XIII

Mary had not minded the hard work; she had never minded that; anyway, the worst of the drudgery was behind them now. A colored couple, Vicey and Dulsa, were living in a shack which Castex had run up from odds and ends of lumber left over after he had finished the new house; Vicey did most of the washing and ironing, and revealed a natural aptitude for cooking, though she either could not or would not learn to clean, in accordance with Mary's standards. Relieved of much laundry and kitchen work, however, Mary did not mind doing this herself, and she was no longer overwhelmed by fatigue at night, or troubled by Brent's obvious exhaustion, when the burden and heat of the day were over. Dulsa was as useful to him as Vicey was to her, and Brent had better machinery now, and a good buggy of his own. To be sure, the herd had doubled in size, but much of it was young stock, which required little care. He was not worrying about money any more, either, for he had doubled the income from his rice, too. The lightening of his load, both physical and mental, represented a corresponding lightening of Mary's, as far as he was concerned. But she was increasingly troubled about Lavinia.

Not that there was anything about the little girl's health to cause her concern. Lavinia was shooting up fast, and she was slimmer than when they had come to Louisiana; but it was a well-rounded slenderness that bespoke normal development, just as Mary's had been at the same age. She had kept the bright coloring of her babyhood and her thick, fair hair was long enough for her to sit on. Mary had been secretly sorry when Lavinia had learned to braid it herself, though she had conscientiously taught her little daughter to do so at the earliest possible age; there was no curl in it, but it was wonderfully soft to the touch, and it had the sweet scent of youth and cleanliness. Lavinia had always been an apt pupil about learning to do things for herself, like braiding her hair and taking her bath and reaching the back buttons on her clothes; she had also learned quickly how to do things about the house, not only dishwashing and bedmaking and sweeping and dusting, but cooking as well. She could already churn fairly well. She could make good biscuits and cookies, and she could prepare the vegetables that she picked from the garden. Moreover, even Anne Villac admitted she could cook rice as though she had been born on the prairie. Under slight supervision, she could baste meat in the oven and take a responsible part in the preserving; it would not be long before she would be able to get a whole meal on the table, in creditable condition and short order. But none of these housewifely talents interfered with her outdoor pursuits. She was on and off a horse at all hours of the day and was both a fearless and a graceful rider; her delighted grandfather said it would be no time at all before she could halter-break a colt and drive a double team. She could give as good as she got in the rough-and-tumble games she played with the Villacs and her other boon companions; and she derived enjoyment out of all their sports, whether she lost or won. But she had made no progress at all with book learning, though she could figure quickly enough in her head. After Mary had saved enough money to buy a piano, and proudly watched over its transportation, arrival and installation, Lavinia evinced no interest in it whatsoever, and soon betrayed the fact that she had forgotten almost everything Jonathan had taught her about music. The discovery that she was also forgetting much of the classical French she had learned with him was made less easily since Mary knew no French herself; but when the lamentable truth of this came to light, it weighed still more heavily on Mary's heart and she determined on swift action.

"Brent, I've got to talk to you about Lavinia," she told her husband one afternoon when Lavinia had gone to spend the day with the Villacs and they were alone.

"Why, what's the matter?" he asked in genuine amazement. "I thought she was as fit as a fiddle."

"She is, physically. But she's growing up completely ignorant."

"Oh, I wouldn't say that! She'd had some schooling before we left Illinois and—"

"How much?"

"Well, not much, but it must have laid the foundations for her to go on by herself. And she goes to Sunday school."

"How often?"

Brent preferred not to make a direct answer to that question. After the Winslows' first Christmas in Louisiana, when the young Villacs and Primeaux had returned full of enthusiasm about the good time they had "passed" at Rayne, in connection with their nocturnal expedition to Mass, Mary insisted that her family must make an attempt to attend services in West Crowley, where they were held, intermittently, in a one-room schoolhouse, not unlike Miss Millie's on the "Island." The Reverend H. Q. White, whose regular church was in Rayne, also ministered, as best he could, to the Protestants of Crowley; and these ministrations supplemented the more-or-less unorganized Sunday school which had already been started. Now a building committee had been formed, land for a church donated by W. W. Duson and operations begun. Brent had promised that, when there was a "real church," he would try to get Mary and Lavinia there more often; but the makeshift arrangements which had hitherto prevailed did not appeal to him. He did not mind "making do" on the farm; when he went into town, he wanted something better. Jim Garland had, admittedly, never been much of a churchgoer and, in this instance, he upheld Brent. Sunday was supposed to be a day of rest, he reminded his daughter, and if anyone needed and deserved this, Brent did. It was not a restful experience to make an early start, in order to get Lavinia to Sunday school, and then to reach home late, partly because they themselves had had rough going into Crowley and back, and partly because the "Reverend" had had the same difficulty getting there from Rayne. In fact, several times when the Winslows had made the effort, Mr. White had not been able to get to Crowley at all. It was all right to risk this sort of thing once in a while, of course, but there was no use trying to make a regular practice of it. . . .

"Once in a while" proved to be at fairly long intervals, and Brent's conscience troubled him about this, though Jim Garland's did not. Brent's parents were far more strait-laced than Mary's; he should have been the one, he told himself frequently and reproachfully, to maintain

141

habits of churchgoing. He told himself this now. But, after muttering something unintelligible, all he said aloud was, "Well, she reads, doesn't she?"

"Very little. We haven't many books, you know. Besides, she's outdoors nearly all the time."

Mary glanced up at the shelf which had been built to companion the one for the clock and the old pewter tea set, which was still used, as it had been for years, not as a tea service, but as the receptacle for petty cash and oddments of household necessity—the sugar bowl for savings, the cream pitcher for current expenses, the other pieces for bits of twine, thumbtacks and so on. Mary's well-worn Bible stood on this second shelf, flanked by Brent's, which was much larger, but which bore fewer signs of usage, though it was important to him and, indeed, to all of them, as it contained a careful record—on the pages provided for this purpose, between the Old and New Testament—of all births, deaths, marriages and baptisms which had taken place in the family for several generations. Lavinia's Bible came next: a much smaller one, with very fine print, which lacked not only these important pages, as Mary's did, too, but the colored maps of the Holy Land, and the Glossary, which Mary's did have. Grandmother Winslow had given it to her and, because it was a present from this stern and stingy old lady, for whom the child had been named, and because Brent and Mary had both been brought up not to look a gift horse in the mouth, they had refrained from commenting on its inadequacy, either to each other or to Lavinia. In fact, their conscientious attitude in regard to it had even prevented them from replacing it, though Mary found it unsatisfactory for the regular reading that she insisted Lavinia should do from it—a chapter every weekday night and two on Sunday.

Besides the Bibles, there was an unwieldy one-volume collection of Shakespeare's plays, also in very fine print; a two-volume collection of Longfellow's *Poetical Works*, which Mary was ashamed to have found more readable; half a dozen very battered novels, memoirs and juveniles —Bulwer-Lytton's *Last Days of Pompeii*, Cooper's *Spy*, Mark Twain's *Innocents Abroad* and *Tom Sawyer* among them; a *Book of Manners for All Occasions* and a *Home Medical Guide;* and finally, the schoolbooks they had all used in Monroe. That was all. They had owned a copy of *Uncle Tom's Cabin* and a *Biography of Abraham Lincoln;* but Jonathan Fant had advised them it would be more tactful not to take these to Louisiana and they had agreed.

Brent's gaze followed his wife's in the direction of this somewhat dreary supply and, after looking it over without enthusiasm, he spoke testily, if truthfully. "We've as many as most people around here, if not more. This isn't a region of readers—it's a region of doers. Anyway, you can buy more books, can't you? We're not all that hard up. And it's good for Lavinia to be outdoors. She's the picture of health. And she's pretty, too. She doesn't seem to be headed for any awkward age. It wouldn't surprise me if she were *quite* pretty by the time she's eighteen."

"And then someone will fall in love with her and she'll get married while she's still ignorant and remain ignorant all her life."

"Good Lord, you are borrowing trouble! Can't you take time yourself to teach her what you want her to learn now that you've got Vicey to help you?"

"I could take the time all right—I *would* take it, no matter what else I left undone, but I don't know enough to teach her what I want her to learn—French, for instance."

"Why, I hear her chattering away with our Cajun friends; I thought she'd picked up a lot of French from them—they talk it half the time. Fleex most of the time."

"She has—that kind. But that's not real French—it's not even good French. I want her to learn to speak it the way educated people do, in France and well—everywhere. Besides, it isn't only a question of books. It's a question of music, too. She's hardly touched the new piano and, when she does, she stumbles through the simplest pieces and jumps up and runs off the minute she can find an excuse for making an escape. She played very well—once—for a child of her age and she loved her lessons. It's a surprise to me—a great disappointment—that she isn't interested any more."

They were just finishing their midday meal when Mary broached the subject of Lavinia's education and they were still sitting at the table. Now Brent drummed on it with his fingers and looked out of the window. He did not want to seem impatient, but he was installing some new pumps, modeled after those with which his neighbors, the Abbotts, had been the first to experiment. He had not been much interested when Castex had spoken to him about these crude contrivances, because his mind was on the house he wanted to build. However, since then, he had recognized their enormous possibilities for developing irrigation, and he was now prepared to try out for himself the

143

system of raising water to the prairie level by means of an endless log chain, to which buckets were attached at regular intervals. He had already secured an old three-horse-power engine and was ready to gear it to an equally old threshing machine cylinder around which the endless chain could run. His hired men were waiting for him and required his supervision. Besides, he privately felt Mary was exaggerating the importance of trivial accomplishments; he did not think it really mattered very much whether Lavinia learned to speak classical French and play the piano like a professional. These acquirements were not like the three R's, of which she already had a rudimentary knowledge and was bound to pick up more, one way or another. He was satisfied to see her so healthy and happy, so handy about the house and grounds and so easy with horses.

"Just what do you want me to do about it, Mary?" he asked eventually. "I can't teach her those things, either. And she couldn't learn them around here, even if she went to one of those shacks they call schoolhouses—you know as well as I do that only boys go to those, pretty rough customers, some of them, too. I suppose the girls do grow up ignorant, the way you're afraid Lavinia will. I remember getting that impression when we first came here, and you asked Primeaux about his daughters' education. But I haven't thought much about it since and they seem to get along all right."

"The girls whose parents can afford it are sent away to school."

"You want to send Lavinia away!"

For the first time, he was roused. The prospect of a house, of barns and fields, gardens and groves, devoid of Lavinia's presence was appalling to him. He forgot about the new pumps and the uninstructed field hands and looked across the table at his wife in consternation.

"I'd miss her just as much as you would, Brent," Mary said earnestly. "Probably more. After all, a mother and daughter are closer to one another, in many ways, than it's possible for a father and daughter to be."

"I don't believe it," Brent said shortly.

"I didn't expect you to," Mary replied with a slight smile. "Just the same, it's true. But I'm thinking of her good—not our pleasure."

"She'd be miserable, separated from us," Brent said, still shortly and even more stubbornly.

"I don't believe so. I think she'd be very happy after

144

she got over her first homesickness. And she could see us quite often. I wasn't thinking of sending her far, Brent."

"Perhaps you'll be good enough to tell me where you had planned to send her."

It was seldom that Brent spoke sarcastically. Mary winced a little, but she continued in her usual calm way.

"I hadn't *planned* anything, Brent, without consulting you. But the place I thought of was Grand Coteau. That's where Miss Millie went. The Sacred Heart Nuns run a very famous school there."

"You'd send her to a *Catholic* school!"

"Lots of Protestant girls go there, too, Brent," Mary answered, curbing her impulse to say that, though Lavinia was, of course, theoretically a Protestant, nothing much was being done to assure her adherence to that faith. "There isn't any proselyting—I've been assured of that," Mary went on. "And those nuns are wonderful women—resourceful and courageous. They kept their school going, somehow, right through the war. Before that, they had all the rich planters' daughters as pupils—all except the ones who went to the other Sacred Heart School, at Convent, on the Mississippi, instead. After the planters weren't rich any more, even when some of them were ruined, the nuns kept right on taking their daughters just the same. The Order of the Sacred Heart regards teaching as part of its vocation."

"I don't know what you mean when you talk about vocations and I don't believe you do, either."

Again Mary smiled faintly and, this time, she suppressed a slight sigh. "I think I do, Brent," she said. "I think we all have vocations, if we're trying to lead good Christian lives—different kinds, but vocations just the same. Let's talk about that some other time though, shall we? All I want you to do now is this: I want you to say you'll keep an eye on Lavinia for a day or two while I go over to Grand Coteau to see the principal—that isn't what she's called, but you know the person I mean. Vicey isn't capable of controlling the child; Lavinia runs pretty wild sometimes, when she's out with that Villac tribe. But if you'd look after her, I could take the trip and find out whether I thought it was really a good place to send a little girl and how much it would cost and all that. It wouldn't do any harm, would it, just to find out?"

"No," Brent muttered reluctantly. "It wouldn't do any harm—just to find out. But you can't make me believe those Catholic teachers would take Protestant girls for nothing, or next to nothing—not now anyhow. After all, the Civil War was over quite a long while ago, though to hear some people around here talk, you'd think it was still going on. And remember, if you do go for a day or two—by the way, just what do you mean by that?"

"I've made inquiries," Mary answered readily. "I can leave Crowley at 8:10 A.M. and get to Lafayette at 8:54. I have to change there, but I have only a half hour's wait before I can start for Sunset. Then that takes only half an hour on the morning train. Connections and service coming back aren't quite so good. I can leave Sunset at 9:22 P.M. and get to Lafayette at 10:35. Then I have to wait until 12:53 A.M. for the train to Crowley and it doesn't get in until 1:38."

"A nice time of night for you to be traipsing around all alone! And a nice time for your father or me to come in from the farm to meet you!"

"That's why I spoke of a day or *two*, Brent," Mary said patiently. "I can spend the night at Grand Coteau—the letter I've had said I'd be welcome to—and leave Sunset about 8:30 the next morning. I'd have to stay in Lafayette all day, but I'd enjoy that. You know I've never been there, and I've heard it's a very pleasant town, with lots of good shops and pretty houses. I could have lunch and look around. Then I could take a train out of there, getting me to Crowley at 6:30 in the evening. That wouldn't be a hard time for you to meet me. Or Father could do it."

"Oh, I'll do it," Brent said grudgingly. "But, as I started to say when you rattled off your train schedule which, apparently, you've studied pretty thoroughly, remember, if you do go for a day or two, that doesn't mean I'm willing you should tell the principal, or whatever she's called, that everything's decided, that we'll send Lavinia there a week from next Monday."

"No, Brent, I won't tell her that," Mary said. And once again, the little smile played around her lips. But this time, no sigh came with it.

The trip to Grand Coteau proved to be quite a formidable journey. Mary got up even earlier than usual for the drive into Crowley, where she was to take the train; and this drive in itself was trying, not only because of the rough road, but because neither Brent nor Lavinia, who both went with her, was in a particularly amiable mood. Lavinia had somehow caught the dreadful words "boarding school" and had shied away from them like a fright-

146

ened filly. The Villacs and Primeaux had just organized the semblance of a baseball team among themselves, and Lavinia was allowed to join in "three-old-cat" and practice pitching, at which she was surprisingly good for a girl; she was sure there would be no such opportunities elsewhere. Brent was still antagonistic to the whole idea, and Mary was acutely conscious of the disfavor with which he viewed her venture and of his sympathy with Lavinia. She would never have expected to be pleased at the prospect of a separation from her husband and daughter; but she was glad when the train's raucous whistle announced its approach to the depot, and she kissed them both good-by with unexpressed relief.

Despite the fact that she had gone into Crowley so rarely, she was already aware of its rapid growth and she had not been surprised to see that eight or ten new houses were being added to the half a hundred she had counted when she was last there; but, having taken no train trip since she went to Rayne and Opelousas for shopping, shortly after the excursion which had brought them all to Louisiana, she looked out of the window with eager interest, once she was settled in the car. There was no crowding this time, so she had a whole wide seat to herself; and there were no unwelcome distractions to interfere with her absorbed observation of the countryside and the towns through which they were passing. There was a great deal of land under cultivation now, and Rayne, which had the advantage of a head start over Crowley, could boast of more stores and larger houses, several churches and a lumberyard. The progress and prosperity of the entire region was unmistakble.

When Mary got out of her car at Lafayette, she found the platform of the depot crowded. Apparently, a good many people had gathered merely to watch the train come in, though she would have thought that, by then, the coming and going of trains was such an everyday sight that no one would marvel at it any more. A number of other persons, both white and colored, seemed to have more or less settled down on the platform to spend the day; games of cards and of craps were both in progress, and the interested players went on and on with their gambling, looking up only to cast withering glances at anyone who jostled against them, or to crack a joke with some passing crony whom they were glad to see. Because of the half hour wait before the train for Sunset came in, Mary had to take her choice between sitting in the stuffy waiting room, where

147

there was nothing to see, or standing on the platform and watching the games, and the people—both passengers and onlookers—who came and went. She found the platform much the more intriguing and it did not seem long to her before the train that went down the branch line came in, together with a new group of onlookers and more evidences of irritation from the gamblers who did not wish to be disturbed at their games. She boarded her car with even more interest than she had felt in making the trip to Lafayette, for this part of the countryside was even more unfamiliar to her. When the conductor came through to punch the tickets, he spoke to her in friendly fashion.

"So you're going to Sunset?" he inquired. "Got friends there?"

"No. I'm going on to Grand Coteau."

"Someone going to meet you?"

"If no one does, I can get a hack at the livery stable, can't I?"

"Sure, sure! Just thought it would be pleasanter, a young lady like you, traveling alone, if you had someone to help you. . . . Ever hear how Sunset got its name?"

"No. I've often wondered."

"Well, it was this way: when the railroad was being built between Lafayette and Opelousas, the workmen were able to get just so far from their base by sunset. So they named the place for that point."

"I see. Thank you for telling me."

"Thought it might interest you. Hope someone does meet you and that you enjoy your trip."

"Thank you," Mary said again.

The friendly conductor moved on to the next passenger, whom he also engaged in conversation, and Mary resumed her interrupted observation of the landscape. When the local finally stopped at Sunset, a courteous, neatly dressed Negro came up to Mary almost instantly and asked if she were not Mrs. Winslow; the Mother Superior at Grand Coteau had sent instructions that she was to be met. He had the carriage waiting.

Mary enjoyed the carriage ride even more than she had the train ride. The countryside was not as flat here as it was around Crowley, and she remembered now that someone had told her *coteau* was a French word meaning hill. Personally, she would have called the landscape rolling rather than hilly; but it gave the illusion of having more height than it actually possessed and it was beautifully wooded. Most of the houses they passed were of moderate

148

size, but they were set in the midst of small groves and gardens and they were not without charm and distinction of architecture. The colored driver pointed with pride to the buildings of St. Charles College as they passed by it, and told her how many boys the Jesuits had at this school of theirs; however, Mary was watching with eagerness for the approach to the Academy of the Sacred Heart, and she listened with more politeness than attention to these details.

"You ain't got you no son, ma'am?" the driver inquired, sensing the reason that the plant he was extolling and the statistics he was reciting made so slight an impression.

"No, just a daughter—an only daughter."

"Well, you sure is goin' to be proud when you sends her to Grand Coteau," the driver told her. "You watch, careful now, thataway. You's gwine to see the *allée* directly and the garden soon—soon afterward. The lady nuns done their plantin' handsome. They pines is mighty high already, and they's got their flower beds laid out shaped like hearts and stars."

The expression "thataway" had been accompanied by a gesture toward the left with a whip, and presently the driver slowed down his not unwilling horse to a walk and pointed a second time. Then, as they came abreast of the pines, he reined in completely, thus affording Mary a leisurely and unobstructed view of a nobly proportioned avenue, with a porticoed chapel at its farther end. The boughs swayed gently in the breeze, and the white façade of the chapel beyond seemed all the more glistening in contrast to the misty green of these waving branches, which bore a deceptive resemblance to those of moss-hung oaks. Mary gazed ahead of her in silent fascination; then, tardily realizing that the carriage had ceased to move, asked a quick question.

"Do I get out here and walk up the *allée?*"

"No, ma'am. I'se just givin' you a chance to see it good. You gets out on de yonder side of de garden. You gwine see that next."

He clucked to his horse and they resumed their leisurely progress. When he reined in again, Mary could not suppress a little cry of joyous admiration. Above and beyond an immense garden, a long white building with pillared galleries extended in gracious amplitude. Little as she knew about architecture, the beauty of its chaste and classical design was not lost on her; but it was the loveliness of the garden which really held her spellbound. Symmetrically spaced among the ornate flower beds and gleaming statues rose camellia plants which far surpassed in luxuriance any that she had seen before. Many of them were as tall as trees, and so laden with blossoms that their glossy green leaves formed only a background for these; yet countless blooms must already have fallen, for the ground beneath was covered with a carpet of pink petals. A snowy image of the Sacred Heart, which stood in the center of the garden, had been banked with flowers and, at the rear, two nuns were busily gathering more, without making any appreciable change in their profusion.

"Ah 'spects Reverend Mother gwine give you a cuttin', iffen you asks her," volunteered the driver. "This time of year, it's so many camellias they comin' right out ev'body's ears."

"I wouldn't dare to ask," Mary said, finding her voice.

"Ain't never no harm askin'," the driver observed. "Us asks for lots of things, and ain't often Reverend Mother says no. . . . Well, you'll be wantin' I should go on again, I reckon?"

Of course, she knew she should go on; after all, she had come to inquire about schooling for Lavinia, not to sit, dazed and idle, staring at a garden. But she was suddenly loath to go any farther, to come back to realities, to face hard facts, after an experience that had taken her into realms of rapture. Her reluctance deepened into awe as she sat in the bare little parlor where the Portress had taken her to await the arrival of the Mistress General. None of the garden's glory had penetrated to this austere apartment. The shades of the undraped windows were carefully drawn, so that the stiffness of the straight-backed chairs and the bareness of the floor and center table were unredeemed by sunshine; and the few old-fashioned pictures on the walls were depressing, rather than encouraging in character. Mary, clenching and unclenching her hands, realized that they were growing colder and colder.

As a matter of fact, her wait was actually a very short one. The parlor door, which the Portress had carefully closed behind her, reopened to admit a nun of distinguished presence whose quiet grace of manner almost immediately put Mary at her ease. She was the Mistress General, this nun explained, and she would be glad if Mrs. Winslow would tell her a little more than she had said in her letter about the child who might be coming to the Academy as a pupil. Rather falteringly at first, but with increasing confidence, Mary told her story: she thought

150

that Lavinia, who would be twelve in the Fall, had made a good start in school before they left Illinois, but since the family had moved to Louisiana, there had been practically no opportunity for book learning and this was very distressing to the little girl's parents. They were not really rich enough to bear the expense of sending Lavinia to the Convent; but their first two crops had brought them in better returns than they had expected and now they had every reason to believe that they would become increasingly prosperous. Therefore, since they felt it so important to give their only child as many advantages as they could. . . .

"I can see that you are very much in earnest about all this," the Mistress General said kindly. She had asked very few questions, and even when she did ask one, she had been careful not to interrupt, but to wait until Mary paused of her own accord. "We are always glad to cooperate here with parents who have their children's welfare so much at heart. I suggest that you and I now go together to see our Reverend Mother and that you tell her the same things you have told me. Of course, I cannot speak for her. But I feel quite confident she will tell you that she will be pleased to receive your little daughter."

After this visit had taken place, with the happiest results, and Mary had been bidden Godspeed by the Superior, the Mistress General suggested Mrs. Winslow might like to go over the premises, to see the classrooms—which were, to be sure, very small and simple—the dormitory with its curtained alcoves, the chapel where nuns and pupils worshiped together, and the oratory which had formerly been the infirmary, where a young postulant by the name of Mary Wilson had been cured, when on the point of death, through the miraculous intervention of St. John Berchmans. Mary showed becoming reverence on being taken to the spot which was obviously hallowed to the Convent and listened with respect to the story the Mistress General told her about Mary Wilson's mortal illness and supernatural manner of recovery; but the atmosphere of the oratory was alien to her and the account of the miracle bewildering; it was her first experience with such manifestations of Catholicism. The Mistress General, far from resenting this attitude, viewed it with sympathetic understanding. It was not easy, she knew, for a young woman like her visitor, to whom she had taken an immediate liking, to grasp such mysteries quickly or easily, and it was better not to attempt any hastening of such a process. With still greater kindliness, she suggested that before Mrs. Winslow had her supper and retired for the night she might like to take a turn through the garden, in order to see it better than she had been able to do from the carriage.

"Oh, may I? It would mean more to me than I can possibly tell you!"

"Why, of course! . . . You're fond of flowers?" the Mistress General asked, leading the way down the stairs and out to the garden through the gallery.

"I think they mean more to me than anything—except people, of course. I try to be a good housekeeper and I hope I am—anyway, my husband thinks so! But my garden's always seemed more important to me than my kitchen. I had one in Illinois with the sort of flowers we grow there—just a few perennials, like roses and peonies, and annuals, like sweet peas and nasturtiums, at first; then later a—a friend helped me to plant and grow more varieties and to arrange them all to better advantage." Mary wondered why she should blush as she said this and, hoping to cover her confusion, she went on hurriedly, "Now my husband's enclosed a small plot of land around our new house with a fence to keep the stock out—a pretty picket fence. And I've laid the plot out in little square beds and bordered them with violets and marguerites. I have three kinds of roses growing farily well in the beds already—Maréchal Niel and Seven Sisters and Louis Philippe—and I'm starting to train some climbing roses, too —Dorothy Perkins—over a trellis. Besides, I have several varieties of camellias started—just ordinary ones like Opelousas Pink and Wax Leaf—and I have bridal wreath bushes and crape myrtle and chinaberry trees. I spend a lot of time in my garden—more than I ought to probably— and it's doing very well, considering. . . . But *this* garden!"

The wonderment was in her face again, the dazzled joy. The Mistress General, pacing quietly along beside her, saw it and spoke with added gentleness.

"We're very fond of flowers ourselves, here at Grand Coteau," she said. "And very pleased when our visitors appreciate them. Now let me show you our oldest camellia tree. It has reached quite a size already, as you can see, and we're expecting it to survive to a ripe old age. Once in a while, we give our friends cuttings from it. Would you care to have one?"

152

"Would I care?" Mary repeated. "Oh, Mother! . . ."

She slept peacefully in the clean, bare little room assigned to her, awoke refreshed to the sound of singing and bells in the distance, and ate, with good appetite and due appreciation of its excellence, the breakfast served to her with silent skill, in another clean, bare little room, as her solitary supper had been the night before. She did not see the Mother Superior again, but the Mistress General placed the promised cutting in her eager hands and the Portress politely escorted her to the carriage which was already waiting to take her to the depot. During the trip between Sunset and Lafayette, she did sums on the back of the envelope containing the letter which had informed her that her visit to the Academy would be welcome; and the time passed so quickly that she was surprised when the brakeman opened the door of the car and shouted, "Lafayette!" She was still more astonished when the first person she saw, after alighting from the train, was Mr. Duson.

"I got in from Crowley just four minutes ago myself," he told her. "So I didn't have to wait long for you."

"You waited on purpose to see me?" she inquired, with ever-increasing astonishment.

"Yes. . . . I heard you'd gone to Grand Coteau—word gets around fast in a place like Crowley, you know. And as I was coming to Lafayette today myself, I thought I'd see if I couldn't be helpful to you in some way. I believe you're not much acquainted here. Also, there's a little matter of business I'd like to speak to you about."

"A matter of business?" Mary echoed incredulously.

"Yes." He had placed his hand under her elbow and was guiding her adroitly toward a waiting hack. "You remember those two lots your husband bought in your name, the day of the auction?"

"Why, yes!" Mary answered, still in growing bewilderment.

"Paid seventy-five dollars for them, didn't he?"

"I believe so. Yes, I'm sure he did."

"Well, I've got a prospect that would like to buy them. He's offering two hundred dollars for them."

"Two hundred dollars!"

"That's what he's offering. But he's well fixed. I haven't a doubt but what he'd go up to three—they're in just the locality he wants. What do you say, Mrs. Winslow?"

For a moment, Mary did not say anything. This was not only because she was still too astonished to speak. It was

153

also because she was thinking hard about those sums she had done on the train. She did not believe Brent would refuse to pay for Lavinia's schooling. But if he did. . . .

"I'd have to consult my husband, of course," she said finally, with a wariness she was very far from feeling.

"Of course, of course! But come to a quick decision between you, won't you? Let me know tomorrow if you can. My prospect's in a hurry. I wouldn't be surprised if you could push him up still another hundred, provided he could get title right away."

Mr. Duson's kind offices continued through the day, but Mary saw nearly everything through a haze and did nearly everything in a dream. Mr. Duson insisted that she should lunch at Rigue's Hotel with him and Mrs. Duson, who had come to Lafayette the day before; and afterward, Mrs. Duson took her to Mouton Frères, a store which carried a much more extensive and attractive line of dry goods than any Mary had seen since she left Illinois. But she was too excited to eat and too intent on safeguarding the money for Lavinia's schooling to enjoy shopping.

Brent was waiting for her at the depot in Crowley; he had missed her more than he would have believed possible, and the kiss with which he greeted her was no perfunctory salute. After a warm embrace, which had in it no hint of self-consciousness because of its publicity, he suggested that they should have supper at the Crowley House. He had gone in there to look around while he was waiting for the train and had been impressed by its great improvement; he had been promised they could have a table to themselves, and fried chicken with all the fixin's. It would seem almost like a party, planned on purpose for them. What did she think?

She thought perhaps they ought to get back to Lavinia, but Brent reassured her. Lavinia was with her grandfather, having a fine time herself; the old gentleman had invited in three or four of the Villacs and Primeaux—Brent wasn't sure which ones—to keep her company, and Vicey had got a good supper for them, too. In the face of all this, Mary could not very well hold out and besides, she was so eager to tell Brent about her experiences that she did not want to lose time in argument. As soon as they were seated at their table, she began her story.

"The Mother Superior and the Mistress General were very kind—very understanding. They said they'd be glad to take Lavinia at the beginning of the next term—that's

154

early in March, about a month from now. The tuition is one hundred and fifty dollars a year—a full year. Of course, for just the last semester it would be only half that much. We can afford to spend seventy-five dollars for tuition this spring, can't we, Brent?"

"I guess so, if we can scrimp on something else," Brent said, reaching for a roll.

Mary drew a deep breath. "I ought to tell you, Brent, that there are a few extras," she confessed. "The cost of board and an alcove in the dormitory is included with the tuition. But there's an entrance fee of five dollars, two dollars for the use of the library, thirty dollars for drawing lessons. Then there's a separate bill for laundry. The Mistress General says there's no set fee for that; some girls get by with as little as twelve dollars and fifty cents a year. But music's another extra—eighty dollars. That makes a minimum of two hundred and seventy-five dollars and fifty cents a year, the way I reckon it."

"Phew! That *is* a heap of money, just for a year's schooling!"

"I know. But, Brent, if you can't spare that much—"

"Well?"

"I saw Mr. Duson in Lafayette this morning. He'd heard I'd be on the train from Sunset and he met it. He asked me if I'd sell—if we'd sell—those two lots you bought in my name. He has a prospect who wants to buy them in a hurry."

"For how much?" Brent inquired, helping himself to more chicken.

"The offer was for two hundred. But Mr. Duson says he thinks it would be increased to three if the prospect could take title immediately. Perhaps more than that. Anyway, the sale would pay for Lavinia's schooling all next year and, maybe by the year after that—"

"Maybe by the year after that I'll be getting still more for my rice. That's what you started to say, isn't it? But listen, honey: we don't sell land to Duson; we buy it from him. I'm aiming to put up a building I can rent out for offices on my business lot, and if those lots of yours are worth three hundred or more now, two years after Crowley was founded, they'll be worth a lot better than that ten years from now. Maybe then we'll talk about getting rid of them. Maybe not. Maybe we'll want them for ourselves— or for Lavinia."

"But what about the school money?"

"Don't you worry. We'll scrape that together somehow.

I know you want Lavinia to have a good education and I do, too. I know you think she'll get it at Grand Coteau and, the more I think of it, the more I'm inclined to agree with you. Not that I care so much about that special emphasis on French and music."

Mary flushed. "How did you guess that I did?"

"Guess! That's what you've been worrying about all the time. That she wouldn't go on from where she started with Jonathan Fant. Isn't it, Mary?"

"I—yes, I suppose it is," she said. Then she began unwrapping the little package she had with her. "It's the most beautiful place I ever saw, Brent," she went on earnestly, if a little hastily. "The *allée* of pines—the long white colonnade—the camellias—why, I never imagined anything like them! They're not bushes, they're trees! And the flowers on them don't fade in the ordinary way—they drop to the ground, still almost whole, in such quantities that they form a lovely carpet. I just stood and looked at them, for minutes and minutes. And what do you think? When the Mistress General saw how I felt about them, she gave me a cutting!"

"Your blue camellia at last, Mary?"

He leaned across the table and took her hand. His voice was still teasing, as it had been all the time she was talking to him. But it was good natured, too. Indeed, there was a warmth in it that had not been there lately, while he was working so hard and striving so doggedly for success. She returned the pressure of his handclasp, looking at him lovingly, and spoke lightly. too.

"No," she said, "it's pink. I'm expecting you to give me the blue one."

CHAPTER XIV

She would have to wait a long time, he told her. He said it good naturedly, so that his response to her remark united the two in a shared jest and, from time to time, they referred to it again. But they were both so preoccupied with matters, far more pressing, throughout the spring, that neither thought about mythical things, like blue camellias, often, much less talked about them. Lavinia's absence had not given her mother more leisure; it had only given her more time to devote to the better organization of her house and the development of her garden.

The furniture which had come from Illinois had been supplemented, not only by the piano which Mary had scrimped and saved to buy, and which silently dominated the parlor, but by a leather-covered "lounge" and two comfortable chairs, together with a huge roll-top desk, which dwarfed everything else in the combination dining and sitting room. This, rather than the kitchen, had gradually become their living center. Matting had been laid on the floor, enlargements of family photographs and chromos hung on the walls, and a big airtight stove provided the requisite heat, just as it had in Illinois, though, happily, for much shorter periods. The room was comfortable, but it was crowded. Mary had her sewing machine and sewing table there and was continually occupied in cutting and stitching clothing, curtains and countless other articles in daily use; her mending basket, always overflowing, stood near by and, while Brent was busy at his desk, she was equally busy with some type of needlework. Often, an entire evening went by in which they did not speak to each other from the time the supper dishes were done until Brent stacked his papers neatly in their pigeonholes, rolled down the top of his desk and announced briefly that they had better be going to bed—a statement which Mary rarely disputed. But the shared silence, far from constituting a strain, represented both a companionship so complete that no words were needed to interpret it, and an ever-increasing mutual sense of endeavor crowned by achievement.

For outdoors, as well as in, there were improvements and expansion. Mary's flower and vegetable gardens were both flourishing, and she was training a grapevine over the porch, partly to relieve its bare look and partly with an eye to future green grape jelly. She was planning an orange grove, a watermelon patch and an orchard which would contain pears, figs and Japanese persimmons— Brent happened to have a special fondness for the latter. She was successfully raising turkeys now, as well as chickens, and talking about a fishpond which they could stock with green trout. Brent had never cared much for hunting, but all the male Villacs and Primeaux were naturally good shots and brought home game from the time they were old enough to handle guns. As they grew older, their skill increased and that of Fleex, in particular, was nothing short of phenomenal. Though he was as wild as ever, he had outgrown his early sullenness and was devoted to Mary; she could count on him to supply her with more game than she could use. Besides, she was learning to lard the meat, supplied by their own stock, and pack it away in large crocks to preserve it. She profited by Anne Villac's example and set a more and more bountiful table.

Rapid as her progress had been, she was hard put to keep pace with Brent. He was no longer hesitant about building, and it was now understood that Jean Castex was to give all the time he could spare to the Winslow farm, with as many helpers as he could get. The carpentry on the cypress slab cabin for Jim Garland and the stable for his horses had quickly been followed by the erection of the seven-room house for Mary, Brent and Lavinia; then Castex had run up the shack for resident hired help. Tramps not infrequently came along and offered to work on the place, but almost without exception Brent refused their services. He had that experiment once, he said rather dryly to Mary, and though it had come out all right, he would rather not risk it a second time. He did not pursue the subject or raise it again and Mary said almost nothing in reply; she still felt vaguely uncomfortable at any mention, however indirect, of Jonathan Fant.

With the elimination of tramp labor, it was obvious that some other provision must be made for carrying on the work. Brent had planted his first crops with no other help than that given by the Villacs and Primeaux—fathers and sons in both cases—and harvested them with the additional help of Jim Garland and Joshua. But even then it had been a struggle. The following year, some distant neighbors—the Sonniers and the Blakes—had come in for the threshing; but now that Brent had more than doubled his planted acreage, less makeshift measures were in order, even though the cradle had succeeded the sickle for reaping, and threshing had been done with a one-horse tread power machine, instead of by hand flail, there must be a reliable man, either married or single, living on the place all the time; and, during harvesting, it would be necessary to supplement the neighborly help by bringing in Negroes from town. The colored population in Crowley had increased so fast that it had kept pace with the rapid influx of white settlers, and the huskier blacks were in great demand as seasonal workers.

"You know I told you, when we first talked about having your father come here, that someday we might need to use our cabin for a bunkhouse," Brent said to Mary. "As I understand it, the owner of a place like ours goes into town every Sunday afternoon and collects as many

Negroes as he needs. They eat and sleep both, in the bunkhouse—they bring biscuit and syrup with them, which doesn't cost much—about eighty cents a week. But they get good wages—as much as sixteen dollars."

"You mean *apiece*?"

"Yes, that's just what I mean and some additional food is supplied. A long table's put in the middle of the bunkhouse and it's carried out to them there by a colored woman. Vicey can do that all right, but I'm afraid you'll still have to do most of the cooking."

"I don't mind. . . . But would you be happy to have our first home used that way, Brent?"

"I wouldn't mind that. We've got a better one now—the one I promised you. The other ought to be used for something."

Mary realized that this was all too true—they were doing well, they were getting ahead, but they could not afford to be wasteful, then or ever. However, the idea of having her first prairie home used as a bunkhouse for Negro laborers was unwelcome to her, and she dreaded their proximity to her present dwelling, both on her own account and on Lavinia's. Her father solved this problem for her, as he had so many others.

"Why not turn *my* place into the bunkhouse and let me move into your first one? I don't need two rooms any longer, now that I don't have to supply storage space for furniture. I'd enjoy being near you, and I imagine you'd enjoy having me, more than you would those workmen from Coontown. Don't start arguing—I know you've got a lot of sentiment about that shack, whether Brent knows it or not. Matter of fact, he does know it, and he's got some himself, only he won't admit it. He's just running true to form, Mary, acting like a husband. Let him be. And let *me* be. I'm running true to form, too, acting like a father. We better make the shift right away, before Lavinia gets home for her vacation. Otherwise, I might have two females to argue with, instead of one. Besides, we'll want all the free time we can get, just to enjoy her company. Pity everyone will be so busy, right then. I'd like to take the family over to those springs at Pointe-aux-Loups I hear so much talk about."

"And I'd like to go. But of course we can't, right in the middle of summer. As to taking over the first house yourself, if you really think—"

"Of course, I really think. And we'll get to Pointe-aux-Loups some other time—though, as a matter of fact, I suppose the first trip I take ought to be back to Monroe. It's two years now since I left there and Sally keeps reminding me of it every time she writes."

It was the first time he had spoken of a possible return to Illinois, and the suggestion came as something of a shock to Mary. She realized that letters were arriving more frequently now, but most of them were addressed to her father and she had never questioned him as to their contents, nor had he previously referred to them on his own initiative. She had no deisre to reopen a closed chapter and she had gradually come to believe that he felt the same way. It was slightly disturbing to her to find that she was mistaken, and she was genuinely disappointed because it was so obviously impossible for her to go to the only "resort" which the countryside afforded; but her disturbance was short lived, for her father did not mention Monroe again and she tried to tell herself that, of course, they would get to Pointe-aux-Loups some other time and that, anyway, she should remember how much she had to be thankful for and not hanker for pointless outings. Anne Villac never seemed to. Except for her rare attendance at church in Rayne, Anne left the farm only once a year, when she returned to Lacombe to celebrate *Toussaint* with her own family and to take personal charge of decorating the cemetery lot and to satisfy herself that this was kept in good condition. Ursin accompanied her and they took some of the younger children with them, leaving the others in charge of the elder ones, who were also held responsible for helping Phares to decorate the little family graveyard back of the orange grove, where his wife and three of his children were buried. But this trip was in the nature of a duty and a pilgrimage, not a pleasure jaunt and, compared to hers, Mary's life was now one of ease and luxury. Moreover, Lavinia was at home again now. Mary had counted the days to that. . . . And then, shortly after the homecoming took place, something happened so exciting that everything else was, temporarily, driven from her mind.

The rice was waist high again now, and more abundant than ever. The day was very warm and Mary, who was in the kitchen preparing dinner unassisted, as Vicey was preoccupied with the ironing, turned around in amazement when Brent burst in on her, half an hour earlier than usual, and with a precipitancy that was uncharacteristic.

"Mary, I want you to come out to the field with me."

"What, now?"

"Yes, right away."

"You mean you need help with the work?"

"No, I want to show you something. I think I've made a discovery."

There was an urgency in his face as well as in his voice. Without questioning him further, Mary told Vicey to keep an eye on the pot roast, and went with him through the yard and the hayfield to the wet patch.

He walked so rapidly that she had hard work keeping up with him, but he did not say anything more until they had neared the field. Then he took her hand and plunged off the levee into the burgeoning rice. He had only gone a few feet, however, when he stopped with the same suddenness that marked everything else he had been doing.

"Look at that!" he exclaimed.

"Yes, Brent, I am looking. It's a wonderful crop, our best yet."

"It is, but I don't mean that. Look at the heads—the flowers. Can't you see anything unusual about them?"

"No, I'm afraid I can't."

"Well, I can. They—the flowers—have opened up, but they'll only stay open a little while, just the way morning glories, for instance, and water lilies open up and then close later in the day. You've seen both of those. Night-blooming cereus, that you've only read about, does the same thing."

Mary bent over to look at the golden flowers more closely. Then she looked back at Brent, with growing wonderment.

"Why, I believe you're right! They do seem to have opened up! I wonder if it's just an accident."

"It isn't. This happens every day."

"Then why haven't you—why haven't we—noticed it before?"

"Because it only lasts a little while each day. Because we've always been so rushed. These flowers bloom at noon, just our dinner-time, and close by one o'clock. This is the third day I've watched them. I didn't want to tell you until I was sure. And then I suddenly felt I couldn't wait any longer. Because, if they do open—"

"Yes, Brent?"

"Nothing. That is, nothing I'm ready to say yet. But I want you to come out here with me at noon every day for a week and watch those flowers. I want you to tell me if you don't think I'm right. Never mind about dinner—we can eat that any time."

161

She was certain he was right; she was able to assure him with proud confidence, after she had watched this phenomenon with him every day for the specified time. He did not again come dashing into the house to fetch her. Instead, he went on with his work, as usual, and, promptly at noon, she walked through the yard and across the hayfield and met him at a corner of the wet patch. Increasingly, the meeting made her think of the time before they were married, when he was courting her; because she could not then wait for his kiss until he reached the house, she had gone out toward the gate or even past it to meet him, secure in the knowledge that, at a given time, he would be coming to see her, as eager, as impatient for their reunion as she was. Every day now as she gazed at the miracle of bloom before her, she had much the same sense of fulfillment that she had had then—a fulfillment not yet complete, but so close to it as to be a visible and tangible thing, for all its mystery. She was still too shy to put this feeling into words now that she was a woman grown, just as she had been when she was a young girl. But she instinctively knew, as she had then, that Brent understood and shared her feeling and rejoiced in it.

At the end of a week, there was no longer any room for doubt about the opening flowers in the mind of either one. Actually, there had been none from the beginning. They had both known, from the first time they had stood there in the rice field together, watching this blossoming, that it was a portent, just as they had known the first time they met as sweethearts, with a mutual sense of harmony and yearning, that someday they must be husband and wife. With this same mutual sense they came closer together now, first reaching for each other's hands and then finding each other's lips. When at last they drew apart, Brent spoke in the voice of a triumphant lover.

"I've always thought that flowers were your department, not mine. I was wrong. Now it's up to me to do as much with mine as you're doing with yours."

She did not ask him what he meant to do; she realized it was doubtful whether he knew himself and anyway, it did not seem to matter. What mattered was that he would do something, the best thing, when the time was ripe. Neither of them guessed that the time would come so soon, or what form it would take.

Brent still went but rarely into town, and that mostly in the slack season. But one day a broken shovel handle resulted in an emergency when Jim Garland had already departed on his usual round of errands and visits. Calling to Mary that he might be late for supper, Brent hitched up the ponies and started for Crowley. When he came back, hours later, he flung the reins to Joshua, lifted a pail covered with wire screening carefully from the buggy and called to Mary. As she opened the door and called in return, her greeting was interrupted by an exclamation of amazement.

"What on earth have you got there?" she asked.

"Bees," Brent replied laconically.

He set his pail carefully down on the porch step and grinned at her. "I happened to glance up, just to see what the weather looked like, as I was coming out of Frankel's," he said, "and what do you think I saw? A swarm of bees on one of the telegraph poles. It came over me what a terrible thing it would be if that swarm should cause a runaway. So I went back to Frankel's and got a stepladder and a broom and a pail. I put the pail on top of the ladder and climbed up to the highest rung myself. After one sudden stroke with the broom, I had dislodged the entire swarm. When the bees were all safely in the pail, I went back to the store and got netting to cover the pail. So there won't be any runaway. But we've got a new colony started. I've wired to New Orleans for supplies—Frankel told me about a firm where I could get them. Frankel knows about almost everything, just as he keeps almost everything. But there's one thing he doesn't know. I told him I was going to set up my new hives in our grove and get an Italian queen. I told him it would seem good to have bees again, that I'd missed them more than anything else I'd left behind when we came here. But I didn't tell him I was going to use them for cross-pollination. I didn't tell him I think I might get new and better varieties of rice with the help of bees."

PART FIVE

Lavinia

July, 1889—November, 1895

CHAPTER XV

From that day on, Brent Winslow was a man with one enduring purpose: the production of rice which, in both yield and quality, should surpass any hitherto grown, no matter where, and the dissemination of this rice to every part of the world.

In the beginning, the yield had not seemed to him much of a problem: since rice was self-pollinating, the more he planted, the more would continue to grow; but the quality would remain the same, unless he could hit on some way of improving it which he had not yet found. To be sure, a great deal had been accomplished by improved irrigation; with this, Providence rice would soon be a thing of the past, for him and other planters. Thanks to the ingenuity of the Abbotts, they were no longer dependent on natural rainfall, but raised such water as they needed from the bayous to the prairies, where the mean level was five feet higher. Their first crude pump had been succeeded by another, consisting of a series of wooden blades fastened to an upright shaft, on the propeller wheel principle, the bladed shaft revolving inside a wooden pipe. A twelve-horsepower engine had replaced the old three-horsepower machine, and the Abbotts were already talking about an additional plant, with a sixteen-horsepower engine. They were ready and willing to supply neighboring families as soon as they had taken care of their own needs and Brent was at the head of their list. But he had never felt that irrigation, despite its great importance in eliminating the hazard of drought, completely solved the problem of improvement. That, he was convinced, must be done by cross-pollination, and until it dawned on him that this might be done by bees, during the brief daily period when the rice flowers opened, he had sought in vain for the answer to the question which his clamoring mind demanded unceasingly.

The single colony in the grove of oaks was increased to ten, to twenty, to thirty, and gradually came closer and closer to the house. The bees went circling over Mary's flower garden and over the fields of clover, and Brent planted a small patch of sugar cane, to provide them with syrup for additional winter food. But though he had so long insisted that flowers were Mary's province and not his, he now established an "experimental garden," beyond the feed pen for the cattle. In this garden, he spent endless hours, for the bees were not slow in finding it, too; and here the various varieties of rice he sought to develop to a state of perfection were planted close together or far apart, depending on the degree of cross-pollination which he had decided was desirable.

But he was not satisfied to confine his experiments to a garden, nor did he feel that cross-pollination was the only answer to his problem; selection must also enter into the picture. The family sitting room became the scene of equally intensive labors, and much of the night, as well as all of the day, was given over to work. Eventually, every picture was draped with sheaves of rice and Mary's sewing table became a testing board. Patiently, hour after hour, Brent would sit at this table, hulling one grain of rice after another, and removing the bran with his thumbnail. This was to see whether there was a "chalky" grain or a "crystal" grain inside. He was perpetually seeking the crystal grains because, little by little, he had learned that they were hard and would stand milling much better than the chalky grains, which would break in the heat. After making his first selections, he would group the hulled rice in little piles, and then he would measure all the grains in each pile, with a small ruler he kept close by, to be sure of getting two that were identical in length. Then he would take those he thought were best and, placing a pin on the top of each pair, run another grain underneath, for assurance that they were the same in thickness, as well as in length. When he was completely satisfied, or as nearly satisfied as he thought was possible at that time, he made his selections for the next seeds he would plant in his experimental garden.

These processes were repeated indefinitely. In his absorption with his experiments, Brent did not notice that

Lavinia was growing up until Mary called his attention to this.

The first time that she came home from school, he had not become so completely preoccupied, and she had not changed very greatly. To be sure, the parlor was no longer quiet, because she played the piano again, for hours at a time, sometimes by herself, but more frequently to the accompaniment of Fleex and his violin. Various members of the Villac–Primeaux tribe, as Brent continued to call it, were practically always present when she was there herself; and when she was not, she was out riding with them, or spending the day at their house, or something of the kind. Brent was not always sure what, but this did not trouble him. He had long since overcome his initial dislike and distrust of Fleex, in the face of the boy's devotion both to his own family and to the Winslows. Disquieting rumors occasionally reached Brent, but these concerned the conduct of the boy elsewhere; Brent took it for granted, and rightly so, that they did not cause him anxiety in Lavinia's case. In fact, he gave the matter of the association between the two very little thought. Then Ursin approached him one day from a very unexpected angle.

"Lavinia, she done put ideas into Claude's head, her," he complained. It was Sunday, and the two men were sitting on the porch, now well shaded by the grapevine. They were drinking coffee and settled—or so Brent had supposed—for a neighborly and harmonious visit.

"What kind of ideas?" Brent asked casually.

"About educate. He got it in his head, him, he's a-goin' off to school. He never would have got no idea like that, no, not unless Lavinia put it in his head, her."

"Well, it doesn't seem to me such a bad idea. He must have learned about all Miss Millie can teach him, by this time."

"An' I tell you frankly, me, that's aplenty for Claude. Maybe it don't look to you like no bad idea he should go off to school, but I can't agree with you, me, I got to speak w'at's in my mind."

"Where does he want to go?"

"St. Charles College in Gran' Coteau, same like the Sacred Heart where Lavinia is, her. She told Claude how that's the place where the boys go, them, that is relations of the girls from Lafayette an' St. Martinville in her class at the Convent. But those boys got rich fathers, them, not no poor farmers like me."

167

"Oh, come, Ursin, you're a farmer all right, but you're not a poor farmer. You're a good one—and a fairly prosperous one."

"Not prosperous enough to send Claude to no college at Gran' Coteau. He got to put the idea right out of his head, him. You tell Lavinia I say so."

The implied rebuke to his daughter irritated Brent, whose affection for Lavinia had a strong streak of admiration in it. Nevertheless, he strove to speak in a cautious and conciliatory way, without betraying his annoyance.

"What about the new college that's just starting up with its headquarters in the Crowley House—Acadia, I think they call it, after the parish. That's a lot nearer than Grand Coteau. If Claude went there, he could come home over Saturdays and Sundays and help with the farm work then. It wouldn't cost so much to send him there, either—you'd have nothing for railroad fare and probably the tuition's cheaper, too."

"I got no reason, me, for Claude to go to no college no place, him. You tell Lavinia what I say."

Again Brent managed to curb his annoyance. He was not only displeased at the repeated reference to Lavinia's idea, on her account, but he himself was beginning to feel that it was not a bad one. Having been won over to the notion that boarding school was advantageous for his daughter, he did not see why it should not be equally advantageous for his neighbor's son; and it was his private opinion that the Villacs could probably afford such an expense as well as the Winslows. Of course, it was different when you had one child than when you had seven; but perhaps none of the other young Villacs would have the same ambitions as Claude. . . .

"I hope the other children aren't giving you any trouble?" he hazarded, seeking to change the subject.

"Not mine, no. Not yet anyways. But Annette, her, she might most any time. Phares' two big girls worryin' him plenty, too, I guarantee you, me."

"They are? Why, I thought they were both very nice, well-behaved girls. Marcelite's very pretty, too."

"She pretty all right. She got her a beau already an' Mezalee ain't, not yet, her. That's part of the trouble, becozz she's a year older. So she say if Marcelite get married first, she goin' to be a nun, her."

"*Get married!* Why, she won't be old enough to get married for a long while yet. And if she's just keeping company with some boy, she may change her mind and decide she doesn't in the least want to marry him, after a year or two."

"She fifteen. Plenty girls get married, them, when they fifteen. That ain't the trouble, no. Trouble is she got a beau first biffo' her sister that's older than her, an' this beau she got, him, he ain't nobody but that Bazinet boy."

"You mean the son of the blacksmith, the one who lives over near where the old trading post used to be?"

"I guarantee you, me. He goin' be a blacksmith, too, him, live over by the tradin' post with his people. Phares don't want his girl should marry with no blacksmith, her, an' live by no tradin' post like she was some Indians. Maybe those Bazinets, them, part Indian, too. I don't know, me. They live there long, long time biffo' we come here, long time biffo' anyone remember."

Again Bent decided it was better not to make any direct answer. This was the first time he had been aware that there were recognized differences in social strata, even on the prairie. The Daigle family, which came from Church Point, but which was beginning to include Crowley in its sphere, far from making a secret of the fact that there were Indians among its ancestresses, was openly proud of this fact; and if rumor were to be credited, the early French settlers in Lacombe had intermarried very generally with the Choctaw Indians, so it was quite likely that Anne had Indian blood, even though Ursin and Phares did not. Indeed, her matter-of-fact acceptance of endless toil, both indoors and out, seemed to indicate that this might be part of a tradition which regarded heavy and menial work as the normal heritage of women. It therefore seemed inconsistent to Brent that the possibility of an Indian strain should be held against Marcelite's suitor, while the trading post seemed to him no less desirable a place to live than the Cajuns' farm, nor the trade of blacksmithing any less praiseworthy than the work of a farmer. Now that he was reminded of it, he realized that the Bazinets had never "visited" casually, either with his family or with Ursin's, and that they had not appeared at *boucheries;* but hitherto, if he had given the matter any thought at all, he would have concluded that the first was more or less accidental and the second caused by the fact that the Bazinets were not farmers. The blacksmith had always been very friendly, from the time the plow was taken there for sharpening; Jim Garland invariably took the horses to him for shoeing, and Bazinet did many other jobs, with unfailing good will, efficiency and dispatch. And now it seemed

169

that his son—Alcée, was that the boy's name?—wanted to marry Marcelite. Trying to put himself in his neighbor's place, Brent wondered how he would feel—years and years hence, of course—if such a contingency should arise in regard to Lavinia and realized, with a sudden pang, that he would be looking higher for her, too. . . . Perhaps the answer would be among those brothers and cousins of her schoolmates, who came from good families in Lafayette and St. Martinville, and who were correctly educated at Grand Coteau. He permitted his thoughts to dwell, not without satisfaction, on this possibility, only to have his reverie interrupted by further grumbling from Ursin.

"Miss Millie, her, she the one to blame. She got the Bazinets followin' her lead wagon to Rayne, same like us. Then the young boys an' girls, except when they in church, be together all eatin' *pâte brisée* an' fried chicken. What you expect, *hein?* Next thing you know, they want to go dancin' together; next thing after that, they want to marry with each other, them. More better when Phares' children didn't never go all that way to church, just let Miss Millie teach catechism after school, boys and girls both, an' wait at home, yes, till the missionaries come to marry an' baptize them. No need to wait too long; those Jesuits is smart, them, they gets around plenty. Me, I don't believe in all this churchgoin', no, not when you got to live in the country. It ain't like when you somewheres near town, no. How Marcelite goin' get a buggy weddin', her, this far from Rayne? That's what she talkin' about now, becozz she been to one when a relation what lives there got married. How we goin' have a party at our house, us, an' a party at the tradin' post, with popcorn an' anisette at both places, an' a white cake for the bride an' a dark cake for the groom? How we goin' to do as much as that an' get them married all the same day?"

"Perhaps one of your relations in Rayne. . . ." Brent began tentatively. Ursin shook his head.

"You snow diggers don't never understand our ways, no. First the girl's family got to give a party, them, an' after that everybody goes to the church in buggies, yes, with the bride in lead buggy, her, by her papa. After they married, the bride an' the groom go in lead buggy, an' everybody has a party by the groom's house where mostly they dance all night, them. Finally, the bride an' the groom goes to their own house. But this young boy, he got no house yet. He got nothin', him."

"Then I should think you or Phares could persuade the

young people to wait. If neither of you could, I should think Anne might."

Ursin snorted. "You ever hear how young boys an' girls wait, them, to marry just becozz they relations want they should?" he inquired. "Maybe they don't get married, maybe something else happen. We don't stand for nothin' like that, no, not in my family."

"No, of course not. But I only thought——"

"Well, you better go think about your bees, yes. You got more thoughts 'bout them that maybe make sense than you got 'bout young boys an' girls, I guarantee you, me. And you tell Lavinia what I say: I don't want she should put no more ideas, no, in Claude's head."

For the third time, Brent managed to refrain from an angry retort, though each time it was harder than it had been before. "You haven't said anything about Fleex and Clement," he remarked. "I hope they're not making trouble for Phares, too?"

"Clement's a good little boy, him; gonna make a good farmer, too, someday, if he don't change like my Claude got changed, goin' against his own father," Ursin replied. Obviously, he was not to be diverted from his grievance. "Fleex, he works all right when he's home, an' he ain't never had no ideas about goin' off to no school, him. But half the time we don't know where he is at. Maybe he playin' that violin of his by some dances; we don't mind that, no. Sometimes he goes to the Sonniers, we don't mind that, neither, us, outside he drinks too much there maybe—those Sonniers they always got plenty to drink, them. Sometimes he goes to the Blakes, too. We don't like that so good, no."

"The Blakes? Why, they're so strait-laced they wouldn't ever take a drink! Don't you remember, when they and the Sonniers have come to help with the harvesting——"

"Sho' I remember, me. They don't drink none. But they got a daughter, ain't how you call so strait-lace other ways, though, her. She could get Fleex in plenty trouble, that one."

With difficulty, Brent suppressed a laugh. It amused him to think that this girl from Iowa, whose family had settled some five miles farther from Crowley than the Winslows, and whose upbringing had been extremely strict, could get the mercurial Fleex into trouble. It even seemed unlikely that things would be the other way around and that he might get her into trouble; though while maintaining its unlikelihood, Brent might have admitted the possibility of this, for Fleex was very good looking now and undeniably "had a way with him." However, the Blakes' principles and the girl's very name—Prudence—which her bearing, at least in public, seemed to personify, certainly argued against such a contingency. But, as Ursin had reminded him, perhaps he knew more about bees than he did about boys and girls. After all, he had been an only child, he had never been in love with anyone except Mary, and their association had been so constant, ever since their childhood, and had ripened so gradually and normally from friendship to ardor and from ardor to passion, that it was not comparable to anything his neighbor was now talking about.

"Let's hope not, anyway," he said pleasantly. "And let me get you some more coffee, Ursin, and something to eat with it. I know Mary baked a chocolate cake yesterday. A nice thick slice of that would go well, for both of us, with the second cups."

Ursin shook his head and rose. "I got to be gettin' back, me," he said. "There's plenty-plenty work even if it is Sunday. Fleex is off again, him, somewheres, maybe to the Blakes; an' Claude got to talk, talk, talk, all the time talk 'bout goin' off to school, so me an' Phares rather work without him, us, even if he's handy enough. Don't forget to tell Lavinia what I said. She got to stop, her, puttin' ideas in Claude's head."

Well, he had not lost his temper in talking to Ursin, Brent reflected with satisfaction, as he watched his neighbor plodding out of sight; but perhaps he *had* better have a word with Lavinia. He could not do so immediately, for she was out, as usual; and when she finally came in, it was so late for supper that he found he was annoyed with her, too. This made it easier for him to upbraid her.

"Where on earth have you been all this time?" he inquired testily.

Lavinia's expression became not only noncommittal, but mysterious. "It's a secret," she said serenely, helping herself liberally to chocolate cake.

"A secret! Well, it shouldn't be. You mustn't have secrets, Lavinia, from your mother and me."

"Everyone has secrets," Lavinia said, still serenely. "And Mother hasn't asked me about this one. Only you. I can't tell you, because it isn't my secret. It belongs to Claude and Fleex."

"I haven't the slightest idea what you mean by that."

172

"It doesn't matter. I don't see why you should want to know about their secret, anyway. . . . Father, did you know thistles were good to eat?"

"I did not. And I wasn't talking about thistles. I asked you—"

"I don't mean the whole thistle. Just the core. I got thirsty, and when I said so, Fleex told me he knew how to take care of that. He stripped a thistle and picked the core for me to chew. It was good. And afterward, I wasn't thirsty any more. Fleex knows a lot about such things, even if he didn't go to school very much."

"Speaking of schools," Brent answered, permitting himself to be diverted momentarily from the subject of secrets, "Mr. Villac is very much annoyed because you've said so much about them to Claude. He says Claude is pestering the life out of him, asking to be sent to St. Charles College. It costs a great deal of money, Lavinia, to send children away to school and their parents are the ones who have to decide whether they can afford it or not."

"Mr. Villac has just bought a very fancy new threshing machine," Lavinia retorted. "He could have made his old one do, and sent Claude to school, the way you and Mother have sent me. The reason he wants to go to St. Charles College is that, if he went there, he and I could see each other oftener than if he went to that new college at the Crowley House. We like to see each other. But he'd rather go to the college in Crowley than not to go to school at all."

"I think it's very praiseworthy of Claude to want to go on with his schooling," Mary, who had hitherto been silent, joined in by saying. "It's tragic enough to see a boy like Fleex, who has so many natural gifts, as Lavinia says, half illiterate, without having Claude grow up ignorant, too. Especially—also as Lavinia says—when his father can perfectly well afford to educate him. I don't understand these Cajuns."

"Well, they don't understand us, so that makes it mutual," Brent retorted. "And *I* don't understand all this nonsense about secrets. . . . I didn't know there were any thistles around here, either."

"There aren't, very near here," Lavinia said, still with undisturbed serenity and still enjoying her chocolate cake. She had now helped herself to a third piece. "That's how I happened to get thirsty, walking so far. . . . Did you ever see a *feu follet*, Father?"

173

"A *what?*"

"A *feu follet*—a kind of fire out on the prairie. Only it isn't on the ground, it's in the air, and usually it's a long way from any house. Everyone hopes it will stay away from houses, because if it comes near that means there's going to be a death in the family, unless someone sticks a knife quickly into the gatepost."

"I never heard such nonsense in all my life!" Brent said explosively. "That really is nothing but what we call a will-o'-the-wisp up north. Who filled your head with yarns like that?"

"Fleex. And they're not yarns. We saw a *feu follet* this very evening. Fleex has seen them quite often, so he knows exactly what to do. He made us run to Miss Millie's schoolhouse, and he told us not to look around; but once I did, and the *feu follet* was right behind us. So then, Fleex and Claude both took hold of my hands and made me run faster than ever, and we got into the schoolhouse through a window Fleex knew how to open. Then we crouched down there with everything shut up tight. After a while, Fleex crawled over to a crack and looked through it and sure enough! We had escaped from the *feu follet*. It lost us when we hid in the schoolhouse. So, after a while, we climbed out of the window and came on home. I wouldn't have been so late if it hadn't been for the *feu follet*.*"

"I've heard just such stories in town, Brent," Jim Garland said soothingly. He had finished his supper before Lavinia came in, and had been sitting in an easy chair, smoking, during the argument between his son-in-law and his granddaughter. "This *feu follet* is undoubtedly just some light caused by gases in the swamplands," he now observed. "But you'd never make any Cajun believe that. . . . So you saw the *feu follet* for yourself, Lavinia, did you? I think that's very interesting."

"Yes, it was interesting. But it was sort of scary, too. That is, it would have been, without Fleex. Even Claude wouldn't have known what to do."

"I should think you'd rather stay in the house, with Mezalee and Marcelite, than go streaking off to eat thistles and run away from *feu follets*, whatever those are," Brent said severely. "And you haven't told me yet—"

"Marcelite wasn't there; she was out somewhere else with Alcée Bazinet. They're a courting couple and they're out together all the time," Lavinia, who was evidently much better acquainted with neighborhood news than her

174

father, informed him briefly. "And Mezalee wasn't good company because she was crying. She wanted to read her missal and she couldn't, that is, not very well. She went to Miss Millie's catechism classes, but she just learned to say what everybody else was saying, without looking at a book much. It didn't seem to matter then, because she could repeat and she has a good memory. But now she's found out she can't be a regular nun if she can't read a missal properly, only a lay sister. She has to know lots of other things, too. Mrs. Villac is very sorry for both girls. She thinks their father ought to let Marcelite marry Alcée; and she thinks her husband ought to let Claude go to school, so that he won't be disappointed, later on, because he's too ignorant to do the thing he's set his heart on, whatever it turns out to be. Mrs. Villac's told both men exactly what she thinks."

Jim Garland burst out laughing. "If that's the case, Brent, the game's up," he said jovially. "And Ursin knows it as well as I do. That's why he was over here, grumbling, all the afternoon. He's bound to give in, once Anne's made up her mind to oppose him. She doesn't do it often, but when she does, nothing will budge her. Claude will start for school about the same time Lavinia does, and Marcelite will be married soon afterward, if not before. You mark my words."

As usual, Jim Garland was very nearly right in all his predictions.

To be sure, Claude was not allowed to go to St. Charles College; but he accepted with gratitude the compromise on Acadia College, which was, at last, grudgingly accorded. Marcelite did not get her buggy wedding; but she was quietly married to Alcée by Father Vialetton, one of the Jesuit missionaries who still rode through the prairie on horseback, and who unhesitatingly upheld her insistence on immediate nuptials, after talking briefly with her and her beloved and their respective parents. The same missionary also talked with Mezalee about her vocation, and advised less precipitancy; she had better wait a few years, he told her. Oh, yes, he understood that she was just as sure she wanted to be a nun as Marcelite was that she wanted to be a wife; but, personally, he did not feel her desire was quite so well grounded. There was just a little jealousy of her sister mingled with it, was there not? *Eh bien*, in Marcelite's case, there was no jealousy and no occasion for any. If Mezalee would wait a year or two, she might find that the right man for her had been a little slow in coming forward, that was all; no doubt he would materialize, all in good time. If he did not, and she still felt she would like to be a nun, the missionary would give her his blessing, after she had given the matter a little more thought. But he hoped she would not content herself with the idea of becoming a lay sister, when some extra schooling was all that stood in the way of being a choir nun. If Claude's father could send him to Arcadia College, certainly her father could do the same for her. Nonsense, it would not be too hard for her! To be sure, the institution was called a college, but its course began with the primary department. Mezalee could make the grade easily, an earnest, intelligent girl like herself. . . .

The good missionary departed, leaving the younger members of the "tribe" much better pleased with the results of his visit than Ursin and Phares. But the Winslows' suspicions that prejudice rather than penury underlay the farmers' objections to their children's matrimonial and educational aspirations was borne out when the cousins announced their intention of buying the Blakes' property, and letting the young couple try their hand at running it —under proper supervision, of course. The Blakes, it seemed, had decided that Acadia Parish did not come up to their expectations; they were going to move on to California, which had supplanted Louisiana in their minds as the Promised Land. This decision, made when a good harvest was at its height, was astounding to many, but not to all. Rumors were flying thick and fast that Prudence had got herself "a bad name." Yes, it might be that Fleex Primeaux was partly to blame for it; but only partly and not at the beginning. There had been other young boys involved—and older men, too. Prudence's strait-laced parents were even more stunned than ashamed; they could not understand how the conduct of their daughter, whom they had brought up in the fear and admonition of the Lord, could have become a public scandal. They did not try to explain it or to brazen it out. They left their good land, dragging Prudence, flushed and defiant, away with them, and leaving a train of sordid stories behind them . . . also a very fine farm, where Marcelite and Alcée were soon happily established, instead of being cooped up in the cramped living quarters back of Marcel Bazinet's blacksmith shop.

"I think if I'd heard that Blake property was for sale,
176

before Ursin and Phares did, I might have bought it myself," Brent told Mary.

"You did buy the timber lot," she reminded him.

"Yes, but I want to plant another field to rice. The wet patch isn't large enough for me any more. And I'm thinking about a canal—not just a ditch, a regular canal. If I had that. . . ."

He bent over his sample grains again, leaving his sentence unfinished. Mary picked up the mending basket she had briefly set aside and went on with her darning. The house was very quiet again, now that Lavinia had gone back to school.

Neither of her parents remembered, until after her departure, that she had never told them where she had gone with Claude and Fleex the day she had slaked her thirst with a thistle core and been chased by a *feu follet*. Brent had been constantly interrupted, when he first asked her about it; and somehow, the question had not come up again, in all the excitement of the missionary's arrival, and Marcelite's marriage, and the acquisition of the Blake property, and the preparations for a year's schooling, not only in behalf of Lavinia, but also in behalf of Claude and Mezalee. Whenever Brent thought of it, the moment was inopportune for further argument and finally, he decided it was a matter of small importance anyway. Why should a man who was involved with great experiments bother his head about the ramblings of three youngsters on a summer afternoon?

CHAPTER XVI

The next summer Lavinia was not at home very much, because she went with her grandfather to Illinois.

He had not brought up the subject of going there again since the day, two years earlier, when he had told Mary he supposed the first trip he took should not be to Pointe-aux-Loups anyway, but to Monroe; and for the second time, she had been lulled into a sense of false security about a closed chapter. Many of the other snow diggers made a practice of returning, more or less regularly, to their old homes; but these were mostly the ones less intent on developing and expanding their new ones than Brent, either because of less necessity or less urge to do so. Next to his wife and daughter and father-in-law, of whom he was also genuinely fond, Brent's heart belonged to his bees; but he did not for a moment allow this obsession to blind him to the fact that his theory of cross-pollination alone would not raise him to the pinnacle of success which he intended to reach, nor could he wait for the seed of his dreams until he could develop this himself. The difficult heights toward which he strained could be scaled only through the mediums of better and more plentiful drainage, better and more plentiful machinery, increased acreage and a corresponding increase of help in planting, harvesting and marketing—together with the best seed already developed, which he could buy or produce by the usual methods. He did not want anything to divert him from his aims; he did not even crave occasional local outings or neighborhood gatherings for amusement. But when Jim Garland suggested it might be a good thing for Lavinia to see something of another part of the country, he agreed with more alacrity than Mary.

"Why, yes," he said, "I think it might be a *very* good thing. You'd stop off in Chicago, perhaps, and have a look around there? Maybe in New Orleans, too? Of course, I've never traveled any to speak of myself, never expect to; but I should think a youngster could learn as much that way as in a schoolroom. If we'd traveled more, Mary and I, maybe we wouldn't have been hunting through old geographies to find out something about Louisiana. If Mary's willing Lavinia should go with you to visit her aunt, I am."

Mary was not altogether willing, but she did not feel she should say so when Brent felt otherwise, when her father obviously wanted to renew old ties, and when Lavinia was straining at the leash to be off. She did not seem to be in the least apprehensive of homesickness or in dread of separation from her parents, an attitude which caused Mary more pangs than it did Brent; and the young girl did not voice—and evidently did not feel—any regret at parting from her accustomed boon companions. Claude and Mezalee, to whom "vacation" meant simply heavy work on the farm, and who had both been looking forward eagerly to interludes with their more fortunate friend, were hurt, and a little jealous, and were too young not to show this; but they went to the depot to see her off, and waved the handkerchiefs bought expressly for that purpose, until the train was out of sight. Marcelite was busy at home with her new baby and Fleex had disappeared on one of

178

his periodic mysterious absences; they could spare Lavinia better than the others could.

When she returned, Claude and Mezalee had already gone back to school, for Acadia College opened early, and she did not have a chance to tell them much about her experiences, until they had faded somewhat from the forefront of her consciousness. In the brief and hurried talks she had with her mother, before she returned to school herself—accompanied, this year, by Annette—she chatted willingly and volubly enough; but she had either failed to notice many things that Mary would have liked to hear about, or else she did not consider them worthy of comment.

"I was crazy about New Orleans, but I didn't like Chicago nearly as well," she said. "And I'm awfully glad you moved away from Monroe. I didn't remember how dismal it was until I saw it again."

"Dismal?"

"Yes. Hardly any trees or flowers or—"

"Why, I had a nice little flower garden," Mary said quickly. "Isn't it still there—on the south side of our house?"

Lavinia shook her head. "If it is, I didn't notice. I was only over there once. The hired man lives there now, you know."

"No, I didn't."

"Well, he does. And Aunt Sally doesn't have a flower garden. She says she doesn't have time for one, with a baby and everything. I don't see why not. Marcelite has a nice little flower garden—not as nice as yours, of course, but still it's pretty, and she takes care of her baby herself. Aunt Sally has a hired girl."

"Is the baby cunning?"

"Not nearly as cunning as Marcelite's. He's too fat. So is Aunt Sally."

"Aunt Sally is too fat!"

"Yes, lots. I told Grandpa I thought so, and he said he'd been afraid she might be, after she got married, because she'd always been plump. Of course, Mrs. Villac's rather fat, too. But *you're* not, Mother. You're not any fatter than I am, and you've been married ever so long."

Mary flushed. She was secretly proud of her figure, and though Brent was sparing of compliments, he occasionally told her, in a tone which implied admiration, that he did not believe she had gained a pound in twenty years. So Sally's pleasing plumpness had taken on more and more

179

ample proportions! In that case, her erstwhile beautiful complexion would be changing, too; the skin which had so often been compared to a rose leaf would soon begin to look coarse and ruddy, if it had not already become so. And a stout, red-faced woman would have little or no allure for a fastidious man like Jonathan Fant. . . . Mary forced herself to ask the question which was hardest for her to put, trying to make it sound casual.

"What about your uncle Jonathan? He hasn't grown fat, too, has he?"

"Oh, no! He looks just the way he did before—that is, the way I think he looked before. I'm not sure I remember exactly. And he was very nice to us when he was there."

"When he was there! Wasn't he there all the time?"

"No, he was gone quite a good deal. And then Aunt Sally cried and Grandpa was cross. And when Uncle Jonathan finally came home they kept talking and talking, after I'd gone to bed at night. I couldn't hear what they said, but I could hear their voices. Aunt Sally's and Grandpa's, I mean. Uncle Jonathan didn't say much. I guess the others were sort of picking on him. I don't see why they should. I guess he just enjoys getting off by himself once in a while, the way Fleex does. I think he and Fleex are something alike."

"What nonsense!" Mary said, almost angrily. "They're not in the least alike. Jonathan Fant is a very cultured, traveled gentleman. Fleex is just a poor, ignorant Cajun, who's never been off the prairie."

"I wish you wouldn't say 'Cajun' like that, Mother. Sometime you might forget and do it when the Villacs or the Primeaux could hear you and you'd hurt their feelings terribly. They don't mind calling themselves Cajuns, but they don't like to have other people do it."

"I know. I'm sorry. I'll try not to. But when you said you thought your Uncle Jonathan and Fleex Primeaux were something alike, you startled me so that—"

"I don't see why you should have been so startled. Fleex hasn't been to school much, I know, and I think he's sorry now, though he never says so. But his mother died and his father didn't realize how important school was. His mother would have. Fleex said she was a real lady, convent bred and everything—a schoolmate of Miss Millie's. But she fell in love with his father and came out to live on the prairie with him and never regretted it, because they were so happy together."

"Who told you all this?"

"Fleex. . . . And Fleex knows all about plants and birds and animals and he's the best shot and sings better and plays the violin better than anyone else around here."

"Lavinia, I realize all that. And I realize he's always been very kind to his younger brother and his sisters and all his cousins, and very thoughtful and helpful, as far as we're concerned. Your father and I are fond of him and I know you are. You should be. But he *is* ignorant and he *is* wild. So when you compared him to your uncle Jonathan—"

"Hasn't Uncle Jonathan any bad habits?"

"Why, of course not!"

While they were talking, Mary and Lavinia had been sorting clothes, placing some aside to be washed or mended, and packing others in the little trunk Lavinia was to take to school. Lavinia laid down the fresh nightgown she was holding and, without saying a word, looked at her mother with an expression that Mary had never seen on her daughter's face before. Again Mary flushed, more deeply this time.

"Well, I suppose he has," she admitted. "Perhaps I spoke too hastily, dear. Of course, even the best of us have a few faults."

"Having a few faults is different from having bad habits, isn't it?"

"Ye-e-s."

"Well I don't know what you think, but I'm sure Grandpa thinks Uncle Jonathan has some bad habits. I've heard him say so. And I know that's one reason he went to Illinois—not just because he wanted to take a trip, but because he thought perhaps Aunt Sally wasn't happy. And she isn't."

"I'm very sorry, Lavinia, to hear all this. After you've gone back to school, and I have more time, I'll talk to your grandfather about it and see if there's anything I can do to help. Meanwhile—"

"Meanwhile," Lavinia said, picking up the nightgown and folding it, "I still think Fleex and Uncle Jonathan are something alike."

Such a similarity, Mary told herself, existed wholly in Lavinia's imagination; it was not unusual for young girls to have fancies, and there was no reason why most of these should prove disturbing to their elders. But Sally's welfare was something else again. Mary gave it a great deal of anxious thought and, when the first favorable opportunity arose, she spoke of it to her father.

"I'm sorry Lavinia let the cat out of the bag," he told her. "I didn't mean to say anything about it—not yet at least. But here's the situation as I see it: Sally wanted to get married and she had her wish, just as your mother hoped she would—every girl ought to get married, if she feels that way about it. I don't need to tell you so. What's more, she wanted to marry Jonathan Fant and she got her way about that, too. She must have known he wasn't as eager to have her as she was to have him, or he wouldn't have shilly-shallied around the way he did. Now Brent was entirely different, when he was courting you."

"Indeed he was!" She spoke joyfully, almost gratefully, a host of happy memories suddenly overwhelming her.

"And *you* were entirely different, too. You used to go out to meet Brent, but if he'd once failed to be there, on his way to see you, it would have been the last time you'd have done it. And you never would have cried and taken on—leastaways where anyone—even your mother and I— could see you. Isn't that so?"

"I suppose it is."

"Well, so I'm afraid what's happening now is only what Sally has coming to her. Jonathan loves the land—he and Brent are alike that way anyhow. And if Sally wouldn't let herself go, the way she does, he'd make a good farmer and he'd try to make a good husband. I'll give him that much credit. But, as your mother said, he'd been a wanderer for a long time when he came to us, and if he gets tried, beyond a certain point, he thinks the remedy is to wander. He may be right, at that. Every man's entitled to some sort of escape from what's hardest for him to take. Your mother's infirmity was the hardest thing for me; I found my escape in my horses. Even Brent's bees are a form of escape from the harder work he knows has to be done. He'll make more progress with his selections than with them. Women ought to be thankful when their husbands don't take to drink for escape—especially when they're driven as hard as Jonathan is."

"Then he doesn't drink or—or run after other women or—or anything?"

"I don't know just what you mean by 'or anything.' But I'm sure he isn't drinking to excess, because I'd have found that out. I probably would have found out if he'd been running after any other woman—that's the kind of news that spreads fastest of all. He just leaves. We've got

182

to hope that someday he doesn't leave for good. But there's nothing we can do to help at present—I've come to that conclusion, after my visit. However, I think I'll go north again when they have that Columbian Exhibition in Chicago. Brent can't afford to miss seeing the exhibits of how rice is grown all over the world. And there'll be lots of other things to see, too, that you and Lavinia will enjoy."

"I'd love to have Brent go, and Lavinia. But someone will have to stay here and look after things."

Jim Garland picked up his pipe and rose. "Well, of course if you feel that way about it," he said.

The summers were flying by, each one faster than the one before. Ninety-one brought forth no radical change at the farm, and again Lavinia was gone during a large part of her vacation, this time visiting friends she had made at school, in Lafayette and St. Martinville. Ninety-two was a banner year for rice. As a result of it, Brent was able to afford all the improvements he wanted—a canal and a share in a big pumping plant, a twine-binding harvester that would do the work of forty men with sickles in the same length of time; and all the Sonniers' land to do it in, which he had been able to buy because they were moving into town to take charge of the mill that was being built, and which would save the rice farmers the trouble of sending their crops to New Orleans. The following year was so preternaturally dry that, even with the great strides made in irrigation, many farmers were hard hit; nevertheless, Brent, who had suffered less than most, felt he could take time off for the World's Fair, and he unhesitatingly accepted his father-in-law's invitation to go; and while he was there, he not only saw all the exhibits that were of vital concern to him as a farmer; he took Lavinia up in the Ferris wheel and around the lagoons in a gondola and riding in a Bath chair and did everything else that she or her grandfather suggested in the way of amusement. It was his first break away from work since he had gone to Louisiana on his inspection tour, except for the dreadful illness which had been the cause of this and which was only a memory to them now. He reveled in every moment of his holiday. The only flaw in his enjoyment was that Mary had persisted in remaining behind, though afterward, he admitted it was just as well one of them should have been at the farm, since there had never been so many indigo weeds, and, without her supervision, the hired hands could have easily—and perhaps, even willingly—overlooked many of these.

As far as the family in Monroe was concerned, Brent could see nothing much to worry about, he was able to tell Mary, with complete sincerity, on his return. To be sure, he had not been there long; but his brother-in-law had been at home throughout his visit and had been civil, if condescending—but that had always been Jonathan's way. It was true that Sally was too fat, and now that there was another baby, a second boy, she kept complaining of overwork, though she had capable help, and a good deal more of it than most farm women in Illinois. On the whole, the land looked well cared for. Yes, Brent was afraid the little old flower garden on the south side of their former home was gone. But what did that matter, now that she had such a fine one here?

Both Brent and Mary had reason to feel increasing satisfaction, not only with their respective gardens, but with their daughter's record at school, which had become increasingly creditable every year. She had made up for her late start with astonishing rapidity and was one of the youngest pupils in the graduating class. Several times she had been awarded the Blue Ribbon, which was the symbol of leadership, and which the winner was entitled to wear for three consecutive months; and her essay on "The Products of Louisiana," in which rice was featured in a form totally foreign to its former stereotyped or occasional mention in such themes, was a source of pride to her English teacher, as well as her parents. It was very generally taken for granted that at the exercises which, at Grand Coteau, were called "The Prizes" instead of Graduation, Lavinia Winslow would sing in the chorus, play the piano and carry off top honors in French and mathematics and none of her classmates begrudged her these evidences of success. What added far more to her popularity, however, was the generous and tactful part she played in preparing for the May ceremony of Crowning Our Lady. As a Protestant, she was not entitled to put the crown in place on the Virgin's statue; and she herself was the first to silence the whispered expressions of regret over her ineligibility and to make the choice of Annette, who had won few prizes and won no Blue Ribbons, seem to the girls, who were entitled to vote, the logical one. Annette, who was pleasant rather than pretty and plump rather than poised, and who had no voice to speak of, would easily have been outdone by several Maids of Honor, even after her elec-

184

tion had been carefully engineered, if Lavinia had not clarified the potentialities of her role for her by coaching her secretly and encouraging her constantly and, without appearing to do so, concealed Annette's lack of musical ability by the dominance and excellence of her own. "Oh Mary, we crown thee with blossoms today" had never been sung, in the memory of the oldest nun, with more clarity and beauty than on this time-honored occasion; and it was Lavinia's face and figure, the sheen of Lavinia's golden hair under her white lace veil, Lavinia's grace in marching and in kneeling, not Annette's, that were treasured in the memories, not only of the religious and the pupils, but in those of all visiting relatives and friends.

Even though Lavinia had now nominally "settled down" at the farm, it seemed to Mary that the girl spent most of her time ranging the countryside, and one night she stayed out so late that Mary became seriously worried. When she finally heard the sound of voices on the porch, she rose and threw a robe around her. Then she went into the sitting room to wait until her daughter came in, her feeling of uneasiness assuaged, but her curiosity roused. One of the voices, of course, was Lavinia's. The other was Claude's. Lavinia's had a note of protest in it, and also a note of weariness; the latter was especially surprising, as the girl was practically indefatigable. Claude's was protesting, too, and pleading.

"I said no," Lavinia declared at last, so clearly and emphatically that her mother heard every word. "If you keep on pestering me like this, I won't go out with you alone again. I'll stay with the crowd. Good night."

The front door opened and closed and Lavinia extinguished the light in the front hall and started up the stairs. The sound of retreating footsteps outside served to give Mary confidence that Claude would soon be out of hearing. She called, softly, to Lavinia.

"Light the candle again and come in here for a moment, dear," she said. "I want to speak to you before you go to bed."

Lavinia turned obediently, relighted the candle and came into the sitting room carrying it. In the dim light, she looked as tired as she had sounded.

"It's very late, darling," Mary said, trying to speak casually and quietly. "I'd begun to be worried."

"There's no reason why you should have been. I'd have been home hours ago, if Claude hadn't been making such a nuisance of himself."

"A nuisance of himself?"

"Yes. He's bound and determined that I should get engaged to him. He's been harping and harping on it. This isn't the first time, either. I've told him that, if he keeps on this way, I won't go to any more dances with him."

"Darling, you know your father and I both like Claude very much. He's a fine boy. It's greatly to his credit that he's done so well at Acadia College and graduated with honors. Now I understand he's had a good job offered him at the new rice mill. His family and friends have every reason to be proud of him. But he must know you're too young to be engaged. I'll tell him so myself—or your father will."

"It won't do any good. He'll tell you Marcelite was *married* when she was younger than I am, not just engaged. He'll tell you lots of girls are. It's true, too. But I don't want to be engaged to Claude. I like him a lot, I always have; I'm just not in the mood for getting engaged to him. . . . Do you mind awfully if I go to bed, Mother? I'm pretty tired. And I do hope you won't say anything to Father about this. Because nothing's going to come of it. And it would mean a lot more arguing, when I've had about all I can take."

"All right, darling. I won't say anything to your father —not now, anyway. He wasn't worried about you—he's fast asleep. And we'd better get some sleep, too. Perhaps we can talk about this tomorrow."

Mary turned this prospective conversation over in her mind many times during the remainder of the night and, the next day, took pains to create opportunities when Lavinia could talk with her confidentially. Lavinia did not improve any of them. She slept late, played the piano for hours, went for a horseback ride with her grandfather and, early in the evening, announced that she was going to her room to dress. This in itself was surprising, for Lavinia was singularly free from vanity, and changed casually and quickly from one kind of clothes to another, when she bothered to change at all. Her mother, who was working in her flower garden, looked up in astonishment.

"I thought you said you weren't going to any more dances for the present. And you were so tired—"

"I'm not tired any more, and what I said was that I wouldn't go to any more dances with *Claude,* if he kept on pestering me. I'm not going with Claude. I'm going with Fleex."

"Fleex! I didn't know he was at home."

186

"He came home today. I happened to meet him while I was out riding. He asked me if I'd like to go into Crowley to a dance tonight and I said I would."

"Well," Mary said hesitantly. "Well . . . if you're going that far, you know I prefer to have you in a group, and I'm afraid you'll be very late again."

"I thought 'groups' just meant people I'd met later, not those I'd known from the beginning. . . . I probably shall be late. But there's nothing to be afraid of."

I'm not so sure, I'm not so sure, Mary kept saying to herself all the rest of the evening. She told herself, at the same time, that it was a very silly thing for her to be saying. She repeated this, both before Fleex appeared, driving the Primeaux' best buggy, and after he and Lavinia had gone off together, laughing and joking and chatting to each other in French. There was no protest in Lavinia's voice now, or any weariness, and she had never seemed in better spirits or looked so pretty. She had put on her graduation dress and done up her beautiful hair in the most becoming way, the way that took longest. Fleex was apparently in very good spirits, too, and he was very neatly dressed, in a new dark suit. He certainly was a handsome boy—no, not a handsome boy any more, a handsome man. He was two years older than Claude, who was about four years older than Lavinia, and that made him—why, Fleex must be twenty-two or twenty-three years old. It was unbelievable, but it was true. He had been away so much, and time had been flying so fast, that Mary had not thought of him as a man before. But now she did. . . .

She made some excuse to Brent about sewing that simply had to be finished and he went upstairs, unconcernedly, without her. Then she sat, her industrious hands for once folded in her lap, watching the clock and listening to its slow, relentless ticking. It seemed an eternity before she heard the buggy drive into the outer yard again. Then she heard nothing else. She endured the silence as long as she could and at last she went quietly out on the porch.

Fleex and Lavinia were standing beside the buggy, while the tired horse drooped in the shafts. They were not saying anything; they were merely looking at each other. In the bright moonlight, Mary could see them clearly, and what she saw made her believe that, in a minute, they would be in each other's arms. But they did not touch each other and they still did not speak, even to say good night, before Lavinia turned and started to walk, alone, toward

187

the house. Then, in that same moment, Fleex turned, too, and Mary saw not only his profile, as she had before, but his full face. In one dreadful flash, she understood what Lavinia had meant when the girl said that Jonathan Fant and Fleex Primeaux were a good deal alike. For that was the way Jonathan had looked, years before, when he had come upon Mary while she was sorting old papers, and told her that it was she he was in love with, and not her sister.

It was the next day that she reminded Brent, as casually as she could, that Lavinia was growing up.

CHAPTER XVII

Brent did not take what she was saying to him very seriously. In fact, Mary felt he was by no means taking it seriously enough. Usually she did not mind when he seemed preoccupied with his experiments; now that she was preoccupied with their daughter, she felt he should be, too.

"What makes you think so?" he asked rather absently. "Mary, do you know I believe I'm finally getting somewhere? Those last grains I measured—"

"I think so because she's acting as if she were—well, interested in being with boys."

"Why, that's nothing new! She's always enjoyed ranging the countryside with Claude and Fleex more than going around with Annette, who's a schoolmate just her age, or staying in the house with Mezalee and Marcelite, who are only a little older. I've told you before that she's something of a tomboy even if she's handy enough when it comes to helping you in the kitchen. She stopped playing with dolls a lot younger than most girls I've known; and she'll never be anything like the needlewoman you are, though heaven knows you've tried hard enough to make her into one. I've always understood nuns were good at that sort of thing, too. They must have tried to teach her and to set her an example at Grand Coteau."

"Brent, you're not really following me at all. A girl isn't necessarily a tomboy just because she doesn't like to sew, any more than a man is necessarily effeminate if he doesn't like to hunt. Lavinia didn't stop playing with dolls because she was a tomboy, either. She had real babies to play with—first Anne's and then Marcelite's. She's crazy

188

about children. She says she hopes she'll have a dozen of her own. Of course that's just a way of talking, but it isn't the way a tomboy talks and it certainly infers that she's given some thought to marriage, too. In the meantime—"

"All right, what in the meantime?" Brent asked, trying to speak patiently.

"In the meantime, she isn't ranging the countryside, as you call it, instead of staying in the house because she's a tomboy. She's doing it because she—well, because she imagines she's in love."

"In love!" Brent echoed. He could not have sounded any more amazed if Mary had told him that Lavinia imagined she could fly to the moon. "Why, she isn't old enough to—"

"She's almost seventeen. I was in love with you when I was seventeen, Brent—when I was fifteen. I never was in love with anyone else."

"You *liked* me, when you were fifteen. That's not the same thing at all," Brent said firmly. "You were just a nice, pleasant, practical kid, a little on the serious side, doing awfully well in school, singing in the church choir—"

Mary wished he had left out that remark about the serious side. It was almost exactly the same thing that Jonathan Fant had said to her years before, about Lavinia. In fact, there was a great similarity about the tenor of everything both men had said. She did not want to be reminded of Jonathan Fant again, after having been reminded of him so poignantly, only the evening before. Above all, she did not want anything to make her feel she and Lavinia were too much alike. Because it was quite true that she had never had any sweetheart except Brent, that she had never wanted any other. And it would be too terrible for words if the only sweetheart Lavinia ever wanted was Fleex. . . .

"Speaking of imagination, who do you imagine she's in love with?" Brent inquired, practically if ungrammatically.

Mary hesitated. She had promised not to say anything about Claude, but nothing had been promised about Fleex. What she had seen, convincing as it was to her, had been wholly accidental. Lavinia still did not know that her mother had watched her and Fleex standing motionless, facing each other in the moonlight. So perhaps it was not a breach of confidence to tell that. At all events, Mary hoped it was not.

"I'm almost sure Lavinia's in love with Fleex," she said hesitantly.

Brent laughed. "Now I know your imagination's working overtime," he said. "If you'd mentioned Claude, I might have believed you. I say I *might* have, though heaven knows even that's improbable enough—partly because they're too young to be in love, and partly because Claude's rather on the stolid side, though he's a pretty decent sort of boy. I shouldn't be altogether sorry, if, five or ten years from now, Lavinia should decide she might as well marry Claude. She could do a lot worse. On the other hand, she probably could do a lot better. I've always had it in the back of my mind, Mary, that maybe one of these young fellows she met when she was visiting in Lafayette. . . . I shouldn't wonder if it had been in the back of your mind, too."

"Yes," Mary admitted. "Yes, it has." Yes, of course. It was natural for parents to be ambitious for their children, to hope that marriage would bring them benefits and advantages other than—or rather, besides—love. The young fellows Lavinia had been meeting in Lafayette had more background of culture and wealth, better educations, wider outlooks, handsomer homes than either Mary or Brent had possessed themselves. They were more like Jonathan Fant. (There he was again, forcing himself to the forefront of her consciousness, when she was determined to keep him out!) "Of course I've hoped that was what might happen," she repeated. "Not just any young fellow in Lafayette, naturally—the right one. I'm sure that among the brothers and cousins of her schoolmates at Grand Coteau. . . . But do you realize, Brent, that she's never asked any of them here? She's visited those girls in their homes, but she's never invited them to visit her in return. I've asked her several times why she didn't. I've even gone so far as to ask her if she thought they wouldn't be pleased to come, if she were ashamed to invite them. And she only told me not to be silly. It's one of the few times she's ever spoken to me that way. She said she was gone so much that when she was at home, she wanted to make the most of it—by which she meant she wanted to make the most of the time she could be with Fleex."

"You say that's what she *meant*. Is that what she *said?*"

"No, but I'm sure—"

"And I'm sure you're being silly, just as Lavinia told you. I'm sorry, Mary. I don't say anything like that to you, either, very often, do I? I didn't mean to hurt your feelings. And I don't mean to cut this short. But I've got to get out to the fields."

Brent did not, however, dismiss the matter of his daughter from his mind quite as completely as his speech and manner indicated. When he came in to dinner, he observed Lavinia carefully. He had not seen much of her since her return from school. For two mornings in succession she had not come down to breakfast, and for two evenings in succession she had gone out before supper. The day before his surprising conversation with Mary, he had eaten his dinner hurriedly, because he was needed outdoors. Now, though he was again needed outdoors, he took time to observe the girl. She was quieter than usual, as far as talking was concerned, but at the same time she gave an impression of restlessness, because she kept looking out of the window. He had not seen her anywhere around the yard or the barns in the course of the morning, so he asked her what she had been doing. She answered that since she got up, which was not long before dinnertime anyway, she had started to make herself a dress. What he had said to Mary about sewing, only a couple of hours earlier, had been with entire sincerity; he had never noticed the makings of a needlewoman in Lavinia. Now he avoided his wife's eyes as he asked Lavinia another casual question. What kind of a dress? A party dress—pink muslin, Lavinia answered. Didn't she have enough party dresses? No, Lavinia said, not if she were going to a dance almost every night. Was that what she was planning to do? More or less. Didn't she think once or twice a week was enough? No, she didn't—everyone in the crowd went oftener than that. Well, as her father, he thought once or twice a week was plenty. Without making any direct response and asking, quite politely, if she might be excused, as she didn't want any dessert, Lavinia rose from the table and, after one more glance out of the window, walked over to the sewing machine. This, Brent now noticed for the first time, was covered with a froth of pink muslin. . . . When he came in from the fields, late in the afternoon, his daughter was sitting in the open doorway, wearing her new dress. He had never seen her look so pretty.

"Lavinia," he said, trying to speak sternly, "you were out last night and the night before and I told you—"

"I know, Father. But I'd already planned to go to this dance. I didn't think you meant me to break an engagement."

"Isn't that rather a solemn way of putting it? Just because you have some sort of vague arrangement with an-

191

other kid that he'll show up here, to take you to a dance, if nothing more important happens to prevent—"

"I don't think anything more important is going to happen to prevent."

"I meant exactly what I said, Lavinia, when I told you that once or twice a week—"

The Villacs' best buggy rounded the turn in the road which led past the grove, the outbuildings and the vegetable garden. It was still fairly distant from the house. But Lavinia leaped up with a speed which suggested that she might be going out to meet it—exactly, Brent suddenly remembered, as Mary had been wont to rush out to meet him when he was courting her.

"There's Fleex now!" Lavinia cried joyously and dashed past her father. Then she stopped as suddenly as she had risen, and stood staring ahead of her as if she could not believe her eyes.

It was not Fleex who was driving the buggy. It was Claude.

CHAPTER XVIII

"But where *is* he?"

"I don't know, Lavinia. None of us knows. He's always come and gone without warning—you ought to remember that. We didn't expect him when he came yesterday morning. We didn't expect him to leave this morning, either. But he's gone."

"Well then, he'll be back. Any minute. It's early yet. You might have waited a little longer."

"Lavinia, I don't think he's coming back. Not for a long while anyway. All his clothes are gone this time. Not that he has many, but he's always left some behind before this —that old coat made out of a blanket, for instance, that he was wearing when we first came here, and the woolen scarves he used to wind around his head even when he was barefoot. Now he's taken those, too. And his fishing tackle and his rifle. They're all gone."

Lavinia continued to stand beside the buggy and to stare unbelievingly at Claude. The joy had already gone out of her voice when she first spoke; instead there had been a note of desperation in it, mingled with the bravado of assumed confidence. Now her father saw that she did not even look pretty any more; something had happened to her face, just as something had happened to her voice. It looked old and it looked hard.

"All right," she said at last, and her voice had changed again. It was not desperate now; it was hard, like her face, and it was not the voice of an eager, sixteen-year-old girl, but of an embittered and mature woman. "If that's the case, I won't be going out to dances, when Father doesn't approve. He thinks I shouldn't go more than twice a week and I've been twice this week already—night before last with you and last night with Fleex. Good-by, Claude."

She turned abruptly and walked back toward the house. Claude, who had got out of the buggy, and Brent, who was still standing in the doorway, spoke simultaneously.

"But, Lavinia, I've come to take you to the dance. You meant to go one more time this week anyway. You were all ready to go with Fleex. I don't see—"

"As long as Claude is here, Lavinia, why don't you go with him? I agree with him that, under the circumstances—"

"You said, just a little while ago, that it was silly for me 'to talk about breaking engagements' when all I had was 'some vague arrangement with a kid my own age.' I had a definite engagement with Fleex, who's quite a lot older than I am, by the way; but I didn't have even a vague arrangement with Claude, who doesn't seem to me enough older than I am to count. I won't have any chance of pleasing you, Father, if you keep changing your mind like this."

She did not actually push past him, because she was so slim that this was not necessary, in order for her to glide quickly and quietly into the house. But the full fresh muslin of her pink skirt brushed against Brent's knees as she went through the door, and he caught a whiff of some fresh, delicate fragrance as she disappeared. He looked helplessly toward the miserable boy standing by the buggy.

"I'm sorry, Claude," he said as kindly as he knew how. "Of course I don't object to having Lavinia go out with you. I just thought she was overdoing things a little, if she tried to take in a dance every night. I'm afraid she's given you a wrong impression—that somehow, she's got a wrong impression herself. In fact, she seems very upset."

"I'm afraid I helped upset her," Claude confessed unhappily. "You see, Mr. Winslow, I'd like very much to be engaged to Lavinia—that is, to have it understood that someday she and I would be engaged. I've kept telling her so, and I'm afraid I've done it too often—that she's grown tired of hearing it. I haven't meant to annoy her, only to make her understand. I care a lot and—" He stopped to clear his throat. "I think you know I've got a good job at the new rice mill in Crowley," he went on after a minute. "I can save money and I mean to. I'll be able to support a wife well, by-and-by. I could give Lavinia a nice home from the beginning and I'd try to be what you midwesterners call a good provider. I was just hoping I could make Lavinia understand this and—well, and also that I thought the world of her. I wouldn't have done it if I thought it would upset her so."

"I'm sure you wouldn't have, Claude," Brent said, still speaking very kindly. "And I want you to know that neither Mrs. Winslow nor I would have put any obstacles in your way—that is, when the proper time came. But you and Lavinia are both very young and—"

"I'm four years older than she is. And I'm so afraid that if I can't persuade her to get engaged to me—I mean to have an understanding about getting engaged—that some other fellow, who's older still, might come butting in. And Lavinia might not know her own mind. She might imagine she liked this other fellow better than she did me, just because she is so young and inexperienced. And then it might be too late to do me any good."

He took a noticeably clean handkerchief from his breast pocket, unfolded it from its neat creases and mopped his forehead with it. Brent guessed that the boy's hands were as moist as his face and he was right; before restoring the handkerchief, which had now lost its pristine freshness, to his pocket, Claude wiped his hands also.

"Well, good night," he said awkwardly. Then he turned, with his foot already on the step of the buggy. "And thanks a lot for saying you don't object. I mean, to having Lavinia go out with me a reasonable amount now, and that you don't believe you'd have any objections to our getting engaged by-and-by. We don't need to go to dances all the time in the meanwhile, if you'd rather we didn't, and we don't need to go by ourselves; we can go on picnics and things like that, with the crowd. I won't come over again for a few days anyway. Perhaps that'll give Lavinia a chance to stop being so upset. That is, I won't come unless we hear something from Fleex. If we do, I'll let her know right away. Because I can't help thinking, Mr. Winslow, that another reason she's upset is because Fleex has gone off without telling her about it."

194

When Brent described this scene to Mary, as well as he could, after they had gone to bed that night, she agreed with him that Claude had behaved very well and that Lavinia had behaved very badly. She did not mention that she also agreed with Claude's surmise about the main reason for Lavinia's upset. Mary thought that enough had been said on that subject already, and she tried to feel hopeful that time would bring about both a satisfactory solution of the mystery and an assuagement for Lavinia's heartbreak.

That it really was heartbreak and not merely disappointment or hurt pride her mother felt increasingly sure. For a few days Lavinia kept close to the house, and her mother was aware that she was still watching and waiting for Fleex, hoping against hope that he would reappear. Then Lavinia herself vanished early one morning, and late in the afternoon she still had not come home. Jim Garland had been given no details about recent events; Brent and Mary had discussed the advisability of taking him into their confidence and had conscientiously decided that, since obviously Lavinia had not taken him into hers, they had no right to do so. Nevertheless, the shrewd old horseman had formed a fairly accurate idea of what was happening, and had kept in closer touch than usual with his daughter and son-in-law. When he sensed Mary's anxiety, he offered to ride over to the Primeaux' place, instead of going into town as usual, and to bring Lavinia back with him.

"What makes you think she's there?" Mary asked quickly.

"I guess I worded that wrong. I don't think she's there. But I think Claude will know where to find her. . . . Don't you remember, Mary," he went on in answer to his daughter's questioning look, "that the three of them— Fleex and Claude and Lavinia, I mean—used to have some kind of a hide-out? All youngsters like to have secrets, whether they keep them or not, which they don't, usually. But this was one they did keep—none of us ever discovered where that hide-out was, though we all tried to, at one time or another. I think that's where Lavinia's gone —hoping to find Fleex. Of course he isn't there—if he were, Claude would have found him already. It would have occurred to him, right away, to look. Then he'd have come back and let us know. Now he'll track down Lavinia for us—you'll see. Of course I won't be so crude as to suggest anything of the sort. I'll just go over to pay a friendly visit, and after a while I'll ask if Lavinia is anywhere around and say that, if she is, she and I might ride home together. As a matter of fact, I don't need any excuse for a visit. There's a perfectly logical reason for one, quite aside from Lavinia's absence. Neither Ursin nor Anne is very well these days. Didn't you know?"

Mary did know, and reproached herself because she had not been the one to make the neighborly visit before this. The last time Dr. Mouton had been to the Winslows' for a social call, he had just come from a professional visit to the Primeaux. Anne Villac was going the way of many another Cajun woman whom he had seen—apparently as strong as a horse and then, having worked like one for half a century or more, meanwhile taking yearly childbirth in her stride, had suddenly reached the end of her rope— well, his similes were getting a little mixed, but Mrs. Winslow would know what he meant. Ursin was greatly astonished—it had never occurred to him that anything like this could happen to his wife. He was also deeply distressed— there was great, if undemonstrative, devotion between the two. It was just as well that Mezalee had been persuaded to put off her project of becoming a nun, and that she had not married some cradle snatcher like that Bazinet boy, the way her sister Marcelite had. She was needed at home, to take up the burden which her ailing aunt was, perforce, laying down. . . .

Jim Garland recalled all this to his daughter before he rode off for the neighborly visit and, while he was gone, Mary sat thinking about it, instead of beginning her preparations for supper, her thoughts temporarily diverted from Lavinia. Brent was staying in the fields very late, these summer evenings, while the light lasted, so she was alone. But long before she expected him, her father returned.

"You'll be glad to know that Anne doesn't seem any worse and that I don't believe there's anything organic the matter with Ursin," he said. "But it's just as I thought: Lavinia wasn't there and Claude said he believed he knew where he could find her. He set out right away and he'll bring her back safe and sound, Mary. Don't you worry. It may be late before they get here, though."

"It seems to me Lavinia's forming a habit of being out late. And it's all very well for you to tell me not to worry. If she were your daughter—"

"I had two daughters, you know, Mary. I must say you never caused either your mother or me much anxiety. But the credit for that goes to Brent as much as it does to you —no parents could ever ask for a more acceptable suitor or a better son-in-law. However, it's been different with Sally."

Mary did not answer. She did not know whether her father was purposely trying to keep her from thinking about Lavinia, by bringing up other troublesome subjects, but whether intentionally or not, that was what he was doing.

"Have you read the latest number of the *Signal?*" he inquired, most inconsequentially, it seemed to Mary.

"No. Why?"

"There was quite an obituary in it on that old Mrs. Arcenaux who lived in St. Martinville—Jonathan's grandmother. She reached an astonishing age and she'd been in her house alone these last years. You remember her husband died some time ago."

"I suppose I must have known it, but if I did, I'd forgotten it. I've never been particularly interested in the Arcenaux. It isn't as if I'd ever met them."

"I realize that. But this article mentioned a grandson— Jonathan Fant—and two great-grandsons—Jonathan's and Sally's little boys—as her sole survivors. Naturally, they'd also be her sole heirs, unless she made some kind of freak will, and that's hard to do in Louisiana. Jonathan didn't come to his grandfather's funeral, but it wouldn't surprise me to learn that he'd come to this one."

"You mean you think he may be in St. Martinville *now?*"

"Yes. That's just what I mean, Mary. I don't believe Sally and the children came with him. I think Sally would have let us know if they'd done that, even though letter writing isn't her strong point. But it wouldn't surprise me, either, if they joined Jonathan there later."

"You think they'd leave our farm and go to *live* in St. Martinville?"

"I said it wouldn't surprise me. I don't see why it should surprise you. You've never been back to our old place since you left it, never wanted to go, for some reason. But you must have guessed that Jonathan was getting tired of it."

She wondered if he were going to add, "You must have guessed that he was getting tired of Sally," and was thankful that he did not. Nevertheless, the unspoken words lay heavily between them.

"Jonathan said, when he came to Monroe, that he was through with the decadent South," she said, knowing, as she did so, that the remark was inadequate.

"Yes. But that was before he'd spent eight long winters in Illinois. Also before he'd inherited a charming old house in St. Martinville which he could run to suit himself —always provided he had any money to run it on. But if he should sell our old farm, I should think he might manage. After all, he's still got the small legacy from those Carolina relatives of his. I have reason to believe he's never touched the capital. And it wouldn't cost him much to live very comfortably in St. Martinville. I don't need to tell you that, Mary."

"You've got to the point where he and Sally are practically neighbors of ours already."

"Oh, I wouldn't say that! All I've told you is that it wouldn't surprise me if. . . . Listen! I think that must be Claude and Lavinia now!"

Unquestionably, there was a sound of approaching hoofs, mingled with that of distant voices. Presently, both sounds died away. Jim Garland and his daughter sat looking at each other in silence, waiting for the next sound. It did not come for some minutes. Then the door opened and Lavinia appeared in its embrasure—alone. She was more or less disheveled and obviously very tired; but both her dishevelment and her weariness were overshadowed by her anger.

"I hope the next time I feel like getting off by myself you won't think it's necessary to send Claude Villac after me," she said. "Anyway, I think I've made it clear to him that, if you try to, and he comes, I'll never speak to him again. To make the situation simpler, I've decided to accept an invitation to make a long visit in St. Martinville. But Claude's gone home now and Father's putting my horse away for me. He happened to meet us out by the gate and he said he could see I'd had a hard ride. He's right, in more ways than one. If you don't mind, I'm going straight to bed. I don't want any supper. I'm not hungry and I'm not thirsty, either. I've been chewing on thistle cores."

CHAPTER XIX

The next morning Lavinia appeared at the breakfast table, acting as if nothing out of the ordinary had happened; and when, with customary efficiency, she had helped with the housework, she disappeared outdoors, also as usual. Mary, who had not succeeded in giving much thought to anyone else, despite the various news items Jim Garland had brought her, went to the front door several times and looked searchingly around; but it was not until nearly noon that she saw Lavinia again, and when she did, the girl was walking beside Jonathan Fant.

With startling suddenness, Mary's thoughts shifted. The first that shot through her mind centered on the fact that eight years had made practically no outward change in Jonathan, whereas probably she herself. . . . He walked with the same unhurried grace, he had the same nonchalant, confident manner, he wore the same kind of clothes, with the same accustomed ease. When he was close enough to the house for her to see his face, she was aware that its clear color was unchanged, and that there were no wrinkles in it, except those that came around his eyes, as well as around his lips, when he smiled. He was smiling now.

"Hello, Mary," he said, as if they had parted only a few hours before, under the most commonplace circumstances. "I happened to meet Lavinia outside, and she said she was sure you'd want me to stay for dinner. I hope she wasn't mistaken?"

"Of course she wasn't mistaken," Mary answered, hoping that her voice and manner were as casual as his, and greatly doubting whether they were. She was conscious, too, of her homemade calico dress, not as fresh as it should have been after her morning's labors; of her roughened hands, to which gardening as well as housework inevitably gave an unkempt look, no matter how much she scrubbed them; and of her plainly dressed hair, which was always neatly done, but which she did not take time to arrange in the elaborate fashion of the day. Then she was aware that she should have added something to such a bald statement; but by this time Jonathan Fant was speaking again.

"I didn't want to be almost next door without dropping in on you," he said. When Mary had told her father, the night before, that he was talking as if Jonathan and Sally were "practically neighbors," she had not felt, in her agitation, that she was speaking in an exaggerated way; but she now thought Jonathan was doing so. After all, St. Martinville and Crowley were forty miles apart by the most direct route. You had to take a train from Crowley to New Iberia, and then you had to drive to St. Martinville; in addition, you had to drive the extra distance between Crowley and the Winslows' farm. Altogether, it was a good sixty miles at least; and immediately after making the remark about being almost next door, Jonathan spoke of hiring a rig in St. Martinville to reach New Iberia, and leaving it at the livery stable in the latter point, before taking the train for Crowley; then about hiring another rig at the livery stable there and of the terrible roads he had gone over to get to the farm—all of which showed very plainly that he did not think the two points under discussion were really so readily accessible to each other, either.

"You must be tired. Wouldn't you like to come into the house?" Lavinia inquired. Of course Mary should have been the one to say that—not that she blamed Lavinia for doing so, since she herself had been so dilatory. "Father won't be coming in unless we send for him," Lavinia went on. "He always stays in the fields for dinner, during the busy seasons. Mother and I did, too, when we first came to Louisiana, but we don't any more."

"Well, I'm glad of that. I'm sure you'd much rather eat, sitting in a comfortable chair, at a well-set table, than grab and gulp at something out in a field," Jonathan said. As always, he spoke pleasantly. But Mary caught the inference that Brent was the type of man who would be satisfied with grabbing and gulping, whereas Jonathan never had been and never would be. "Don't let me interfere with Brent's industrious habits," he went on. "I can see him later—and you two will be plenty of company for me at dinner."

"We can ask Grandfather to come over," Lavinia suggested. "Usually he only comes to midday dinner on Sundays. And weekdays he's in town for supper most nights —he has lots of friends there, so he doesn't eat with us more than two or three times a week, unless we ask him to, specially. But of course he'll want to see you."

"And I'll want to see him. But I don't need to right away. There'll be plenty of time. Probably he's started his dinner already. I know he likes to eat early. . . . Is there some place I could wash?"

Lavinia led him through the house and upstairs to the spare room, to which Mary sent Vicey with a can of hot water. There was no obvious lingering along the way; but Mary felt sure Jonathan had taken in all the details of the household arrangements, and that he felt these not much more tasteful than those in the cottage in Monroe where

200

they had originally met. In fact, almost the first thing he said, after they were seated at table, revealed this.

"I see you still have a parlor."

"Yes, but we use it more than we did the one we had when you first knew us. And Lavinia plays very well now. I hope you're not so pressed for time that you won't be able to hear her."

"I'm not in the least pressed for time. I'd be delighted to hear her. This evening perhaps? . . . I also see that you eat in the sitting room now, instead of in the kitchen."

"Yes, the kitchen's separated from the main house by a dogtrot—possibly you noticed? And, with colored help. . . ."

"I'm glad you've got help of some kind, but this still tastes like your cooking, and there never was a better cook than you are, Mary. . . . What are all those gimcracks over on your sewing table?"

"Brent uses that for his experiments in selection now," she explained.

"And these experiments are successful?"

"They're going to be. . . . Jonathan, you haven't told us anything about yourself yet. I'm sorry to hear you've lost your grandmother as well as your grandfather. Of course, she was very, very old, wasn't she? So her death couldn't have been unexpected. But it breaks your last link with your old home, doesn't it? That's always a wrench."

"I hadn't looked at it that way. The Arcenaux house is mine now. I thought I might find some use for it."

So Jim Garland had been right! Mary drew a deep breath, not trusting herself to speak, and waited for Jonathan to go on.

"Of course it's been neglected, but it was beautifully built in the first place, as all those old houses were, and it's got beautiful things in it." He glanced around him at the room in which they were eating—a room in a house which had not been beautifully built in the first place, by long and toilsome slave labor under skilled and enlightened direction, but hastily knocked together by a village carpenter; and which had nothing beautiful in it, either, except the sheaves of rice which hung over every one of the chromos and "enlargements" which were still the only pictures on the walls. Her home had seemed very beautiful to Mary until this minute; but now she saw it as Jonathan was seeing it—cluttered, overcrowded, tasteless, ill-arranged—and she was angry because he had made her see it that way. "I could sell enough of the furniture and orna-

ments in my grandparents' house to put it in good order,"
Jonathan went on. "They managed to salvage a considerable amount of its contents when they lost the plantation. I
shouldn't wonder if they hid some from their creditors.
Anyway, there's enough silver and crystal and porcelain
for two or three families, to say nothing of the customary
chandeliers and girandoles and *garnitures de cheminée* and
what have you—all imported, of course. Then, besides the
French pieces, there's furniture by both Seignouret and
Mallard. I could get a good price in New Orleans for as
many such trappings as I wanted to sell—or of course I'd
be delighted to give you as many of them as you thought
you could use."

"It's very kind of you. But we really don't need anything. Brent's doing well now—better and better every
year."

Jonathan glanced around the room again and Mary
blushed. She might have imagined it, of course, but she
thought Lavinia was observing both her mother and their
guest with a great deal of attention, as if the girl were
aware of some undercurrent beneath the seemingly serene
surface.

"I'm glad to hear it," Jonathan said pleasantly. "In fact,
I'd heard it already—not only at the livery stable in Crowley, where I went to hire a buggy, but on the train—the
conductor asked me whom I was going to visit—and in St.
Martinville, when I explained that I wanted to come over
here because I was related to the Winslows—that is, by
marriage. . . . I didn't think you needed help, Mary. I
was only suggesting that I'd like to give you a little present
of some sort. However, as the idea doesn't appeal to you,
we won't go into it any further. . . . Well, as I was saying,
I think I could dispose of enough furniture and ornaments
so that I could afford to repair the house and even to
make it very attractive. Then it would be agreeable as a
part-time residence."

Again her father's words came back to Mary with renewed force: when Jonathan said he was through with the
degenerate South, that was before he had spent eight long
winters in Illinois. Again she waited a minute before she
tried to speak. "You mean for your own family or for
someone else?" she asked eventually.

"For me. Of course, I must go back to Illinois now. The
crops are all planted, and I can't leave them to rot in the
fields—perhaps you've forgotten that we don't have abundant Negro labor in Illinois. But in the autumn, I might

take a vacation from farming. I don't know how Sally'd feel about coming along and bringing the children. I haven't had a chance to consult her, of course, since I inherited the house."

"I should think she'd be delighted to come. Besides, how could she manage on the farm without you, in the wintertime?"

"You managed alone, didn't you, Mary, when Brent was so sick?"

"For a little while. And on one place, not two. Besides, Lavinia was older than your children, and anyway, she went to stay with Brent's parents. There isn't anyone to whom Sally could send the two little boys. The comparison's unfair, Jonathan."

"Well, perhaps it wasn't accurate. I didn't mean it to be unfair. I was only speaking in generalities."

You were telling me, Mary said to herself, *that you're tired of my sister, that you're looking for an excuse to get away from her, that you don't really care what happens to her, or even what happens to her children—your children. And somehow you'll manage to come and spend next winter in St. Martinville and leave them behind. You'll say you have to settle the estate . . . to repair the house . . . to sell all those beautiful things you don't want or need, and that I won't accept as gifts . . . you'll make it all sound perfectly plausible. I don't know how yet, but I know you will. . . .*

"Could we have a look at your flower garden?" Jonathan Fant was saying. "I had just a glimpse of it as we came in, and it looks to me as if you'd done wonders, considering the lack of time and material. But you'll at least let me give you some of my grandmother's camellias, won't you, Mary? There are too many of them now—they can't get proper attention. I think I told you she had some of the very first camellia plants that were brought to Louisiana by the Jesuits—I mean, of course, that one of her ancestresses had them. And each generation has added to them until there's quite a display. They're as big as trees now and very beautiful. You must come to St. Martinville and see them—those and the other sights. I understand you've never been there and I don't expect to leave for at least a week longer. Of course, this isn't the best time for transplanting—November would be better, and I hope to be back by then. But meanwhile you could make your selections. And it might interest you to see the house."

"I'm going to St. Martinville to make a visit," Lavinia

203

announced. "Right away. A girl named Clotilde Dufour, who was a new pupil at Grand Coteau this year, has invited me, and I wrote her this morning, accepting. Perhaps you know the Dufour family?"

"Of course I do! Their house is right across the street from mine! What a pleasant coincidence! And how fortunate for me that I'll have company on my trip back!"

"I'm afraid it'll take me several days to get Lavinia ready," Mary said hastily. "She didn't tell me about this visit to St. Martinville until last night, and she's only been back from school a few days. Her clothes will have to be put in order and—"

"Why, Mother, it won't take us any time at all to do that! If we hurry, we can get it all done this afternoon. And I'm sure Uncle Jonathan meant to stay at least overnight. If he didn't, he couldn't see Father or Grandfather or anything on the place. You did mean to stay, didn't you, Uncle Jonathan?"

He looked from Lavinia, who met his glance brightly, toward Mary, who was also gazing at him steadily, but with a very different expression. "Why, yes," he said, "I did mean to stay overnight—at least—if I were invited, and I hoped I would be. Am I, Mary?"

"Lavinia's already invited you," she said with no feeling of regret for her lack of graciousness. "But I'm afraid there won't be time for me to go out to the garden with you just now, if at all. Since Lavinia wants to be ready to leave for St. Martinville tomorrow, I'll be terribly busy all the afternoon. She will, too. But I'm sure Father'd like very much to show you around. Let's go over to his house, shall we, so he'll be sure to know you're here before he starts into town?"

CHAPTER XX

There did not seem to be any reasonable objection she could offer. Jonathan Fant was Lavinia's uncle—only her uncle by marriage, to be sure, but in the eyes of the world that was practically the same thing. How could there be any more logical escort for a young girl? Surely it was much more suitable for her to go to St. Martinville with her uncle than to make the trip alone. She had gone to Lafayette once or twice alone, but that was only half as far; moreover, her father or grandfather had always taken her to the station in Crowley and personally put her in the care of the friendly conductor; then, in Lafayette, she had always been met by someone in the family of the girl she was about to visit, often by the entire family. When she made the trip to and from Grand Coteau, her mother had always accompanied her; Mary and the nuns had become very good friends and she was expected to remain overnight; her room was invariably ready and waiting for her. But she had not been invited to visit the Dufours, who were total strangers; it would be awkward, both for them and for her, if she appeared unannounced, equally awkward if she withdrew from the scene and the Dufours learned afterward that she had been alone and without hospitality in St. Martinville.

She hesitated to say anything to Brent about her distaste —almost amounting to a distrust—of the arrangements that had been made. Obviously, he did not share this distaste; otherwise, he would have said something on the subject himself and found some way of preventing, or at least retarding, Lavinia's departure. On the contrary, he told Mary privately that he thought it was a very good thing for Lavinia to get away from the farm just now. She would find distractions in St. Martinville—reputedly the gayest among the small cities in southwest Louisiana— which would take her mind off Fleex and his mysterious disappearance, and also off Claude and his persistent suit. Perhaps the young fellow they had been visualizing as just the right one for Lavinia might be found in St. Martinville instead of Lafayette. Does this Dufour girl have a brother?

Mary did not know and, when questioned, Lavinia revealed that she did not know, either. Her manner plainly indicated that it was a matter of complete indifference to her anyway. But she made her preparations for departure with a fresh appearance of zest and when Joshua brought Jonathan's buggy up to the walk the next morning, her wardrobe was in perfect order for her visit, as she had said it would be. At the same moment that the Winslows came through the garden with their guest, Jim Garland emerged from his house, waving a small bag and calling out to them.

"Just a minute! Hold on there! I've decided I'd like to go along. There's room for me, isn't there?"

Nothing had been previously said about such a plan and he confessed, when he caught up with the others, that he had not thought of it the evening before, when they had all been sitting around chatting together. "I took the notion in the night," he said. "I've never been to St. Martinville, but it's occurred to me more than once that I'd enjoy it. Now of course I've got an added reason for wanting to see what sort of place it is, if Lavinia's going to spend a lot of time visiting there, and Sally and Jonathan and the children are going to be living there part of each year . . . also, the added advantage of a son-in-law who can put me up. . . . Why not let me drive, Jonathan? I know each inch of these roads by now, and I can spare you some of the worst bumps. . . . You sit between your uncle and me, Lavinia—we'll ride easier that way. Why, you don't take up any room at all! Are we all set now? Well then, let's be off!"

Mary watched them out of sight with mingled feelings of relief and regret. Somehow she felt that Lavinia's visit was likely to be a long one, and she had so greatly looked forward to having the girl at home again, after the winter's separation! But as Bent said, the change of scene would probably prove a distraction, and now that her father was going along, she felt no lurking disquietude about the trip. She did, however, feel genuinely sorry for Claude, to whom Lavinia had not even sent a farewell message. Obviously this was the day when she, Mary, should make her long delayed visit to the Villacs and the Primeaux; Brent agreed with her heartily when she said she thought so. She must take her time about it, too, he told her. It was a long while since she had been there. He would understand if she were not home for supper. . . .

She did not get home for supper and it was obvious, on her return, that she had enjoyed her little outing and that she felt the better for it. Claude had been very reasonable, she told Brent. Of course the boy was sorry not to have seen Lavinia again before she left or even to have heard from her; but he thought she was quite right to take advantage of her uncle's presence to make the trip. Anne had not looked as badly as Mary feared she might; but she was fretting lest she would not be able to get to Lacombe for *Toussaint;* she had never missed a year since she and Ursin had moved away, and though of course they had plenty of relations to look after the family lots, that was not the same as doing it themselves. Mary, who had never mastered the schedule of Catholic feasts and fasts, had asked to be reminded when *Toussaint* came; and when told, not until November 1st, she had laughed and said *of course* Anne would be well enough to go by that time. Then Anne and Ursin had laughed, too, and had agreed with her. . . . Mary did not believe Mezalee had a beau yet, or that she really wanted one; it was more probable that when she thought she could be spared —and her girl cousins were getting very handy about the house—she would again bring up the subject of entering a convent. . . . Clement was growing into a fine big boy. It was hard to realize he was almost as old now as Claude had been when the Winslows first came to Louisiana. . . . All of the younger children were well. . . . Phares thought there would be an unusually fine crop. . . .

November seemed to arrive with surprising swiftness that year and Mary was partly right: Anne did manage to get to Lacombe for *Toussaint*, though it was more of an effort for her than anyone, except Dr. Mouton, guessed— not even Ursin realized. Meanwhile, Jonathan had returned to Illinois to see the crops in and was back in St. Martinville—alone. Sally and the children would come later, he told Jim Garland and the Winslows, rather vaguely. There was a surprising amount of repair work to be done in the Arcenaux house, so they would not be comfortable there for the time being; and he had been lucky in finding a reliable couple to stay with them at the farm while he was gone. He did not come over to see his relatives-in-law very often, but he kept in touch with them through Lavinia, who was spending a good deal of time in St. Martinville, though it developed there was no potential suitor in the Dufour family or, as far as her parents could find out, elsewhere on the horizon. She did not seem discontented when she was at home, and she was never actually rude or unkind to Claude a second time; eventually, she went out with him on the same basis that she did with other young men who lived in and near Crowley. But she made a great many visits, in Lafayette as well as St. Martinville, and finally she announced that she would like very much to go to New Orleans and continue her education.

This announcement was almost as much of a shock to Mary as it was to Brent. "But, Lavinia, you've graduated already," she said in a bewildered way.

"At Grand Coteau. I'd like to do more advanced work than I could there."

"In what, darling?"

"Well, especially in music. I've been to the opera two or three times, when it's come to St. Martinville. I'd like to go regularly, all through the season. And study with a really good teacher—perhaps one of the members of the orchestra, or one of the performers. I don't mean just the piano. I mean some other instrument, too, and singing. I'd like to be with French people, to speak French all the time. I don't mean with Creoles. I mean with the people who come over from France every year, with the French Opera."

"But, Lavinia, where would you *live?* We haven't any family in New Orleans, any friends even. And I'm not sure that those people who are connected with the opera are just—I mean, I'm afraid—"

"All right. That's what I'd really like to do, but if you'd be any easier, I'd settle for the next best thing. That new college for girls, Sophie Newcomb, makes special arrangements for students to board with private families that have been approved. It doesn't believe in dormitories. I read all about it in a college catalog that I saw in the Perets' house at Lafayette. It says 'parents and guardians are advised to consult with the secretary in regard to the suitable placing of their daughters or wards.' "

"But, Lavinia, you're not a student at Sophie Newcomb."

"I could be . . . I wouldn't even have to be a regular student—I mean, one taking the full curriculum—if you didn't want me to. I could just take one or more special courses. Sophie Newcomb has them in all sorts of things —languages, chemistry, art, psychology—and they start in the second and third quarters. I'm too late for the second, but I could get in on the third—it doesn't begin until February. 'Although students are strongly urged to take one of the regular courses, it may nevertheless occur that, for various reasons, some will decide to pursue a partial course or confine their work to a single branch. For such special students provision will be made.' That's exactly what the catalog says."

"You seem to have learned it by heart."

"I have, practically. . . . Of course, chaperones are provided for the opera and things like that. Besides, it isn't as if I wanted to run around with boys. It isn't as if Father couldn't afford it, either."

Mary was silent. Of course Brent could well afford to send Lavinia to New Orleans; he was doing better and better every year, and though he was constantly adding to his land, his stock and his buildings, he was also thriftily saving and making investments beside those represented by his farm. He had carried out his plan of erecting a commercial building on the business site which had been "thrown in" by the Dusons when he bought his first two

208

lots in Crowley, and this now had a well-patronized shop on the ground floor and various offices upstairs; the rental he derived from these alone brought in a substantial income. He had declined all offers of purchase both for this site and the building on it, and he had continued to advise Mary against selling the two lots in the "residential section" which he had bought in her name, though these could have been sold many times over and for many times what had originally been paid for them. Someday, he stoutly maintained, Lavinia would want a house in town, with ample grounds about it. But to Mary it looked less and less as if Lavinia would ever want a house in Crowley, with or without ample grounds. Her startling idea about going to New Orleans seemed to her mother like an additional—and unfortunate—indication of this.

"I'll speak to your father, of course. But I'm almost sure what his reaction will be. I'm almost sure he won't approve. And I don't, either, darling. It seems to us—"

"It seems to you now that I'd be happier if I got married. Evidently parents are always sure that the opposite of what their children want to do is best for them. When I felt like going to dances, you and Father didn't want me to. Now that I don't care whether I do or not, you'd like to have me, provided I went with just the right person, of course, just the kind of man you'd choose for me—not the kind I'd choose for myself."

She spoke with such bitterness that Mary was increasingly disturbed. It was not only undutiful, it was unnatural for Lavinia to talk like this—to feel like this. Well brought up, normal young girls did not defy their elders or lose their taste for the pastimes suitable for their age, merely because their first sweetheart had proved unacceptable and unworthy. Dealing with a grown daughter, she decided, was infinitely harder than dealing with a husband or a father; the problems posed by one slim, pretty girl were more difficult to solve than any of those presented by farming or pioneering. When Brent stubbornly refused to so much as discuss the project Lavinia had broached, and even Jim Garland, for once, had no solution to offer, Mary tried to believe the question was closed, only to find herself thwarted. Support for Lavinia came from almost the last quarter where her distracted mother would have expected to find it.

She had begun to make a point of going to see Anne at least once a week, and more often than not, Anne was in bed. The dreadful word "cancer" was never spoken between them, but its import now loomed ominously in their lives. Nonetheless, Anne joked about being lazy, just as she had joked about having babies, and she discussed Lavinia's attitude as lightheartedly as she did everything else.

"Like I tol' you when I first come on the prairie, me," she informed Mary, "you got to get you your baby every year, sho'. Then you don't be so scared 'bout it, no. You ain't never got used to it, account of havin' no mo' except jus' one. So now you worryin', you, worry-worry-worry, 'bout that one account she the onlies' one you got, stead of havin' maybe a dozen to pass the worry dish on, an' divide it up so each of them, yes, get a li'l bit fo' herself, her."

"Wouldn't you worry if one of your girls wanted to go streaking off to a big city?"

"Not me, no. All I got to do is tell my relations, them. They would take care of her good, yes."

"But I haven't got any relations in New Orleans."

"That's too bad, yes. Me an' Ursin, we got plenty-plenty relations, us, the same relations as Phares, him. But I got to tell you, me, we got plenty-plenty other relations, too. Adeline's relations."

"Adeline's?"

"Sho', you don't know 'bout Adeline? She Phares' *defint* wife, her."

"I suppose I must have known her name was Adeline. But I'd forgotten. She died before I came here, you know."

"Yes, sho'," Anne said again. "That was why we come, me an' Ursin an' the children. But you heard 'bout Adeline, didn' you?"

Mary hesitated. Now that she was reminded, she recalled that Lavinia had said once, Fleex's mother was a "real lady," that she had been in the same class at Grand Coteau as Miss Millie and that she had broken loose from her background and had come to live on the prairie with Phares, because she was so deeply in love with him. It was Adeline who had given her little girls their lessons when there was no school to which they could go; it was she, unquestionably, who had left her children a legacy of grace which their cousins did not possess. Marcelite was a beauty; Mezalee had managed to keep a mystic quality of spirituality in the midst of overcrowding and earthiness; Clement was a winning and handsome boy. Even Fleex, who had turned out so badly, did not lack charm. In fact, he had far too much of it, as well as great talents, however uncultivated and misdirected. Reluctantly, Mary remembered not only his lavish gifts of the game which was the outward and visible sign of his superb marksmanship, and his intimate knowledge of every creature of field, forest and stream; but also, the sound of his singing, that first night on the prairie, when the music he made had followed her and her husband and their child all the way to their new home. . . .

"Yes," she said at last, "I heard about Adeline. I remember now."

"Well, she had plenty-plenty relations in New Orleans, too, her. All you got to do is write to them, tell them you an' Mr. Winslow is our friends, they fix everything up for Lavinia."

Again Mary hesitated. "Are they close relations?" she inquired, after a pause.

"Close enough. Why you ask?"

"I couldn't help thinking that if they were really close they might—well, they might have heard from Fleex."

It was the first time she had spoken his name to Anne since his disappearance. Anne sat up in bed, adjusting her pillows so they would support her better. There was a gray tinge now to her swarthy skin, which made it look coarser than ever, and gray threads in her black hair, which she made less effort than ever to keep tidy, now that she was so far from well. But her essential goodness and wisdom and courage still illumined the countenance which, without them, would have seemed so commonplace.

"I got to tell you frankly, me, I don' know whether they ever heard from Fleex, them, or not," she said. "I got to say, they ain't all that close, so they'd be likely to hear. Fleex's *gran'père* an' his *gran'mère* is both dead since long-long ago, an' his po' *maman* was an only child, without no brothers or sisters, her, jus' like you' Lavinia. But w'at I really got to say, me, is how glad I am, yes, you at last open you' mouth to me 'bout Fleex. Fo' I don' know how long, I been hopin', me, you would say something, account it's such a pity Fleex went away, him."

"Yes, it is. Especially the way he did."

"That ain't w'at I been studyin' on, me, no. W'at I been thinkin' 'bout is Lavinia; thinkin' an' thinkin', and feelin' so sorry, yes, she never married with Fleex, her, an' be happy like Adeline done when she marry with Phares, her."

"But, Anne—"

"Me, I already know real good every word you fixin' to say, yes, so you don' got to say nothin' 'bout it, account it

211

is better a young girl gets married with the man she got in her heart, her, even if she too young-young yet, an' even if he ain't good enough fo' marry with her. Even then, I tell you frankly, it's better they get married with each other, them, than that she should die."

"Why, Anne, Lavinia didn't die!"

Anne gave Mary a long look. "Maybe when you say 'dead' you don' mean the same thing, no, w'at I mean when I say 'dead,' me," she retorted. "But you got to admit, you, yes, that on the night when Lavinia was waitin' fo' Fleex to come, an' it wasn't Fleex who come, but only Claude, him, it like to killed her, yes. Almost, anyway. But that ain't what I got in my min', me, when I say something killed her. W'at I got in my min' was the letter she fin' in that li'l hidin' place they got when she go there, her, fo' to look fo' him. W'at killed Lavinia, I guarantee you, me, was when the letter say Fleex ain't comin' back no mo', not never, him."

"Anne, what makes you think that's what has happened?"

"How you mean think? I don't think, no, me. I say w'at I know! W'at I know is how, when Claude found Lavinia, him, she was still a-readin' that letter Fleex wrote her, in French. They mostly talked French together, them, anyways. You mean you ain't even knowin' that, *hein?* Fleex talked real good French, not no gay-gay French like us, no, but real French w'at he learned from his *maman* biffo' she die, her. Claude never read the letter, no, account it wasn't wrote to him, but Lavinia, she tol' him w'at it said in the letter. I expect, me, she had to tell somebody, or else she'd bus' in two pieces maybe. Fleex wrote how she got to forget all about him, yes, an' how he's goin' take an' go 'way on some ship, him, without he even tells her good-by, account if he tries to tell her he won't be able to leave, no, not never. Then he say he love her plenty-plenty, but he was jus' a no-'count, ig'rant swamps Cajun, him, an' she was a fine lady, educate in Gran' Coteau an' all, an' even if he did think, him, how maybe they could be like his papa an' *maman* some ways, he done make up his min', him, it wouldn't never work, no. He say they can't run off, them, an' get married with each other like Phares an' Adeline done, account no priest wouldn't marry them, not never, lessen he talked first with you an' you' husban', him, an' you both would be boun' an' fixed in you' mind to say no."

"A priest married Marcelite and Alcée without any delay at all," Mary interrupted.

"Sho, he did, but they both Catholics, them, an' Phares fin'ly give in, an' said yes, him. You know why he had to do so, *hein?* Sho' you do. You boun' to."

Mary colored. "I suppose so," she said reluctantly. This was something else that had not been discussed and she did not want to discuss it now. Whatever the Villacs and the Primeaux and the Bazinets might have admitted privately, among themselves, they had continued to maintain elsewhere that Marcelite's first baby had been premature and Mary and Brent had stoutly supported this declaration.

"Well, don' you feel glad, you, I mean real-real glad, Lavinia don' marry like Marcelite, so soon like the priest can get here, him?"

Mary recoiled. "Of course, nothing like that would have happened to Lavinia," she said swiftly.

"Tha's jus' the same w'at Ursin thought, him," Anne retorted dryly. "He say no things like that couldn't never happen, not in his family, no. But I tell you frankly, me, things like that could happen in every family, yes."

"But if Fleex and Lavinia had run away, they could have been married by some Protestant minister or some justice of the peace or—" Mary began, desperately seeking to change the subject.

"An' you know w'at, then? Fleex wouldn't think he was married at all, not him, no. Some things like that would be worser even as the others, I guarantee you. Fleex been gone with other girls anyway, him, like any wild young buck goin' do, yes. Like with that Prudence, her. But I guess you right when you say he wouldn't do some things like that with Lavinia. An' besides where could he take her? Not to that secret place in the swamp w'at they call the hide-out, no. How would they get stuff to eat there, them, I ask you? He would have been 'shamed to bring her here, to us, crowded jam-jam like we live, us. An' he would have been mo' 'shamed yet, to bring her on you' house. Maybe he's got the idee you shut the door in his face an' won't let them come in—an' maybe that's jus' w'at you would do, yes, if he brought Lavinia there to stay wit him on you' house. The young boys an' girls, they can't homestead no mo', them, like his papa an' *maman* done. Anyway, you know how you felt 'bout Fleex, especially 'bout him marryin' with you' daughter, her. Fleex know it, too. You feel kind of that way 'bout all us Ca-

213

juns, 'ceptin' maybe Claude, him, even if us two—you an' me—been friends fo' the longest, us. But 'bout Fleex you feel like that most of all, I guarantee you, me."

"Anne, you're not being fair."

"I don' know 'bout no fair, me, but I know 'bout w'at's truth, yes. Truth is w'at I'm sayin', an' I'm sayin', me, that all w'at counts for life and livin' in Lavinia is dead. Maybe you don' say it, no, but I say it, me. Maybe Lavinia will get married anyway, after a while, her, maybe even to Claude. I hope so, me. I would want Lavinia for my daughter. But gettin' married with Claude won't count for her, not never, no, like gettin' married with Fleex. You know w'at I think, me? I think if a young girl can't have love an' educate all two, she better off, her, if she got love an' ain't educate. But it's too late, I tell you frankly, to study on that now. So you jus' as well let Lavinia go to New Orleans, yes. Ursin an' Phares an' me we fix it for her, us, I guarantee you, me. We got plenty-plenty relations."

CHAPTER XXI

A week or so after this conversation took place, Phares trudged over to the Winslows' farm for one of his periodic visits and informed his hosts, as they sat drinking coffee in the cluttered sitting room, that he had been called to New Orleans on business and that Annette had "worried" him until he had agreed to take her along.

"Mezalee the one belongs to be goin', her," he said. "Clisson an' Haydee Labadie, where we goin' stay by their house, us, is Adeline's relations, so Mezalee is the onlies' one they blood kin to, them. I tell you frankly, me, they been writin' for the longes' how they want to see her, too, account they ain't never laid one eye on her, no, not since she growed up from a little-little girl. I also got to say she don' never get to go nowheres, her, an' she got a right to. Only she won't leave Anne, no, so Annette goin' have this here fine trip. W'at I'm really tryin' to say, is how me an' Annette would be mighty glad, us, if you let Lavinia come along. W'at you say, *hein?*"

"Oh, Father, please!" Lavinia exclaimed, jumping up from the place near the window where she had been listlessly turning the pages of a book which she was hardly pretending to read, even before the visitor arrived. Impulsively, she put her arm around Brent's shoulder and bent over to rest her cheek against his. While he realized the caress would not have seemed so spontaneous except for the purpose that prompted it, nevertheless it pleased him. He did not worry about Lavinia as much as Mary did and she irritated him more; his deepest devotion had always been given to his wife rather than his daughter. But he loved her dearly, also, though he was too reserved to show his fondness as easily as Jim Garland did; and he had been genuinely, if secretly, concerned by her strange conduct during the last few months.

"Look out, Lavinia, you'll upset my specimens," he said, not crossly, but cautiously. Then he looked over the board at which he had been working, as if to assure himself that nothing had been disarranged, before he turned to his caller. "You're not planning to be gone more than a day or two, I suppose?" he then inquired, still speaking cautiously.

"Not me, no. But this yuh business that got to be settled ain't goin' be fixed up not in no two days. But I got it in my min' to come home soon, in one day, mebbe two, an' then go back to town again to finish up with business. So I got the idee, me, that if them young girls is havin' a big-big time in N'Yawl'ns, an' the Labadies invites them to stay, why not let them have the chance, an' I would bring them back, me, nex' time when I go down on the train."

"Well," Brent said. "Well—what do you think, Mary?"

"I think it would be a fine outing for the girls, just as Phares said," Mary answered quietly. Nothing about her manner indicated what else she was thinking: that this business that had come up was too opportune to be wholly accidental; that, unless she were greatly mistaken, Anne had somehow contrived, from her sickbed, to see that Phares was suddenly summoned to New Orleans where, in the natural course of events, he did not go once in a blue moon, and where, as far as she knew, he had never been called on important business before.

"My *defint* wife's papa an' *maman* is both dead now, them," he told the Winslows, apparently unaware that Mary was already possessed of this information. "They never give her nothin', not after she marry with me, no; they so boilin' mad they rather their onlies' chil' should suffer, her, than they should help." He paused, shaking his head as if over sad memories, and continued as if unconscious that his words might be applicable to any other case. "They lived with these Labadie relations all together

215

in one *p'tite maisonette*. Them's the same relations, a brother an' sister, we goin' visit with, us. *Defint* Adeline's papa an' *maman,* biffo' they die, them, give every las' thing they got—their half the house an' ever'thing else they own—to Clisson an' Haydee Labadie, to make sure it wouldn't be not one thing left to Adeline an' her children. I don't know no law, me, but it's got something with a law-talk name—"

"Donations *inter vivos,*" Lavinia said unexpectedly.

"Tha's exackly it!" Phares exclaimed, looking at the girl with respectful amazement, while her parents' glances betrayed that they shared this. "How you come to know 'bout it, will you tell me, yes?"

"From Uncle Jonathan," Lavinia informed him. "He told me that a lot of the beautiful things in the St. Martinville house were given him before his grandparents died and that this was a very advantageous arrangement—to the heirs, I mean."

"Mebbe so. Me, I don't know no law, like I already said. Anyway, Clisson an' Haydee ain't never marry with nobody, so now they gettin' old, by nobody gets no younger, an' it must be they got to thinkin', them, how nobody don' know w'at's goin' to happen with their nice *p'tite maisonette,* an' all those prit-tee things they got in there, them. Who goin' get all that when Clisson an' Haydee comes to die? Strangers mebbe? Mebbe even Yankees. . . ."

"What started them thinking?" Mary could not resist asking, sure that Phares would say he did not know. She was right. He shook his head again.

"Mebbe they got a bad conscience, them, fin'ly, though I got to admit, me, I don' understand how come they conscience hurtin' now as long as it ain't never hurt biffo' now. Anyway, Clisson he set hisself down to write, him, an' say he wants we should talk 'bout the property, us. I tell you frankly, me, it wouldn't surprise me the firs' li'l bit, no, if he an' his sister Haydee ain't made up they min's to leave it to my children, or at least to one of them. If it got to be one, I want it should be Mezalee. Clement, he goin' get my share off the farm; me an' Ursin got our understandings on that, us, for the longes'. Marcelite got not even one thing to worry her, no, at least not 'bout money. That Bazinet boy she got married with is doin' plenny good, him. I got to admit it. He's doin' plenny better'n I ever expect' he would, me. An' Fleex—" Phares stopped and, for the third time, shook his head. "No use to even

216

talk 'bout leavin' nothin' to him, no, when we got no idee, us, where he is at. Tha's a bad one, him, even if he is my son. But Mezalee, her—"

"Mezalee's a saint on earth," Lavinia said quickly. "But what would she do with a nice little house and all the pretty things in it? She won't even go and see them."

"I got to admit you' right 'bout that, yes. Mezalee don' wan' one thing in this yuh worl', her, outside of be a nun; an' w'at use a nun has for *maisonettes* full of prit-tee things, *hein?* But mebbe it should go to all four, anyway, an' so far like that goes, how I know w'at Clisson an' Hay-dee got in they min's, them? Mebbe they got plans tha's different like mud is different from money. But I got to admit, me, they good Cath'lic people w'at wants to do the right things, yes, an' they boun' to have something besides the *maisonette,* too. They both been teachin' music fo' the longes', them. . . . You got some trouble with you' lungs mebbe, Mary? I don't like to hear nobody coughin' like that, me. You got a right to take care of it real good, yes."

"A cake crumb went down the wrong way, that's all," Mary said, recovering her speech. "When are you starting, Phares?"

"In the letter he talks like he wants me to come soon-soon," he said thoughtfully. "Mebbe nex' week, yes."

"*Next week!* Why, Mr. Primeaux, don't you think you ought to start tomorrow? If that letter's so terribly urgent—"

"Lavinia, Mr. Primeaux knows when he ought to start. He has the farm to think of, too."

"There isn't much work on a farm in January. And I'm sure—I'm absolutely positive—that those Labadies are thinking of willing their property to someone in the Primeaux family. I don't believe there's a moment to lose."

Simultaneously, Brent and Mary reproved Lavinia. But Phares did nothing of the sort. He eyed her with increasing attention and respect.

"Lavinia got it right, her," he said. "Not tomorrow, no. I wouldn't have no chance, me, to get ready by no tomorrow. But the day after. . . ."

Not since the afternoon when Lavinia had made herself a frilly pink dress and piled her golden hair high on her head, singing as she did so, while she prepared to go danc-ing with Fleex, had Mary seen her daughter so happy. The girl fairly flew around the house, not only as she gathered together her belongings and packed them, but as she per-formed the usual humdrum household tasks, in which she had been proficient from childhood, but in the accomplish-

217

ment of which, of late, she had shown so little spirit. She insisted that before she left her mother with no other help than Vicey, she must sweep every room, she must wash the curtains, she must tidy the closets and cupboards and bureau drawers; she declared she would not be satisfied if she did not leave everything in perfect order and she did exactly that. Nevertheless, she found time, every few hours, to go to the piano and play a merry little tune; and toward nightfall, she made a tour of the stables with her grandfather and went horseback riding with him. After supper, she ran ahead of her parents as they accompanied her on a farewell visit to Anne and Mezalee and the younger children. Then, throughout the six-hour train trip, she chatted so merrily that both Phares and Annette assured her that it had not seemed like any time at all between the moment when they left the Crowley depot and arrived at the one in New Orleans; and she was still chatting merrily when their hack drew up in front of the Labadies' little house on the Rue de Quartiers.

It was unlike any place she had ever seen before and, from the moment she entered the side door, which led directly from the alleyway into the drawing room, she was charmed with her surroundings and excited by them. The little house—the Labadies called it their *maisonette*—was two rooms wide and two rooms deep; and Clisson Labadie explained to Lavinia, in his gentle, quavering voice, that it was made up of twin houses that had been thrown together, so that, originally, each had been only one room wide though each had its *cabinet* over the wine cellar, its loggia at the rear, and its kitchen and slave quarters on the farther side of the patio. The *cabinet,* Lavinia discovered, was actually an extra bedroom, a tiny one, reached from the big one by a short flight of stairs, but inaccessible in any other way. The one thus connected with Mlle Labadie's room was where she and Annette were to sleep, while M. Primeaux would occupy the one over M. Labadie's.

For one person, a *cabinet* was not really crowded, but two could hardly squeeze into the small space it provided, which, Annette and Lavinia both declared, made it all the more amusing and attractive; and the furnishings of their nook, like those in all the rest of the house, were the most exquisite either had ever seen. They had barely had time to wash their hands and faces at the beautiful porcelain bowl on the washstand, when they were summoned to dinner by a Negress so immense she had difficulty in wedging her way up the narrow stairs, and who informed them, with a broad grin, that her name was Mignon. Then they went down to the loggia, which had been enclosed to serve as a dining room and, sitting side by side at a gateleg table, feasted on the most delicious food they had ever eaten: turtle soup, grillades, baked cushaw and French cream cake.

Mignon kept waddling in, puffing and panting, from the kitchen on the farther side of the little patio, and every dish that she set down in front of M. Clisson or Mlle Haydee to be served was still piping hot and each seemed more delicious than the one that had preceded it. There was a great deal more, still heavier and more beautiful, on the sideboard. The porcelain was all of the fragile, flowered variety, edged with gold leaf; and the damask napkins, richly embroidered with monograms which matched those on the tablecloth, were enormous. The girls had both visited in well-ordered houses, larger and more pretentious than this one, in St. Martinville and Lafayette and on near-by plantations; but they had never seen such elegance, combined with such accustomed ease, as at this perfectly appointed table. They were both a little overawed by it at first; but Phares was totally unembarrassed, and M. Clisson and Mlle Haydee were both so friendly that the *malaise* was of short duration. The brother and sister resembled each other closely; both had soft white hair, soft white hands and soft brown eyes; both spoke English correctly, but slowly, and with a pronounced accent, and seemed delighted when Lavinia said, rather shyly, that she understood French and that, if they would rather talk in that language. . . . Then they hastened to compliment her on her command of it and, above all, on her excellent pronunciation, which they insisted was extraordinary. Both were dressed in deep black, as if in first mourning for some near and dear relative; but no reference was made to any recent loss and, eventually, it transpired that their latest bereavement had occurred more than a year previously, when an aunt by marriage had died of old age. Mlle Haydee's somber attire was relieved, to a certain degree, by the fine diamonds in her pierced ears, which were rather long, at her wrinkled throat, which was likewise rather long, and on her slim fingers, which were long, too; all were slightly out of proportion to her well-set head and her slight, firmly corseted figure; but somehow they seemed to add to her air of distinction. Her brother's immaculate white linen, so stiffly starched that it looked as if it had been glazed, lightened his mourning in the same way that his sister's diamonds did hers; and there was no mournfulness about either their manner or their conversation. On the contrary, nothing could have been more genial in its assurance of welcome and its insistence on a leisurely visit. Phares must not think of hurrying back to the farm, now that he had, at last, come to New Orleans; there were matters of great importance which they wished to discuss with him, but not, of course, this first evening. *Les affaires sont les affaires,* M. Clisson admitted; but the time for *affaires* was in the morning—the late morning—after a sound sleep and a hearty breakfast; and it would take several mornings to cover all the ground he had in mind. Besides, these charming young girls must see something of the city—the waterfront, certainly, where they would view the big sailing ships and ocean steamers; the Spanish Fort, where there was a Ferris wheel comparable to the one in Chicago and a restaurant built right out over the water; Audubon Park, where the Cotton Centennial Exposition had been held only a few years before to celebrate the hundredth anniversary of the first bale of cotton shipped from New Orleans to a foreign port. Besides—did they know?—Audubon Park was part of the Deboré estate where Etienne Deboré had first granulated sugar and it was important on that account, too; no doubt, a hundred years from now, Mr. Winslow's experiments with rice would be equally famous, and there would be celebrations with electrically lighted buildings in one of the big parks at Crowley, in just the same way that big buildings, electrically illuminated inside and out, had been the main feature of the Cotton Centennial Exposition. But however that might be, such sightseeing as he had in mind was a part of a young girl's education. And then, of course, there was the opera. The Labadies still retained the small *loge grillée* which their dear parents had had before them. Were the young ladies interested in music? Lavinia very greatly so? Why, that was splendid, she must certainly take advantage of the cultural opportunities afforded by this visit! And even if Annette did not care so much for the cultural side of things, she—and Lavinia, too, for that matter—would enjoy the Carnival Balls. It was too bad they had missed the Twelfth Night Revels, and by so narrow a margin, too! But fortunately there were other balls still ahead—Momus and Proteus, of course and, on Mardi Gras, Rex. . . .

"You forget, Mlle Haydee, these young girls ain't goin' to stay but a few days, them. You're talkin' like they was goin' to impose on you all winter."

220

"Impose? Impose did you say, Phares? Never! It would be our pleasure and our privilege to have them remain as long as we can keep them contented. *Bien entendu,* you will feel you should return to your farm when *les affaires* have had your attention. But these sweet children—what *affaires* can there be which will take them back to the prairie?"

None, of course, Lavinia said to herself. She was still doing so when Mlle Haydee led the way into the drawing room for coffee; and she continued to repeat it, mentally, during the musical interlude which followed, with Mlle Haydee at the piano and M. Clisson at the violin. Even when she "obliged" by performing herself—to be complimented on her playing as warmly as she had previously been complimented on her French—her mind was not on her music. It was on Fleex, as it generally was. Miraculously, she had managed to get to New Orleans, and she had not told any lies, either, when she said she wished to continue her education. The desire was sincere, and if it did not have the same intensity as another desire, well, that was her own secret and she had a right to keep it. Now she would manage to stay where she was until she had found the man she sought. Sooner or later, the ship which had borne him away would bring him back. She would study hard, she would practice faithfully, she would scrupulously observe the proprieties. But all the time she would be waiting for Fleex.

CHAPTER XXII

M. Clisson maintained what he called his *bureau* in the tiny room on the ground floor of one of the twin slave quarters and, all the next morning, he and Phares were closeted there, presumably discussing *les affaires*. Meanwhile, Mlle Haydee was occupied with the pupils who arrived, in orderly sequence, exactly an hour apart, and the two girls were thrown on their own resources. It was mild enough for them to sit in the patio and they were both enchanted with it; nevertheless, they might have found time hanging somewhat heavily on their hands if Mignon had not kept emerging from her kitchen in the quarters opposite, to answer questions and supplement her replies with unsolicited information.

"How do you use the space about the *bureau* and the

221

kitchen?" Lavinia wanted to know. "There must be rooms up there, too."

Mignon put her hands on her hips and rolled her eyes. "Ain't nothin' but *greniers*," she told them. "Unfinished attics. Slaves used to sleep there, of course, and most anything was good enough for them."

"Does anyone sleep there now?" Lavinia inquired.

Mignon grinned. "I ain't sayin' I don't catch me a little daytime nap once in a while," she admitted. "I got me a shakedown in the *grenier* over my kitchen. But nights, I likes to go home to my man and my chillun. I got six head."

"And what about the *grenier* over the *bureau?*" Lavinia persisted. "I don't see why that couldn't have been fixed up and used for a *garçonnière*, like on the big plantations."

Mignon's grin broadened. "I don't know nothin' about big plantations," she asserted. "I's a New Orleans nigger, me. And it ain't never been fixed up, same like the house is fixed up. But it do have a real bed in it and a chair and a commode. Seems like I remembers some young man slep' there once in a while—long time ago."

"What young man?" Annette asked, interested in her turn.

"I disremembers his name," Mignon said vaguely. Then, with more sprightliness, she added, "Lands sake, doesn't I smell something burnin'? I got to be gettin' back to my kitchen," and she waddled off with a speed surprising in one of her size.

Eventually Phares and M. Clisson emerged from the *bureau*, both looking very important, and Phares offered to take the girls to Audubon Park while M. Clisson, who went to his pupils' houses, instead of having them come to his, like his sister, was out giving lessons. He was going back to Crowley the next day, Phares said; but he would be returning in about a week, to settle *les affaires*, which, so far, he had only discussed tentatively with M. Clisson; he now wanted to talk them over with Anne and Ursin. Meanwhile, the girls could take advantage of the Labadies' invitation to extend their visit. No doubt they would enjoy the opera, though he, personally, did not care to attend it; and it appeared that a few nights after the performance of *Romeo and Juliet*, that newly organized Krewe, the Elves of Oberon, would be giving their first ball, to which M. Clisson might be able to secure invitations. Probably the young girls would enjoy that, too. . . .

"I'd enjoy it more if I had something fit to wear," An-

222

nette told him. "Lavinia and I would rather go shopping on Canal Street than see Audubon Park. Wouldn't we, Lavinia?"

"Well, I'm willing to do either," Lavinia said agreeably. What she really wanted was to see the secretary of Sophie Newcomb about special courses; but, very wisely, she had decided to wait until after the departure of Phares before broaching this subject. "We do need new dresses, though, Mr. Primeaux—I mean, materials for new dresses. I can run them up in no time, if there's a machine in the house. If there isn't, I'm sure we could find a seamstress somewhere who'd make them quickly and reasonably. Probably that would be better anyway. She'd know more about the latest styles than we do."

"You' papas they done give you *d'argent* fo' to buy silks an' satins by the hay-wagon load, them, mebbe, no?"

"They gave us some," the girls replied in unison. "They knew—"

"W'at you tryin' not to say is like so: Mary, she done tol' Brent, an' Anne, she done tol' Ursin, I guarantee you, me," Phares said, still sarcastically. "In this yuh time young folks, them, don' never think 'bout nothin' only spend, spend, spend money, instead of save, save, save money, like us used to do, us. It's education, or either it's clothes, or either it's something else, as long as somebody got to spend, spend, spend. Boys is plenny bad, I got to admit, yes, but girls is even worser."

"None of your children has asked you for any money," Lavinia reminded him. "All Marcelite wanted was to get married and all Mezalee wanted was to be a nun and all Fleex wanted was to run away. But you haven't been pleased with any of that, either. You're not even pleased with poor little Clement, who only wants to stay on the farm—you say he's getting lazy. I don't believe parents are ever pleased with what their children want to do."

"You look yuh, now Miss Lavinia, with all that sassy talk," Phares said sharply. "I got to promise you this much, me: was you my daughter, you wouldn't please me, no, not one least li'l bit. It's no wonder you' papa an' you' *maman*, them, is so worried to death about you."

"The only thing that ever worried them about me was that they thought I wanted to marry your son."

"Sho', I know, me, an' he run out from you. Mebbe he had plenny mo' sense, that boy, him, than we give him credit fo' havin'. So you an' also Annette can go spend all the *d'argent* you' papas had to work hard-hard fo', them.

Also you got a right, yes, to get to Canal Street by you' own selfs. Me, I ain't goin' with you, no, I guarantee you."

He turned on his heel and walked away. The ill feeling engendered by this verbal duel would have continued through the evening, if M. Clisson, scenting that something was needed to ease strain, had not produced some exceptionally fine Burgundy from the *cave,* and if the two girls had not been so full of chatter about their afternoon shopping. They had not experienced any difficulty in finding their way to Mr. Holmes' fine store, having carefully followed Mlle Haydee's directions about walking to Royal Street and then taking a streetcar—the first in which they had ever ridden. After they had chosen their materials— yellow taffeta for Annette, green surah for Lavinia—they had taken these to the seamstress recommended by Mlle Haydee, and she had shown them the latest fashion plates that had come in from Paris and had agreed to make up the silks very quickly in the styles the girls had chosen. The dresses would not be ready for *Romeo and Juliet,* but as they were to sit in a *loge grillée* that did not matter so much; and the seamstress had promised to put forth her best efforts to have the new finery ready for the Ball of the Elves of Oberon.

Phares departed the next morning before the girls put in an appearance, and the report which he took back to the prairie was not particularly satisfactory to either family there. Yes, he admitted, he and M. Clisson had talked about *les affaires;* but, despite what he had previously said in New Orleans about being in a hurry to talk things over with Ursin and Anne, he now insisted that he would wait until matters were more nearly settled before he said anything about the first conference in the *bureau.* The young girls were spending money like drunken sailors, though, since they were not his daughters, he supposed he should not comment on that either; he would say, however, that Lavinia should be taught to mind her manners. Had she been rude to the Labadies? Mary inquired in alarm. Oh, no; to the Labadies she had spoken as gently as a cooing dove; it was to her interests to do so. But she had talked back to him, from whom she had nothing to gain—or so she apparently thought; and she had better apologize or, sooner or later, there would be a *crise.* Mary hastened to apologize for her; Brent, who resented any remarks uncomplimentary to his daughter unless he made them himself, merely said that Lavinia was like Ursin: she had to speak what was on her mind.

A letter, received a few days later, disclosed a certain amount of what was on her mind: perhaps her parents did not know, Lavinia wrote them, that Annette would be quite ready to go home after a week or ten days. Pierre Peret, that boy from Lafayette who had a cowlick and sat on his hands when he got embarrassed, and who was now working in the new bank at Crowley, had been making eyes at her for quite a while; she thought he would suggest buying the *alliance* almost any time now. At all events, she wanted to give him the chance, because she was also very much smitten, though Lavinia could not understand why she should be, and she had not confessed this until they had snuggled down in the *cabinet* together—such close quarters were conducive to confidences. As for Lavinia she hoped very much that her parents would let her stay on with the Labadies, who were cordially urging her to do so. Mlle Haydee would give her music lessons and French lessons, too, right there in the house; and she could take special courses in literature and art at Sophie Newcomb. M. Clisson would see her on and off the streetcar himself—he could arrange the lessons he gave in such a way that they would correspond with hers. The Labadies would take her to the opera once a week or oftener and, at least as a spectator, to the major balls—they would not promise seats in the call-out section, though even that was a possibility. As a matter of fact, Lavinia did not care much whether she had an opportunity to dance or not, it was the other things she cared about, the serious things, though of course anyone would like to see the tableaux and the parades, once any way. Mlle Haydee was writing by the next mail—there were so many pupils scheduled for that day she hadn't been able to catch this one—and she would invite the elder Winslows to come and spend a day or two at the *maisonette* as soon as Mr. Primeaux had made his second visit and Annette had gone home. After that, there would be room for other guests. So Lavinia hoped her father and mother would let her stay on at least that much longer. Nothing needed to be definitely decided until then, except it was true they would like to know, as soon as possible, at Sophie Newcomb, whether she was going to take those special courses. . . .

Mary read the letter first and then handed it to Brent. He went through it twice, slowly, before he looked up and gave it back to her.

"You think we ought to let her stay, don't you, Mary?"

"Yes, I do. That is, I think we ought to accept the invitation, and if everything looks all right to us. . . ."

"Very well. If that's the way you feel about it, I'm willing to give my provisional consent."

Everything not only looked "all right," but almost ideal. Nothing that Lavinia had written about the Labadies, the *maisonette* and the advantages which both offered to their daughter seemed in the least exaggerated to either Brent or Mary; the opportunities provided by special courses at Sophie Newcomb, while rousing them to less wholehearted enthusiasm, were certainly satisfactory. It was agreed that Lavinia should go home briefly in April, between the third and fourth quarters of the college year, but that she should make her headquarters with the Labadies until after Commencement in June. Brent put in a good word for Claude: this was the slack season at the rice mill; the boy might be able to get down to New Orleans once in a while. Would M. Clisson and Mlle Haydee be willing to have him come to see Lavinia occasionally? There was no engagement, not even a definite prospect of one, though it was increasingly evident that, in the case of Annette, matters were different. But Claude was a declared suitor and, as far as Lavinia's parents were concerned, an acceptable one. In fact, they rather hoped that, in time, he might succeed in diverting her thoughts from one who had been less acceptable and whom, they were afraid, she had never wholly dismissed from her mind. Of course, both Labadies hastened to assure the Winslows; Claude would be welcome at any time; he could sleep in the loft over M. Clisson's *bureau*. In fact, it had been occupied every now and then by his cousin Fleex. That, *bien entendu*, was before Fleex had behaved so badly and run off to sea; it was in the days when he had come in from the prairie for an occasional brief visit in New Orleans. He had always appeared unannounced and uninvited, but the Labadies had made him welcome for the sake of his dead mother and his dead grandparents, God rest their souls! Even then, his character and his conduct had left much to be desired, however. He was unpredictable, he was unreasonable, he was unreliable. Moreover, he was given to sudden outbursts of anger and had a bad name in the Quarter because of the quarrels in which he had figured publicly, while still a young boy. In short, the Labadies had put up with a good deal from Fleex. Now that he had brought real disgrace on the family, naturally he could no longer

226

be received at the *maisonette*. The Winslows would understand. . . .

They did understand and they understood also that the Labadies had divined the identity of Lavinia's unacceptable suitor. Nothing more was said on the subject. Mary went back to her flowers and Brent to his experiments, convinced not only that they were leaving their daughter in good hands, but that everything pointed to a satisfactory solution of the situation, as far as Lavinia, Claude and Fleex were concerned. It had not occurred to them to question Mignon, making it worth while for her to answer them; still less did it occur to them that Lavinia might have done exactly this.

"Well, you promises not to tell M'iz Haydee nare word an' I tell you," Mignon had cautioned her.

"Of course I won't tell," Lavinia had said urgently. "If it comes to that, you make mighty sure *you* don't tell her you told me, or that I asked. The way you run on, you're a heap more likely to tell her without meaning to than I'd ever be to tell her on purpose."

"Well, Mist' Fleex he been here all right. He been here lots," Mignon confided, lowering her voice. "I don't mean he been to the house, no, like he used to come. But he come to N'Yawlins plenny times, account the boat he on come to N'Yawlins plenny times."

"Which boat is it?"

"One 'em bananny boats that make a roun' trip to some heathing bananny land ev'y three-fo' weeks. But he never stay here no longer'n it take to get shed of the banannies they brings up the river, turn de boat 'roun' with whatever they done loaded in her, an' go back fo' mo' 'em banannies."

"You mean he's a sailor?"

"Fiah'mun, M'iz Viney. Lease-a-ways, 'at's what 'ey tell me."

"Who tells you?"

Mignon's features set themselves in stubborn lines.

"'*Ey* tells me. Peoples tells me," she said with an air of finality. "An' 'at's all I knows 'bout it."

"Oh, no, it isn't," cried Lavinia, sensing her error. "I don't really care who told you, Mignon. All I want to know is what they told you and it must be more than that. I mean, wasn't he ever in town more than two or three days at a time? And how come anybody happens to tell you about one fireman on a steamboat? . . ."

"Not no steamboat, M'iz Viney. Steamboats is on the

river. This here a banany boat, a banany boat goin' t'all 'em heathing lands 'cross the sea."

"All right, on a banana boat. Do they talk about all firemen and sailors on all the banana boats?"

"Nome, 'ey sho' 'nuff don't. 'Ey talks 'bout Mist' Fleex, though by him all the time fightin' when he got a few 'em son-kick-yo'-mammy drinks in him.'

"Fighting?"

"I mean! He the fightines' gemman when he come ashore an' get to drinkin'! I mean!"

"Yes," Lavinia agreed slowly, and almost absently, "he would be."

"Tha's how come he stay here longer'n no three-fo' days, one time. He stay here thutty days, jes' like the judge say."

"You mean they put him in prison?"

"I mean! Smack spang in the jailhouse. Not the big one. The yuther one, what they calls the house of attention, where he got to work cleanin' out 'em ol' gutters an' such as that."

"And Mlle Haydee never found out?"

"She wa'n't in town, nor neither M. Clisson, by it was last summer the time of the big fever when ev'body that could left the city done it. Tha's how come Mist' Fleex to get put in the jailhouse, too."

"Oh, I thought you said it was for fighting."

"Tha' wa'n't no mo' 'n the start. For drunk an' fightin' 'ey puts gemmens in jail over night tillst 'ey cools off an' sobers up. But this here time of the big fever doin's Mist' Fleex's boat was helt up at the konteen station 'cross de river. . . ."

"Konteen?"

"Somethin' like 'at, anyways. A place where 'ey shuts peoples up when 'ey got fevers an' such."

"Oh, quarantine."

"Yas'm, konteen. Ain' nobody 'lowed to get off no boat when it in konteen, but Mist' Fleex don' hol' with 'at, so he slip off an' come 'cross the river on the ol' Third District ferry, an' go in one 'em Decatur Street saloons an' get in a fight like always when he got some 'em son-kick-yo'-mammies inside him, an' the patrol hack come dang-dang-dang an' the police taken him on de pree-sink station house like always to let all 'em gemmens sober up. But when 'ey fin' out Mist' Fleex he from 'at ol' boat what jest come in from some heathing land or 'nother, they say, 'Hah! So you done jump konteen, is you, so us gwine teach you a lesson, by us got yaller Jawn too bad 'thout no dirty name jumpin' konteen on us.' So they taken him to night co't an' the judge say fifteen days for pullin' a knife in a fight an' fifteen days fo' jumpin' konteen an' he hopes Mist' Fleex stays long enough to get the yaller Jawn his own se'f. Yas'm, M'iz Viney. 'At's azackly what the judge say, an' Mist' Fleex stay in town thutty days 'at time, an' he got out befo' M'iz Haydee come back, so she never knowed."

"Mignon! Does he still come in on that same boat?"

"Nome, not's I know. Way I heard, he lost the job account he got to stay on the house of attention an' miss the nex' trip. But he got some kine job on a boat to some 'em heathing lands 'cross the sea, only farther off, by he don' come back near so often no more."

"He'll come back someday though."

"Yessum, M'iz Viney, likely he will."

"Well, when he *does*, if—if—they—you should hear anyone speak of it—will you tell me, Mignon?"

"Maybe. But maybe 'ey'd want a little somethin'—"

"Five dollars?"

Mignon's lids dropped. She shrugged her shoulders and turned as if about to leave the corner of the patio, well out of earshot from the *maisonette*, where she and Lavinia had been talking.

"Ten?"

Mignon turned back, but still did not raise her lids.

"Twenty?"

"I reckon for twenty they might say somethin'," she admitted. "Twenty-five make it surer though."

"All right. Twenty-five."

"And I'd have to have some beforehand, for a promise like."

"All right. I'll give you ten right now as a promise."

This meant there would be no masquerade costume for Mardi Gras, no new dress for the Rex Ball. Brent was allowing his daughter enough for all reasonable expenses, but extensive bribery did not come under this heading. Nevertheless, Lavinia did not bewail the sacrifice such an expenditure entailed or begrudge a cent of the money that Mignon pocketed so greedily. If double the amount had been demanded of her, the girl would somehow have found the way to get it.

Because she was so confident that, sooner or later, she would have news of Fleex, and that this news would be the prelude to their reunion, she was able to await these tidings without obvious impatience and, for the most part, without undue restlessness of spirit. She really enjoyed her music lessons with Mlle Haydee, in which she made rapid progress, and her courses at college, where she quickly acquired new friends; and at the operas she attended, her pleasurable excitement sometimes rose to such a pitch, while watching the ill-starred lovers on the stage and listening to their impassioned arias, that she was able to forget, momentarily, that she had been crossed in love herself. It was only afterward, when the last ardent duet had been sung and the storm of applause had died down and the splendid curtains had swung together for the last time, that she remembered again, with redoubled poignancy, and with a sudden stab of longing and pain. On such nights she lay for a long while sleepless, rebellious at the solitude of the *cabinet* which at first had seemed so lovely to her and yearning to be with Fleex, even if they had no other shelter for their love than the little hideout they had built, as children, in the swampland.

If there had been someone in whom she could confide, these interludes of rebellion and yearning would not have seemed so unbearable; but, of necessity, they were as secret as they were searing. However, she did not allow them to affect her visibly and she kept all the promises she had made: she studied hard, she practiced faithfully, she scrupulously observed all the proprieties. The parents of her college friends, to whose homes she was invited, found her a suitable companion, in every respect, for their daughters, and encouraged her visits. Both M. Clisson and Mlle Haydee were delighted with her; they told each other that surely *le bon Dieu* must have had a hand in bringing this lovely young girl to brighten the *maisonette* in their old age; it was the compensation he was giving them for their own childlessness. They glowed with pride over the good marks that she received at Sophie Newcomb; they gave little soirées so that she could play to their relatives; they drew back the grille of their loge at the opera for the first time in many years, so that their acquaintances would realize they were again welcome to drop in between the acts, and so that everyone in the audience would have a chance to admire the fresh beauty and modest bearing of the Labadies' protégée. When Claude came to visit, they made him welcome and created opportunities for him to see Lavinia alone. Normally, they would have felt that closer chaperonage was indicated; but with such a decorous young girl, such a correct young man, surely there was no need for constant surveillance. . . .

Claude did his best to improve these opportunities, but he did not make much progress, partly because he did not feel any real enthusiasm for Lavinia's new-found interests and pleasures, and could not seem to pretend that he did; if he could have, these would have furnished numerous topics of conversation, to begin with, and various occasions for pleasurable outings in consequence. He had no dress clothes and did not think he should spend the money to buy any; this precluded his attendance at any ball or at any evening performance of the opera; and though he did accompany the Labadies and Lavinia to a matinee of *Aïda,* he not only yawned but actually drowsed through the second act, and said afterward that the "Triumphal March" was the only piece he enjoyed. Not *Celeste Aïda?* —Lavinia wanted to know. Not that heavenly duet at the end? They both sent shivers all over her! Why no, he had not shivered at all; it was all make-believe, very improbable make-believe at that. He could not understand why she should be so excited over it. . . . As for the "Study of Form with Line and Clay" and "Elements of Shading in Charcoal," which absorbed Lavinia in her special course of Normal Art, and the essays on "Epic, Lyric and Dramatic Poetry," which she was required to write in connection with her detailed work in Literature, he was so obviously baffled by her discussion of these that she soon abandoned all efforts to talk to him on such subjects. He was willing to take her to the waterfront and, at first, he shared her enthusiasm for such excursions: the river packets lined up at the landings; the steamships from all parts of the world; the great array of merchandise—sugar, molasses, lumber, hemp—these were indeed a proud and astonishing sight. The endless state of turmoil caused by the Negroes who handled these wares and the drays which brought them to the riverside appealed to him less; so did the strange mingled smells of tar and smoke and sisal; and he could not understand why Lavinia wanted to know where every ship in port had come from and how long it was likely to remain in New Orleans. When he eventually realized that she wanted to spend most of her time on the banana wharf, rather than the sugar landing or the cotton landing, and grasped the fact that her curiosity about Central American products had something to do with Fleex, he was no longer willing to satisfy it. In fact, he blundered so badly that he and Lavinia quarreled, for the first time since the day he had gone to find her in the swampland hide-out.

"Lavinia, you're not serious about this, are you?" he asked, as they sat down to rest on a stringer, after having wandered about for an hour or more, during all of which time Lavinia had been avidly seeking information.

"What do you mean, serious? About what?"

"Well, you're not asking all these questions with the idea that they might help you to find out something about Fleex, are you?"

"Of course I am. Don't you want to find out what's become of Fleex?"

"Not particularly. But even if I did—"

"Don't you want to know whether he's alive or dead, sick or well? There are all kinds of dreadful diseases in those Central American countries, a lot worse than yellow fever in New Orleans. After all, Fleex is your cousin; you and he grew up together almost like brothers. I should think you'd want to know what's happened to him."

"But, Lavinia, we don't even know that he's gone to Central America. We don't know where he's gone. And obviously he doesn't want us to know. If he did, he'd tell us—he'd have told us long ago. And of course we did grow up in the same house, but I—well, I never cared for him the way Clement did, for instance. I never liked the way he acted—especially with girls, if you must know."

"I've always known how he acted with girls. I don't need you to tell me. He didn't act the same way with every girl, either. If you think he acted the same way with me that he did with that Prudence—"

"No, of course I don't think so." Claude was blushing brick red by this time; however, he went on doggedly. "But I don't like the way he acted with *you*, if you must—"

"There isn't any *must* about it. In fact, I'd much rather not listen to all these things you're trying to tell me. What you're not saying, and what you ought to say, if you're so determined on telling the truth, the whole truth and nothing but the truth, is that you were always jealous of Fleex. That's why you didn't care for him as much as poor little Clement, who'd give his eyeteeth to know what's happened to his idol. Not because of anything Fleex did—because of the way you felt. You knew I was in love with him and still you wanted me to get engaged to you."

"Lavinia, I. . . . You couldn't get engaged to Fleex. You couldn't marry him. He saw that, even if you didn't. And I thought you'd get over caring for him. I mean, that's what

232

I thought in the beginning. For a long while after that I thought you *had* got over caring for him. In fact, I thought so until just now. You could have got engaged to me, you still could. You could get engaged to me today. You know I want to marry you more than I want anything else in this world."

"I haven't got over caring for Fleex. I never shall. I wish somehow I could get that into your head. If I could, maybe you'd stop plaguing me to get engaged to you. Maybe you'd even have sense enough to stop wanting to marry me. You don't want to marry a girl who's in love with another man, do you?"

"You could care for me in a different way. You *would* if you'd only give me a chance to show how much I care for you."

"Good heavens, I don't *want* you to show me! Come on, let's go back to the *maisonette*. There's no use sitting here arguing. People are beginning to stare at us. And listen! I don't think there's much sense in your coming down next week. I'm going to the Proteus Ball Monday night, and masking on Mardi Gras and—"

"You're not going out in all those rough crowds alone, are you?"

"Of course not."

"Well, I just couldn't help worrying a little. Because I thought the Labadies were a little too old to go in for that sort of thing any more and—"

"They are. But several of the friends I've made at Sophie Newcomb go in for it. The girls' brothers and other suitable escorts take them. Sometimes their parents as well —the parents aren't all old and decrepit, you know. As a matter of fact, I'm not going masking with any of them though. I'm going with my uncle."

"Your uncle—you mean Mr. Fant?"

"Of course—who else would I mean? He's the only uncle I've got."

"Somehow I don't think of him as your uncle," Claude muttered. "After all, he's only your uncle by marriage, isn't he?"

"Yes, but I don't see what that's got to do with it. Anyway, he's coming down from St. Martinville Monday and the Labadies have invited him to dinner before Proteus. Then Mardi Gras he and I are going masking and to the Rex Ball. But this hasn't anything to do with what I started to say, which was that I think I'll be terribly tired afterward. Besides, my essay on lyric poetry isn't going

233

very well, so altogether I know I'd better spend next Saturday and Sunday either resting up or studying. There must be lots of things you can do in Crowley, even if this is the slack season at the mill. Why don't you find some other girl and make up a foursome with Pierre and Annette?"

"They don't want a foursome, they want a twosome," Claude said despondently. "And that's what I want, Lavinia. *All* I want."

"Oh, let's go home!" she said impatiently, jumping up from the stringer and rapidly threading her way among the casks and barrels and coils of ropes with which the wharf was cluttered. And for once Claude realized that it would be worse than useless to argue with her.

Apparently Jonathan Fant had not felt it was necessary to economize on evening clothes. At all events, when he presented himself at the Labadies' house Monday evening, he was already attired for the ball; and a flowing cape, lined with white satin, which he surrendered to Mignon with an air of nonchalance that commanded her instant admiration and respect, added to the general effect of elegance. He realized he was a little early, he said, as Lavinia came hurrying ino the drawing room to meet him. He did hope he was not *so* early as to cause any inconvenience. Not at all, she assured him, a little breathlessly. To be sure, M. Clisson had not quite finished dressing yet, but that was because he had been delayed by a pupil who insisted on having a lesson, even if it was the day before Mardi Gras—just imagine! And Mlle Haydee had stepped out to the kitchen because, though Mignon was a wonderful cook, she could not *quite* be trusted with the *baba au rhum*. . . . Well, Jonathan could quite understand. A certain ingredient did, automatically, have to go in to the making of a *baba au rhum*—an ingredient with which very few cooks could be trusted, and the more accomplished they were, the less trustworthy, like some persons who belonged in quite different categories. He said all this with a humorous lightness which was a great relief to Lavinia, after the rather heavy going she had had with Claude; and then Jonathan added he must make his eagerness to see her his excuse for arriving so soon. Quite obviously New Orleans agreed with her, he went on, chucking her under the chin and then tilting her head back a little and looking laughingly into her face, before he lowered his eyes and looked, with even greater attention, at the rest of her person. He had always thought she did her

234

hair very well; but now her coiffure was really bewitching! And certainly she had learned a great deal about fashion in a very short time not that the dresses she had run up on the old sewing machine were not creditable, in their way; but this confection she was wearing tonight had real style. Besides, she had the figure to set it off—the figure and the skin. It was all to the good, in his opinion, that she was now showing rather more of the latter than she used to. As he said that, his hands moved from her chin to her neck and from her neck to her shoulders, and came to rest, briefly, on her bosom, before he withdrew them and said it seemed a long time since she had been to St. Martinville. He had been kept there much too closely with his restoring and redecorating and replanting; now that was all done and he could hardly wait to show it to her, though he supposed he would have to, at least until she came home between the third and fourth quarters. Meanwhile, he thought he could break away every now and then and they must see some plays together. It was too bad she had missed *The Marble Heart,* given for the first time in New Orleans just before she reached there—a wonderful play with a title which should have a special appeal for her. Why? Well, wasn't *her* heart marble? Jonathan was sure Claude Villac thought so and he was rather inclined to think so himself. But perhaps there was some secret flame which could be made to glow through alabaster. Why, from the way she was blushing, he believed there was! Would she give him a glimpse of it? There, there, he was talking a lot of nonsense! All he had meant to say was that James O'Neill was an even better actor than Robert Mantell, and that the former would be playing *Monte Cristo* at the Grand Opera House in about two weeks. Jonathan could certainly get down again about that time. Would Lavinia care to see the Dumas play with him? Fine! Well, now that he had looked *her* over, could she show him a little more of this charming house while they waited for their host and hostess? He had enjoyed his first glimpse of it so much that he wanted to see more.

"It's very small. There really isn't very much more to see," Lavinia told him. "And of course we can't go into M. Clisson's room now, as he's still dressing. We'll go through it on our way to dinner in the loggia though, so you'll see it then. In addition to those, besides the drawing room, where we are now, there's just Mlle Haydee's room and the little *cabinet* where I sleep, above it."

"Well, couldn't I see those? You said Mlle Haydee was in the kitchen and you're certainly not sleeping now."

She most assuredly was not. She was feeling very wide awake and happier than at any moment she could remember, more at ease, more relaxed. Jonathan Fant had always given her that feeling, just as he had her aunt Sally —at least, that was certainly the feeling he had given Aunt Sally in the beginning, and it was unfortunate, as well as puzzling, that this had not lasted, just as it was puzzling and unfortunate that there were some people to whom he never seemed to give that feeling. But Lavinia's thoughts did not dwell very long on Aunt Sally, or on any of those other people. She was too wide awake, too happy, too relaxed.

"I don't see why you couldn't," she said. She went over to the door leading into Mlle Haydee's room and knocked. There was no answer, so she waited a minute and then knocked a second time. As there was still no answer, she opened the door and went in. Jonathan Fant followed her.

He glanced around him with obvious appreciation: at the massive half-canopied bed with its matching dressing table and washstand of rosewood, at the tall *armoire à glace*, the *étagère* with its fragile ornaments, and the *garniture de cheminée* on the mantelpiece. "It's all charming," he told Lavinia. "Charming—and complete, except for a *lit de repos*. I'm surprised not to find that here—almost every well equipped Creole bedroom has one."

"This bedroom had one, too. But Mlle Haydee had it moved into the *cabinet* for me. It takes up less room than a regular bed."

"And do you repose well in it, Lavinia?"

"Usually."

"Not always?"

"No, not always."

"Well, of course a *lit de repos* is very narrow. You would be more comfortable, I believe, in a full-sized bed —a very soft, wide one, with large fluffy pillows. That's the sort that is still prepared for Creole brides."

"But I'm not a Creole or a bride, either, you know, Jonathan."

He sighed. "I know. It's rather a pity, too. You wouldn't have a marble heart, if you were a Creole, and you might not be quite so singlehearted, either. But Creole or not, you'd be a lovely bride." His look swept over her again and then he turned, smiling, toward the little staircase.

"Is that the only means of getting to your virgin's bower?"

"It's not a bower. It's a *cabinet*."

"My dear child, don't be so literal. I know what it's called. I've been in this type of house before. Also in one or two old Virginia houses where they have what's called a safe room."

"A safe room?"

"Yes. It doesn't have a door into the hallway—only one into the main bedroom, occupied by the father and mother of the family. The unmarried daughters occupied the safe room. No intruder could reach it, you see, without crossing the parents' room first. At least, that was the theory. But accidents happened sometimes. I heard about one girl who jumped from the window straight into her lover's arms, and about another who received her lover in the room that was supposed to be so safe—he wore moccasins as he went through the connubial chamber and never made a sound. There were other cases, too. I always hoped someone would write a story about them—someone with a real feeling for that sort of thing."

"Why don't you write it?" Lavinia inquired in fascination. "You have the feeling."

"Yes. But not the talent or the drive. It takes both to write books, unfortunately. I'm just a wastrel—they told you that from the beginning."

"Only my grandmother Winslow. And I never believed it."

"Didn't you, my dear? No, I don't think you did. And I'm very glad. But I'm afraid your grandmother Winslow isn't the only one who holds that opinion now." He sighed, but lightly, as he had been speaking. "Well, I've been in one of those safe rooms, but at a time when it was empty, unfortunately. My interest in the house was wholly architectural—or at least was supposed to be. Like my interest in this house, which is even greater, especially as I've never been in one of those *cabinets*. But I've changed my mind. I'm not going to suggest that we should try to go to yours now. Somehow, I don't think the Labadies would feel my interest was wholly architectural or even wholly avuncular."

He put his arm around her and kissed her, just as he had done dozens of times, since he had married her aunt. It had always seemed natural to Lavinia, and to everyone else in the family, that he should caress her in this way, when she was a little girl, and no less natural, at least to her, after she began to grow up. Now, for the first time, she felt there was something different about the embrace. She was not exactly startled, but she was surprised. Jonathan, as if instantly aware of this, let his arm drop without pressing his hand against her waist, and spoke to her with some of the lightness gone from his voice.

"I really believe you are inaccessible, at least for the time being, and I'm glad of it," he said. "As I remarked before, safe rooms have been proven insecure, and bowers are notorious as love nests. But I have great faith that your *cabinet* is inviolable. Don't disappoint me or disprove my words. . . . Come, let's go back to the drawing room. I can hear a door opening somewhere. I'm sure M. Clisson has finished his dressing and that the drawing room is where he'll expect to find us."

Lavinia enjoyed the masking on Mardi Gras and she was thrilled with the performance of O'Neill in *Monte Cristo,* and with the other plays which she and Jonathan saw together in the course of the late winter and early spring. As he had predicted, he managed to "break away" from St. Martinville every now and then, and every time he came to New Orleans he spent at least one evening in Lavinia's company. Apparently, he also managed to visit Crowley occasionally, since when Mary took one of her rare trips to New Orleans, for the opening of the Annual Flower Show, she told her daughter, with an excitement rare to her, that Jonathan had given her a wonderful present.

"I thought you wouldn't accept presents from Jonathan," Lavinia said with the logic which so often proves both exasperating and embarrassing to parents when it comes from their adolescent offspring.

"Not valuable furniture and ornaments," Mary hastened to explain. "That was what he suggested, when he began to do over his house in St. Martinville, you remember. A lady—I mean any woman of refinement—never accepts gifts like that from a gentleman, unless he's closely related to her."

"But Jonathan *is* closely related to us. He's married to your sister—my aunt."

"That isn't close *enough,* Lavinia. Besides, how do I know that Sally may not want some of those beautiful things herself? She hasn't seen them yet. But it's always proper to accept presents of flowers and candy and music and books. Never jewelry or wearing apparel or anything of permanent value."

"I should think some books might have just as much value as a lace scarf or a garnet brooch. . . . Never mind, Mother, I see what you mean. Which of the four things that are proper did Jonathan give you?"

"He gave me a beautiful camellia—one that's just been introduced into this country."

"A blue one?"

"Lavinia, there isn't any such thing as a blue camellia. You know that."

"Oh! I've heard you and Father talking about blue camellias, so I thought—"

"You didn't think any such thing," Mary retorted, her annoyance for once getting the better of her natural calm. "You know we were just using that as a symbol for things we wanted and knew were impossible to get. This is another *pink* camellia—the most beautiful one I've ever seen. It's called Pink Perfection and that's an ideal name for it. We were a little later than we should have been, getting it into the ground, but there were some blooms on the plant when it came and I've had a few more since then. Next year, with any luck at all, there'll be masses of them."

"I'm glad you're so pleased. And I'm glad Jonathan has at last found a present that you'll accept. And I'm glad the camellia's pink. Father doesn't seem to be making much progress these days. So I'm glad he can keep his joke or his symbol or whatever you choose to call it about a blue camellia. . . . Mother, don't you think we ought to be getting started for the Flower Show? Washington Artillery Hall is quite a way from here and we don't want to be late for the opening."

Mary was only too glad to put an end to the conversation by starting for the Flower Show and she thoroughly enjoyed it, from the moment she stepped between the palm trees at the entrance and ascended the staircase lined with various exotic plants remarkable for their foliage. Once in the main hall, the single exhibit, comprising sixteen varieties of ferns, seemed to her most extraordinary; but the giant violets with long stems and large blossoms made an even greater impression on her because of their beauty. She had hitherto not tried to do very much with lilies; now, after seeing the diversity of these displayed, she began to visualize their possibilities for her garden; and she made a mental note to try using the striking effect of crimson American Beauties and snow-white Pearl-de-Jardin side by side.

Owing to the lateness of the season, camellias were not featured, but this did not seem to disappoint her; the thought of the new Pink Perfection which had now been added to the older varieties in her garden, which was awaiting her there, and which was more beautiful than any other she had ever possessed or even seen, up to that time, was completely satisfying to her. Lavinia teased her again, saying she was showing signs of impatience to get home, instead of being eager to stay over for the concert by Gilmore's Famous Band, as she had promised to do. Mary indignantly denied the charge; of course she was going to stay over for the concert; the fame of its new conductor Victor Herbert had already spread to Crowley, and she would not miss hearing him for anything. Or seeing him? Lavinia inquired. Everyone said he was terribly good looking. When the curtain went up at the Grand Opera House, disclosing the handsome young leader with his uniformed corps of musicians effectively grouped around him, Mary readily agreed that, for once, everyone was right. It was almost as thrilling to look at him as to listen to him, especially when he laid aside his baton and appeared as a soloist, playing his violoncello with spirit as well as artistry; his audience quickly succumbed to the spell of his glowing mood. Jonathan, who had again "broken away" from St. Martinville to escort Mary and Lavinia to the concert, began to tease in his turn. They had both fallen for the intriguing young conductor, he said. What would he do with two fallen females on his hands? Take them to the French Market for coffee before you take them home, Lavinia suggested instantly. With a light laugh, he agreed, and continued his banter all the time they were sipping their *café au lait* and eating their sugared doughnuts. When they reached the *maisonette*, he opened a package that he had left there before they started for the concert and took from it a variety of sheet music. It had occurred to him that a pleasant way to bring the evening to a close would be for Lavinia and himself to play some of the selections to which they had listened at the concert; so he had bought several of the arias which had been arranged as duets for the pianoforte. Mary's mood became almost as glowing as Herbert's while she sat listening to a "Minuet" by Scharwenka, a *"Fantasie"* by Servals, "The Shadow Song" from Dinorah and fragments from Grieg's *Peer Gynt*. She had not realized that Lavinia

240

had made such progress, that she could read music of this importance at sight. Or was she reading at sight? Had there been some previous practice in the form of duets, either of these arrangements or of others requiring comparable skill? The thought troubled her vaguely. . . .

He had still one more piece of sheet music in this package, Jonathan said, when he finally rose as if preparing to leave: a "Camellia Polka," composed by Hilmara. He had found it in an old collection which had belonged to his grandmother and which had come to St. Martinville from New York via Philadelphia. There were various other polkas in the collection: a "Flirtation Polka," a "Coquette Polka," a "Pride Polka," a "Picnic Polka," a "Happy Family Polka." Well, of course the first two would not do for Lavinia at all, since she was neither a flirt nor a coquette. (What exactly was the difference between the two? Did she know? He didn't.) The "Happy Family" was obviously still in the future, and though the "Pride" or the "Picnic" might serve the purpose, he had thought the "Camellia Polka" especially appropriate for her mother's daughter. And see, here was another piece that he had almost overlooked—a very short one of quite different origin. He did not know how that one had fallen into his grandmother's hands. He passed it to Lavinia and, leaning over her, read the superscription aloud:

"LA LINDA CAMELIA"
COMPUESTA y DEDICADA a la SRTA. D.ª ADELITA
FONT por JOSE DESIDERIO MACIA
PUBLICADA por EDELMANN y C.ª CALLE de la
OBRA-PIA N.º 12
HABANA

"*Habana, Habana,*" he repeated dreamily, "how much more musical the Spanish name for that city is than ours! We must all go there someday—no doubt the camellias *are* surpassingly lovely there, too. Play '*La Linda Camelia*' for me, Lavinia—that isn't a duet, as you see. Your mother and I will listen. Then, afterward, play the 'Camellia Polka' and perhaps your mother will dance with me."

"What nonsense!" Mary said, flushing. "You know perfectly well I've never danced, in all the years you've known me."

"Well, couldn't you begin again?"

"Of course not. I'm nearly forty, much too old for dancing. And I never danced a great deal, even as a girl. It

241

wasn't as customary in Illinois—our part of Illinois any-how—as it is in Louisiana."

"I see. Well, I'm glad you moved to Louisiana before it was logical that Lavinia's dancing days should begin, because she's a very good dancer. There are some other pieces, not polkas, in the collection that might interest her from that angle and others allied to it—'*Le Souper* Waltz,' 'Midnight Waltz,' 'Reverie,' 'Magic Belle,' 'Romance.' I'll bring those to you some other time, Lavinia. As I said, the camellias seemed especially appropriate for tonight, when your mother's here, but there are lots of other nights. Now go ahead and play for us."

It was very late when he finally took his leave and Mary was silent as she and Lavinia made ready for the night. The narrow *lit de repos* had been removed from the cabinet for the period of Mary's stay, and the bed which Annette and Lavinia had shared, on the occasion of Lavinia's first visit, reinstated for the convenience of mother and daughter. The cramped quarters inevitably encouraged greater intimacy than usually existed between them. When they lay side by side in the darkness, Mary found that she could speak with unwonted freedom.

"You've seen a good deal of Jonathan this winter, haven't you, darling?"

"Not all this last winter. Not until just before Mardi Gras."

"What I really meant was, since you left home. You've seen him fairly often since Mardi Gras, haven't you?"

"Yes. He's been very kind to me."

"You've never thought, have you, that he was a little too kind? That his attentions weren't just prompted by kindness, but by—well, attraction? An attraction that might not be for the best, that might even be dangerous? I mean, he's an older man, a married man, and you're just a young girl. Sometimes. . . ."

"You're not worrying because he gave me those 'Camellia' selections, are you? You said yourself that music was one of the four things—"

"Yes, I know. But there was something about the way he gave you that Spanish piece and talked about going to Havana—"

Lavinia did not answer instantly. Then she said, "Mother, did you ever hear the story about the poor woman who had to go out to work and leave her family of small children behind?"

"I'm not sure which story you have in mind."

242

"This one is about a worried mother who told her children not to put beans up their noses while she was gone. They'd never thought of such a thing. But when she came home that night, they all had beans up their noses."

Again Mary was silent. The relevance of Lavinia's story was all too clear, but she was puzzled as to what she should say or do next. Of course, it was unwise for mothers to put ideas into their children's heads when they were better off without these. On the other hand, how did you guess whether the ideas were already there or not? And if they were there, how could you be sure that the children knew they were dangerous? While she was still turning these questions over in her troubled mind, Lavinia spoke again, with a strangely mature tolerance, as if she were the mother and Mary the daughter.

"Please don't worry, Mother. I do think Jonathan's attractive, as well as kind—in fact, I've never seen but one man that I thought was more attractive. But I happen to be in love with the other man. So, even if Jonathan weren't married and a lot older than I am, and even if his attentions were ever so much more marked than they've been so far, I wouldn't want to encourage him. Not even to the point of an *amitié amoureuse*."

"You know I don't understand French, Lavinia."

Lavinia refrained from saying that it seemed to her there were a number of things her mother did not understand. "I know you don't," she contented herself by replying. "So I'd put it into English if I could have. But it's one of those things you can't translate literally. *Amitié* means friendship and *amoureuse* is loving—the kind of loving that's between sweethearts. But you couldn't say 'enamoured friendship,' could you? It would sound silly."

"Yes, it would. And that kind of a friendship would *be* silly. It would be—"

"Please don't say dangerous again, Mother."

"Very well, I won't. . . . Where did you learn this expression, anyway?"

"I found it in a book. Not one of my schoolbooks. The kind one of your classmates lends you secretly and that you hide under your pillow. But *amitié amoureuse* didn't sound silly to me. It sounded exactly like the kind of friendship I might have enjoyed with Jonathan if I hadn't been in love with Fleex."

"Oh, Lavinia, Fleex has *gone!* He's gone for *good!*"

"Don't you think we'd better try to get some sleep,

243

Mother? Don't you think we've talked long enough without getting anywhere?"

Again Mary found herself forced to confess defeat as far as Lavinia was concerned. She was deeply worried and she prolonged her stay in New Orleans, hoping that she might find another occasion to broach this delicate subject more successfully. But Jonathan did not appear again, Lavinia did not mention either him or Fleex again and no favorable opportunity arose for further discussion. At last she went home, still troubled and still unequal to coping with the causes of her anxiety. She did not guess that Lavinia was equally discouraged and equally troubled. For the hush of Lent had followed the hubbub of Carnival, and Commencement had brought the fourth quarter at Sophie Newcomb to a close and still she had heard nothing from Fleex. Then apologetically, almost timidly, Mlle Haydee told Lavinia that all her pupils and her brother's had left New Orleans now, because the dread season of yellow fever was again at hand; and since it was their custom to close the *maisonette* for the summer and go over to the Pass, they were afraid. . . .

There was no help for it. Lavinia must go home, confessing defeat to herself, if to no one else. She must take her place in the cortege of Annette's buggy wedding, she must stave off Claude's more and more urgent importunities, she must be a dutiful daughter to the parents who had given her so much and to whom, so far, she had given little in return. For the first time, as she watched her father planting the rows of rice in his experimental garden under the hot sun, or bending over his measuring board in the long monotonous evenings, she recognized a kinship with him and his soul's sincere desire which she had not felt before. He also was waiting and searching; to him, as to her, the wait seemed endless, the search vain. With the recognition came a new tenderness and a new tie. But neither sufficed to make her feel she could confide in him or to still the clamor in her heart.

CHAPTER XXIII

Annette's romance was as satisfactory to her family as her cousin Marcelite's had been disappointing; everything about it progressed in the most approved way. Pierre Peret's father made a formal Saturday afternoon call on the Villacs, in the course of which he outlined, without undue reserve, the fine qualities and glowing prospects of his son, and paid ponderous compliments to Annette. The visit was not unexpected, so proper preparations had been made for a company supper, at which Pierre and Annette were placed side by side and, at the end of the evening, he presented her with a picture of himself. Her blushing acceptance of this was regarded as a sign that she considered herself betrothed to him. Next, Pierre, with his father and mother, who had a fine house in Lafayette, met Ursin and Anne at Mr. Krauss' new jewelry store and together they purchased the *alliance* for which Annette's finger had been carefully measured. Then, before it was duly put on in the presence of the assembled relatives, the apparently solid band was pried apart by inserting a thin blade at the almost invisible notch on one side, and it divided to reveal that actually it was made of two narrower bands, indivisibly linked together, one engraved with the initials P. P. and the other with the initials A. V.

"It fits, doesn't it, *chère?*" Mme Peret asked solicitously. "You must be sure to tell us if it doesn't. Mr. Krauss will exchange it for another immediately, even though it has been marked, if it's either too loose or too tight. That's his guarantee with every *alliance* he sells."

"It fits perfectly. I wouldn't exchange it for anything," said Annette, looking down at the *alliance* and then up at Pierre with radiance in her face.

She was so absorbed in both that she forgot it was time for refreshments until she saw that Mezalee was beginning to serve cherry bounce. Then she jumped up, confused and blushing still more deeply, and tried to make amends for her neglect by being especially helpful, and proving to her future mother-in-law that she was going to be a competent housewife and hostess.

As the company sipped cherry bounce, a date for the wedding was discussed and by the time coffee and cake made their appearance, July was decided upon as a propitious time. The younger children would be out of school for the summer by then, and of course they all wanted to take part in the cortege; moreover, the enlargement of the house, a project on which Ursin and Phares had embarked at their joint expense, would be finished; there would be three new rooms, fine for the wedding party. Anne, whose demands were so few and far between, had been saying occasionally, over a period of years, that they really needed a *salle,* now that there were so many courting couples, actual and potential, in the family; and that, since she and Ursin occupied the big front bedroom, it did not seem fair that Phares should indefinitely share one with all the boys who did not sleep in the cramped *grenier,* reached only by a steep outside staircase leading up from the porch. A lesser consideration, but one worthy of being taken into account, was that Mezalee also deserved a certain degree of privacy, in return for her many sacrifices, instead of sharing a chamber with all the younger girls. Moreover, it appeared that Anne had always secretly pined for a house with two front doors, such as adorned the more pretentious Acadian dwellings, though it was only recently that she had made this hidden aspiration known.

Her husband and her cousin agreed between themselves that she should be humored in all these respects; indeed, if Anne had asked for a *salon* as well as a *salle,* and three more bedrooms instead of two, these would have been added; and, once started on their program of expansion, they dismissed frugality from their thoughts, at least as a primary guiding principle, for the first time in their lives. Moreover, since their friends all hastened to give them a *coup de main,* the improvements progressed rapidly. The façade of the house was widened to permit the erection of the *salle,* with its own front door, beside the master bedroom, and back of the latter, two more bedrooms came into being, each with its own chimney piece. Mezalee had always done her best to keep the house clean with brick dust and homemade soap, and the *armoires* sweet smelling with vetivert; but it had been a losing fight with the handicap of overcrowding that existed. Now her patient industry was at last rewarded and her high standards realized. As the kitchen and bedrooms became less cluttered, it was easier to reach into all the corners with her broom and to scrub the floors to bone whiteness; and the new quarters were soon the object of studied and prideful adornment. No longer were paper flowers, chromos of the Sacred Heart, and photographs depicting various members of the family at the time they married or made their First Communion, the only embellishments the house could boast. There were mirrors over the chimney pieces, hand-painted vases, *veilleuses* and loudly ticking clocks on the mantelshelves. A step forward had been taken in the direction of interior decorating—not as elaborate, of course, as if they had had a company *salon* as well as a family *salle*—designed not only to keep abreast of the family's ever-increasing prosperity, but of its corresponding progress in culture.

This did not mean, however, that any of the time-honored customs connected with an approaching marriage were abandoned. Carding parties, at which the guests prepared the cotton for gaily striped blankets, became the order of the day, to assure Annette the traditional twelve of these in her trousseau; and the results were striking, for sometimes as many as twelve different colors appeared on a blanket in inch-wide woven stripes. Rugs, bedspreads and curtains were also busily prepared, and the most solicitous attention of all was given to the bride's wearing apparel, which all her friends and relations had a part in fashioning. When the great day came, everything she put on for her marriage, except her net veil and her crown of artificial flowers, was the product of their loving hands.

When the first wedding guests arrived, however, she was still in her oldest workaday clothes, ostensibly oblivious of the reason for their presence. Not until Anne, with equal ostentation, reminded her that she was about to be married and that it was high time she began to dress for the ceremony, did she stop washing dishes and sweeping floors. Then all the young girls who had come to the house flocked around her, offering her superfluous pins to stick in her lace-trimmed undergarments and white silk dress—pins which they would reclaim, as soon as the ceremony was over, on the theory that this would bring them good luck in getting husbands themselves. They were so insistent and so vociferous about these talismans that it was only after several efforts that Annette escaped and went into the *salle* to kneel for her father's blessing, and listen to the homily which he solemnly pronounced on her duty to her husband and to the children she would bear him.

The Perets had come over from Lafayette the evening before, to spend the night with the Winslows, and there had been dancing of *rondes,* singing of ballads and general merrymaking at Phares' house until the wee small hours. No one got much sleep or expected to have it. By early morning, the yard was filled with buggies, and when the procession started from the house to the church, there were nearly thirty of these in line, Annette and Ursin in the first, Anne and Mr. Peret in the second, Mrs. Peret and Phares in the third, and Pierre, with Claude, who was to be head groomsman, in the fourth. Lavinia and Odile were the bridesmaids, Pauline the flower girl, Clement the page and all the bride's brothers the groomsmen. Some of the buggies were filled to overflowing. Odey, Onezime and Olin squeezed onto a single narrow seat, Marcelite and Alcée had their two children with them, and many of the guests managed to make room for more numerous offspring. Though this multiple occupancy reduced the number of buggies somewhat, every foot of space was taken on the two long rails at right angles to the church where horses were hitched; and dozens of townspeople, who had not gone out to the prairie before the ceremony but had come to the church on foot, were waiting at the door to see the cortege arrive and were shouting to each other in a vain attempt to make themselves heard above the clamoring of the bell. Inside, the pew of the little mission chapel proved entirely inadequate to accommodate such a throng; the side aisles were full of standees and it was with difficulty that the central one was kept clear for the bridal party to advance to the altar.

When the ceremony was over, the order of precedence for the occupants of the buggies was changed, for Annette and Pierre, as the newly wedded pair of course rode together, as did the father and mother of both bride and groom, and Claude, without the necessity of maneuvering, became Lavinia's logical escort. Never, since the disappearance of Fleex, had he seen her in so blithe a mood. She had entered fully into the spirit of the *ronde* dance and ballad singing the night before and he was ready to hazard a guess that she had taken an equally merry part in the morning's pin sticking, for, through the thin partition that divided the *salle* from the girls' bedroom, he had recognized her voice in the midst of the babel. He decided to ask her whether he had been mistaken or not when they were on their way home that night, if her gaiety did not wear thin in the course of the long day that was ahead of them. To be sure, she still looked delightfully fresh, as well as bewitchingly pretty, though he doubted whether she had been to bed at all; but the bridal dinner and the bridal ball were yet to come. As the house of the Lafayette Perets was too distant for practical purposes, as far as these festivities were concerned, the groom's aunt and uncle Peret, who lived in Crowley and had the largest house there, had offered to open this for the occasion. The feasting would go on for hours and hours, that was certain; and countless healths would be drunk, countless cakes cut and countless songs sung before the ball began. Then Annette would have to dance with every male guest, or offense would be taken; and every married woman, as

248

well as every young girl, would have her turn on the floor. It would be midnight at least before Pierre and Annette would manage to slip away to the new little cottage that was in readiness for them. As the day wore on, Claude felt no surprise because his sister was standing up so well to a celebration which was something of an endurance test; after all, it was part of their tradition and he had seen many another Cajun girl do it before. But he realized that however much Lavinia might enjoy occasional participation in such observances, the exhilaration she derived from this one might not be lasting.

He need not have worried. Again she seemed to take the keenest interest and feel the keenest pleasure in everything that was happening; and though she, too, danced with every male guest and it was, indeed, well after midnight before she and Claude left the Perets' house, she still looked as fresh as when they had started out that morning, and she kept singing snatches of the old song which had brought the banqueting to an end with all the convivialists joining in:

> *"J'ai promis dans mon jeune age*
> *De ne jamais me marier.*
> *Aujourd'hui je trouve l'avantage;*
> *Mes parents l'ont conseillé."*

Unrebuked, he put his arm around her shoulder. "Will I get pricked if I come too close?" he inquired, with a light-heartedness he had never before felt in her presence.

"You might. I managed to get quite a lot of pins. Do you think it's worth risking?"

"I do, for true."

"All right. But don't blame me then."

Cautiously, though with increasing courage, he lowered his arm and tightened his grasp. Evidently, the pins, if they really were secreted about her person, were not so placed as to interfere with this pleasant progress, and Lavinia herself did nothing to hinder it.

"I love to hear you sing," he murmured in a voice of great contentment. "And I've always liked that tune. But the words are pretty silly, aren't they?"

"I hadn't thought. Just like you, I think the tune's nice. . . . What words do you think are silly?"

"About promising myself in my youth that I wouldn't ever marry. Annette never made herself any such promise—she's been dead set on getting married for ages. I bet

249

most girls don't do anything of the kind. You never did, did you, honey?"

"No, I never did."

A different note had suddenly crept into her voice. *No, Claude said to himself, you didn't, because you thought you were going to marry Fleex. But you've begun to stop thinking about that—you must have.*

"Do you think the rest of the verse is silly, too?" Lavinia asked. "The lines where the girl says she's decided to act on her parents' advice?"

"No, I think that part's very sensible."

His spirits were soaring again. *Lavinia's begun to realize she might as well listen to Mr. and Mrs. Winslow*, he told himself triumphantly. *She wouldn't have mentioned those lines about parents' advice if she hadn't.* And Lavinia went on singing:

> *"La ceinture que je porte*
> *Et l'anneau d'or que j'ai au doigt*
> *C'est mon amant qui me les donne*
> *Pour finir ses jours avec moi."*

"But you aren't wearing a gold ring, Lavinia. I wish you were. Because that part of the song isn't silly, either."

"No. It's all right to wear one—when the time comes."

When the time comes! Then she did still think it might come! His arm slid to her waist and closed firmly around it. She laughed.

"I *am* wearing a belt, you know, even if it wasn't given me by my sweetheart. And you'd better be careful."

The warning came just too late. He had pricked himself hard. Instinctively, he whipped away his arm and sucked his bleeding finger. But when Lavinia laughed again, he did, too.

"Even if I didn't give you a belt, '*J'ai passé devant ta porte,*'" he said, quoting another old song, "couldn't you put that pin somewhere else?"

She felt for it cautiously and, after she had drawn it out, held it up for him to see in the moonlight. Then she tossed it over the side of the buggy.

"I still have enough left for good luck," she said and added, "anyway, I didn't want to be the next to get married."

"No, but you'll get married sometime soon."

"I suppose so."

He put his arm around her waist again. There were no more pins in her belt. He took up the refrain of the song

250

where she had left off and then switched to *"La Noce de Josephine."* Singing it together, they went on home.

Anne had admonished the members of her family, both individually and collectively, that they were not to talk to the Perets about the state of her health; if the latter noticed that her skin was a queer color, of course that could not be helped; but she hoped they would lay it to a naturally poor complexion. They were not so dull witted as to do this, nor had it been possible to curb Dr. Mouton's tongue as completely as those of Anne's husband, her children and her cousins. But the Perets respected her wishes; they said nothing to indicate that they realized the almost superhuman effort she was making, or that they feared she might collapse before the long-drawn-out festivities were finally over. Ursin, whose own fears on that score were more acute, watched over her with pride in her fortitude and dread of its consequences; but though she made no further effort to stay up or even to get up after the wedding, it was not until weeks later that he saw a noticeable change in her. When this happened, he made a hesitant suggestion.

"Dr. Mouton, he ain't helpin' you none, Anne. I think it's time we got in a *traiteur*. Maybe neither he wouldn't help none, no, but it don't do no harm if at least we try, us."

In the absence of an immediate and violent objection, Ursin guessed, and rightly, that Anne had entertained a similar idea herself, but that, for some reason, she had been hesitant about voicing it.

"I ain't never hear about no *traiteur* here'bout, me, no," she said finally. "Where you goin' find one, out here on the prairie?"

"Nobody don't have to look on no prairie, them, for no *traiteur*, no more than you got to look for a doctor. There's *traiteurs* in Mermentau an' also in Crowley, too, same as in plenty other towns, I guarantee you, me!"

"You know one so you could call his name?"

"Sho'! Archange Blanchet."

"Archange . . . that's a good name for true."

"From what I hear, he's plenty good, him."

"Well, I guess I give you right. Go see will he come. Like you say, mebbe he don't help, but neither the doctor did, him, so it wouldn't do no harm, no."

Ursin went to Mermentau the next day and brought Archange Blanchet back to the farm with him. The healer had come willingly enough. He was an emaciated old

Negro with a benign countenance, a snowy, abundant head of hair and snowy, abundant whiskers; his manner was respectful, his speech hushed. After entering Anne's room and talking to her with gentleness while looking at her intently and making the sign of the cross, he beckoned to Ursin and withdrew to the kitchen, meanwhile taking a small bundle, which proved to contain herbs, from its place of concealment on his person. He would need a frying pan, some water and some salt, he announced, still speaking almost in a whisper. Mezalee was nowhere to be seen. She had so greatly disapproved of this visitation that she had actually refused to have anything to do with it and failed, for the first time in her docile and dedicated life, to lend a helping hand. Claude, who might likewise have raised objections, was at the rice mill and the younger members of the family at school; there was something desolate about the vacancy and silence of the kitchen, which was usually the scene of such lusty and noisy good cheer. Ursin had no difficulty in locating the one simple utensil Archange had requested or in supplying the salt and water, and he was glad, rather than otherwise, not to have Claude present; but he was upset by Mezalee's attitude, as well as her absence, and his disquiet persisted as he watched Archange bending over the hearth and adding herbs from his bundle to the boiling water while making cabalistic signs and murmuring to himself. Ursin was still more alarmed when the *traiteur* finally lifted off the fire the frying pan, from which the contents had now partly boiled away, and poured what remained into the cloth which had formed the bundle.

"W'at you goin' do?" Ursin inquired abruptly, as the *traiteur* started back toward the sickroom, carrying the bundle with him.

"S-s-sh, not so loud! Ah's just goin' to have the patient pass this over where she got the most pain."

"It'll burn her! It'll hurt like fire from hell!"

"It ain't goin' do no such thing. Don' you interfere with me now, man! Iffen you do, the spell be broke."

Ursin said no more, but kept close beside Archange, prepared to act quickly. Anne herself made no objection when the *traiteur* handed her the steaming bundle and told her to rub it over her body, under the bedclothes. Ursin saw her wince once or twice, but she did not cry out and no tears had come to her eyes when, after a few minutes, she handed the bundle back to the *traiteur,* who set it down beside the bed.

"You pass it over a couple times mo' an' then hol' it still

252

till it gets col'," he told her. "Ah goin' leave you now. But Ah goin' give you some string to hol' in you' han'. You got to slip it through you' fingers an' every time you comes to a knot, you got to stop an' say a prayer. Which you want, a string with three knots for the Trinity or a string with seven knots for the Saciments?"

"A string with seven knots," Anne answered.

Ursin did not like the sound of her voice; she spoke with clenched teeth, as though she were in pain. She *is* burnt, she *is* in pain, he thought to himself; but he did not dare to say it aloud, for fear of breaking the spell. He drove the *traiteur* back to Mermentau and, on his return, was confronted by Mezalee, who had emerged from her hiding place, wherever that had been, and who spoke to him angrily and reproachfully.

"She's suffering, she's blistered. I've given her some of Dr. Mouton's medicine, the kind that makes her drowsy, and when she's asleep, I'm going to put some cloths, soaked in oil, on her body. I'm going to tell her that's part of the treatment—I won't say *whose* treatment. And I'll let her keep her string—for now, anyway. She's pretending it's a kind of rosary, and I suppose there's no great harm in that. But I'm going to start saying novenas for her in the hope that good will overcome evil. But don't you dare have that *traiteur* here again! What he did to her was almost exactly what he'd have done to a horse with the colic—except for the string, of course!"

On his return from the rice mill, Claude added his expressions of displeasure to Mezalee's; but Ursin needed no further reproaches; he was troubled enough without them, though Anne seemed to feel no resentment over what had happened. Indeed, she declared that the blisters amounted to nothing, that they would heal presently—as indeed they did—and that they were a sign the disease had been "drawn out," where it could be seen and exorcised, instead of doing its evil work inside her. She lay in bed, contentedly fingering the knotted string and declaring that she was certainly better. Ursin tried to tell himself that it had not been a mistake to send for the *traiteur* after all and, for a time, buoyed up by Anne's attitude, he very nearly succeeded. It was not until several more weeks had passed that she said anything which could be interpreted as an admission of renewed pain and increasing weakness.

"I don' see how I'm goin' to get to Lacombe for *Toussaint*," she finally told him. "I been studyin' on it an' I just know I can't make it. You'll have to go without me, *cher*."

"If you ain't goin', I ain't goin', either," Ursin said stubbornly. "I ain't leavin' you, when you're all that sick, not for *Toussaint* nor either nothin' else."

"Ursin, we ain't never missed once, us, all these years."

"I know. But I guess a time got to come to everybody when they misses. It ain't like we didn't have no relations right there, either, which they could look after things for us."

"We got no relations right there no more, us, no. Slidell is plenty far from Lacombe."

"Why, Anne, it ain't only a few miles, I guarantee it."

"That's too far for 'em to keep close watch of the candles an' such. An', anyway, they got their own tombs, them, to look after, ain't they?"

He tried to make a feeble jest. "Their own tombs? How you mean their, *hein?*"

Well, he knew what she meant well enough, Anne said, her voice rising in the sudden temper that had so often flared up when she was young and strong, but which so seldom made itself felt in these days. Ursin answered sharply, not because he was angry, too, but because he was deeply worried, and did not know how else to make her understand that nothing would induce him to be absent from her for three days, which, at the very least, was what a trip to Lacombe would mean. Anne interrupted him.

"You know, Ursin, don't you, I ain't thinkin' just about my people's graves no mo'? I'm thinkin' 'bout my own, too."

"Now, *chère*—" he began, the sharpness all gone from his voice. Anne interrupted him again.

"It don't help none, not no mo', no, to be pretendin', Ursin. Not between you an' me, leastways. To other people, we got to keep on pretendin'. I got to give you right on that, yes. But husban' an' wife, that's different. So: the two of us, you an' me, knows real good I ain't got much mo' time to live, me, an' even if we ain't talked too much about it biffo' now, you bound to know I want to be buried in some real cemetery, an' not in no hole somebody digs in the prairie, no. With Adeline it wasn't like that; you got to admit it. She done buried three little children, her, there on that prairie, an' I feel in my heart, me, she wanted to be close to where they was at, yes. But thank God all our children is livin' an' healthy like anything. So when your time comes, like it's got to come some day, Ursin, you an' me will be all two together in a fine tomb, an' not some place where maybe it ain't even consecrated ground."

"Phares says Father Vialetton come on purpose—"

"Sho' I know, me. But you bound to admit he never come 'til he could get to come, an' the way it was, ridin' all over like he had to do, him, he couldn't always get to some places on time, no. You got to remember how he was late marryin' Marcelite an' Alcée, even when they had plenty-plenty more missions around by that time."

"No, I ain't forgot." Ursin spoke shortly. Even in the midst of his concern for his wife, he could not help betraying the resentment he still harbored over the tardiness of that marriage.

"I guarantee you, me, he was sorry, but sorry don't help nothin', no, after something's done happened. Sure, I know Adeline an' Phares baptized the babies their own selves, them, when Father Vialetton couldn't come. But Fleex let it out one time, an' even if Phares ain't never said it was true, him, I tell you frankly it's bound to be so, how biffo' the ground got consecrate' by the priest, a storm blew down two of the little crosses an' they ain't never been sure, them, if the new ones was put up right."

"They got a real for-true cemetery in Crowley now, them," Ursin reminded her. But he knew before she answered that the reminder was useless.

"You mean to tell me, you, an' right to my face, even, you think that's some real cemetery, *hein?* A place where they buries Protestants an' snow-diggers right side by each with good Cath'lic Cajuns, even? A place where they got no family tombs, no, not even the first one, them, only just graves an' markers an' like that? I been to see it with my own two good eyes, me, with weeds all around an' no sign of whitewash or anything even for *Toussaint,* no! I couldn't rest easy in no such place, me, an' you got to give me your promise, right now, biffo' God His own self, you won't never-never bury me in no Crowley cemetery."

"All right, I promise—if you should be the one to die first."

"You know good in your heart I'm goin' die first, me. An' you also know real good I got plenty other reasons for not wantin' nobody to bury me on no prairie or no imitation cemetery like that Crowley place. I want to be with my own people, people I got a right to be proud of an' I am proud of."

"Yes, I know. I promise, Anne."

He took her hand and, for a few minutes, they both sat silent. Then Ursin cleared his throat and made a hesitant suggestion: if Anne did not think their family relations at

Slidell could look after the family lot to suit her, on *Toussaint,* would she let Claude try to do it? He had been going with them to the cemetery year after year, ever since he was a little boy. They had taken him even when he was a baby. He would have to do these things when they were both dead and gone. Perhaps it would be just as well if he began now.

Ursin braced himself against another outburst, but it did not come. Anne lay back on her pillows and appeared to be pondering his suggestion without actual antagonism. When she finally answered, she spoke with comparative mildness.

"You suppose he could get off from the mill, him?" she inquired.

"Positive, I guarantee you, me! Not to go to some dance, maybe, no, or like that. I know they says Tibier is a slave driver, him, an' he sure works his men hard, hard. But he is also the kind of man what understands how you feel, yes, if somebody explains. An' Claude could easy do that. Claude got a pleasant way to speak, him."

"That pleasant speakin' never got him all that far with Lavinia."

"You ain't grievin' on that, no, are you, Anne?"

"Sho' I am. Claude's a one-girl boy, him. I want to see him married an' happy like he got a right to be."

She did not add, "before I die," but Ursin knew what was in her mind. It was in his mind, too. He sighed and turned from his wife, who was apparently beginning to feel the soothing effects of the medicine Dr. Mouton had left for her earlier in the day, and which Ursin himself had been giving her, according to instructions. When he was satisfied that she was sleeping, he crossed the floor quietly and closed the door leading from their bedroom to the porch after him. Then he went straight out into the yard. Claude, who rode back and forth to the mill every day, had just unsaddled his horse and was coming toward the house. His father stopped him.

"Your *maman* ain't feelin' so good," he said. "No, don' go in right now. I think she's fixin' to get a little nap. But she's been talkin' to me 'bout *Toussaint.* She say she ain't goin' be able to go to Lacombe this year, her, no, an' I tell you frankly, me, I ain't about to leave her an' go no place without her. Not me. So you got to go, Claude, an' you got to tell Tibier right away, him, how you got to be away three days, startin' October 30th."

"Of course, I'll go if that's what you and *Maman* want. And I'll tell Tibier right away. He won't be too glad, I expect—that's one busy time at the mill. But never mind. I'll go anyway." Claude spoke with the confidence of one who was making good at his job and who knew he would be hard to replace. "Who's going with me?"

"I expec' you got to go alone by you'self, yes. Annette can't leave her husban', not right after they got married, an' neither Pierre would have the same reason to leave the bank like you would the mill. Odile can't get away from Gran' Coteau, no—them nuns is plenty strict 'bout vacations; an' the others is all too young, them, to help an', anyway, they in school, too."

"Yes, that's so. Well, I sort of hate to go alone, but I guess there's no help for it."

He's thinking what a grand thing it would be if Lavinia would go with him, Ursin said to himself. *I hope he doesn't tell her that though—it would just give her another chance to turn him down and she's done that half a dozen times already. If I was in his shoes, I wouldn't even ask her to go to a picnic in the woods or for a boat ride on the Mermentau River. But I suppose he will, the young fool. I suppose he'll go right on asking for sorrow. . . .*

Ursin was right in one respect: the young fool did go right on asking for sorrow. But in another respect, he was wrong. Lavinia did not turn Claude down. She said she would be glad to go to Lacombe with him.

CHAPTER XXIV

He was almost stunned by the readiness of her answer. The request had represented a forlorn hope, based not only on her sympathy for his mother or her friendship for him, but on her appreciation of the unusual, the picturesque and the spectacular, whether the form it took was grave or gay. He had never forgotten the expression on her face during the Procession of the Lilies, which took place every year at Grand Coteau on the Feast of the Immaculate Conception, when the pupils, all dressed in white, wearing filmy veils on their heads and carrying lilies in their hands, marched two by two through the gallery of the main building into the chapel and placed their lilies in vases before the altar, saying, as they did so, "O Mary, I give you the lily of my heart. Be thou its guardian forever." Lavinia had never shown the slightest sign of a leaning toward Catholicism; yet not one of her schoolmates had had as rapt an expression during the service, or had pronounced the dedicatory words with as much feeling as she did. The same intensity, the same fervor had marked her singing and her manner on the occasion of the May Crowning of the Virgin and Claude had noticed much the same evidences of emotion on several other occasions. Apparently, there was something within her that cried out for release and that found it only when she was temporarily a part of some experience alien to the well-ordered but unstimulating life that she normally led. There was nothing in Crowley which even remotely resembled the celebration of *Toussaint* at Lacombe; as far as that went, there was nothing like it even in New Orleans, where every cemetery was a mass of bloom on that occasion, and people went in droves to visit among the tombs of their departed relatives, whom they did not seem to think of as dead on this Holy Day of Obligation. Claude had heard that, in Barataria, where the lights in the cemeteries were reflected in the Bayou des Oies, and the people, led by their priests, circulated, singing, among their newly whitewashed tombs all night, the spectacle was an unforgettable one and he could well believe it. Still he did not see how it could have the same supernal quality as the one at Lacombe, where the graveyards, large and small, were secluded in the forests, and you came to a lighted clearing when you least expected it, if you did not know your way, or caught a fleeting glimpse of radiance, which made you think of *feu follets*, somewhere in the distance. . . .

Of course Lavinia knew about *Toussaint* in Lacombe: she had heard the Villacs and the Primeaux talk about it for years, both before and after the annual pilgrimages made by Ursin and Anne. But these conversations had been incidental; they had never been prompted by a purpose. Now, as Claude talked about the glow of sunset behind the pine trees, and the eerie effect of mystery, created by the oncoming dusk, and the first intermittent glimmerings of light, widening to brilliancy, in the dark forest, he dwelt on details never mentioned before and became preternaturally eloquent in his descriptions. But he did not and could not believe that anything he said would really be effective, when Lavinia interrupted him.

"I'd like very much to go," she said simply.

"You would!"

"Yes. I've always wanted to, ever since I first heard about it. But you never asked me before."

He stared at her, too astonished to speak. Here was something Lavinia had wanted to do for years, something

258

that he could have made it possible for her to do, and he had never even thought of such a thing. He had failed to have her with him, he had missed seeing her excitement and her wonderment, all through his own stupidity.

"Of course, I've an added reason for wanting to go now," she went on. "Naturally, your mother would feel badly to have you go alone and there doesn't seem to be anyone else who could go with you." He wished, momentarily, that she had said, "naturally, *you* don't want to go alone," but his tinge of regret because she thought of his mother and not of him was swallowed up in his sense of rejoicing, because she actually was going, for whatever reason. Then she said something that put a sudden damper on his joy.

"I'm going back to New Orleans in a few weeks and —"

"You're going back to New Orleans!"

"Yes. Mother's willing and she's talked Father into being willing, too. The danger from yellow fever is practically over already—there wasn't much of it this year anyhow—and Mlle Haydee has invited me to come and stay at the *maisonette* again and go on with my music lessons. I may take another special course at Sophie Newcomb, too—that isn't decided yet, nor how long I'm going to stay. But what I started to say was, when you interrupted me, that you could come to the Labadies'—I'm sure they'd be delighted to have you again—and spend the night. Then we could take a morning train for Slidell—there is a morning train, isn't there?—and have dinner with your family there before we went on to Lacombe. What's their name? Bachemin? Well, the Bachemins would be glad to have us for dinner, wouldn't they? And to have us spend the night, too? And I suppose they'd lend us a horse and buggy to go to Lacombe?"

"Of course," Claude said, over and over again, in answer to her questions. He could not find the words to say anything else. He was still too stupefied. He had thought it would be so hard, and it had been so easy. Perhaps there were other aspects of his relationship to Lavinia which were not as hopeless as he had begun to fear they were. Perhaps everything would come out all right after all, and not in the dim distant future, either. Very soon. He began to believe that Lavinia did love him, but did not realize it yet. From there, it was easy to take the next step and believe that she did realize it, that it was he who had been lacking in understanding and perception.

The following weeks were the happiest in his life; even

his mother's decreasing strength and increasing pain made little impression on him, partly because Anne saw to it that he was, as far as possible, kept unaware of both; and partly because his absorption in Lavinia crowded everything else from his consciousness. He was working long hours at the rice mill, twelve hours a day or more all of the week except Sunday; and the only reason he was not working on Sundays, too, was because Mr. Tibier, unlike the managers of most rice mills, thought such labor contrary to the biblical injunction to keep holy the Sabbath day. But Claude managed to see Lavinia, two or three times a week, late in the evening, and Sundays he was free to spend wholly with her. All through the golden weather of early autumn, they went on outings together: bicycle parties to the Crowley Pumping Plant; boating trips on Bayou Nezpiqué; visits to the springs at Pointe-aux-Loups; picnics in the woods near Lake Arthur; excursions down the Mermentau River to the lake itself on the *Agnes T. Parks,* which they jokingly called a yacht, but which was really a rice barge. To be sure, all these outings were made in groups and not in the solitude *à deux* which Claude craved; but he was spending more and more time in Lavinia's company, and occasionally he did succeed in detaching her from the party, even though all such groups were chaperoned with care. At such times, she nearly always seemed gay and friendly, as she had on the night of Annette's wedding, though she adroitly evaded caresses and pleasantly changed the subject when it showed signs of leading toward topics she was unready to discuss. But Claude told himself, with increasing lightheartedness, that at last he was making progress.

Even after Lavinia went to New Orleans, he continued, by taking night trains, to be with her almost weekly; and he lived from one meeting to the next. She never again suggested going to the waterfront, and he told himself, with growing conviction, that she had really forgotten about Fleex at last; moreover, to his immense satisfaction, she had not resumed her courses at Sophie Newcomb; instead, beside her music and French lessons with Mlle Haydee, she was continuing her study of art with a private teacher. This seemed to Claude an infinitely less binding arrangement than a connection with a college. Once having started on a course, naturally anyone would want to finish it; but private lessons could be terminated at any time, for any sound reason—an engagement, for instance. A short engagement. He told himself that probably Lavinia herself had such an easy termination in mind, when she decided on private lessons instead of college courses.

Naturally, Tibier grumbled when Claude asked for extra leave. But a second rice mill was under construction in Crowley now, and a rumor had reached the ears of the grim old manager of the Columbia that the promoters of this second mill had already made Claude a tentative offer. Tibier was afraid this was true, especially as Jim Garland was one of the stockholders; Claude was too efficient, too faithful and too reliable for Tibier to dare run the risk of losing him. Grudgingly, the man let his employee go.

Claude arrived in New Orleans on October 30th in time to take Lavinia out to dinner at Antoine's. The next morning he rose and went to Mass and Communion. When he returned to take her to the train, there was a new quality in the sense of exaltation which had pervaded his being ever since she had agreed to make the pilgrimage with him.

They reached the home of his maternal uncle Cénas Bachemin in comfortable time for the ample dinner that had been provided for them, and Claude could see that Lavinia was making a favorable impression on his mother's family from the very first. She had enjoyed the two-hour trip from New Orleans immensely, she said: the fishing boats on the Lake had fascinated her and the drawbridge had been up, to let a schooner loaded with charcoal through—another novel and intriguing sight. And what a beautiful garden the Bachemins had! She hoped her mother, who had much greener thumbs than she did—she held up her pretty hands for inspection and shook her head dolefully—could come and see it sometime. Her mother's garden was very large now and had lots and lots of roses and camellias—different kinds—in it; but it didn't have sassafras. Good filé was hard to get in Crowley, and as for that delicious drink, sarsaparilla, they never had it at home. Lavinia could not remember when anything had tasted so good to her as this beverage that Mrs. Bachemin was serving with dinner. Would it be possible to put some in bottles and take it home, or wouldn't it last that long? Wonderful! Some for the Labadies, some for the Winslows, some for the Primeaux and Villacs. . . . Lavinia would not be at all surprised if this sarsaparilla drink did Mrs. Villac a world of good.

The Bachemins had already been over to Lacombe, they assured Claude; he would find everything in order at the family lot—ground cleared, tombs whitewashed, candles in place. They would not go again that evening; but the buggy would be brought around at four—why, it was almost that now! They were sure Claude could manage all right without them. Though Cénas spoke in a grave tone, appropriate for the discussion of tombs, he could not refrain from giving Claude a knowing look, behind Lavinia's back; and when Claude responded with a smile, Cénas permitted himself to wink.

The sun was still fairly high in the heavens when the buggy was brought around. Without questioning him, Lavinia allowed Claude to help her into it; but when, almost immediately after starting, he took an abrupt right-angle turn in the road and headed toward Lacombe, she looked at him inquiringly.

"I thought you said the grave lighting didn't start until dark."

"Just dark, not good dark. We'd best start now if we aim to see the beginning. And anyway, I thought you seemed interested when I told you that the sunsets here are kind of special when you see them through the pines. But I don't need to tell you they don't last all that long."

"No. Mother's often said one of the things she misses most in Louisiana is the long twilights."

"She doesn't miss the long winters though, does she?" Claude inquired with a grin. He thought he had probably scored there. But he was mistaken. It was certainly hard, he reflected, to score with Lavinia.

"Yes, she does. It's only on Father's account that she's glad of the milder climate. Of course, she'd be glad of anything that was good for him, or helpful to him in any way. But she says she used to love the cold darkness closing in, after the long twilight, and the sense of being snug and secure, in a warm room, after the chores were done, no matter how freezing it was outside. Sometimes she'd go to the kitchen door and open it for a minute, not just to get a breath of fresh air, but to have an added feeling of coziness and comfort afterward. I can remember her doing it, too. I don't remember many things about Illinois, but there are a few that are still very vivid to me and that's one of them. Besides, I've often heard her talk about it, since. I think she's still a midwesterner at heart."

"I believe you are, too."

"What makes you say that? How do you know what midwesterners are like, anyway?"

"Good Lord, Crowley's full of them, isn't it? Full of people who *were* midwesterners and only came south because they thought they'd better themselves by doing it, not for any love of Louisiana—just the way your father did."

"Don't you dare say anything against my father! He's one of the most intelligent, hard-working, persevering men that ever lived. If it hadn't been for him and men like him—"

"I didn't say anything against your father. I know he's a wonderful man. I only—"

"What about the people who were trying to sell the land that was going begging and the 'house lots' in a city that didn't even exist? They couldn't get anyone in Louisiana to take them as a gift! If it hadn't been for the midwesterners they'd have been ruined—their great 'real estate' venture would have been a complete washout. I'd like to know if *they* weren't trying to better themselves, when they put all those ads in our weekly papers!"

As usual, Lavinia's reasoning was all too sound. She had not lost her temper, as Claude's mother still sometimes did, in a way that made her lose her head as well. She was angry, but it was the sort of anger which only served to increase the clarity and conviction with which she was always able to argue a point. Claude, who had built his hopes on the supposition that at last he had found an occasion which would lend itself to romance, rather than logic, did not even try to retort. He was too discouraged. For a few moments, they jogged along in silence, and when Claude glanced surreptitiously in Lavinia's direction, he noticed that her cheeks were somewhat flushed and that her lips were set in a straight line. The flush was becoming and inviting; but the expression of her mouth was forbidding. There was nothing about it to suggest that it might yield to a kiss, much less respond to one. And a kiss on her cheek was not what he wanted. . . .

It was Lavinia who broke the strained silence and, when she did so, she slipped her arm through his and drew a little closer to him. The effect of this unexpected gesture was so heady that it took a minute or two for Claude to recover enough to answer her next remark collectedly.

"There it is! The lovely light you told me about! Oh, Claude, it · is beautiful—that crimson sky behind those dark pines. I'm glad we came!"

"You mean—just so we could see that light?"

"No, of course not. We're going to see lots of other things, too, aren't we?"

She withdrew her arm and his excitement slackened, his soaring spirits fell. So that was all it was, still, as far as

263

Lavinia was concerned. They had not come to be together, they had not come to share a magic spell. Well, he might have known it was merely her usual response to the stimulating, the exotic. . . .

"Yes," he said flatly, "we're going to see lots of other things, too. We'll see groups of people starting for the cemeteries any moment now, walking along the road and carrying their candles and their flowers."

He had hardly finished speaking when just such a group came into view around a bend. As these people were walking in the same direction as the buggy, only their backs were visible. But presently another group appeared, coming from the opposite direction, their faces in plain view beneath their scarves and hats. A few, who were bareheaded, had straight black hair and Lavinia asked an interested question.

"You said these people were Indians?"

"I said many of them were part Indian. There was a Choctaw settlement here before there were any whites, or any blacks, either. There aren't many purebred Indians left though."

"Then nearly all these poor people are crossbreeds?"

"I suppose so."

"That has a sad side to it, hasn't it?"

"Yes it has. They won't go to the Negro schools or the Negro churches. That was a Negro church we passed, just a few minutes ago. Probably you didn't notice it. There was no reason why you should have. There wasn't a light in it."

"So the people who go there bring their lights here instead?"

"You could put it that way. . . . We may as well follow the ones ahead of us and turn in at that wood road they're taking. It's sure to lead to a cemetery."

The two groups had converged and were slowly disappearing amidst the underbrush which rose, in a tangled mass, beneath the tall dark trees. To Lavinia, this underbrush looked impenetrable; she could not understand how the people who had aroused her pity could force their way through it. But no snapping or crashing sounds proclaimed their progress; only the faint gleam from the candles they were beginning to light revealed it; when Claude turned the buggy again, the girl could see a narrow clearing, hardly wider than a path, which seemed to lead nowhere except into the depths of a forest. It immediately proved to be as rough as it was narrow; exposed roots humped over it and recent rains had made ridges on it and furrows in it. Their faithful old horse plodded slowly along, but occasionally he stumbled; and though Claude drove as carefully as he could, it was impossible to prevent almost incessant jolting and jarring. Every now and then an especially rough movement threw the boy and girl closer together; but when that happened, Claude did not experience the same joyous thrill as when Lavinia had suddenly seized his arm. This contact was not caused by something she had done spontaneously; it was accidental and inevitable and there was nothing to indicate that she welcomed it. However, she did not complain; indeed, though she did not say so, he sensed that she was beginning to fall under the eerie spell of their surroundings. The crimson light was fading with its accustomed swiftness, but it was not quite gone, even yet; and above the pale rose which still lingered after the radiant glow, a few stars had appeared, and a young moon was swinging up into the calm sky as this darkened from pale turquoise to deep sapphire. Against these celestial splendors, the pines stood out, less sharply than against the sunset, but with increasing majesty. It was very still. Only the quiet tread of the marching people and the creaking of the buggy penetrated the silence; and even these, like the minor sound of the horse's hoofs, seemed muffled in some mysterious way by the engulfing forest. The marchers did not speak to each other, except in whispers. When Lavinia spoke again, unconsciously she whispered, too.

"Are you sure we're on the right road?"

"We must be. If those people ahead of us didn't know this led to a cemetery, they wouldn't be taking it."

"And you've taken it before, too, haven't you?"

"Yes. Dozens of times. If I hadn't, I wouldn't have brought you here. I wouldn't have known there was a sight worth seeing at the end of it."

If she were bent on being reasonable, he could resort to logic also. But he resented the necessity. His resentment made him momentarily careless and he slackened his hold on the reins. Their horse stumbled in a rut, deeper than any that had previously furrowed the road, and, in his effort to right himself, plunged still more deeply forward. The buggy rocked back and forth. Again Lavinia was thrown against Claude and, this time, she clung to him.

"Is it much farther?"

He could not answer instantly, because he was giving all his attention to his horse. When the poor animal finally regained its footing and staggered forward again, Claude replied with assumed nonchalance.

"I don't think so. I think in a minute or two you'll see a clearing, with more lights. These people ahead of us probably aren't the first ones to come and they won't be the last. The early comers will have started placing their candles around the graves already. It's surprising how much light they give. Anyway, you're not afraid of the dark, are you?"

"No, of course not."

"Nor of anything else?"

"No, but—"

He noticed she did not say, "Of course not," a second time and the "but" seemed significant. He tried to look at her more closely, to see if her lips were still closed in the same firm line as before. However, at first, there was not enough light for him to do so. Then, as the first glimmer from the clearing came within range, he saw that there had, indeed, been a change in her expression. Her lips were slightly parted now and he thought they were trembling a little, too. He reined in his horse.

"I think this is about as far as we can go in the buggy. I'm going to turn it out of the road a little, if I can, and hitch Mac to a tree. Wait a second, and I'll help you down."

She did not decline his proffered help, as she often had in the past. He knew well enough that she did not need it. Dozens of times he had seen her rise buoyantly from her seat and spring lightly over the wheel, landing no less lightly on the ground. But this time, though she was as nimble as ever, she landed in his arms. She made no show of trying to disengage herself and neither did he try to detain her. He realized that she was not thinking of him at all, just then. She was looking back, over the rough road, where, sure enough, another group, larger than the other two, were now advancing. Then she turned toward the clearing and, after gazing at it in silence for a moment, walked slowly toward it, wonderment in her face.

The great square, surrounded on every side by tall trees, had suddenly opened up before her. A few tombs, freshly whitewashed, rose starkly above the bare ground; but these were the exception. For the most part, the woodland cemetery embraced only graves, laid out in neat rows with narrow aisles between the rows, each grave encased in a low white wooden frame and outlined with candles, nearly all of which were already burning brightly. The people

266

who had entered the enclosure while Claude was hitching his horse had gone rapidly from grave to grave, illuminating the ones for which they were responsible; they had also placed great clusters of flowers, most of them artificial, in front of the tombstones or on the graves themselves. In the latter case, they painstakingly avoided any disturbance of the crosses, made from small twigs of evergreen, which had already been laid lengthwise on the slight elevations of earth framed by the wooden palings. By and large, the candle lighting and flower laying were done in silence; but when the work was nearly finished, groups began to form again and, at last, there was the renewed sound of voices, subdued at first, but gradually growing louder. Some of the mourners were speaking only in French to each other—not a patois, but a language which, though somewhat localized as to certain expressions, was still clear and pure. Other groups were talking in equally limpid English. Only occasionally was there an exchange of comments or greetings in Negro dialect. Some of these were reproachful.

"Which you first wife's grave, Montie?"

"Cain't rightly remember. Over yonder someplace."

" 'Over yonder someplace!' And you makin' out you love her so you like to die of grief when she passed on."

"Cain't nobody grieve forever."

Certainly the speaker did not seem to be doing so. He had his arm firmly around a comely girl, one of the few dressed in noticeably bright colors. She was snickering, and she wriggled in his grasp; Lavinia stared at her briefly in unconcealed distaste and then walked quickly away. Claude saw the look and understood the withdrawal. For the first time, he felt something akin to appreciation of Lavinia's aloofness. She would never cheapen herself, either for him or anyone else; whoever won her would know that she came to him utterly unsullied in both mind and body. . . .

She had gone on a little ahead of him now and he had to walk quickly in order to catch up with her. At first the people to whom the cemetery belonged had left the two strangers severely alone, not exactly avoiding them or treating them as intruders, but letting them see, very plainly, that they were aliens in a gathering otherwise communal. Now a neatly dressed man, clearly of Indian extraction, detached himself from his companions and spoke to them.

"You want to see Pa George's grave, don't you?"

"I don't know. Is there something special about it that we should see?"

It was Lavinia who spoke. The bronze-faced man looked at Claude instead of her as he answered.

"Maybe you wouldn't think so. We do though. We make a grave for Pa George every year."

"You *make* a grave for him every year! Why should you do that?"

The man sighed softly. It was plain to him that this strange lady did not—and either would not or could not —understand. Again he looked at Claude, this time hopefully.

"Because he hasn't got one of his own. No one knows where Pa George is buried or if he's buried at all. Pa George was drownded and we never found his body. So every year we fix him a grave, like I said. I'll show it to you."

Without waiting for them to accept or decline his offer, he led the way to a corner at the extreme end of the cemetery, where a "grave" was heaped high with flowers. Evidently the candles on it had been among the first to be lighted, for some of them had burned almost down to their sockets and some had already gone out. A kneeling woman was carefully replacing these with fresh ones. She went quietly on with her task, not looking up at the approach of visitors. "Do you know where he was drowned?" Claude asked the Indian, feeling that he should say something and not knowing what else to say.

"Somewhere on the bayou. It runs right back of us here. You can see it if you step that way. Before we had our road, we brought our dead here in pirogues to bury them. Unless we never found them, like Pa George."

"Would you like to see the bayou?" Claude asked, turning to Lavinia.

"No thank you. I think. . . . That is, we've seen all of the cemetery now, haven't we? I think I'd like to leave."

So it had been in vain, after all. She had felt something of the spell, while they were going through the woods and when she first saw the clearing. But it had not been strong enough to hold her. Perhaps something had upset her—the giggling girl in the trifling man's embrace, the story of the grave which was "made" afresh every year, the unexpected nearness of the treacherous water. Claude did not know; he could only grieve because he had failed again. He thanked the man who had told them about Pa George and started up the nearest aisle, between the rows of lighted

268

candles. Suddenly Lavinia stopped and spoke to him in a hushed voice.

"Have you noticed how many of the graves are very small? So many poor little babies. . . ."

He had not noticed it before, but now that she spoke of it, he did. Perhaps that was what had upset her. She was very fond of children, he had long been aware of that. Perhaps the thought of little lives snuffed out, many of them doubtless through lack of enlightened care, had made her feel there was more tragedy in this place than she could bear. But he did not ask her and she did not tell him. It was not until they were back in the buggy, jolting over the rough road again, that she asked another question.

"Are we going to any more cemeteries like that one?"

He hesitated. "Just as you say. The larger ones are all more or less alike, except that, in some, the Negroid strain shows up most among the mourners, in some the Indian, in some the French. And, of course, there are a lot of little cemeteries, too, where just one family is buried. But there's a good deal of sameness to those, too. I think when you've been to ours—"

"Shouldn't we have gone there first? After all, that was the one we came on purpose to visit!"

"I know. But I wanted to keep that for the last."

"Why, Claude?"

He hesitated again, groping for the right words, and then blundered along, conscious that he was expressing himself inadequately. "I thought you'd enjoy seeing the big ones—well, not enjoy them exactly, because of course there's always something sad about a cemetery. But I thought you'd find them thrilling—the setting and the lights and the crowds and all. Especially the crowds."

"You were right. I did find them thrilling."

"I'm glad. . . . But I didn't think there'd be anything *personal* in the way they affected you. And I thought perhaps there might be, in the little cemetery where my mother's people are buried."

"You're right about that, too, Claude."

He was comforted and encouraged by the sudden gentleness of her voice. "There won't be any crowds now," he went on. "Just you and me. I wanted it that way at the end, after the sun had gone down and it wasn't first evening any more. Night's different from sunset and dusk. I wanted to be alone with you and my people when night came on."

"I think I see what you mean."

Again they drove on without speaking to each other and this time the silence was longer. At last, Claude slowed down by the side of the road.

"There it is, a few hundred feet back."

Lavinia followed the general direction of his gaze. At first, she could see nothing except a blur of radiance and something large and white looming up in the midst of darkness. Then she was aware of a huge white tomb, brilliantly illuminated, and a low, lighted rectangle, which must mark a grave, on either side of it. Beyond one of these rectangles rose a tall white cross and all were encircled by the overhanging branches of pine trees. Above them the moon and stars shone brightly in a sky which was now as black and smooth as onyx.

"It's very beautiful," Lavinia said softly.

"I hope you won't find the going too rough, getting to it. There isn't any road. In fact, there isn't even much of a footpath. Two or three times a year, a man we've hired hacks his way through the underbrush and clears up the cemetery. Just before *Toussaint* the tombs are whitewashed. Uncle Cénas has always seen to that, ever since *Maman* and Papa moved away. Then on *Toussaint* itself, the candles are lighted. *Maman* and Papa have always done that themselves, until now, but Uncle Cénas arranged to have it done, today, by Emil Gremillion, who lives nearby, so that you and I would have a chance to go to one of the larger cemeteries first and still find the candles lighted when we got here. They don't burn all that long."

"I hope your mother won't mind because you didn't do it yourself."

"No, she won't mind. Probably she won't even ask. But if she does, I'll tell her why Uncle Cénas had it done for me and she'll be pleased to think you had a chance to see more of the Lacombe celebration than if we'd only come here."

"Well, now that we are here, aren't you going to help me out of the buggy?"

"I warned you, there isn't even a decent path."

"If a man can get through the underbrush, I can. I'm not as big as the average man. I don't need as much room."

"Then you *really* want to go there?"

"Of course that's what I want. That's what I came for."

There was enough light now, from the luminous sky, for him to see her expression, and he could not doubt that

270

she was telling him the truth. He guided the buggy closer to the underbrush, located a tree to which he could hitch Mac and stepped down. Then he held out his arms and Lavinia sprang into them. This time they closed around her, pressing her close to him, and she remained quiescent in his embrace. He could have kissed her now, he realized, and she would not have resisted that, either. But even while he held her, he realized that the moment for this, though it might be near, had not yet come. He released her.

"The path won't be wide enough for us to go abreast," he said. "So I'll lead the way. But you'd better keep hold of my hand. And mind the roots. Don't try to hurry."

They could not have hurried, even if they had tried. It was rough going, and several times Claude stopped and asked Lavinia if she wanted to turn back. Each time she said briefly that she did not. When they finally reached the clearing, her shirtwaist was torn, the coils of her hair were loosened and her face was scratched. In spite of the solemnity of the setting, Claude looked at her with something akin to amusement.

"Do you know this is the first time I've ever seen you when you didn't look as neat as a pin?" he asked.

"This is the first time you've ever taken me through a bramblebush. How did you expect me to look?"

"I didn't expect. I didn't think about it at all, because I didn't feel too sure you'd come—all the way. But I don't mind telling you I'm very pleased that you did and I think you look simply wonderful—about a thousand times prettier than you ever did before."

He gazed at her with eyes of love, untinged by the bitterness and disappointment which had engulfed him so short a time before, and almost instantly he knew that there was something akin to love in the eyes that met his. Perhaps it had been there earlier and he had been too blind to see it. No matter; he saw it now. He was sure of it. Lavinia smiled and his heart missed a beat.

"The standard of that cross is big enough for us to sit down on, isn't it?" she asked. "There wouldn't be anything sacrilegious about doing that, would there?"

"Of course not. And we can stay as long as you want to."

He had started to say, "We can stay all night if you want to," and then had bitten back the words. But he felt sure, in his new-found confidence, that Lavinia had known he started to say this and had not minded, even though of course she would not have done it. She seated herself at the foot of the cross and he sat down beside her and put his arm around her again.

"I want to stay long enough to hear about your people who are here," she said quietly.

He noticed she did not say "your people who are *buried* here." She had begun to feel that close communication with the dead which made them seem alive again, and which gave those who were really living that sense of shared immortality, just as he had hoped she would and as he had feared she would not.

"Well," he said, "my great-grandfather André de Bachemin was a French officer, on the colonial governor's staff. I guess he cut quite a figure in New Orleans, and it seems like he played the field for a while. But none of the belles in his own crowd who set their caps for him had any luck in tying him down. Then one day when he was passing by the Tremé Market he saw a very beautiful girl sitting between two squaws. Most of the women who came to this market with their wares were Lacombe Indians—they brought basketry and filé powder, and heron breasts that were used as dusters. But this particular girl plainly wasn't an Indian and André was rather intrigued at seeing her among them. So he made inquiries and found out that she was the daughter of a white market hunter."

"A market hunter?"

"Yes. A man who hunted on purpose to supply the market. It wasn't an unusual occupation in those days. This one was rather a lone wolf. No one knew very much about him—where he had come from or what his real name was—and he didn't seem to have any family except this one daughter, Auriette. However, it didn't take the officer long to find him. The market hunter went parading up and down the street, with his gun on his shoulder and eight or ten pairs of fat ducks draped over the long barrel. He must have cut quite a figure, too, in his way, and his daughter was a great help to him—she attracted a good deal of attention herself and she could keep more of his game on display, when she was seated among the squaws, than he could sport on his gun. André bought a couple of mallards from him, and then said casually he wished he had some pappabottes to go with them. The hunter said all right, come along, or something of the sort and took him right up to the girl. It was as simple as that—to start with."

"But it didn't stay simple?"

272

"No. André almost immediately suggested that he'd like the girl for a *placée* and came mighty near getting shot for the suggestion. You know what a *placée* was, don't you, Lavinia? I'm almost sure the Labadies' house must have been built for one and probably they've told you."

"Yes, they have. They explained that a *placée* was a girl who had a 'protector' to whom she wasn't married, but who took good care of her," Lavinia said with suitable reticence. "Never mind what the Labadies told me though. Go on with your story. I'm very much interested in it."

"Are you really? And you're not uncomfortable, sitting here so long? Or cold or—or anything?"

"No, no, no! So I suppose, when he found he couldn't get her any other way, the French officer married the beautiful girl who sold him the game that her father shot?"

"He was only too glad to marry her. He was terribly in love with her. He just hadn't thought of it that way at first. But he was furious when none of his fine friends would have anything to do with her. So he resigned his commission and shook the dust of New Orleans from his feet and went into partnership with his father-in-law. Then he built a house for his bride in Lacombe, where she could be among the Indians who were so fond of her."

"And they lived happily ever after?"

"I guess they would have. But you see, Auriette died the next year when—when her baby was born."

"And that was when the beautiful tomb was built? On purpose for her?"

"Yes. Her husband said she should have the finest tomb in Lacombe, even a finer one than any of those people in New Orleans who had been so mean to her. He got the materials for it himself and built it himself. And of course, when he died, he was buried there with her. The baby was my grandfather—he and his wife are buried in the smaller tombs on either side. But *Maman* told Papa years ago that, when she died, she wanted to be buried in the big one with André and Auriette. She says André would have known she was worthy of respect, even if she did pioneer on a prairie and didn't have much book learning. Just as he knew that Auriette was worthy of respect, even if he found her sitting in a market among the squaws. *Maman* wants Papa to put another inscription on the tomb, underneath Auriette's epitaph, and worded just like that one, except for the names and dates."

273

The candles were burning low now. Lavinia put her hand on Claude's arm and spoke softly.

"I didn't look at the inscription when we came in and I can't see it clearly from here. Will you tell me what it says?"

> *"AURIETTE DE BACHEMIN*
> *ÉPOUSE BIEN AIMÉE*
> *DU*
> *CHEVALIER ANDRÉ DE BACHEMIN*
> *SON VEUF INCONSOLABLE*
> *ÉRIGE CE MONUMENT*
> *À LA MEMOIRE*
> *D'UN ESPRIT PUR FIDÉLE ET COURAGEUX*
> *JUSQUÀ LA MORT."*

" 'Beloved wife, pure of spirit, brave and faithful until death,' " Lavinia whispered. "Yes, I—I think I understand why your mother wants to be buried in that tomb. And I think she ought to be—that she deserves to be. When she dies, you'll bring her here, won't you, Claude?"

"I've promised. And you'll come with me then, too, won't you, Lavinia?"

He was conscious of the tears on her face when she lifted it for his kiss. But he did not try to question their cause. It was enough for him that she did not draw away when he took her in his arms. The candles sank lower and lower in their sockets. Neither Claude nor Lavinia knew when these flickered for the last time and went out one by one.

PART SIX

Lavinia, Claude and Fleex

November, 1895—November, 1905

CHAPTER XXV

Claude was still in a state of ecstasy when they started back to New Orleans the following day and, though Lavinia was very silent in the course of the trip, he neither thought this strange nor took it amiss. He knew that she must be tired, not only because the emotional experience of the previous night might well have left her exhausted, but also for the less dramatic reason that she had taken a tiring journey, met a number of totally strange people, seen a number of totally strange sights and, meanwhile, had almost no chance to rest. He was pleased, rather than disturbed, when she went quietly to sleep while looking out of the car window, and slumbered peacefully, with her head resting on her hand, until they were almost into New Orleans. When she finally woke, looking first confused and then startled, he spoke to her soothingly.

"You've had a nice nap, honey. I reckon you needed it. You were plumb worn out. I'll see you home, of course, but I won't come in. . . . You'll go back to Crowley with me tomorrow though, won't you?"

"Why—I hadn't thought. Do you want me to?"

He laughed happily. "I don't want to let you out of my sight, not a minute that I can help it. But that's not the only reason I want you to go back to Crowley with me. I want to tell your folks and mine that you're going to marry me and I want you there with me when I do it."

"All right. I guess I should be. But I can't get ready to leave New Orleans for good tomorrow morning, Claude. I couldn't wind things up that fast—arrange to stop my lessons and pay my bills and say good-by to everyone who's been kind to me."

"I'll wait over a day, if that would help."

275

"It would help. But I couldn't do everything there is to do in just one extra day. I couldn't even get packed. I'll have to come back to do that because—well, because I seem to be awfully tired."

"All right. I'll wait for you, but I won't come around bothering you until evening. You take the extra day now, just to rest and tell your teachers and your friends that you're needed at home. You don't have to tell them why. I'd rather the family knew first, wouldn't you?"

"I guess so," Lavinia said again. Then, more positively, she added quickly, "Yes, of course, I would."

"All right. We'll go home together and tell them. Then, later on, you can come back and pay your bills and do your packing and all that. I'll come with you. We'll have another nice trip together."

The next twenty-four hours dragged by slowly, but he kept his promise and did not go to the Labadies' house until the following evening. Mignon, who opened the door for him, grinned broadly in welcome as usual, but handed him a note while she talked to him.

"Po' lil' M'iz Viney, she wore out and that's a fact. She ben mos' crazy with the headache. Ah been sittin' by her, puttin' old handkerchief wrung out in cologne water and ice on her head and tellin' her she'd feel better when the sun went down. Sho 'nuff, she gone to sleep now. You ain' goin' for to wake her up, is you, Mr. Claude?"

"No, of course not," he said, speaking in a flat voice and opening the note. It was very brief:

Dear Claude:

I'm sorry, but I just don't seem able to get up. I never had a headache before in my life, but this one has me beaten. Mignon says she thinks it'll pass in the night and I hope so. If it does, I'll get up early and pack enough things to last me until I can get back for the others. Don't try to come here in the morning. I'll meet you at the train unless the miserable old head won't let me. If I'm not there, please go ahead without me and I'll come on to Crowley the first day I can and let you know beforehand when that will be.

Love,
LAVINIA

He walked slowly away and spent an almost sleepless night, the prey to all sorts of vague worries. It was true that, as far as he knew, Lavinia had never had a headache before; could she be sickening for something? . . . And the note, besides bearing the ill tidings of her indisposition, did not read to him like a love letter; most girls, even if they were not feeling well, would make their first written message to their fiancés reveal their happiness in their betrothal—or so he supposed. Did she feel she had acted too impulsively under the spell of the *Toussaint* celebration? He had counted on the probability that she might be greatly moved by it, and that this emotional turmoil might react to his advantage, because he had seen this happen several times before. But he had forgotten that often, after some special occasion, which had moved her deeply by its solemnity or exhilarated her by its gaiety, she had been more reserved than usual for several days afterward. The *Réveillon,* following Midnight Mass, which she had finally persuaded her parents to let her attend; the festive breakfast of *pâte brisée* after Odile's First Holy Communion, which she had insisted on attending, too; the Procession of the Lilies and the Crowning of the Virgin at Grand Coteau, in which she had taken part herself; the parties preceding and following the buggy wedding of Annette and Pierre, at which she had been such a radiant bridesmaid, and her ride home with him afterward; even the more hilarious gatherings at Crowley and Rayne, especially if she had been to them with Fleex—all these had resulted in an aftermath of restraint. Most marked of all had been her withdrawal after a dance at Arnaudville, to which she had gone on horseback with a gay group, starting out from Carencro, where several of the girls were spending a few days with a schoolmate and where the boys had joined them. They were delayed in getting off because their supper was so bounteous and there was some pleasant loitering along the way, for which the deplorable condition of the roads, after a heavy spring rain, offered a welcome excuse. By the time the merrymakers reached the dance hall, there was no room anywhere near it for them to hitch their horses, so they were obliged to do this at some distance from it. The boys had on high boots, but the girls peeled off their shoes and stockings before they dismounted and waded barefoot through the mud toward the entrance of the hall, where a wrinkled, white-haired colored man was waiting with a tin tub and a towel to wash and dry their feet. The mud had come halfway up to their knees; the girls had been obliged to lift their skirts high, and to accept support from their escorts so that they

277

would not bog down. Claude remembered how Lavinia, who was usually so self-reliant, had clung to Fleex, looking up into his face and laughing with every difficult step forward, and how close Fleex had stood to her, while the old man washed her feet and ankles and calves. Claude had come close, too, completely forgetting that by so doing he was neglecting the girl he was nominally squiring, and he had seen how disturbingly pretty all this part of Lavinia's person was. Then he had turned away, embarrassed and ashamed; nice girls were not supposed to uncover their limbs and, if through accident or necessity they were obliged to do so, young men who respected them were expected to glance in another direction. But neither Fleex nor Lavinia had been embarrassed or ashamed; they had gone on looking at each other and laughing together and when Lavinia was finally shod again, they had gone arm in arm into the dance hall, where three musicians were rendering rollicking tunes on a triangle, an accordion and a drum, and had stayed together almost the whole evening, locked in dance after dance. It was obviously only afterward that Lavinia had thought of her bare legs and her unblushing behavior; but then she apparently dwelt on it with self-reproach for a long time—at all events, she avoided Claude so pointedly he was convinced that was what she was doing. Illogically, it had not occurred to him until now to wonder whether she had been equally constrained with Fleex. . . .

The fears that had long been dormant in Claude's mind and that had been lulled into blessed oblivion the night of *Toussaint* were suddenly and violently aroused. Was she thinking about Fleex again, yearning for him again, after having put him out of her thoughts so successfully that she had almost forgotten him? Or *had* she put him out of her thoughts, *had* she almost forgotten him? This was what Claude had thankfully assumed for some time and this was what her surrender at *Toussaint* seemed to confirm. Surely what had happened then could not have served to resurrect a dead love for another man! She had never embraced Fleex as she had embraced him, Claude, beside that candlelit tomb, or been so embraced, by Fleex or any other man, except Claude himself. On that, Claude would have taken his oath. Though he was not her first love, at least he was her first lover. He tried to take comfort from this certainty throughout his tormented night. . . .

To his unspeakable relief and not a little to his surprise, Lavinia was already waiting for him at the station when

278

he reached there the following morning. She greeted him with apparent pleasure, assured him that Mignon had been right, her headache had begun to improve the minute the sun went down, and that now she had had a good night's sleep, she had never felt better in her life. She chatted companionably all the way to Crowley, confirmed her willingness to have Claude tell their respective families about their engagement immediately and, when they said good-by to each other for the time being, left him immeasurably happier than he had been the night before, and inclined to be slightly ashamed of himself for having made mountains out of molehills.

Both the Winslow and the Villac families were delighted with the news of the engagement, but there was a decided difference of opinion regarding the length of time which should elapse before the wedding. Mary and Brent said firmly that it was impractical for it to take place before spring. It would require several months, Mary insisted, to prepare a proper trousseau; Lavinia had never possessed a hope chest, and it was impossible to get a supply of sheets and towels hemmed or hemstitched, to say nothing of getting them embroidered, in less than six months, especially since leeway to make the bride's clothes must be taken into consideration. Brent might have objected to such a stipulation as representing a waste of both time and money, if he had not been equally determined that Lavinia should begin her married life in a home of her own, and that this should be the finest residence in Crowley.

"I couldn't take my wife to a nice house when we were married," he said stubbornly, "and when we came to Louisiana, she didn't even have rudimentary comforts, the first year. She hasn't any more than the bare essentials of comfort now—can't have, out here on the farm, and this is where we've got to live—where we want to live, as far as that goes." He paused to glance around the cluttered sitting room, with the sheaves of rice drooping over the pictures and his measuring board wedged between his pigeon hole desk and his wife's sewing machine. The look conveyed no discontent or discouragement; there was something akin to dedication in it, though Claude was too young to realize this; but there was also a consciousness that, though the room represented industry and progress, it was neither commodious nor beautiful, and Claude did realize that. "This is where my work is, this is my home," Brent continued, turning to look squarely at Claude. "But your work isn't out on a farm; it's in a town that's growing

279

by leaps and bounds. And that's where your home and Lavinia's is going to be. I can afford to give my daughter the best there is and there's no reason why she can't have most of the modern conveniences in Crowley now. Besides, I'm not thinking just of the present; I want the place I build for her to be her permanent home, one she'll be just as proud of at forty as at twenty. Of course, she'll want to keep on improving it, as fast as improvements are possible, and she may want to enlarge it, if you and she have a big family, as I hope you will. There'll be plenty of room for that because it's going to have ample grounds. But it'll still be the same house—the one her father gave her for a wedding present. And it takes time to build the kind of house I have in mind."

"Is it the same kind of house Lavinia has in mind?" Claude ventured to inquire.

"It is," Brent said shortly. Then, recognizing that he had been unnecessarily abrupt, he added, more agreeably, "Of course, Lavinia wants you to be pleased with the plans, too, Claude, and I think you will be. We'll go over them together."

"Well, thanks," Claude answered, speaking rather shortly in his turn. "Is it all right to ask—is the location decided on, too?"

"No, but there are several available that you can choose among, if you make up your mind quickly. I've already talked to Duson."

"I wanted to give Lavinia one of the two lots her father bought in my name when we first came to Crowley," Mary interposed. "That is, subject to your approval, too, Claude. But Mr. Winslow doesn't think that's a good idea, for several reasons. For one thing, he doesn't think it would be big enough. So then, I suggested that I give her both lots, and he said he still wanted some town property kept in my name and that, anyway, the two wouldn't give room enough, either."

"For heaven's sake, how much room does he think we need?"

"Well, of course, you'll want a stable for at least two horses, and land enough for both a vegetable garden and a flower garden and pasturage for a cow."

Claude looked from his future parents-in-law to his betrothed, hoping for help.

"I want to get married," he said. "I'd like some say in how and where I'm going to live, for the principle of the thing—any man would. But when you get right down to it,

280

I really don't care very much, as long as Lavinia is satisfied. What I don't like is being put off like this. It's taken me forever to get Lavinia to say she'd marry me, and now you want me to wait forever before she actually does it. I don't think that's fair."

"Not forever, Claude. Just a few months," Lavinia said. "You couldn't leave the mill now, right in the busiest season, long enough for us to take a wedding trip. Why, you had hard work persuading Mr. Tibier to let you off long enough to go to Lacombe!"

"A wedding trip! Where do you want to go on a wedding trip? Is that all decided, too?"

"Of course, it isn't. I meant to talk it over with you as soon as we had a good chance, and I didn't think we had had yet. But we can do it right now, if you want to. What would you think of New York?"

"New York!" Claude exclaimed. If she had suggested the South Sea Islands, he could hardly have been more surprised. Most of the honeymoon couples of his acquaintance, who took any kind of a trip, did not go farther away than Lake Arthur or Pointe-aux-Loups and did not prolong their stay beyond a week; many went immediately to their own little cottage after the celebration connected with the buggy wedding had ended, as Annette and Pierre had done. Claude looked at Lavinia in consternation.

"Well, New Orleans wouldn't be any special treat to me any more," she said, as if that were the nearest point she had been considering. "But if the idea of New York doesn't appeal to you, I'd be willing to go to Washington instead. I thought maybe we could do both—that is, if we waited until the busy season at the mill is over."

"I don't believe you really want to marry me. I think you just want a trousseau and a house and a trip," Claude said, with sudden, uncontrollable anger.

Of course, he was instantly sorry, not only because he would not voluntarily have been rude either to Lavinia or her parents or seemed ungrateful in the face of the Winslows' generosity, but also because he knew Lavinia was quite capable of saying, if that was the way he was going to take it, perhaps, after all. . . . But he had hardly finished his muttered apology, when, to his great relief, all she said was she thought they had talked about future plans enough for the moment, and that it was a shame to waste such a lovely day indoors—what she wanted was a good gallop. Claude did not feel that horseback riding afforded ideal opportunities for lovemaking, especially at the pace Lavinia, who rode better than he did, liked to cover the countryside; but at least it was preferable to the sort of heated argument which led to nothing but acrimony. Besides, Lavinia made no objection to swinging around by the Primeaux's house on their way back, and there he knew he would have plenty of staunch allies, should any debatable subject come up. However, the visit, made at Anne's bedside, passed off pleasantly and uneventfully. It was not until his return, after seeing Lavinia home, that his mother called him back into her room and, on her own initiative, began to make pointed remarks and ask leading questions.

"I got plenty pleasure, me, to see Lavinia this here evenin', Claude. That young girl, her, she gets mo' prettier all the while, yes. On top ever'thing else, she got plenty sense, an' I guarantee you, me, she's a good girl, too. But why she never said nothin' 'bout when you two fixin' to marry with each other, *hein?* Not one little word she say, nor neither you, Claude. Me an' Papa ain't goin' poke 'round, us, no, in w'at ain't our business, but I got to admit we both been thinkin' the weddin' better be soon-soon, so you wouldn't run into Advent. Ain't that right, Claude?"

"There isn't any question of our running into Advent—or Lent, either, for that matter. Lavinia doesn't want to get married until late spring."

With her characteristic gesture, Anne pulled herself upright among her pillows, wincing visibly as she did so. "Not till spring? Not till late-late spring? W'at she means not till late-late spring? Ain't that young girl Lavinia got good health, no?"

"She's in splendid health. But you see—"

"You an' me, we not talkin' 'bout the same things, us, Claude. We got a right not to be bashful, no, when it's time to talk frankly, like a boy an' his *maman* got a right to talk. W'at I mean, ain't that young girl ready fo' no man, her, like she got a right to be at her age? Ain't she maybe not wantin' you or either no other man for a husband?"

"Of course, she is. Of course, she does," Claude answered quickly. He was angry again partly because, to his intense annoyance, he was blushing, and partly because he did not feel too sure that his words carried conviction, since he did not speak with complete assurance. Lavinia greeted him with a kiss, as a matter of course, whenever he went to see her now; but it was affectionate rather than ardent, and though he had tried to tell himself this was because at least one member of her family was apt to be present at the time of his arrival, he was not altogether successful; the kiss with which she bade him good night, at which time they were nearly always alone, was not prolonged or passionate, either. When they were driving together in a buggy, going to and from dances, he held the reins in one hand and kept his free arm around her waist; but that was the custom with any courting couple, whether they were definitely engaged or not. She did not remonstrate when he stopped the horse, at some opportunely lonely or secluded spot, of which there were a good many —fortunately, from his point of view; and she did not resist the caresses for which he thought these places offered so obvious an advantage. But he realized that she would have done so if these had become either daring or intense; and she never actually seemed to welcome them, much less to invite them; neither did she spontaneously, from time to time, slip her hand into his, lay her head on his shoulder or rub her cheek against his. So far, he had not once succeeded in recapturing the mood or reawakening the response that had glorified the night in the woods at Lacombe for him.

"Then why she don' go 'head, her?" Anne persisted, breaking in on these unsatisfactory reflections. "I guarantee you, me, it ain't you that's holding back, no."

"No, I've said everything I could to persuade her to change her mind. And she won't. Besides, it isn't just Lavinia who's holding back. Her mother doesn't want her to get married until her trousseau's finished, and it seems that dozens and dozens of things have to get made and embroidered—you probably understand about all that better than I do. And her father doesn't want her to get married until he's built her a great big house in Crowley on a huge lot that isn't even bought yet. Then there's still another hitch. Lavinia wants to go to New York and Washington for our honeymoon, and of course I can't leave the mill, right in the busiest season."

"I ain't never heard no such foolishness in all my whole life, me, no! W'at you say about that, Ursin?"

Ursin had been peacefully sleeping, on his side of the bed, when his son came in, and had progressed from slumber to drowsiness and from drowsiness to dazed bewilderment while this conversation was going on. Now he roused himself to agree with his wife on all points, but most emphatically on the subject of the wedding journey.

"Where she think you goin' get money for some *cuyo-*
283

nade like that?" he inquired. "She maybe thinks it don' cost plenty to go traveling? I tell you, frankly, me, it cost like hell."

"Her grandfather's offered to give us the trip. But I don't want to be beholden to her family for everything. And I do have a little money saved up. I was putting something aside even before I got my raise and you know I'm getting eighty dollars a month now. I suppose I could manage that part. A nice ring costs plenty, too."

"Not all that much, no. It don't take but only eight dollars fo' the *alliance,* yes. You know w'at? We got a right to be setting a day soon, us fo' to go buy that."

"I wasn't talking about the *alliance.* I was talking about a diamond solitaire in a Tiffany setting. That's what Lavinia says all her stylish friends in New Orleans have when they get engaged. We're going to pick it out together at Griswolds' when she goes back to get her things. I want her to have as nice a ring as any girl she knows—the same way her mother wants her to have nice clothes and her father wants her to have a nice house."

"I got no idea w'at you talkin' 'bout, me, with you' diamond solitary Tiffany settles. Somebody 'round here is gone crazy, an' I tell you frankly, it ain't me, no. You know w'at? You goin' send that young girl, that Lavinia, here to me. I'm goin' have a talk with her."

"It won't do any good. It'll just make her mad."

"You hear me, Claude! You do like you' *maman* say. You ain't got so old an' big yet, no, not you, so you know more an' better than w'at *maman* an' me knows. *Maman* got to say w'at she got in her mind, yes, an' neither it won't hurt that Miss Educate to hear it, no. An' now it's time to say good night an' *fais dodo.*"

Claude did not need to make an issue of having Lavinia see his mother. She still went back and forth between the Winslows' house and the Primeaux' as frequently and naturally as she had always done; and now that Anne was in bed so much of the time, her room had become the usual center for visiting. The problem was to keep the other members of the family out of it while Anne spoke her mind, without letting them or Lavinia know there had been a definite plot to do this. That meant making sure the visit took place when the youngsters, who went to a new, near-by school for both boys and girls, were disposed of in this way; when Ursin and Phares were both intensively occupied out of doors; and when neither Marcelite nor Annette had come to visit. With only Mezalee to handle, the problem would be easy. But several days went by before the stage was set to suit either Claude or his mother, and a delay of this length, just then, seemed to him like an eternity. Even the fact that during the interval Brent invited him into town, for the purpose of looking over the desirable lots that were being held, and pointedly consulted him as to which he preferred, did not serve to placate him. Neither did the house plans, which Lavinia spread out on the kitchen table, asking very pleasantly what he thought of them and inviting him to make suggestions for changes.

"They're all right, I guess," he conceded. "But what I want to see is the house, not the plans for it. And who's going to build it? Castex doesn't do carpentry any more. Why, Frank Blanc is building a house for *him!*"

"Frank's going to build ours, too, as soon as he finishes the one for Jean Castex."

"And when's that going to be?"

"I don't know exactly. As soon as he can."

Decidedly, it was time for Anne to intervene, if her intervention was to bring results, and she kept assuring her impatient son that it would. She had got results lots of times, with Lavinia's mother among other people; of course, she could get them with Lavinia. All they had to do was to make sure she didn't get interrupted while she was talking. . . .

At last the opportune moment arrived. Ursin and Phares went to Rayne to buy lumber, and that meant they would also visit their relatives at the same time. Marcelite's three children were all down with the mumps, so she could not leave the house, and Annette had gone to stay with her mother-in-law in Lafayette while shopping for her expected baby. Mezalee, in whom Claude confided, instantly showed herself co-operative and understanding.

"Of course I'll help, any way I can, Claude," she assured him, in her gentle, pleasant way. "I know exactly how you feel about wanting to get married."

"You do?" he blurted out in surprise. "Why, I didn't know you wanted to get married! I thought—"

"You thought I wanted to become a nun? Yes, and I've had to put it off, over and over again. That's why I understand that it's hard for you to wait."

He stared at his cousin, his astonishment tinged with sympathy. Yes, of course he remembered now that she had said, years ago, she wanted to be a nun; but that was when Marcelite had become infatuated with Alcée, and

285

everyone's attention had been diverted by her headstrong and upsetting behavior. Afterward, when Marcelite was safely if unsuitably married, Father Vialetton, the missionary priest who had performed the ceremony, had encouraged Mezalee to continue thinking about a vocation; at the same time, he said she should have more education before she entered a convent, that there was no reason why an intelligent girl like her should content herself with being a lay sister. So she had gone to Acadia College and had graduated with much higher honors than either Lavinia or Annette had taken at Grand Coteau. Then, just about that time, Annette had become absorbed in her eminently desirable suitor and Phares had decided to enlarge the house, so they could have the right kind of a party before the buggy wedding; and, after the wedding, Anne's condition had become rapidly worse. Someone had to lighten her burden, both with the actual housework and with the care of the younger children, and Mezalee was obviously that person. The housework had grown heavier, instead of lighter, with fewer hands to do it; and though the youngsters required less physical care, except during the emergency caused by illness or accident, they were more and more of a responsibility. Odile would not be able to graduate from Grand Coteau in June unless her marks improved, and she was already older than most of the girls in her class and the prettiest and most popular of all the cousins; her suitors, as well as her marks, presented a problem, not because she was acting recklessly and prematurely in selecting one that was unacceptable to her family, like Marcelite, but because she kept half a dozen, all more or less eligible, on tenterhooks; the resultant rivalries culminated in a succession of scenes which no one, except Odile herself, enjoyed. Onezime had given his father no peace until he was allowed to go to St. Charles College, and now he was determined to be a priest instead of a farmer; he did not propose to submit tamely, as Mezalee had done, to interference or even delay when he was sure he had a vocation. Neither Odey nor Olin had recovered satisfactorily from a siege of scarlet fever which had laid them low the previous year. Odey had been left a little deaf and this handicap was increasing; it hampered him in his schoolwork and made him the butt of cruel jests among his classmates. Olin had been delicate ever since the attack and was the object of both concern and disappointment to Anne, who could not reconcile herself to the fact that any of her children was puny. Clement, whose idol had always been Fleex, was determined to be as much like his long-lost brother as possible and, consequently, played hooky on every possible occasion; his father and uncle, who had both set their highest hopes on him, during his docile and industrious childhood, as far as the farm was concerned, were in a constant state of irritation and anxiety on his account. Pauline had been hopelessly spoiled by everyone and was completely unamenable to discipline. . . .

With all the problems created by these conditions, Mezalee dealt kindly and competently, while ministering to her aunt's needs and cooking, cleaning, sewing and weaving for the entire household. She had been doing it all so long now that Claude, like the others, with the exception of Anne, took her role as the domestic mainstay of the family for granted. Until so unexpectedly reminded, Claude had honestly forgotten that she had ever aspired to any other; it came as a complete surprise to him that the abandonment of a vocation had been a source of lasting grief to her, that she still yearned for the dedicated detachment of a cloistral existence.

"Why, Mezalee, it never occurred to me—" he began awkwardly. Then, because he realized that whatever he said would be not only inadequate, but clumsy, he decided that it was useless to go on. "Well, anyway, thanks a lot." He put his arm around her shoulder and patted it gently. As she looked up at him, smiling responsively, he thought there were tears in her eyes. But her lips were not even quivering.

When Lavinia dropped in, later that same afternoon, Mezalee was weaving a coverlet. She stopped the loom and invited her caller's opinion of the pattern.

"It's lovely, Mezalee," Lavinia said enthusiastically. "But then, everything you make is exquisite. I can run things up in a hurry, on the machine, but when it comes to any kind of handwork, I'm no good at it."

"No one can be good at everything," Mezalee reminded her, with no apology for the triteness of the remark. "Think of all the other things you do well! Claude says you're the best rider and the best dancer in the parish and that, given a little more experience, you'll be one of the best cooks."

"I'm afraid he's prejudiced. He enjoys riding and dancing with me, and he can't wait to see that I get more experience in cooking."

"There isn't any reason why he should, is there?"

"No. Except that it takes time to get ready for the wedding and everything. You remember how it was with Annette."

"Yes, I remember." Tactfully, Mezalee refrained from saying that these preparations had been made in short order, all things considered. "I'm glad you like the bedspread," she went on. "I meant to give it to you for a wedding present, if you did. And I've been meaning to tell you —I'd love to help with any hand sewing you want done. I could get through a lot of it in odd moments and, as you've just said, it isn't one of the things you like to do best."

"I shouldn't suppose you had any odd moments."

"You'd be surprised. But I'd better get on with this bedspread if I'm going to have it done in time. Won't you go right on into *Tante*'s room? She's all alone and I know she'd love to see you."

Anne did, indeed, appear to be delighted at the sight of her prospective daughter-in-law. She heaved herself up in bed with such apparent vigor, smiled so beamingly and held out her arms with such an expansive gesture of welcome that Lavinia decided she must be feeling better than she had in a long while. Then she continued to hold the girl's hand and stroke it affectionately from time to time, after Lavinia had drawn a chair up close to the bed and sat down.

"Claude done told me, him, all 'bout those fine-fine lots you' papa bought," Anne said enthusiastically. "You must be glad in you' heart, yes, you got them a'ready, an' don't need to wait, no, to find a good place for buildin' a home. Did you maybe bring the plans with you, *chère*? I would be proud, me, to see how you' house goin' look, yes."

"I'm sorry, I didn't. My uncle Jonathan has them just now."

With admirable self-control, Anne refrained from comment. She had never cared for Jonathan Fant and she had said so more than once. But she realized this was not the moment to do it again.

"He thought he could suggest some improvements in them and I was glad to have him, he has such good taste," Lavinia went on. "But he'll bring them back the next time he comes over from St. Martinville and then I'll show them to you."

"I got to say I'm hopin', me, he hurries, hurries, hurries," Anne permitted herself to say. "Frank Blanc, him, is ready to go to work soon-soon, ain't he? Monday ain't too quick, no."

"Why no! He has that house he's promised to do for Jean Castex first and—"

"Oh, Jean Castex, Jean Castex, Jean Castex! He ain't no king, him. He don' mind waitin', no. Why, he even say to Ursin how he don' mind livin' in the house where he is at, him, for a while yet. It ain't like he got no house, same as you an' Claude ain't got one. Nor neither he ain't waitin', him, to marry nobody, no. But him an' that Frank Blanc, too, I guarantee you, me, they knows how it is with young couples. They knows young folks got to hurry, now, an' Frank told Ursin, too, him, he fixin' to push you' new house right fast-fast-fast."

"I hadn't any idea there was so much talk going on about my house."

Anne tightened the clasp on the hand she was holding.

"Now you got to admit, yes," she said genially, "everybody is glad-glad when a nice young boy an' a nice young girl, them, is ready to marry. Everybody feels like they got to help out all they can, yes. I'm almost crazy, me, I got to lie here like some log, when I want to get up an' help, 'specially when I got so much happy thinkin', me. I say 'Thank you, *Dieu Seigneur,* I don' got to worry none, me, 'bout Claude like I got to worry 'bout Odile, her. Claude got real good knowledge, when he find the right girl, her, to make up his mind he goin' marry with her so soon like she say yes, her.' Now she done said it, so there ain't nothin' to wait for no more, no. That Odile, she don't make up her mind. I tell you frankly, I think I'll be dead, me, biffo' that girl make up her mind, an' then I won't never have no chance, no, to see her settled down like a young girl ought to be, her."

"Why, of course you will! What makes you say a thing like that?"

"Account I am dyin', me. You an' me both knows it, us. An' don' you go wastin' no sympathy on me, no. I don't need nobody to feel sorry for me. I ain't afraid of w'at is comin', not when I know for true that Claude, him, has got the right wife, the wife w'at is goin' to make that boy happy, her. So I'll be dyin' happy, me, with Claude an' his wife settled down, them, in a fine new home that is a present from his wife's people, so I can see them, me, start keepin' house, with plenty-plenty room for a big family, an' plenty-plenty room for company besides."

Lavinia did not answer. She could not deny that she

knew Anne was dying; she had known it when Claude pleaded with her to go to Lacombe; she had heard Dr. Mouton speak of it half a dozen times to her father and mother. However, she had not realized before that Anne's condition should have any affect on her own plans. She had not been consciously selfish. But, since she was genuinely fond of Anne, she now reproached herself for her thoughtlessness.

"I got to admit, me, that mostly I'm thinkin' 'bout Claude," Anne went on after a short silence which she seemed to feel in no way awkward or surprising. "But I'm thinkin' 'bout Mezalee, too, some, me. She's a good girl, that Mezalee, an' it ain't right, no, she should give up her whole life to her cousins, no. Maybe if they was brothers an' sisters, yes. But not no cousins. Onezime ain't goin' to be no trouble, him. I got a promise, me, from Ursin, an' also Phares, they won't pester him no more, no. They goin' let him do like he wants an' be a priest. It won't be too long, no, biffo' they will be proud, them, they got a priest in the family, just like they already proud how Claude, him, is doin' so good in the rice mill an' Annette's husband, him, got a job in the bank."

"Yes, I think they will," Lavinia agreed.

"Looks to me, *chère,* like we thinks the same way, us, 'bout almost everything," Anne said contentedly. "I expeck, me, we both know that Odile, her, is goin' make up her mind, one of these here days, which boy out the lot that's hangin' 'round her like they was sheep at a salt trough, them, she goin' pick out for a husban', her. Then she or either Annette could give Pauline a home, yes, on account I tell you very frankly, me, Pauline's all that contrary maybe Ursin or neither Phares or neither both, them, could manage her."

"Yes," Lavinia agreed again.

"One little bitty young girl more to take care of won't make no difference, no, not when folks got lots of their own kids like they'll have soon-soon," Anne continued. "Odey an' Olin is the onliest ones I got to worry about, me. Not Annette an' not either Odile, them, could take care of Odey an' Olin, no, not if Mezalee goes ahead to be a nun. I mean a real nun, me, one that makes public vows like they say. I guarantee you, me, I think she got them vows already made in her heart, yes. Don' you think so, too, *chère?*"

"Why, I don't know. I hadn't thought of it."

"That's why I'm tellin' you, me, go right ahead an'

think now. Think how that girl looks, yes, an' how she dresses an' talks an' acts, her. I got the idea, me, that's partly on account of she ain't never in this world forgot her *maman* was a lady, like that Marcelite, her, done forgot, an' I hope she is good an' ashamed of herself for it, me. But when it comes to Mezalee, it ain't only how she talk an' act, no; it's mostly on account she wants to be a nun." Anne's comment was a command; Lavinia had no alternative but to obey; and, with her essential honesty, she had to admit that Anne was right. Of course, Mezalee did not wear a habit; but she invariably dressed very simply, sometimes in gray with a white collar and cuffs and a white apron, but usually all in white, though this must have represented a tremendous amount of extra work for her, when she was already overburdened. Her expression was serene, even under the most adverse circumstances, and she never raised her voice, or spoke sharply or shortly, no matter how greatly the children tried her patience. Moreover, she carried herself with a dignity and composure that were extraordinary, considering her upbringing. There was, indeed, something about her bearing and manner not unlike the bearing and manner of the nuns at Grand Coteau. Lavinia admitted as much, with astonishment at her previous blindness, though without hesitation, in answer to Anne's question.

"But," she added, "I don't think she'd go ahead and be a real nun until all the boys are grown up. And even if she did, I think Annette and Odile would be just as good to Odey and Olin as they would to Pauline."

"You got to remember they got rules," Anne reminded her. "You can't wait, no, till you get to be some old lady biffo' you go in no convent. Maybe they don' want you should die on 'em, no, right after you go in, first thing. An' I got to admit you' right when you say Annette an' Odile, all two, them, would be good to the po' young boys. But they don' have the knowledge, them, nor neither the patience, an' Mezalee knows it, her. But you—you're different. You could see for sure Odey got the right treatment to make him hear again, maybe. Anyway, you could cheer him up an' give him *courage* when the other boys, those devils, them, they teases him. An' I got a feelin', me, Olin might get well if he was where they got some good doctors, them. You could make sure, *chère*, I know, me, that they both went to some good doctors, *hein?* I got no doubts, me, you would do that, even if you had to take them to N'Yawlins to get doctored right, them."

"Why, yes," Lavinia said slowly. "I'd do my best for the boys—if it were really my responsibility."

"Sho' you the one that's goin' be responsible, yes. If you was 'shamed of how Cajun families do, you wouldn't be marryin' with no Cajun boy, no. An' I tell you very frankly, me, no Cajun girl in this livin' world, no, would leave her husban's little brothers without nobody to give them the right care, not if her husban's mother, her, went an' died. With us, *chère*, it ain't just one man, him, an' one girl, her, w'at's married with each other, no. It's the whole family w'at counts, all two of the families, an' the families looks out for everybody that's in the families, them. That's the way we do, us, an' it's a good way, I guarantee you, me."

"I know. And I'm very fond of Odey and Olin, you know that. But I wish you wouldn't keep talking about dying, Mrs. Villac."

"You better start callin' me *mère*, so it will come more easier later," Anne admonished her. "An' I ask you to tell me, please, why I ain't supposed to talk about dying, me? When you talk 'bout something, it's more easier to plan for it, yes, an' get ready for it, an' I tell you frankly, me, I'll die lots happier if I got everything lined up like it ought to be. It's the same thing, yes, with you. You got to admit, don' you, *chère*, you'll be more happier married if you got everything planned out an' lined up like you an' your folks want—the clothes an' the house an' all like that. Same way with Mezalee, too. I don' see, me, why Mezalee ain't got the right, same like you an' same like me, to make plans to get everything lined up the way she wants to have it, her. You got to promise me, please, that when I'm gone, me, you'll tell Mezalee how you'll take Odey an' Olin to live by you an' Claude, if she wants to go ahead an' be a real nun, like she always been sayin', her."

Lavinia swallowed hard, but she did not hesitate. "All right," she said, "I promise. I'll do everything that's necessary or best for Odey and Olin, if Mezalee goes into a convent, but she may not want to, after all. She may just want to go on thinking about being a nun in her heart, the way you said. Because she may not want to leave Clement. You haven't said anything about him. And you did say, when you started talking about the others, it would be different if they were her brothers and sisters. He *is* her brother."

"Yes, an' he's Fleex's brother, too, ain't he, him? I didn't think, me, nobody would have to remind you, no, to be good to Fleex's brother, not when he's the spittin' image of the one that's gone an' left us. Me, I tell you frankly, I thought that would be just nature."

A note of scorn had come into Anne's voice. It gradually softened when she went on after stopping to look steadily at Lavinia, who met her gaze for a moment and then turned her head away.

"Well, I see I don' have to say no more about that, no. I see you goin' take care of Clement like he was you' own brother, yes, an' not just your husband's brother. An' you'll straighten him out, *chère,* so he won't be no trouble to his papa an' his uncle like he is now, him. You got to look on it like this: Clement's the onliest one his papa an' his uncle, them, got to depend on to keep this farm like it got to be run. They can't depend on Onezime, on account of he's too weak, him; he ain't no stout young buck what can do heavy work, no. An' that poor little Odey, him, can't hear good enough to understand w'at they tell him to do. I got a feelin' in my heart, though, me, that you will do all w'at is right, yes, an' never mind if it makes you happy or if it don'. I know something else, me. I know it real good-good-good. I know you'll be plenty more happier, *chère,* if you put that Fleex, him, right out you' mind for keeps, outside of sayin' to yourself, yes, how you goin' see to it his little brother grows up to be a credit an' not no disgrace, no. An' here's something else w'at I know, me. I know marryin' with Claude ain't goin' to be like w'at it would have been if you could have married with Fleex. I told your *maman* that long ago. But you done give you' promise to Claude, yes, an' I know right in my heart you goin' keep that promise. You goin' keep it account it's right, not account it's happy for you. You ain't happy, no. You thought you forgot all about Fleex, him, didn't you, *chère?* But when Claude started makin' love like he got the right to do, him, you boun' to been thinkin' 'bout how it would have been if it was Fleex, an' you was wishin' it was, yes. I ask you very frankly, me, ain't that right, Lavinia?"

"Yes," Lavinia whispered, so softly that Anne could hardly hear, though even without hearing she would have known what the girl was saying. "I'm sorry, but it's true. That's just what I did. That's why——"

"Never mind, *chère.* You don' need to tell me, no. An' I tell you this, I tell it frankly, me. I'm sorry for you, yes. I'm glad for Claude, sure, account he is my son, but I know in my heart, me, that you need help an' sympathy more than me right now. I guarantee you! Now I tell you w'at you got to do, *chère*. You got to say to you'self like so: 'I loved Fleex an' Fleex loved me, him. But Fleex never loved me enough, no, to stay here an' work out some way to make everything be right. He run away, him. Me, I tried all I could to get him back, but it was like chasin' some *feu follet*. Exackly like chasin' some *feu follet*. But Claude wasn't like that, no. Claude never run away, him, an' he never will. I never had to chase Claude when I found out he loved me. Not Claude, no. He chased me, that boy, yes, an' that's how it belongs. An' anyway, Claude's real, a man, him, flesh an' blood, not no dream 'bout somebody I ain't seen in too long to remember an' ain't goin' see no more, me, not never. So I'm goin' marry with Claude, me, an' stop all this foolishness. I'm goin' to be a real good wife, an' make him happy, an' bimeby I'm goin' to be happy too, me. Everybody goin' be happy. An' Claude's *maman* goin' be the most happiest one of all, her!' "

Nothing more was said about a wedding before Advent, which was, after all, now almost at hand; but preparations were soon astir for a wedding on Christmas Day. It was now obvious to everyone that, no matter how great an effort she made, Anne would not be able to get far from home this time. However, when Father Gassler, the resident pastor at Iota, was consulted, he said that, under the circumstances, he would be glad to perform the ceremony at the bride's home. This would not be the first time he had done so, by any means, in the case of a mixed marriage. Yes, of course, theoretically these always took place at the rectory; but there was none connected with the little mission chapel in Crowley as yet, and its lack constituted a valid reason for making concessions. Anne was completely satisfied with this explanation, into which the condition of her health had not entered, at least verbally; and the question of the bride's dress and those of her attendants—Odile and Pauline—had hardly been settled when Anne began to discuss her own. Ursin was surprised, since he had taken it for granted she would wear the same one she had worn to Annette's wedding, but he raised no objections; as in the case of the additions to the house, he was mournfully aware that, if her wishes were to be met at all, this would have to be in the very near future.

"Me, I don't say too much, no. But one thing I'm goin' say, I guarantee you. This here is one time I got to have a different color dress. A green dress. Green is the most good color for Christmas, so I got to have a green dress, me."

"Sho', sho'. If you got to, you goin' to, yes. The girls, them, can get you some pieces w'at they call samples the very next time they goes to Crowley. How 'bout that? Tha's goin' satisfy you, maybe?"

"Not no Crowley. This here got to be a real soignée dress, from the finest silk they got, yes. Silk from Mouton Frères in Lafayette. An' you got to go with the girls to pick it out, too."

"What I got to go to Lafayette for, me? I don't know not one leas' li'l thing, no, 'bout pickin' out no silks, Anne. You know that good as me."

"Sho' I know it, me. But you got to go account green silk ain't the onlies' thing I got to have, no. I got to have some pearl beads. I mean pearl beads to wear."

"Hein? W'at you say, you? Pearl beads?"

"That's true like the Bible. I ain't never said nothin' biffo', me, by I knew you got so much to pay fo', yes, with seven kids w'at got to be educate, an' land w'at got to be paid fo', an' a house w'at got to be made big-big-big all the time, yes, an' that trousseau we give Annette for her *dot.* But now I got to tell you frankly, me, all my livin' days long I been wantin' pearl beads, so this time . . . maybe . . . you got to admit, you, that we got no expenses fo' Claude gettin' married like if he was a girl, no. An' you got to admit, you, that Lavinia's a real-real lady, her, same as Adeline. You got to admit, you, that in one way she doin' us lots of credit, yes, when she marries with our son, him, so we got to do her lots of credit, too, us. Ain't that right, no?"

Ursin's voice was husky, but firm.

"Sho' that's right. It couldn't be no righter if the priest himself say it in the church. You' right like everything, Anne, yes, an' I'm goin' with the girls to Lafayette, me, an' so soon like they got some silk sample pick' out fo' you, them, just so soon we go by Mr. Krauss an' they can help me pick out them pearl beads."

"I don't want some young girls, maybe, to pick out no pearl beads for me, Ursin, no. I—I—got the idea, me, I want you should be the one to pick out my beads. You would do it fo' me, no?"

"I will do it fo' you, *yes.* I guarantee you, me."

There was some division of opinion about both silks and

beads. Lavinia was in favor of a very soft pale green fabric with a smooth silvery finish, while Odile and Pauline were both sure their mother would prefer a bright emerald-colored brocade; and Lavinia favored tiny milky beads that looked like real pearls, while Ursin and his daughters were far more attracted by large pink globules, which bore no resemblance to these whatsoever. When samples of the two materials and both strings of beads were brought back to the farm for Anne's inspection, Lavinia insisted that her future mother-in-law should not be told whose choice was for which, and Anne unhesitatingly applauded her daughters' and her husband's. So Mary found time, despite all she had to do at home, to make up the emerald green brocade from a paper pattern of Anne's choosing, and the pink globules lay, embedded in an open white satin box, on the sick woman's bedside table, where she could look at them as often as she chose.

She spent countless hours in doing so, with ever-increasing satisfaction, and once in a great while she took them out of their satin box and fingered them, with almost the same reverence she gave her rosary. But it was not until Mary had the green brocade ready to fit that Anne tried the pearls on. Her natural lack of tidiness had been intensified by her long illness; it required firmness as well as tact on Mezalee's part to persuade her that her hair must be brushed and braided, her face and hands washed. But when the day came for the fitting, she submitted without protest to careful hairdressing and to a sponge bath, and after the skillfully cut dress had been adjusted to her figure and the pearls clasped around her neck, she asked, for the first time in months, for a mirror.

To her family and friends, who saw her constantly, the change in her from day to day, though admittedly for the worse, had at no time seemed startling. To Anne herself, the transformation in her appearance came as a dreadful shock. She had never been pretty and, consequently, she had never been vain of beauty; but she had prided herself on the vigor which had permitted her to work without fatigue in the fields, as well as in the house, to minister unaided to the needs of a large family and to take childbearing and child-rearing in her stride; she had known that this hardihood was reflected in her face and figure and she had gloried in it. Now, not only was the last vestige of her amazing vitality gone; in its place were the disfigurement wrought by disease and the unmistakable signs of disintegration. Mercifully, she did not realize that the glowing colors of her triumphantly chosen finery intensified the effect of these telltale ravages; nevertheless, she had received a terrible blow. She turned from the mirror, which Mezalee was holding up for her, and swallowed hard. Then she looked at Mary and caught the unvoiced sympathy in her friend's expression.

"Tha's such a beautiful, beautiful dress you made fo' me, Mary," she said. "I ain't never had no dress that pretty in all my life, no, me. An' the pearl beads is just w'at I been wantin' fo' the longest, ever since I been a young girl, me, so far like I can remember. But now I got to get back on the bed. I expeck it must be maybe some excitements that got me all this wore out. Rest—tha's w'at I'm needin' now, so close the door, Mezalee, yes, when you goin' out. Rest . . . I got to rest, me."

Only the members of the two families were present at the marriage ceremony, but Anne, wearing the green dress and the pink pearls, was among them. And it was a sizable group for, of course, the Bazinets and the Perets were members of the family now; and Sally had, at last, come on from Illinois, bringing her two children with her, for the exciting prospect of a wedding had been too strong a temptation for her to resist. Then all the best friends of both families were added to the gathering for the wedding breakfast, which was also Christmas dinner, at the Winslows' house; and it did not seem unnatural to anyone that Dr. Mouton should be among these or that he should leave immediately after dinner, for he was a busy man and had patients to see, even on Christmas. If anyone thought it was strange that the elder Villacs left at the same time, no one said so. It was a beautiful balmy day, and all the other guests lingered around the festive tables which had been set up in the first little old house and the parlor and sitting room of the new one—Brent's measuring board had been carefully carried upstairs to the spare room, and so had Mary's sewing machine; and the old leather couch had been put out on the porch, where there was still another table. So everyone had enough room to sit down and feast. There was wild goose as well as wild turkey, both with wonderful rice dressing, and great dishes of scalloped sweet potato, flavored with orange; there were dozens and dozens of fresh, homemade rolls and loaf after loaf of light bread; there were preserves and pickles and jellies and jams and half a dozen different kinds of pie; there were freezers full of ice cream and others full of cream cheese, and gallons of coffee; and, of course, there was a white cake for the bride and a dark cake for the groom and *dragées* for the children. When Lavinia went upstairs to change from the beautiful snowy dress, with the balloon sleeves and the full-gored skirt, which was the very latest style and vastly becoming to her besides, into the blue traveling suit—another creation of Madame Sophie's in New Orleans—the guests were so replete with good food they could hardly bestir themselves to stroll out into Mary's garden, where her camellias were in full bloom, and prepare to throw old shoes after the decorated surrey in which Jim Garland was going to drive the bridal pair to the depot.

Nothing more had been said about a wedding trip to New York. It was Lavinia herself who had remarked that she could not think of a nicer place to go than over to the Pass, but that she was sure she and Claude could see all they wanted of the Gulf Coast in a week's time. No one did much work at a rice mill or anywhere else between Christmas and New Year's. But on the second of January Claude would be back at work again and she could start getting straightened around in their new house. It was practically done, just a little papering and painting still unfinished. She preferred to oversee these finishing touches herself while she was unpacking the wedding presents and finding places for the unbelievable quantities of cut glass among them. . . .

The bride and groom surprised everyone by getting back on New Year's Eve, instead of a day later. That, Claude announced, had been Lavinia's idea, too; she said that as long as Christmas had been spent at her house she wanted to spend New Year's at his. There was a great deal of scurrying around and some rather broad jesting while everyone made ready for the extra doubling up that was necessary in order to provide the newlyweds with a room to themselves. They were finally assigned to the one normally occupied by Mezalee and Pauline which, though smaller, was pleasanter—and took less time to tidy up!—than the one Claude had previously shared with Odey, Olin and Clement. Mezalee always managed to have fresh white muslin curtains at her window and a fresh white linen bureau scarf on her dresser. Now the beautiful new coverlet, which was just done, was quickly spread on the white iron bed, over new sheets and blankets that were hand woven, too. Lavinia told Mezalee, and meant it, that it was a much prettier room than any she and Claude had been given at the Pass, and that she was only sorry they had not come to occupy it sooner.

It was hours before anyone retired for the night, however. The entire family gathered in Anne's room, and Mezalee showed Lavinia how to make the "Queen's Sauce," their favorite nightcap, which they never failed to drink on New Year's Eve and other great occasions, and which they always made over an open fire.

"Of course, it isn't what *you'd* call a sauce," Mezalee explained, standing by the chimney piece, as she stirred white sugar and beaten eggs into milk which she had previously brought to a boil, but which she now set over a low flame where it would not boil any more. "It's a drink —a sort of eggnog—the very best kind." Her father uncorked a whisky bottle and handed it to Mezalee, who bent over to go on with her stirring, as she slowly emptied the liquor into the custard. Then Odile brought cups, and Mezalee poured the hot, fragrant mixture carefully into them; Pauline, with equal care, took the cups from her, one by one, and passed them around. Anne was the first to raised hers for a toast to a happy New Year; and when the answering chorus had died down, she added, "Now we goin' sleep, us, I guarantee you it will be a fine sleep, yes, account everybody gets a fine sleep after they drink Queen's Sauce. *Allons,* everybody, *fiche moi le camp!* Everybody exceptin' only Claude an' Lavinia, them. Claude already knows w'at the Queen's Sauce is good for, yes, outside of puttin' folks to sleep. But maybe Lavinia ain't never heard 'bout it, so I'm goin' tell her right now, me."

She drew the bride down beside her and whispered to her, but it was a stage whisper that everyone could hear, and everyone laughed, Lavinia with the others. "I guarantee you, me it don' never fail, *chère,*" Anne said. "Nor neither I ain't the only one. My *maman* had nine an' my *gran'mère,* her, she had twelve, an' they both said the same, them, 'bout the Queen's Sauce. . . . Now you got to sit by me a little while yet, *chère.* Maybe you could tell me about the Pass. We never got there, us. I mean me an' Ursin. We always planned to see that ocean, but somehow . . . I guarantee you, me. . . ."

Her voice trailed contentedly away into silence and she closed her eyes. As all the others, except Lavinia, trooped away, Mezalee beckoned to Claude and he, too, went into the next room.

"Dr. Mouton stopped by again this afternoon, before you and Lavinia got here," she said. "He keeps *Tante* more or less under opiates all the time now, of course. He told me he'd be back tomorrow, but he didn't think she'd suffer any tonight and she hasn't. I believe it's been one of the happiest nights of her life."

"Same here," he answered emphatically. "All right, Lavinia and I will stay with her a while, like she asked. She might rouse up long enough to ask a few questions. If she doesn't pretty soon though, we could go to bed, too, don't you think so? After all, we might bother Papa if we stayed too long."

He grinned and went to rejoin his wife at his mother's bedside. As he sat down beside Lavinia and put his arm around her, she nestled closer to him, laying her head on his shoulder and reaching for his hand. Here, at last, was the spontaneous gesture, the unmistakable sign that his caress was so welcome that she was impelled to return it. He had waited and waited for this and now it had come. When he leaned over to kiss her, he found that her lips were already seeking his. Nothing that had so far happened between them had thrilled him like this. Not that Lavinia had sought to prevent or delay their union on their wedding night; but he had sensed her instinctive defensiveness, her involuntary recoil from complete self-abandonment. He had striven to remember that he must show her he understood, that he must be gentle and not precipitate if he were to help her pass beyond the barriers which kept her from being wholly his in such a way as to rob the memory of all reproach. And he had succeeded. He was conscious of her gratitude to him, of the increasing ease with which she accepted the marriage relation; but still he had not yet felt that he could take her swiftly and passionately, and hold her fast until the force of his desire had spent itself; much less had he felt that she was ready and waiting to be so taken and so held. Now the great moment had come and he could not seize it. He must wait until he was sure his mother no longer wanted him; he must pray that his beloved would still yearn for his dominance when that maternal need was past. . . .

At the end of an hour Anne was still sleeping peacefully. Ursin, who had unceremoniously climbed in beside her, was also sleeping, though somewhat less silently. Claude rose, his arm still around Lavinia, and together they tiptoed out of the sickroom and into the one that had been so lovingly prepared for them. When they, too, fell asleep at last, still in each other's arms, it was to sink into the deep, dreamless slumber following the assuagement of

300

mutual passion. They were still sleeping when Mezalee came in and stood by their bedside, looking down at them long and fondly before she waked them.

"You mustn't feel that I've come to bring you sad tidings," she told them then. "You mustn't grieve. This is the way she hoped it would be, after she'd lived to see you married. *Tante* never woke again or spoke again after she told you she wanted you to stay beside her."

CHAPTER XXVI

The only previous time that Lavinia had been seriously affected by the loss of someone close to her had been when her grandmother Garland died. She had been a child then, carefully shielded from all the dreadful details connected with preparations for burial, and the memory of the funeral services themselves had become a dim and distant one. Even if all this had not been so, she would have been utterly unprepared for the proceedings which followed Anne's peaceful and merciful release from suffering and, granted the experience which would have mitigated her bewilderment, she still would not have been able to suppress entirely her instinctive recoil from many of the observances which were traditional to the family into which she had married.

Mezalee lingered only a few minutes after telling Lavinia and Claude what had happened—just long enough to give her cousin the support of her sympathy and to make him feel that she shared his deep sense of loss. Lavinia tried to speak the same sort of soothing words and to supplement these with compassionate caresses; but, for the first time, Claude appeared hardly aware of her, or aware in a way that seemed to indicate she did not count. He did not actually shake off the arm she put around his shoulder, or draw his face away from hers when she laid her cheek against his; but he began to dress hurriedly, while tears he did not try to wipe away ran down his unshaven cheeks and he made no effort to control the sobs which shook his solid frame. As soon as he was sketchily clothed, he opened the door and went into the *salle,* leaving Lavinia, who was still struggling with the clasps of her corset and the strings of her petticoat, behind him in the room which had so recently been the scene of their most joyful and spontaneous union.

To her, it seemed disrespectful to approach the dead woman, whom she had so sincerely loved, without first bathing and clothing herself with even greater care than usual and, above all, without tidying her long hair, which always required a good deal of time to arrange properly in the morning and which she knew was now in a state of complete dishevelment. However, such proper arrangement involved unbraiding, combing, brushing, rebraiding and fastening in place; and sensing that she, too, was expected to make haste, she started to pin it up, as best she could, without competely undoing it, when there was a knock at the door and Mezalee came back into the room, with a clean white cloth in her hand.

"You'd rather I didn't cover it up yet, wouldn't you, *chere?*" she said, glancing from Lavinia to the one tiny glass in the room.

"Cover it up? You mean the mirror?"

"Yes. Didn't you know that was our custom? We veil the mirrors as soon as possible after a death in the family. But I see you need this one to do your hair. Just let me know as soon as you've finished. I've already veiled all the others and stopped the clocks and emptied the vases."

"Stopped the clocks! Emptied the vases!" Lavinia exclaimed, realizing that for the second time within a few moments she was repeating, in her astonishment, something Mezalee had said to her, and telling herself that she must try not to keep on doing it.

"Yes. Time has stopped for *Tante,* so it must stop for us, too, at present. And *N'Onc* holds to the old belief that if water is left in vases that are in the house, the soul of the dead may drown before it reaches Purgatory."

This time, Lavinia said nothing. She was quite incapable of speech.

"The neighbors will start arriving at any moment to help us make our mourning," Mezalee went on. "They'd think it very strange if all these things weren't done before they arrived."

"People will be coming here to sew today?" Lavinia asked, echoing Mezalee's words for the third time before she could stop herself, and trying hard to hurry with her hair, which seemed to become more unmanageable by the moment.

"Oh, yes. Everyone will try to be helpful. We couldn't possibly do it all by ourselves. But I don't think we ought to wait for two persons who aren't relatives to lay *Tante* out, as long as there are none who live near by. I spoke to

N'Onc about it, as soon as he had closed her eyes, and he agreed that, under the circumstances, I had better do it, with your help. Could you come with me to her room now?"

"Yes, of course."

Mezalee fastened the cloth she had brought with her carefully around the little mirror and they went into the *salle* together. Olin, Odey, Onezime and Clement were setting up the tables which, so short a time before, had been used for the marriage feast. Evidently, Odile and Pauline were busy in the kitchen, for not only the usual pleasant aroma of morning coffee while brewing, but the scents given forth by various hearty foods were wafted toward them. Claude was nowhere to be seen and, as Mezalee realized that Lavinia was looking for him, she explained his absence.

"He's gone to tell your father and mother and grandfather. And—I hope you won't think this is strange—he's going to tell the bees, too."

"Tell the *bees?*" Lavinia had given up trying not to echo what was said to her.

"Yes. Of course, they're not really our bees, but you belong to our family now and, in a way, your parents do, too. So we thought—we hoped—they wouldn't mind tying a little piece of black cloth on each of the hives. We call it *faisant le deuil aux mouches à miel.* *N'Onc* still holds to another old belief: that if the bees aren't taken into the confidence of the family where there's been a death, they'll all leave their hives. And if anything like that happened, it would be a terrible calamity for your father as he has more than a hundred colonies now."

"Yes, it would," Lavinia managed to say.

"Next, Claude will go to the Bazinets' and one or two other houses. *N'Onc* and *Père* went to tell Marcelite and Alcée before they started into Crowley to see the undertaker Mr. Toler. Alcée promised to tell all the other neighbors, and to go to Mermentau and Iota, after he'd brought Marcelite here. And Mr. Toler will see that our friends and relatives in Crowley and Rayne and other near-by places are told."

It seemed to Lavinia that both Claude and Alcée must have ridden with extraordinary speed. She and Mezalee had not finished washing and dressing Anne's lifeless form when the first overcrowded buggy came into the yard, discharging no less than three women and two little boys. The little boys went into the yard to play and were soon joined by numerous other young companions. The women had all come prepared to sew, but first they went into Anne's room, making the sign of the cross with one hand and carrying a dried frond, left over from the previous Palm Sunday, in the other. They stopped beside the bed, partly to pray and partly to make comments and ask questions.

"Ah, the poor soul! One sees how greatly she has suffered. Indeed, it seems as if her suffering still continues."

"I do not agree with you, Ambrosine. To me, she looks perfectly at peace. I believe she has already been through her Purgatory and has entered into Paradise."

"I saw no knife sticking in the gate post and there have been more *feus follets* about than ever before at this time of year. I hope every precaution was taken to safeguard the poor invalid, but I cannot help feeling some oversight may have occurred."

"Oh, no! The knife has now been taken out, but it was thrust into place the minute the *feus follets* were observed. And I am sure that was as soon as they began to flutter anywhere near by."

"Is this still her own mattress, the one on which she died, where she is lying, Mezalee?"

"Yes. Lavinia and I had only just finished shrouding her when you came. But *Père*'s bed has been stripped, his mattress is ready to bring in. While you go into the *salle* and have some coffee, before you start sewing, the boys will help us lift her off this one and place her on the other and Lavinia and I will dress the bed properly and light the vigil lamps. I am sorry we could not have everything done before you arrived."

"I think I will not start my sewing until after the mattress has been changed. I wish to go outdoors and see Anne's burn. It is important to watch the direction to which the smoke blows. I hope, *chère*, it will not be toward your parents' house."

The last remark was addressed to Lavinia, who was experiencing more and more bewilderment as well as more and more revulsion every minute. She had been afraid, several times, during the process of handling her mother-in-law's inert body, that she was about to become violently sick. Now the precipitate appearance and prying curiosity of these total strangers, who spoke in a patois so broad that she could hardly understand it, familiar as she was with local dialect, seemed to her not only inquisitive, but

304

ghoulish. She made a determined effort not to betray her feelings and she succeeded; but her relief knew no bounds when she saw, amidst the buggies which were beginning to fill the yard in even larger numbers than they had for Annette's wedding, her parents' surrey swinging into line. She rushed out of the house and, as soon as Mary, who was alone, stepped to the ground, the girl flung her arms around her mother's neck and buried her face in a comforting shoulder.

"I was fonder of her and closer to her than any of these outsiders," she said in a muffled voice. "I don't mean the family, of course. I mean all these strange people I've hardly ever seen before, except at First Communions and weddings. Some of them I haven't seen then. But *I* feel like the outsider. Even Mezalee's doing the strangest things —stopping clocks and emptying vases and covering mirrors. Now they're burning Mother Anne's mattress and watching to see if the smoke goes toward your house—or where. They believe that the direction it takes will show the place of the next death. And I had to help—undress her and dress her again, when she couldn't help herself."

"I know, darling. I was afraid this was going to be very hard for you. I came as soon as I could. And your father's coming, too—when he has the little pieces of black cloth tied on all the hundred-odd hives. He was glad he could do something to show his sympathy, and he wouldn't have known what would mean the most to them, if Claude hadn't come and told us. Your grandfather's gone into town—he knows so many people he thought perhaps he could be of the most service there. Look, I've brought my sewing machine with me. Let's get two of the boys to carry it into the *salle,* shall we?"

All day long people were assembling, drinking coffee, eating *cushcush et caillé* and biscuits drenched in syrup, singing sad songs, going into the chamber where Anne lay dead, to evoke memories of their long association with her and lament the ending of this, then coming out again with their handkerchiefs half hiding their faces before resuming their singing, their stitching, their eating and drinking. As time went on, gumbo and boudan sweet-dough pies were added to the more solid refreshments and, less openly, homemade wine and spirits to the coffee. Every room in the house was filled; so were the porch and the yard. *But when night comes, they will go home,* Lavinia said to herself. *They will go away and it will be quiet here again, and Claude will come back and, this time, I will be able to comfort him, when everything is dark and peaceful and we are alone. There will be no hot love-making, as there was last night; just tenderness and compassion between us. . . .* But though some of those who had come from a distance did go home, many others stayed, and there was eating and drinking all night long, interrupted by frequent recitations of the rosary, designed to subdue any trend toward hilarity. When Claude finally returned, bringing the coffin, made in the lumberyard, with him, he and Lavinia did not go into the little room which might have been such a haven to them; they sat on straight chairs all night, with other members of the family, around the candlelighted bed where Anne lay in the strange, motionless state that Lavinia had helped to provide.

Early the next morning, a crude hearse, to which everyone referred as the *corbillard*, came into the yard, drawn by two black horses and driven by one of the men who worked in the lumberyard. The buggies, already reassembled and filled with black-clad mourners, readily fell into line behind it. This time, Ursin, with Olin, rode in the first one; in the next two were Odey and Onezime, Lavinia, Claude and Pauline, followed by Annette, Pierre and Odile. Then came Phares with Clement and Mezalee, Marcelite and Alcée with their children, the Winslows and Jim Garland, the Bazinets and all their tribe. The day was unseasonably warm, the road into Crowley seemingly even rougher than usual; and, after the long Requiem Mass at the little mission church, still remained the task, which there was no provision to perform privately, of encasing the crude coffin in a still cruder box for shipment to Slidell, and the inevitable overnight wait at New Orleans before the sad journey could be completed and the final interment could take place in the forest cemetery at Lacombe.

The Bachemins had done all they could in preparation for this: the tomb of Auriette and André had been opened for the reception of Anne's coffin, the tiny cemetery plot put in the same exquisite order it would have received for *Toussaint*, the rough pathway through the woods from the road to the clearing freed of branches overhead and roots underfoot. But it was impossible for the *corbillard* from Slidell to enter the forest, and the last part of Anne's journey was made on the shoulders of her widower, her sons and her cousins. The local priest was not content with a brief service of committal; he felt that the occasion called for a long eulogy. By the time the burial was over, it was too late to start back to New Orleans. The night was spent at Slidell with the Bachemins, whose house was not sufficiently large to accommodate all the Crowley relatives in any sort of comfort, though they did the best they could by providing makeshift sleeping arrangements, putting all the men in one room and all the women in another. Claude would have found solace in Lavinia's presence now; but it was denied him except in the company of the entire family; by the time they reached the *maisonette*, where they were to stop for dinner, Lavinia was by no means the only member of the group who was almost frantic with fatigue; everyone was more or less almost overcome with weariness, as well as sorrow. The emotional excitement which had sustained the mourners at first had been engulfed in exhaustion. And still the journey back to Crowley remained to be faced. . . .

Eventually, Lavinia succeeded in drawing Claude aside and hesitantly suggested that perhaps it would be better for her to stay over and collect the belongings which had never been removed from the Labadies' house since *Toussaint*. At first, Claude declined to consider such an arrangement; so she excused herself from the dinner table and went up to the *cabinet* to do what she could in the way of packing before train time. Presently, he joined her there.

"I think you're right, after all," he said reluctantly. "I hate to leave you behind. I'd stay with you, but I know *Père*'s counting on me to see him through his homecoming —it's going to be a pretty hard one, all around. But I'd rather have you stay now then come back after I'd got you to Crowley. Our house is practically ready for us, and it'll be harder to break away, once we start moving in. And of course you want your books and music. Besides, I know it isn't fair to the Labadies for you to leave your things here forever. They might need the room for someone else."

"Yes, that's what I thought," Lavinia said. She tried to smile, and though she did not do so very successfully, the attempt encouraged and comforted Claude. He laid his cheek against hers and whispered that he was going to be terribly lonely without her—it had been bad enough the night before and tonight it would be even worse. A peremptory call from the room below reminded him that it was almost train time; did he want to miss it and make everyone else do so? He was keeping them all waiting. . . .

"I'm afraid you are holding them back, dear," Lavinia said, making a conscious effort to show him that it was not she who was trying to hurry him off, that it was- not her wish his last kiss should be shortened. Somewhere at the back of her mind was the fear that if she had been sufficiently responsive he would have known this instinctively, that he would have needed no reassurance; and because the fear, however latent, was there, she tried all the harder to render their parting as painless as possible for him. "It's only for one night you know."

"Yes, but I didn't think there were going to be any nights when we'd be separated ever again."

"Why, there are bound to be, sometimes! You'll have to go away on business and—"

"I'll take you with me. . . . Promise me you won't miss the train tomorrow, darling"

"No, but you'll miss the one today if you don't go down this minute. They're getting annoyed with you, Claude."

"I haven't annoyed you some way, have I, honey?"

"No, no, of course not! But you must go! Really you must. . . ."

"Well, come down with me, won't you? And wave to me from the window? Another two or three minutes won't make all that difference in your packing."

She had said good-by to the others before she came upstairs, because they had been trying to get off even then, and she had thought it would expedite matters if there were one less person present. Another round of farewells would delay things still further, and Claude's people would blame her, mentally, though they would not say anything, for holding him back. She did not mind taking the blame for him, but she wished that neither he nor she had deserved it. With the same uneasiness behind the wish which had made her fear, a few minutes earlier, that she was not sufficiently responsive, she bent over backward, trying to do the right thing, the kind thing. She ran down the stairs and told everyone how sorry she was that she had kept Claude so long and yes, she realized they mustn't stop for anything more now, good-by, good-by. . . .

She parted the curtains and stood waving as the Primeaux and the Villacs got into the waiting hacks. Claude, with his foot already on the step of the second one, turned to make sure she was really there and to throw her one last kiss. Then someone reached out from inside the hack and pulled him in and slammed the door and they were off. Involuntarily, Lavinia sighed.

"It's wonderful to be so much in love, isn't it, *chère?*"

Mlle Haydee, who was also standing by the window, asked softly and, Lavinia thought, a little enviously.

"Ye-e-s," Lavinia answered. Of course it was wonderful, of course she should be glad and thankful that she was happily married, that she would not have to lead a life barren of love, like the kind old lady beside her: But she was so tired that she was not glad about anything or thankful for anything. She was not really sorry Claude had gone; she was too numb with fatigue. In so far as she wanted anything, she wanted to be alone, to lie down, to sleep and sleep and sleep, and forget about having become a wife and having come face to face, for the first time, with death, and having taken a long, hard, sorrowful journey, all within the course of ten days.

"Why don't you rest for a little while, *chère,* before you start your packing?" Mlle Haydee said, still speaking very gently. "You look exhausted, and no wonder, *pauvre petite!* You have been under a great strain. It will be very quiet in the house and that will be good for you. I must go out, to give a lesson to a pupil who could not come to me because of a cold, and of course Clisson has already been obliged to excuse himself, in order to keep to his schedule. Moreover, before we knew you would be with us again, we had promised *Cousine* Ernestine that we would have dinner with her, before going on to a meeting of the Athenée Louisianais afterward. We would gladly have canceled this engagement, if we had thought our presence here would alleviate loneliness which would be painful to you. We still can. But almost the first instant I saw you, I thought solitude was what you wanted—what you needed. Solitude and rest. Was I wrong?"

"No, you were right. I *am* very tired and—yes, I do feel as if I'd like to be alone for a little while."

Her eyes filled with unwelcome tears, which she tried in vain to wink back before they showed on her cheeks. Mlle Haydee patted her shoulder.

"There, there, my dear! Go and lie down. I will tell Mignon not to disturb you for the present. And after a good rest, you will feel so refreshed that you will be able to work all the faster."

"I think you're right. I think I had better lie down for a little while. It's silly, of course, to be so tired. But I am. Tireder than I ever was before in my life."

"Dear child, that is quite natural. *Allez reposer vous.* And do not worry about sleeping past dinnertime. Mignon will bring you something on a tray, whenever you call her."

Conscious as she was of her weariness, Lavinia had not realized that she was actually overwhelmed by it until she started up the little stairway. She stumbled as she went, and was obliged to cling to the slender banister for support. When she reached the *cabinet* she flung herself down on the bed without even taking off her dress, though she fumbled at the fastenings to undo the tight collar and loosen the belt. As she did so, the *alliance* slipped off and fell, tinkling, to the floor.

"It must have been too loose, after all," she murmured to herself. "I must take it back to that nice Mr. Krauss." It was her last conscious thought before she fell into deep, dreamless slumber. She did not get off the bed to pick up the *alliance*, nor reason that she had not realized before it was too loose because it was held in place, most of the time, by her engagement ring. She had been warned that she must be very careful of the Tiffany setting, that it must be cleaned regularly and methodically, and that, unlike the *alliance*, which must never be taken off, it must always be removed when she had her hands in water or was doing any kind of dusty work. She had been scrupulously careful in her observance of this advice; when she washed clothes or dishes, when she bathed, when she swept and "tidied up," she took off her engagement ring and put it in a safe, near-by place until all this was done. Since her marriage, she had not been doing much housework, so the necessity of securing the *alliance* had not been especially evident; but that afternoon she had taken off the engagement ring, because the books and sheet music she was preparing to handle were dusty. She had not thought of putting it on again when she went downstairs with Claude—indeed, she had thought of nothing but speeding him on his way. She had not thought of it when she came back upstairs. She had been past thinking of anything.

It was a long time before she emerged from the abyss of deep slumber and reached the realm of dreams at the borderland between sleep and drowsiness. When she did, she dreamed that her name was being spoken in tones of infinite yearning, and that she was being kissed, at first very gently, on her brow; then less gently, on her throat; and then, not gently at all, on her mouth. The sound of her name was sweet, in her dream, and the kisses were sweet, too, so sweet that she wanted to return them, in all their increasing strength. They were different, too, from any real kisses she had ever received, and she tried, in her dream, to understand why this was. Hazily, it seemed to her they must be like the kisses she had expected Fleex to give her, and that she had expected to return, the last time she had seen him, when they had parted without kissing at all. Then gradually she realized that she was not dreaming any more, that the kisses were real; and it came to her, not hazily or slowly, but in a flash, that there was a new quality in Claude's lovemaking, something that had never been there before, even in his most passionate moments. Again she realized, as she had that afternoon, that she must be very careful not to let him feel she was reproaching him, though this time he had missed the train and inconvenienced many other persons because of his overpowering desire to be with her. Above all, she must not let him guess how much she had wanted to be alone.

"So you came back?" she murmured, still contending with her drowsiness and striving to inject a note of welcome into her voice.

"Yes, of course I came back. You knew I would, sometime, didn't you?"

With a swiftness that was terrifying, she was wide awake. Stifling a scream, she struggled to free herself. The light in the room was very dim, for dusk had fallen while she was sleeping. The form bending over her, the face so close to her own, might well have been Claude's, as she had taken for granted, for all she could see. But the voice was unmistakable. It did not belong to Claude. It belonged to Fleex.

CHAPTER XXVII

She could not speak again, she could not make another move. Now that her delicious drowsiness was gone and the cobwebs of dreamland swept away, her consciousness was dreadful in its clarity: Fleex had come back. Fleex had come back and she was married to Claude. She was married to Claude. . . .

"Say yes, of course you knew I would, darling. I know I told you I wouldn't, in the stupid letter I wrote you; but you must have realized that was only because I didn't have anything to offer you then, not even a place to take you, and didn't see how I ever would have. But the minute my luck turned. . . ."

311

The minute his luck turned! Then it had turned, he did have something to offer her, a place to take her. Not that it would ever have mattered to her, if he hadn't. It was Fleex, just Fleex that she had always wanted. . . .

"Well, all right. Don't say anything yet if you'd rather not. Just let me go on kissing you. I'm sorry I startled you. But, *mon coeur,* it's been so long!"

Somehow she must break away from him. But he was holding her so tightly that she could not sit up, much less get off the bed, and his mouth had closed down on hers so hard that she could not even free her lips until the kisses ended, and they went on and on. He would not willfully hurt or harm her, she knew that. But there were so many things he did not know, so many things he was taking for granted. He had no idea she was married, he had never dreamed she would not wait for him. Moreover, he seemed unconscious that there had been an attempt to escape from his embrace, or even that there had been a deliberate lack of response to it. Perhaps, while she was still dreaming, or thought she was, she had reacted more spontaneously, more ardently, than she realized; and afterward, perhaps he had been so dominated by his own desire that he had been unaware of anything else. Or perhaps he believed she was overwhelmed by the unexpectedness of his arrival and could not instantly give expression to her joy, but that, as soon as she had recovered from the first shock of his unforeseen presence, her yearning for him, like his for her, would find rapturous release after long denial.

She was still perforce supine in his embrace as these tumultuous thoughts went racing through her tortured mind. Then, at last, of his own accord, he slackened his hold on her and straightened up. "I had to have that first of all," he said. "And of course I've got to have a lot more. But meanwhile, I want to see you. I haven't had a good look at you yet."

There was no bafflement in his voice, no doubtfulness, no anxiety. It was the voice of ecstasy and of triumph. There was only one means of lighting the room, a single bulb suspended from a cord and inadequately shielded by a china shade, which hung directly over the bed. He reached for the little metal chain attached to the fixture and tugged at it. As he did so, Lavinia managed to straighten up and get to her feet. Then her fingers flew to the loosened opening of her dress. But quick as she was, Fleex was quicker. He caught her hands and held them imprisoned.

"Don't," he said. "Everything about you is so lovely. You can't blame me for wanting to see all I can."

His hungry eyes were devouring her, from her shining, disordered hair and flushed cheeks, to her lips, redder than he remembered them, and redder than they would have been now, he knew, if he had not kissed them so long and so hard. Then his gaze shifted to her slender throat and white neck and came to rest on the hollow between her breasts which the open dress had partially revealed.

"Mon coeur," he said again, *"je t'en prie. . . ."*

"My heart"—the most precious, the most intimate form of endearment! He had used it for the second time. And now he was coupling it with an entreaty. They had always used the familiar form of "thou" when speaking to each other in French—that was natural; all children, all members of a family and close friends did so. The French was natural, too; it had always been their custom to use it when they were alone together. But he had never called her *mon coeur* before tonight, he had never begged her for any privilege or any favor. How could she deny him now? The very fact that he could so easily have taken her, when—as she knew only too well—he would have taken almost any other girl whom he desired, made it all the harder. For this was something of which desire was only a part, though the desire was there, crying for assuagement. This was love, the kind of love everyone had told her Fleex was incapable of feeling, the kind of love she had finally allowed everyone to persuade her she was waiting in vain to receive.

"I can't," she said brokenly. "Fleex please—please don't say that to me again. Please don't even kiss me again."

"Please don't even kiss you again! Are you crazy? Mignon told me the Labadies wouldn't be home until late, that they were having supper with a cousin and going to some kind of a meeting afterward. We've oceans of time. I suppose that eventually we'll have to go down to the drawing room and put in a decorous appearance. And of course I'll announce that we're going to be married right away. Meanwhile, however—"

He was still holding her hands imprisoned. But now, as he looked down at her, there was less intensity in his face than when he had first seemed bent on devouring her with his gaze. His expression was happier, his manner easier; they were those not only of a man very much in love, but of a man confident that his love was returned and that the moment of its fulfillment was at hand. And though he had been so careful to avoid giving any impression of force, there was an air of authority about him that was entirely new, the air of a man who had an unquestionable right to expect that his orders, or even his suggestions, would not be disregarded. Lavinia, who had been too preoccupied otherwise to pay any attention to his clothes, now noticed for the first time that he was wearing a neat uniform, which fitted him well and which was suited to his coloring and figure. From her observations of the water-front, she thought it might represent some sort of a minor but responsible position on one of the banana boats, unremarkable in itself, but nothing short of extraordinary considering the past record of its wearer.

"Meanwhile," she added swiftly, afraid, not without reason, that this slackening of pressure might be only temporary and that she must seize upon it, "I'd like to ask you what else Mignon told you besides the Labadies' plans for the evening. Obviously she told you where you'd find me. Did she tell you how I happened to be here?"

"She said you'd been studying in New Orleans all last winter and part of this winter, too. She was pretty vague about it all. Naturally she would be. I'm afraid Mignon isn't very familiar with the details of learning."

"And I'm afraid there are a few other reasons why she was vague," Lavinia spoke scornfully, but the words were not out of her mouth before she realized she had no right to blame an ignorant colored woman for what had happened. She had bribed Mignon to find out, through every means at her disposal, when Fleex came to New Orleans, and she had never countermanded that order. Why should she be the one to assume that Mignon would recognize the fact that for Lavinia marriage would have to make a difference? With the almost unfailing instinct of her race, Mignon had scented a romance, and had done so with added relish because this had evidently been unsanctioned and ill-starred from the beginning. It had doubtless not even occurred to her that any fruition of it, now, would be unthinkable. She was probably terribly proud that she had at last found M'iz Viney's man for her, the one M'iz Viney really wanted, and had brought them together under conditions which were so propitious—a house empty except for them and night coming on. . . .

"Would you care to tell me what you think those reasons were?" Fleex inquired, still speaking easily and smilingly.

"No, I won't take the time right now to go into reasons. I'll stick to results."

"Just as you say. But couldn't we sit down while you do it?"

The only place they could sit, side by side, in the tiny room was on the bed and instinct quickly told Lavinia they must not do that. She had managed to slip off it once; she doubted very much whether she could do so a second time. She freed her hands and reached behind her for the one chair in the *cabinet*. But, before she could sit down in it, Fleex had done so, drawing her onto his knees. The chair had arms, it was wide and soft cushioned. Fleex shifted his position until he was sure Lavinia was comfortable. It was almost impossible not to lean back against his shoulder. But she tried to remain as detached as possible.

"Evidently Mignon didn't tell you that I stopped here on my way back from Lacombe to pack up my belongings because I'm returning to Crowley for good," she said, unsuccessfully making an effort to sit upright.

"No, she didn't. And of course you're not. You're coming with me to Central America, on a honeymoon trip. I've got it all arranged. I thought I'd have to go all the way to Crowley to tell you so, and it was a real break to find out that I wouldn't need to, that you were right here in New Orleans. Can't you relax, darling? We'd both be so much more comfortable if you would."

"I want to look at you while I talk to you. How did you find out that I was in New Orleans?"

"It seems that Mignon has a lot of cronies along the waterfront. Before one of them had finished telling me to get in touch with her right away, another one came along to tell me the same thing. I couldn't leave for Crowley until morning anyway because we didn't dock until the afternoon train had gone and—"

The afternoon train had gone! If the boat had docked just a little earlier, Claude would still have been at the *maisonette* when Fleex reached it. If the message from the dock hands had not been delivered to Fleex until the next day, Lavinia would have been gone herself. But Mignon's cronies had been too well bribed to risk displeasure at the source of their revenue. . . .

"And I thought I might as well come up here to see her," Fleex was continuing. "I didn't have anything else I especially wanted to do. I've rather had my fill of hitting it up at dives. And besides, now that I've got this job as third engineer—"

315

So that was what the uniform meant! He wasn't a stowaway, a tramp, a common seaman. He was an officer, a junior officer to be sure, but still an officer. And she had been led to believe. . . .

"It may be just temporary. The regular man came down with dengue just as the boat was leaving Puerto de Oro and they had to have someone. They grabbed me for lack of anyone better. I've learned quite a lot about machinery this past year, so I took an examination of sorts and they gave me a certificate. I don't suppose I could have got it in a place where they'd have been more particular, but I believe I can make good and, in that case, I can get the same kind of a job on another boat of the same kind, if the other man gets well and wants his job back. Maybe even a promotion. And haven't you ever noticed? If you have one piece of bad luck, you generally have two or three running. It's the same way with good luck. Actually, the first thing Mignon told me didn't have anything to do with you. It seems she's been eavesdropping."

"Eavesdropping?"

She managed to twist around so that she could face him. This time Fleex did not try to prevent her freedom of movement.

"Yes. She was intrigued when M. Clisson invited my father down here and stayed shut up with him in his *bureau*, talking about *affaires*. So she—well, she must have listened on purpose, and of course she wouldn't understand what she overheard, any too well. We've agreed that there are some things she's vague about, purposely or otherwise. But apparently there's no doubt that the Labadies have made a will in favor of all my parents' children. The original idea was to cut me out, because I was such a ne'er-do-well. But Mezalee insisted that wasn't fair. So I'm to get this house. Of course, Marcelite's fixed with Alcée and Clement will have the farm and Mezalee's just waiting for the time when she can go into a convent. So it seemed logical that I should have the house and the others the money. You'd like to live in the *maisonette*, wouldn't you, darling? I've always thought it was quite pretty."

Would she like to live in the *maisonette!* In this charming house where she had been so happy, except for missing and wanting Fleex, in the city where she could do all the things she most enjoyed, in the company of the kind of people she found most congenial! And with Fleex for her husband—Fleex, whom she would have been willing to marry, even if they could have had no other home than a shack in a swamp! She did not answer, she did not trust herself to answer. But Fleex did not seem to mind, he did not even seem to notice.

"Well, I believe we'll enjoy ourselves here very much, later on. Not that I'm in any hurry to see the Labadies go to their graves. They've always been very kind to me—that is, they were until they decided, like everyone else, that I was quite hopeless, and even since then they've been fair, or tried to be, if Mignon's got things anything like straight. But let's not talk about them any more right now. I mean, what really matters is that you're here, that I'm here, and that we haven't seen each other in months and months and that we're terribly in love with each other."

"I'm sorry, but there are some things that matter a good deal, too." Lavinia had found her voice at last, and though she spoke with difficulty she did so with determination. "You didn't ask how I happened to be in Lacombe and, obviously, Mignon didn't tell you that, either. I went there for Anne Villac's funeral."

His expression instantly changed. "I'm sorry," he said gravely. "Sorry she's died and sorry I didn't get in a day sooner. I'd have liked to show my respect by going to her funeral. She was always very good to me—very forbearing. I was really fond of her, though I'm afraid I didn't always act as if I were—in fact, I know the way I did act must have troubled her a good share of the time. Perhaps it's just as well I didn't get to Lacombe after all. I might not have been especially welcome. I know I'm the black sheep of the family. And then, Claude was always so damned jealous of me. It must have been bad enough for him to lose his mother, without finding out at the same time that he was going to lose you. I don't think he ever really believed he would."

"No, I don't believe he ever did. And he hasn't."

"What are you talking about? Of course he has."

For the first time Fleex spoke roughly. There was no help for it. She could not prolong the delay, she could not soften the blow. She must tell him, straight out, as quickly as she could, even though by doing so quickly she had to do so cruelly. Somehow she managed to slip from his arms and stand, facing him.

"Claude and I were married on Christmas Day," she said.

CHAPTER XXVIII

It was the very general opinion that Claude and Lavinia Villac were outstanding among the young couples, not only in Crowley and on its outlying farms, but as far west as Lake Charles and as far east as New Iberia.

They were devoted to each other, to their children Prosper and Anne Marie, and to all the members of the Primeaux, Villac and Winslow families; but their interests were not confined to their immediate circle of relatives. They had a host of friends, whom they made welcome at their pleasant, commodious house, and whom they went out of their way to help in times of trouble; and beyond this ever-increasing group of acquaintances, their kindliness and co-operation encompassed the entire community. They were public spirited, they were charitable, they were farseeing; they believed in the future of Crowley and earnestly desired to do their share toward its growth and its improvement. In a place which had its fair share of small-town gossip, jealousies and factionalism, the young Villacs escaped enmity and even criticism. Everyone liked them and wished them well; no one begrudged them their happiness and their prosperity.

The house which Brent had given his daughter for a wedding present was in every way suited to be a center of prodigal hospitality, as well as one of comfort and convenience for the family itself. To be sure, outside, the Perets' house gave the impression of being larger. It was two full stories high, not counting its attic and its cupola; it had various excrescences in the form of balconies and bay windows and it was elaborately adorned with woodwork, cut to resemble Hamburg edging. The young Villacs' house, on the contrary, was a story and a half structure, surrounded by a deep gallery supported by graceful pillars, and it was only upon entering it that its true size was revealed. A wide central hall separated the parlor and sitting room on the right from the library and dining room on the left; the hall was attractive in itself, handsomely wainscoted and furnished, and it provided both the free circulation of air, which kept the house cool except in the hottest weather, and the possibility of privacy in the other rooms, the taste for which Lavinia had inherited from Mary. If the bride had felt free to follow her own inclinations

318

and Jonathan Fant's advice, she would have had only one long spacious room at the right of the front door, instead of two smaller square ones, and she would have followed one color scheme throughout those that adjoined each other and kept all the woodwork light. But Claude obviously expected each room to have different wallpaper and scrollwork of dark polished wood and Lavinia, having won the point about the simple columned gallery, as well as the wide entrance hall, gave in pleasantly on this phase of interior decorating, and was rewarded, not only by Claude's pride in it, but by the approbation in which it was generally held: the library ceiling particularly, which was ornamented by a design of golden garlands surrounding crimson squares on a background of buff, was a feature which brought forth special admiration, as were the mahogany frets surmounting the portieres of crimson velour separating the library and dining room. Each room had a fireplace with an elaborate mantel and a small grate, the latter concealed, when not in use, by a plate of wrought iron depicting a scene at a well; but throughout cool weather, open coal fires burned cheerfully everywhere, except in the modern kitchen—complete with soapstone sink and running water—where the coals were confined in a mammoth range, which was polished with the same regularity as the brass and the silver. Upstairs, there were four large dormer bedrooms, ranged two by two, with a hall between, like the rooms downstairs, and, over the kitchen, a real bathroom, a linen room, and a sewing room which could be used as an extra bedroom in case the others were all in use, which they frequently were. The old New England furniture, so long hidden from view, had at last come into its own again; and the treasures, which Jonathan Fant had, many years before, found relegated to the Garlands' attic, gave grace and distinction to the new habitation, so proudly erected in the little southwestern city which had come into being through the vision and the perseverance of two men.

It had been a foregone conclusion, on the part of those who had known her from childhood, that Lavinia would be a model housekeeper; she had always been quick and handy when it came to cooking and cleaning and, had it been necessary, she could have dispensed with servants altogether and still found time for church and club work without neglecting either her children or her home. Since she could well afford household help, however, she had it, and apparently not only possessed the rare knack of getting "clean corners and light biscuits out of the same Negress," but the still rarer ability of winning her helpers' faithful devotion, and keeping them on indefinitely, when nearly everyone else was complaining about high wages—actually up to three dollars a week!—incompetence and unreliability. Her cook Verna—one of the numerous progeny of Vicey and Dulsa, who had been so long with her parents—came to her when she married and had been with her ever since. Her children's nurse Callie was added to the staff when Prosper was a baby and had also stayed on and on. With Verna's help, Lavinia set a table that was without peer anywhere in the parish; under Lavinia's supervision, Callie kept the house in spotless order, laughed off the labor of mountainous washings and guarded her young charges with loving zeal.

It was admitted that Lavinia did not have the same gifts for gardening as her mother, who possessed a magic touch with flowers, and who now had a show place, as far as her many and flourishing varieties of camellias and roses were concerned. Nevertheless, Lavinia's yard was a credit to her and a source of satisfaction to the neighborhood. It was surrounded with day lilies, which bloomed in golden profusion all through the spring, and beyond the day lilies rose crape myrtles, which cast their shadows over it on the hottest summer days. In less abundance, but with the promise of plenty, were paper-white narcissi in January, Japanese quince in February, wisteria in March, Creole lilies in April, gardenias in May, asters and chrysanthemums in October, holly in November and December, camellias all winter, roses practically all the year. Mary Winslow had helped select and plant these flowers, but once they were started, it was Lavinia who took the responsibility for them, doing some of the work herself, and capably superintending the yardman Sylvester in the rest of it. Besides the flowers, the yard also contained sago palms, a flourishing young live oak, which someday would become a magnificent shade tree, a pomegranate which was less beautiful in itself, but which had an exotic quality that gave it distinction, two pecan trees, two magnolia trees and several pines and sweet olives. The Villacs' neighbors told them—and each other!—that all these trees, shrubs and flowers would eventually make this a show place, too, the handsomest one in Crowley; and they likewise applauded the good sense which had caused the young couple to devote part of their property to practical purposes. Back of the stable was a flourishing kitchen garden, where vegetables of one sort or another throve throughout the year, and pasturage for a gentle, purebred cow, who moved slowly about on her tether as she munched the abundant grass, and stood quietly to be milked, night and morning.

Lavinia's grandfather had insisted on giving her a small personal allowance from the beginning. Sure, a man wanted to feel he was supporting his wife, Jim Garland told Claude easily; on the other hand, it hurt a girl's pride to go running to her husband for money every time she wanted a postage stamp or a new ribbon; such trifles did not come under the same heading as groceries and taxes, for instance. He—Garland—had always been sorry Brent would not let Mary accept such an allowance; it would have made things a good deal easier for her in the first years of her married life; Garland hoped Claude would not require Lavinia to go without what she really needed or overtax her strength as her mother had done. When it was put to him in this way, Claude yielded instantly; the last thing he wanted was to have his adored Lavinia doing without or overtaxing her strength.

As a matter of fact, there was very little danger of either, for financial reasons, since Claude was doing very well himself. He had risen quickly from the position of assistant manager to manager of the clean rice department in the Columbia Mill; and eventually he left it to become general manager of the Monrovia Mill, at a better salary than was usually associated with such a position, but which the Monrovia was quite able to afford, since it was well built, well equipped and already extensively patronized; though it had been in operation only a short time. Tibier was sorry to see Claude go; but he was too just a man to harbor hard feelings over an advancement which he himself would not have been able to offer, for Claude's job was now better than his own. Besides, it was generally known that Jim Garland controlled much of the stock in the Monrovia and that he was buying up more all the time; and though Garland was a shrewd businessman, and would not have given the boy a boost if he had not been worth it, merely because he was a relation, no one could blame the old gentleman for seeing that his granddaughter's husband was put in charge of this mill, since Garland was serving his own best interests and those of the other stockholders by availing himself of Claude Villac's industry, intelligence, integrity and experience. To be sure, there was some criticism among the more strait-laced, because it was an open secret that much of the money Garland put into the mill did not come from his horses, but from his poker games. However, since several of Crowley's most prominent citizens were regularly numbered in the group with which he habitually played at the Elks' Club, and since these gentlemen also used their winnings for investments, there was not much which could safely be said by less successful persons on that score. Neither could there be open objection to the well-known fact that Garland was regularly putting the additional stock he acquired in either Claude's or Lavinia's name; if he preferred to do this, instead of giving them a more stereotyped form of present on Christmas, birthdays and other anniversaries, and that was what they wanted, after all it was a family affair.

The young Villacs' progress to greater and greater prosperity and prominence had been uninterrupted and steady. On the personal side, the happiness of the young couple had, inevitably, been clouded occasionally, though this had seldom been obvious even to the members of their respective families, except during the first year, when Lavinia's prompt pregnancy had terminated in a miscarriage. In itself, the miscarriage was surprising, considering the radiant health she had always enjoyed; the fact that it was an extremely painful one, that her convalescence was slow and that it was several years before she conceived again, was still harder to understand; she seemed the embodiment of easy and abundant maternity, unmarred by any physical mishap or by a depressing aftermath of one. Lavinia could never be persuaded to talk about her disappointment; and she always managed to change the trend of conversation when anyone else attempted to do so in her presence. But other women, particularly older women, delighted in discussing it among themselves. Some of them were sure she had worked too hard, above all that she had moved too much furniture around and lifted too many heavy objects when she was getting settled in her new house; she should have let all that go until after the baby's birth. . . . Others blamed her physical activities less than the burden of responsibilities she had so quickly assumed. Nearly every Saturday she had gone out to spend the night either with her father and mother or with Claude's family; and though the former visits were probably relaxing, the latter certainly were not, because she was trying to help Mezalee as much as possible and, in any case, the ride over the rough roads was a jolting one. When she did not go out to either of the farms herself, she brought Clement into town to stay with her and he was a handful. At least once a fortnight she had gone to Grand Coteau, and there had been a marked improvement both in Odile's conduct and her scholarship as a result of these prodding visits; but they took a good deal of Lavinia's strength, too. On top of all this, after a consultation with two of the best local doctors, she had taken Odey and Olin to New Orleans to see a specialist, and had made arrangements for appointments and examinations at regular intervals thereafter. Olin was already obviously less "puny" because of the excellent and enlightened care he was receiving; and though Odey's improvement had not been as striking, he was either hearing better or was learning to cope better with his deafness. The efforts which resulted in all these improvements must in themselves be "worrisome" to Lavinia, and train trips to Sunset and New Orleans could be just as fatiguing as too much physical exertion. . . . Still other gossipers hinted, in whispers, that perhaps Claude had not been as "considerate" as he should have been, under the circumstances —not that he would willingly have harmed a hair of his beloved wife's head; but he was terribly in love, and perhaps no one had warned him that when a young woman was in a delicate condition, her husband must be very careful. Of course, Lavinia herself would not have tried to restrain him; she would have believed that it was her duty to "submit" to conjugal embraces, no matter how importunate these might be. She should have been warned, too, and evidently no one had done this in her case, either; she had a duty to her unborn child, as well as to her husband and, conscientious as she was, she would certainly have heeded good advice on the subject. Well, it would be a sad thing if she never had a baby now, but in one way or another she had certainly risked such a calamity. . . .

As several years went by, and even the most observant neighbor could detect no change in Lavinia's trim and graceful figure, there was much nodding of heads and many sighs expressive of sad foresight. Then came the incredulous realization that her figure was not what it had been, and next that there was a definite reason for the loss of its grace and trimness. To do the gossips justice, everyone was delighted to find that they had been mistaken in their doleful prognoses. Prosper's birth, which was attended by no undue difficulties, was hailed as an event calling for general rejoicing. When Anne Marie was born, three years later, everyone was equally pleased. A boy and a girl, that was a family! No one suggested that it was a smaller one than popular opinion had considered probable or ideal.

To a very great degree, the children themselves were responsible for this widespread satisfaction. What they lacked, numerically, they made up in many other respects. To begin with, they were both beautiful, each in an entirely different way. Prosper had thick dark hair, snapping black eyes and bright red cheeks; he had been a bouncing baby and he continued to be large for his age. But he soon outgrew his infantile chubbiness and shot up, tall, straight and slender; he was quick as a cat in his movements, equally quick of wit, and merry, not to say roguish, in manner. He loved his parents wholeheartedly and was easier to manage than his high spirits and superabundant vitality would have indicated; but it was to his little sister that he gave his most worshipful devotion. She was a tiny, dainty little creature, who had inherited the fair coloring of her mother and her maternal grandmother, but who had far more winsomeness than either of them had ever possessed. Her golden locks framed her rosy face in such soft curls that everyone was tempted to touch them; her blue eyes looked out trustfully on a world which was not only friendly but adoring; her disarming smile embraced all of her small safe universe; her gentleness was such that it impelled a gentleness in return. She quickly became the darling of her parents, her grandparents, her aunts and uncles and the neighborhood at large; but dear as she became to these, it was to her brother that she was most precious of all. The expression of her slightest wish was a command to him; her mere presence sufficed to make him happy; there was nothing he would not have tried to do and be for her sake.

Acadia College had burned to the ground just before the turn of the century, but there was a good primary school in Crowley by the time Prosper was old enough to attend it, and when he was gone for part of every weekday, Lavinia had more time to spend on interests outside her home. Callie had never succeeded in handling the spirited little boy without help from his parents, but she had no trouble at all with Anne Marie and the two were very happy together; so Lavinia had no hesitation in leaving the baby girl in Callie's charge. Moreover, Lavinia's responsibility toward other members of the family was now slackening. Odile had surprised them by making a quick decision among her suitors after all, selecting a personable and persuasive visitor from the East and leaving to live in New

York—of all places! Onezime had become a priest and had been assigned to a parish in the Delta. Olin had so far outgrown his early physical handicaps that he had played baseball at L.S.U. and had made such a success of it that he had secured a position in one of the minor leagues and had drifted away from his family. Odie had done equally well in his studies; he was still a little deaf, but so slightly that it did not trouble him much any more and many of his associates were hardly aware of it; much to his father's disgust he had insisted on staying on at the University to take postgraduate courses. Clement, however, had partially made up for this defection; though he had finished a high school course, because Claude and Lavinia insisted upon it, he had done so with difficulty and they had realized that it was futile to suggest that he pursue his studies any further; he was now his father's right-hand man on the farm. Pauline had also remained contentedly at home and had become a very good housekeeper. In consequence, Mezalee had been released at last; and unabashed because she was so much older than any of the other postulants, she had triumphantly completed her novitiate and taken her final vows in the Order of the Sacred Heart.

This orderly pattern gave Lavinia plenty of leisure for church and civic work. In the years before Prosper's birth, she and Claude had taken occasional trips; but she could not leave the baby while she was nursing him nor did she wish to; neither did she wish to drag him around from one place to another when he and she could both be more comfortable at home. After he was weaned, she and Claude left him from time to time, very briefly, in the devoted care of Mary, Pauline and Callie; but Lavinia was always so much gladder to return to him than to leave him that Claude soon stopped urging her to do so, and, by the time Anne Marie was born, he had stopped such urging altogether. There was no place where they could be so contented and so well off as in their own pleasant home; why on earth should they go away from it?

A similar feeling governed their social activities. They were fond of their friends, but they were so much fonder of each other that, without ever seeming inhospitable or unsociable, they managed to keep a good many evenings free from engagements. During the busy season, Claude was sometimes obliged to return to the mill after supper; but this was now the exception rather than the rule and, even between the long working hours from "can to can't," he tried to wedge in a romp with his children and a quiet

325

hour with his wife. She was never out at the time of his homecoming—in fact, she managed, without giving offense, to keep her attendance at morning coffee parties and afternoon card parties to a minimum, and make up for her absence from these "dove" functions by going with Claude to the evening parties for mixed company which they both enjoyed. She was always waiting to receive him, smiling, composed and very pleasing to look at. There was a good drink ready for him and a good supper underway; and afterward, when the children had been put to bed, he and she had a game of checkers or cribbage together, or she played the piano while he read.

It was because this leisurely and agreeable pattern was so well established by the time Claude had become general manager of the Monrovia Mill that Lavinia was mildly surprised when he came home one evening, obviously in a hurry, and told her he thought they had better cut their drinks short and have supper as soon as Verna could get it on the table; he would have to go back to the mill as quickly as he could. She made the necessary adjustments without comment. However, when she heard him tell Sylvester, as the latter came in with the milk, to hitch up the buggy, she was still more surprised; Claude sometimes rode to the mill, but he almost never drove, except in very bad weather. The day had been mild and clear, the sunset beautiful; the moon was almost at its full and would soon be up. She was tempted to suggest going with him; but Callie had already gone off duty for the day, Verna had been promised release the minute supper was over, to attend a camp meeting, and this was one of the weeks when Clement was at the farm because of extra work there. Of course, she could not leave Prosper and Anne Marie alone in the house. Neither could she refrain from asking a question.

"You're driving? Taking someone with you?"

He nodded, without answering otherwise and turned toward the dining room. Evidently he had decided to cut out the drink altogether and get on with his supper.

"There isn't anything wrong at the mill, is there, Claude?"

"No. But I really ought to stay late, this time of year, oftener than I do. Tonight I must. There's a shipment for Vera Cruz overdue already. I've got to make sure it catches the morning eastbound. And I can't be, unless I'm there myself. I may have to go to another warehouse, too,

326

if my shipment's short, and take one of the boys who hasn't a horse of his own. That's why I want the buggy."

"I see."

She was not sure that she did. First he gave the impression that he was taking someone with him immediately, to the mill; then he spoke of going to another warehouse later. There was nothing actually contradictory between the two, but somehow they did not quite seem to fit. And it was not like Claude to have his shipments overdue. His reputation for prompt delivery was one of the strongest points in his favor. There was something here that was not fully understandable or explained and it worried her a little; but she would have to wait for an understanding or an explanation. Obviously, this was not the time to harass her husband with questions, when she guessed that something was troubling him already, though he did not say so. She saw that he had some supper in record time, putting off the children's until after his departure and sending them into the sitting room to play parcheesi. Then she went to the hall closet for his overcoat; it might turn colder before he started home—you never could tell at this time of year. She kissed him good-by and watched him hurry out to the waiting buggy before she turned back to the hungry children.

After their supper, she read aloud to them, superintended their baths, heard their prayers, tucked them in for the night and sang to them. Prosper was old enough to look after himself now; but he was apt to bathe somewhat sketchily if his mohter did not keep an eye on him, and he enjoyed the period of companionship after he was in bed, when she sat beside him in the dimly lighted room, either continuing to sing his favorite songs or replying to the questions which arose in his active mind and which had gone unanswered during the day. His demands upon her were apt to be varied in character and Lavinia was not always able to cope with them; but she did her best.

"Tell me the names of all the battleships you can think of," Prosper now urged. Lavinia had not much information about battleships and she had never known her son to show particular curiosity about them before. However, she could recall some of those which had figured prominently in the Spanish-American War and she recited these, to Prosper's evident satisfaction.

"Sing 'Now the Day Is Over,'" was his next request. It seemed to bear no logical relation to the former one, but it was easier to satisfy; Lavinia knew the old hymn from beginning to end. Prosper interrupted in the middle of the third verse.

"Do you think Jesus ever really does give children bright visions of Himself?" he inquired.

"Why, yes. I'm sure He must."

"Then why hasn't He given any to me?"

"I don't know, dear."

"Did He ever give any to you?"

"No."

"Or to Daddy?"

"Not as far as I know."

"Then I don't want to hear any more of that song."

"Very well. Do you want to hear something else instead, or will it be all right if I go downstairs now?"

"I don't want to hear any more songs, but I want to ask another question. There are lots of different kinds of liquor, aren't there?"

"Yes, lots."

"Well, tell me the names of all those you can think of."

Lavinia knew more about alcoholic beverages than she did about battleships. Before she had finished enumerating them, Prosper was comfortably drowsy. Without protesting against her departure, he permitted her to kiss him good night. Anne Marie was already sound asleep. Lavinia went back to the sitting room and picked up *The Lightning Conductor,* a best seller which, somewhat belatedly, had reached Crowley. But though she had enjoyed it very much when she started it the evening before, it did not hold her attention now. She kept thinking about Claude and his preternatural haste in returning to the mill, about his unconvincing explanation for its reason.

She put down her book and went to the piano, turning the pages of the new edition Claude had given her of *Songs Without Words* and choosing from them at random. Very few of these seemed to have any appeal, either, though Mendelssohn was one of her favorite composers. Eventually she closed this volume, too, and began to strike stray chords. While she was doing so, the telephone rang.

She leaped up to answer it, a quiver of fear forking through her. Telephone service had come early to Crowley; even the outlying farms were equipped with it and Lavinia made a practice of calling up her mother every morning directly after breakfast. But it was not yet in the frequent use, supplanting personal visits and business letters, which it subsequently received, and it almost never

328

rang late in the evening. Her fingers trembled as she picked up the receiver.

"Hello!" she said, fearful that even the one word was not spoken steadily.

"Hello, Mrs. Villac. This is Tobe Bennett. Could I speak to your husband?"

Tobe Bennett—*the sheriff!* This time Lavinia was sure her voice was unsteady as she answered.

"He isn't here, Mr. Bennett. He had to go back to the mill right after supper—he'd been late in getting off a shipment to Vera Cruz. There—there isn't trouble of any kind in town, is there?"

"Not a bit," Bennett assured her heartily. "It was just —well, a personal matter I wanted to see him about. I knew he was at the mill—fact is, I left him at his office, looking after that shipment. He was so busy he couldn't talk to me then, but he said he'd pass by my house to see me on his way home and I thought maybe he'd forgotten, it was getting so late. I wanted to catch him tonight if I could—in my own interests, you understand. He'll probably be along any minute. If he isn't, I'll call him at the mill. Sorry to have bothered you. Good night, Mrs. Villac."

"Good night," Lavinia said, hanging up the receiver.

As she did so, she glanced at the clock. Half-past ten. Crowley kept early hours; even half-past nine would have been late for a personal visit. It was true that Claude and Tobe Bennett were on friendly terms; but she could not imagine why the sheriff should have needed to see her husband on a private matter that could not wait until morning. She was tempted to telephone the mill herself; but it had never been her habit to break in on her husband's business hours and she resisted the impulse now. Nevertheless, she found she could not go back, either to her book or her piano. She went to a window and stood staring out of it unseeingly, until she heard footsteps on the garden walk. Then she ran to open the door. The words of welcome already on her lips ended in a scream of horror.

CHAPTER XXIX

Lavinia had been right in believing that something was amiss when her husband came home, but no guess she could possibly have made would have given her the solution of the riddle. A little before six, Claude had been sitting in his office, a "stone" spread out before him, a smaller one in his hand. Actually, the stone was the top of a lard pail, filled with emery cement. The one he held was a smaller one, cast from the same material in the general shape of a blackboard eraser. He was spreading rough rice over the flat stone, rubbing the grains vigorously with the smaller one, and then examining the hulled grain to grade it, and he was feeling well pleased: most of the small samples he had tested so far seemed to be well above the grade his rough rice buyer had assigned to the rice as a whole.

Conscious of another presence, he looked up and saw that the sheriff was standing in the door, his brown corduroy jacket open to reveal the star pinned to his shirt and the holstered revolver at his belt, a wide-brimmed white felt hat pushed back on his head. Claude hailed him cordially.

"How!" he exclaimed grinning. "Come in and light. What you got on your mind this far ahead of election time?"

"Not a hell of a lot, Claude, but it's something you can help us out on. I mean help a lot. It's about Fleex Primeaux."

Claude did not answer instantly. When he did, he spoke guardedly. "I haven't seen Fleex in years," he said slowly, "but he's my cousin and we grew up as close as red beans and rice, Tobe. I don't know what you've got on your mind, but if it's what I think, just bear in mind the old one about every man skinning his own skunk."

"Oh, hell, Claude, it's not all that serious. You know how Fleex has always been when he gets liquored up. He's a fightin' fool. He's had trouble several times in the city. That's no secret."

"If he's in trouble now, I expect I'm on his side. I just thought I'd tell you." Claude turned to a doorway. "Beebee!" he shouted to some unseen functionary. "Bring in a little coffee for the high sheriff and me."

"What I'm asking you to do is to keep what's no more'n a loud belch in a windstorm till yet from becoming one ungodly mess. It's Fleex I want you to help."

"Well, tell it to me. I'm listening," Claude invited. The two men paused while a white-thatched Negro shuffled in with a tray on which were two small cups, a gray granite-ware coffeepot, also small, a large cup of sugar and a jug

330

of hot milk. They helped themselves and sipped the aromatic brew.

"Like I said, I'm listening," repeated Claude.

"Well, it's a short horse and curried real quick. Believe it or not, Fleex is second engineer on the *Portero*—that's one of the Blue Fleet's banana boats. So he got into town a couple of nights ago, all fitted out in a tailor-made uniform and go-to-hell cap with gold braid on, and runs into that potbellied Polydore Lasseigne. You know him, don't you?"

"Sure. I made him an offer on his crop this fall, but he was bound and determined he would sell it in the city."

"Well, they run into each other in some cabbyray or other right along the fringes of the District, and they were both drinking. Polydore's a loudmouth when he's sober, let alone with booze to oil his jaws; and Fleex—well, if you don't know 'bout Fleex and how he is when he's drinkin', there's no use me trying to tell you."

"All right, Tobe. All right. So what happened?"

"Exactly what you'd expect. Mr. Loudmouth and Mr. Tough Stuff got in a fight and it wound up with Loudmouth on the floor."

"God Almighty, not dead, was he?"

"Him? Hell, no! Scared to death, maybe, but not cut to death. A stab here and a slit there, and blood enough to make him faint dead away at the sight of it, but nothing they couldn't stitch up and tell him to go home and sleep off the rest of it."

"Well, if that's the way it is, what's troubling you?"

"Fleex evidently thought it was worse than that, because he joined the bird gang and flew the coop. Nobody knows where. Of course, I got my ideas like a person would have, but officially I don't know nothing about it, see? Now I could get hold of the sheriff of St. Landry, and get him and me both to raise a posse and drag the parts of the swamps where he's likely to be; sooner or later, he's bound to come out for supplies or for a drink or something. But if he sees a gang like that coming toward him, he'll think he's wanted for something a lot bigger than just a Saturday night cuttin' scrape and somebody's liable to get shot bringing him in. Then the fat will be in the fire for true enough."

"So you want me to get word to him some way? . . ."

"Cut it out, Claude. I want you to go by yourself and tell him to give himself up because there's nothing but a barroom brawl against him. I already talked to that worthless tub of guts Polydore Lasseigne, and he says he ain't got no idea of going to the city to testify against Fleex, so they don't even have a case against him. Maybe give him ten days at the House of Detention for the usual drunk and disorderly. I'll see to it they don't make any fugitive from justice charges."

Claude absently stirred the hulled grains on his emery stone with the tip of one blunt finger.

"This'd be between us?"

"On my dead mother's grave I promise."

"I've got an idea where somebody might find Fleex. Course, it might not be the right idea, but the worst that could come of a try would be a failure. So this is what I'll do. It's most suppertime, and I'll go up to the house and tell Lavinia I've got to come back to the mill to get out a shipment for the morning eastbound, else it'll miss the boat for Vera Cruz. That way she won't worry; this time of year I ought to work all hours, anyway. But you back me up in it. If it comes to the clutch, you've got to swear I was working here."

"Kee-rect!"

"I'll be leaving the house by before seven and, if Lavinia asks me what I'm taking the buggy for, instead of walking to the mill, I'll spin her some kind of a tale about having to go to some warehouse if my shipment's short. And, if my idea's the right one, I'll be back with Fleex before ten. Before half past, anyway."

The steady clop-clop rhythm of shod hoofs was muffled by the soft dirt of the roadway once Claude turned off the main traffic route in the direction of Prairie Jeunesse. The harvest season had been dry; blessedly so from the point of view of farmers and millers. But, as the way led deeper and ever deeper into the back country, puddles and deep ruts and other areas of standing water became more frequent and larger.

Over and again the wheedling cry of killdees, rising abruptly from the marshy flats where they were resting, broke the stillness; occasionally the harsher, more rasping cry of a jacksnipe. It would soon be time to go afield in pursuit of such game—plover, snipe, papabottes and the timberdeedles with their staring, shoe-button eyes. Lavinia enjoyed these seasonal tidbits and was skillful in preparing them for the table. She had always been fond of woodland delicacies, Claude recalled; it must have been somewhere in the very area he was now traversing that Fleex had first introduced them to peeled thistle cores. Come spring, he must not forget to bring her some of these greens.

Well, that had been long ago and times had certainly changed. More and more of the wet lands were cleared, ditched, diked and planted to rice with each passing year, and Crowley—why, Crowley was a city! You couldn't find a vacant bit of ground anywhere along the four wide avenues leading to the courthouse square—not until you got way out from the business section; and on each Saturday, buggies were ranged hub to hub along the hitching racks.

Claude had long since ceased to be jealous of Fleex, indeed he had almost forgotten that rivalry had ever existed between them and that Lavinia's persistent preference for Fleex had been a source of resentful anxiety. She never mentioned his name any more, unless someone else did so first; it seemed obvious to Claude, when he thought about the matter at all, that she had practically forgotten his cousin, at least in connection with romance. But doubtless she would be glad to see him again. Personally, Claude felt it was too bad Fleex had not been minded to settle here and grow with the country. Perhaps, once this hodgepodge about Lasseigne was cleared up, he might yet be persuaded to do so. Believing he had killed Polydore would certainly throw a good scare into Fleex, and that might be a very salutary experience indeed, with no real harm done to anyone.

The horse splashed into the shallow bed of a tributary of Bayou Nezpiqué, which must be forded. Claude let the animal rest a few moments before urging it up the steeper bank which led to a short stretch of relatively high ground on the far side. He was very near the point where he must leave his buggy and proceed on foot. It would be a sorry sort of joke on him if Fleex had not sought sanctuary here, but had holed up in New Orleans, or maybe Lacombe, until he could make his way safely aboard ship. All that time and trouble, the roundabout excuses to Lavinia, and getting mired from head to foot for nothing!

A youpon copse, to one of whose saplings Claude tethered his horse, had taken over most of the high ground about the tumbledown cabin which had once been Miss Millie's "Island" schoolhouse. Even in the moonlight, the tangle of branches, which would be encrusted with scarlet berries before Christmas, showed glints of red, intermittently brightened by the fitful gleam cast by fluttering *feus follets*. Claude had never seen so many of them in one place, but he had long since ceased to consider their radiance a sign of ill omen. He stopped to pat his mare's cheek affectionately and then strode off into the swamp.

He certainly wasn't dressed for it, he thought to himself ruefully. If Lavinia was still up by the time he returned, he would have a lot of explaining to do, as to why and how and where he had become covered with mud. Even in the dry season, there were some sloughs that must be waded, and there was one stretch of *flottante* he would not be able to negotiate in full daylight without an occasional misstep into the bottomless mire. But he would think of something. If not, he would tell her the truth. After it was all over, it would not hurt her to know. And he would feel much better when he had confessed his lie and the reason for it.

The swamp noises multiplied as he made his way more cautiously; the deep wah-wah-hronnn! of a bullfrog, the coughing roar of an alligator, the startled whoee-whooee of a *grosbec,* the terrified-child scream of a rabbit gasping out its small life in the murderous talons of an owl. He made his way to the edge of a slough he would have to wade. The black surface of the water, like volcanic glass, gave back the reflection of the stars more clearly here, in the shadowed darkness, than in the moonlit sky itself. As he stood motionless, a doe picked her way daintily down to the water's edge, two month-old twin fawns nuzzling against her for protection. He waited until they left; he had no desire to frighten any mother with her two children.

Then he went on—floundering where he could not help it, wading watercourses where he must, upbraiding himself for the clumsy way in which he moved through the clashing palmetto leaves in a veritable uproar. Of course, Fleex might not even be at the cabin, now but a short distance off. If he were there, he would certainly taunt Claude for having forgotten all his woodcraft and making more noise than a railroad train in going through the swamps.

He must be almost at his journey's end. He could feel he was on rising, firmer ground. Just beyond the next open glade would be the hideaway. One of his shoes had become unlaced. He bent over, raising his foot to a fallen cypress log, before sending a halloo across the glade to call Fleex, if Fleex were there. He never knew what made him look up; some whisper of alien sound, perhaps simply some premonition of peril. He saw a stab of flame, but by the time the heavy crump of a shotgun blast reached him, he had sunk down through a black and bottomless well of agony into oblivion.

CHAPTER XXX

The previous evening had started well for Fleex; he was conscious that his new uniform set off his spare, wide-shouldered figure to good advantage, and proud of the two narrow gold stripes denoting that he was now second engineer. It had taken him a long time to win his promotion, because he had so often fallen from grace; but at last he had got it and he was determined that he would soon get another. With this in mind, he did not seek out his usual shoreside haunts on Decatur Street, but walked away from the river and along the broad, brightly lighted way of Canal toward what had once been the city's landward rampart and hence was still called Rampart Street.

Here he paused for a while, and looked appraisingly over the pedestrians who seemed to revel not merely in the comfort of cool weather, but even more in the freedom to mingle with one another now that the worst of a yellow fever epidemic had waned with the first frosts. Forgotten were the grim vehicles piled high with bodies that no one had time or material to coffin decently, the carts sprinkling carbolic acid along the open gutters, the air of desolation that wrapped a city from which all who could leave had fled.

He turned at last into Rampart Street, frontier of the Tenderloin beyond which stood the close-built bordellos of Storyville. From brightly lighted doorways of saloon and cabaret came the jungly bounce of dance music, the tinny crash of mechanical pianos, or the high-pitched voices, strident rather than seductive, with their unvarying strumpet call of "C'm'on in, honey!" A current favorite of the prize ring, followed by his entourage of sutlers, shouldered his way into the establishment whose proprietor was reputed to be "Mayor of Storyville" and was as riotously welcomed as, a few years hence, battle scarred and penniless, he would be hustled off the premises.

Fleex turned back toward the river on Customhouse Street. At a doorway decorated with live oak greenery and Spanish moss, beneath a sign proclaiming the establishment to be "The Vineyard," he turned in. A number of conspicuously dressed young women who all wore, among other things, ostrich plume hats and heart-shaped lockets on chains so long the baubles dangled at the level of their knees, swerved toward him. He beckoned to one and led her to an otherwise unoccupied table for four; its gray-grimed cloth was bare except for one plate on which rested what had once been a sandwich. The Vineyard's proprietor, careful to maintain cordial relations with the authorities in the matter of regular cash contributions, was thus enabled to practice thrift in having his saloon licensed as a restaurant where food was served—the petrifying sandwiches, of which each table displayed one, furnished proof of it.

"Bourbon—bottled stock, and bring the bottle," said Fleex to the waiter. "None of the rotgot you serve across the bar, understand."

"Whisky and plain water," said the girl.

Fleex knew that she would receive a glass of water colored by a few tablespoonsfuls of cold tea and that he would be charged a dollar for it. But that was part of the price. He would also be charged for the sandwich with every round of drinks that was ordered. A plain steel, wooden-handled steak knife lay beside the plate; the fork which should have been there was missing.

"How long you going to be in port, honey?" asked the girl mechanically.

"Long enough," Fleex grinned.

The shrill voice of a singer proclaiming that "I wuz bawn in Vawginya, that's the state that'll winya, if ya got a soul inya," drowned out the next question and the girl's affirmative answer. It did not matter. He would make sure he was taken to no creep or clip; the music, the lights, the girls and the laughter were like a draught of heady wine after Puerto de Oro, and the unswept cantinas along the sandy shore, with no choice except between tequila and veeskie-cocktaileys.

He flexed his muscles under the trim new uniform jacket. This was home, and no place like it. Something that might have been a shadow, or the half-caught echo of a single high note plucked from a guitar—something unsubstantial—flashed for a fractional instant across his inner consciousness and was gone as swiftly as it came. He tried to recapture it for he felt it had been sweet to the eye, to the ear, to his entire being. But it was gone. Then, abruptly, someone called his name.

"Fleex! Fleex Primeaux! The stallion of the wil' herd his own self, yes!"

He glanced at the speaker, a ruddy, pig-eyed man, whose naturally stocky build was already running to corpulence, although he was still young. The look was without recognition.

"I'm supposed to know you?" he asked incuriously.

"You bet you' whole goddam life you been knowin' me," retorted the other. "You done try to kill me once account of a fight we was havin' us, over a no-good little piece call' Prudence. I'm from the prairie in Acadia Parish, me, same as you. My name Polydore."

"Well, by God, I wouldn't have known you!" exclaimed Fleex, his expression lightening perceptibly. "Pull up a blonde and sit down. What the hell you doing here? Don't you live by Crowley any more?"

"Sho do I, me. Got a wife and three kids; maybe four, but I didn't count since last night when I left home, and another one li'ble to be born most any minute."

"Then what brings you to town?"

"Man, I can sell my rice yuh in N'Yawlins for too much more than those bastards in Crowley and Rayne will give. That's what I been doin' today, me, and now I got a pocketful of rocks, and I'm gonna be a wil' young buck before I go back tomorrow and settle down. Course, they got some place outside Crowley on the South Side these days . . . but a man gotta be careful when he got a wife and three kids, maybe four, special if his wife is one slowpoke gal from the prairies."

Fleex had been eyeing the speaker with growing distaste as the rambling and slightly tipsy conversation proceeded. But the shrill-voiced singer took charge of the situation once more, asking what sounded like, "Are you sincere, are you sincere, why won't you call me your deeeeerie?" Fleex waited until the din subsided and then he asked, rather ominously, "What's the matter with girls from the prairie?"

"What the hell, you can answer that better'n me," retorted Polydore. "We had a fight over one what wasn't worth powder to blow her to hell, when we was kids, us, didn't we? And from all I hear you nearly got caught with 'nother one only you made a fast-fast getaway in time, and not like. . . ."

Obscene phrases from the banana ports leaped to Fleex's lips even as he lunged across the table. *"Hijo de puta! Cabrón!"* he snarled as the table turned under his weight and toppled plate and sandwich to the floor. But Fleex caught a flash of glinting metal and swept the steak

337

knife into a hand that rose and fell. The rest was confusion, a babel of high-pitched screams, the drum of heavy feet across the floor and one flash of what had been beefy, red-faced Polydore a moment earlier, blood welling from a gaping wound in his chest and a slash along the side of his neck. His eyes, open but unseeing, were rolled back in their sockets, his face no longer ruddy but waxen. . . . .

Fleex was unobtrusively worming his way through the legs of those pressing forward to see what had happened. Outside, whistles shrilled and the loud, trilling sound of night sticks sounded an alarm against the pavement. But Fleex had reached a back courtyard by this time. He caught sight of a doorway, obviously used for the disposal of garbage, and tossed into an open trash barrel the steak knife he still held in his hand, then stepped from one littered courtyard to another, until a dimly gaslit hallway gave him egress to a quiet street.

He mingled with the crowd on Canal Street as soon as he could, worked his way toward the river and then upstream toward the banana docks. He knew he should change his uniform before he could hope to escape the hue and cry that must, by now, be out against him. This was no mere drunk and disorderly brawl. Those wide, unseeing eyes, rolled back in a waxy countenance, and the pool of blood spreading its grim verdict over the soiled, sawdust-strewn floor, had brooked no denial. But even as he approached the Felicity Street wharf, slipping along the shadows cast by brick walls enclosing cotton press yards, he heard the clanging bell of a patrol wagon, as the shod hoofs of its two horses clattered over the great granite blocks of the street paving.

The hunt was up already, then. Someone must have identified him; one of the hangers-on who might have recognized him from earlier barroom brawls. He headed away from the river, made his way along Parkerson Square with its low date palms, and walked upstream along the huge arc of St. Charles, until an owl car, bumping along with one flat wheel, overtook him; then he rode undisturbed to the end of the line.

Here he once more slipped into the shadows and made his way unobserved to the near-by levee. Dawn was almost breaking when he reached the Kenner interchange, a switch track on which fright cars could be shunted from the Southern Pacific to the Valley Railroad. While brakemen with dancing lanterns broke a freight train into short sections, each of which was pushed onto a huge car ferry, he climbed onto the roof of a boxcar.

Daylight broke over the slow, jolting freight train at Lafourche Crossing, where the chuffing little engine took on water. Fleex glided into the rank growth that bordered the Tomswood Plantation switch, waited until the train pulled out and, seeing himself in a deserted area, drank deeply from the taplike faucet of a rain-water cistern. Then he retreated into the undergrowth, feeling a sense of security in the swamp which was such familiar territory to him and so little known to any probable pursuer. He dozed and rested through the day on a pallet of Spanish moss piled over a bed of broad palmetto fronds. When the first freight train stopped at the crossing for water, he slipped into an empty gondola and was still there when the train trundled into the outskirts of Rayne. Here he left it, sustaining a nasty fall, for he was on a Red Ball—a through freight—which would make no stops between Lafayette and Lake Charles, except to go into a passing switch when letting a fast passenger train go by. But he dared not let himself be seen at Crowley, where there was such a switch. If he had been identified, the alarm would be out for him at Crowley, too.

He would have to hole up again through the day. He dared not risked being seen crossing the open prairie to the deep swamp in the Stewpan Cove area, through which he could still make his way blindfolded. But he clubbed two jumbo frogs along the banks of a slough, still shrunken from the drought and heat of autumn, and broiled them on sticks over a small fire of dry cypress bark, which glowed like punk with almost no smoke. By nightfall, he knew he was safe. He was not even worried about the drenching moonlight that silvered the open grasslands he must traverse. Before midnight, if all went well, he would have a change of clothing, a gun, food and a secret hiding place in which he could maintain himself against a small army.

When at last he came within sight of the cabin, it appeared, at first glance, far more dilapidated than he remembered. He paused in thick undergrowth at the edge of the clearing to take careful stock of the structure—little more than a hut—of weathered gray cypress slabs, set on cypress pillars to raise it above the temporary flood levels left by heavy rains in the wet season. Some cypress shakes were missing from the roof, but these spots he could thatch with palmetto. The pillars appeared sound enough,

339

however, as he peered into the blackness beneath the cabin, searching for some trace of movement. But, as his sharp, forest-trained vision adjusted itself to the darkness, he could see through to the other side of this space and no signs of alien presence appeared there. He stepped cautiously into the open, then strode to the steps, mounted them and entered the cabin, which was instantly flooded by moonlight.

He could see there was dry wood in the box by the old stove; that had been one of the rules they had observed even as children: the woodbox must be left well filled on departure. Who could say how long these stove lengths had been there? They might be the very ones he had put there himself, twelve years earlier. More probably, by this time, the existence of the cabin had been discovered by some stray trapper. It was also possible that Claude still went there occasionally, though Fleex doubted it and he felt sure that Lavinia never did. It didn't matter. What mattered was that he was there himself, safe and sound, and that a supply of fuel was ready at hand.

Fumbling in one of the storage boxes, he closed his hand on the smooth, cool metal of his old acetylene headlight. He examined its various parts hastily, noting with satisfaction that all seemed intact—even the flexible tube from a small belt tank for carbide and water to the reflector with its gas jets, attached to a band worn about the head. With this light Fleex had formerly shined many a frog, rabbit, *bécasse* and deer. At the moment, the device was useless; its few bits of carbide had long since caked into inertness. But that was a lack he could soon replenish. Meanwhile, a box of candles was still on hand; so were some canned beans, a glass jar of dried beans and another of green coffee. A tin of sugar was intact and a small lard pail was well filled with flour, though this was probably too weevily to be used.

He lighted a candle and, shielding its flame with one hand, began a search for dry clothing. Again, he was fortunate; he found overalls and a jumper rolled together and, well cached inside the bundle, a pint bottle of whisky, almost full. He took a long drink, then stripped quickly to the skin, stuffed his muddy outer garments into his discarded shirt and knotted its sleeves about the bundle, so that it could be stowed above the ceiling joists for the present. He hoped no pregnant cotton rat would decide to establish a well-shredded maternity ward there.

He had found no shoes, but he was now dry and reasonably warm and the whisky had been a boon. He took another drink and continued his inventory. His shotgun, an old hammer-firing single, but serviceable enough, was still where he had stowed it deep in a nest of well-oiled rags, and so were a dozen buckshot shells. The food problem would thus solve itself. Tomorrow, he would pot a deer. There was enough salt to preserve whatever meat he did not use before it turned too *faisandé*. Now to make coffee and warm a can of beans. Meanwhile, another drink. . . .

He paused, setting down the bottle, almost empty. . . . Something big and clumsy was moving out yonder . . . coming closer and closer to the cabin through the palmettos. Something or someone? Or how many? A posse already? He had been observed at Rayne, perhaps, when he fell from the Red Ball freight; if so, the entire countryside might be raised against him by now.

He brought the flat of his right palm down on the candle flame, mashing it into extinction. Then, carefully, he opened one of the wooden shutters so that he could peer out, while he fumbled a buckshot shell into the breech of his shotgun by touch, and slid the long barrel across the window sill for a stable rest. Steady now; the noise might be made merely by a stray cow. If so, she would serve even better than deer.

But it was not a cow. It was a man, thickset and stocky, wearing a wide-brimmed, light-colored felt hat. Fleex could make out no features, for, as the newcomer stepped into the open, he bent forward as if to fasten a shoelace, so that Fleex could see no more than the crown of that light-colored felt hat above the unwavering sight-bead of his shotgun.

Silence closed down on the swamp, a silence which seemed all the deeper after the blasting roar of the weapon. Finally it was broken as a voice, seemingly disembodied, sounded in the riven night.

"That'll show 'em. I can't get strung up any oftener for a dozen of those sonabitches than for the two I got already. I'll have plenty of company before they cut me down. But in the open—and fighting back. Not any business of being fed up and washed and stuffed like I was somebody's hog being fatted up for the *boucherie*."

As the voice trailed off into silence, there was a barely perceptible stir in the vegetation. Then a dim form materialized in the glade and Fleex, barefooted, stepped out into the open and trained the muzzle of his shotgun on the motionless figure lying at the edge of the water.

341

"Too goddam bad you can't go back and tell them about it," he muttered. "I'd better take you off and bury you, else the carrion crows are likely to bring too many others to this spot at one time. Wonder do I know him?"

He turned the body over and, in the moonlight, looked down on his cousin's face.

CHAPTER XXXI

"Christ Almighty! It's Claude!"

The anguished words, half whisper and half groan, were torn from Fleex's throat. He did not even know that he had uttered them, as he sank on his knees beside the still form. Then he began to babble frantically. "I never meant to do it, not to you! I wouldn't go to hurt you, I swear on my mother's grave I wouldn't. You got to listen to me, you got to tell me. . . ."

His desperate appeal was voiced without volition; it was based on no wild belief that there would be a response to it. Claude was clearly unconscious. Nevertheless, Fleex continued his incoherent pleading as he ran a groping hand over his cousin's chest, hoping against hope to find signs of life. The hand was instantly covered with blood, but under it he could feel a spasmodic rise and fall. His heart bounded with sudden joy.

"I didn't know it was you!" he cried. "You got to believe that, Claude! Can you hear me, man, can you?"

With a stab of relief that was like a sharp pain, Fleex saw the fallen man's head turn slowly. His eyes fluttered as they opened, but once their gaze was fixed, it was surprisingly clear, and presently a twisted smile tugged at the angle of the lips.

"Yes, I hear you," he whispered reassuringly. Then his voice, weak at first, became stronger and steadier. "I know you never meant to do it. And I'm not bad hit. You used to shoot straighter than that."

"Don't joke, man, you've got blood all over you. Your shoulder's punctured. I've got some clean cloth in the cabin, I'll tie it up. Are you hit anywhere else?"

"My leg, I think. Maybe my chest, too. And I've got a hell of a headache. One of those slugs must have creased me. But it'll take a lot more than that to keep me down. Help me up, so I can sit on that log."

Fleex leaned his shotgun upright against the log, then

stooped and slipped sinewy arms under the recumbent figure and eased it gently down again. A swift examination showed that Claude was right: his head revealed only a slight contusion; but blood was flowing as freely from his leg as from his shoulder, and there was another bullet puncture at the right side of the chest.

"That one don't look so bad though," Fleex said thankfully. "At least, it isn't bleeding as much as the others. Will you be all right if I leave you long enough to go and get that cloth?"

"Sure. You only hit me with four buckshot out of eleven in that shell," Claude gibed. "If I were a buck, I'd be clean across the parish line by now."

"I said, don't joke about it." Fleex had gone quickly into the cabin, returning with some white cloth which he tore into strips and bound tightly around the thigh and shoulder wounds to stop their bleeding. As he worked, he went on talking.

"I'm so thankful I didn't kill you, I'm almost ready to give myself up for butchering that fat son of a bitch, Polydore Lasseigne, in New Orleans. You see, I thought the posse was after me for murder. That's how I happened—"

"You'll give all hell up," Claude exclaimed with sudden spirit. "I came out here to tell *you* about Polydore. You didn't need to run away on account of him. He isn't even bad hurt. Just a stab here and there, Tobe Bennett—he's high sheriff now—told me. Tobe says there isn't even a case against you, because Polydore hasn't any idea of going to the city to testify. You might get ten days in the House of Detention for being drunk and disorderly, but that would be all. Tobe promised there wouldn't be any fugitive from justice charges. But he was afraid, if he sent a posse after you, you'd shoot somebody and get shot yourself. So he asked me to look you up, and I said sure—"

"I wouldn't shoot you! That's what you told him, isn't it? And then that's just what I did do! Well, it's done now, and I've tied you up as well as I know how."

"You did fine, too. So the next thing is for me to stay here, all quiet and easy, while you hustle to town and get some men with a stretcher. I'm not hurt too bad, but I couldn't walk far."

"You're not staying out here alone. You and I are staying together and I'm getting you to a doctor quick."

"Not to a doctor. To Lavinia. Home. When I get home, Lavinia'll see to everything. She's wonderful. She'll get hold of a doctor. Besides, I want to get into my own bed."

For the first time, since he had found Claude, words did not come pouring out of Fleex's throat; instead, he had to swallow hard before he spoke.

"Sure," he finally managed to say. "That'll be best—to get you home first and have Lavinia send for a doctor and look after you while we're waiting for him to come. How'd you get out here—in a buggy?"

"Yes—left it by the old cabin on the 'Island' where Miss Millie used to keep school. Remember how we hid there from the *feus follets* one evening when we were children? It's a queer thing, they were flying all around it when I came out tonight."

Again there was a slight pause before Fleex answered. Then, though he spoke with an effort, he did so with resolution. "Yes, I remember," he said. "All right then, I'll carry you out to the buggy and drive you into town. Maybe I don't shoot as good as I used to, but I could still carry you to the schoolhouse and juggle pool balls while I was doing it. Just let me slip into my shoes, and we'll be off."

As gently as possible, he helped Claude rise, and slung his cousin across his shoulders in the "fireman's carry" that had been a feature of every boat drill in which he had taken part since he ran away to sea. Then he made his way, steadily and carefully, through clashing palmettos, across small waterways and over fallen logs to the "Island," where the buggy was hitched near the old schoolhouse, the patient horse drooping in the shafts. Painstakingly, Fleex lifted Claude into the seat.

"There you are!" he said with well-assumed cheerfulness. "Now, just as soon as I unhitch this crowbait of yours, we'll be on our way into town. Feel like you can take it if we drive easy over this first rough stretch?"

"Take it! Getting this far, I expect I could drive back to town myself."

"Don't talk like you didn't have all your marbles," Fleex retorted, getting in beside his cousin and encircling the wounded shoulder with his right arm, while taking the reins firmly in his left hand. "I'll drive you into town and get you to your house, so the doctor can tie you up *right* —not clumsy like I did it—after Lavinia has you settled in bed. All you have to do in the meantime is to take it easy and show me where you live. Remember, I haven't been to Crowley in more than ten years."

"That's ten years too long. But you won't have any

344

trouble finding your way. They never did change the original layout, even if Crowley's almost a city now."

For a few minutes, he spoke with pride of the wonderful progress that had been made in his home town. Then he lapsed into silence. Fleex had to remind Claude again that he would need to know the exact address; after that, of course he could find his way there all right. Claude gave the address and added a description of his home and its grounds, again speaking with pride. After that, he fell silent a second time. Every now and then Fleex asked, "How you making out?" and invariably the same, "Hell, I'm all right." But Fleex did not feel so sure of it. Once on the highway, he forced the tired horse to a faster gait and, under his breath, murmured the long disused prayer which he had learned at his mother's knee: *"Sainte Marie, Mère de Dieu, priez pour nous, pauvres pécheurs, maintenant et à l'heure de notre mort!"*

"Pray for us *now!*" he muttered. "Never mind about the hour of our death—that's a long way off—it's got to be. Pray for us now, Holy Mother!"

Claude was leaning more heavily against him and Fleex shifted his position slightly, hoping to give the wounded man greater ease. Was it a mistake, he wondered, to try driving so fast? Inevitably, it meant more jolting, for even the best part of the road was rough; but he did not dare risk a moment's unnecessary delay and he gave a smothered exclamation of relief as he realized that they were at last approaching their destination. Only a few lights were burning in West Crowley, the Negro section of the town, though here and there a sudden glow of lamplight revealed colored couples dancing with abandon to the blare of a Gramophone, or a group of dusky men drinking and dicing around a table; and the road was no better here than it had been out in the country. Fleex would have to get nearly to Parkerson Avenue before he could hope for any improvement; then he would have to keep track of the streets he passed and figure out the relation of their numbers to the alphabetically named avenues. Of course, that should not be too hard; but the character of the place had changed so completely that he was bewildered. He had left a straggling, unkempt village; he had returned to a trim, pleasing town, with well-painted houses set in the midst of carefully tended lawns, behind neat fences; there was something baffling about the complete unfamiliarity of it all. Moreover, he was still hampered by his inability to see exactly where he was, for most of the houses in this section, too, were in darkness, and there were no street lights. But Claude, who had been silent for so long that Fleex thought he might again have lapsed into unconsciousness, suddenly struggled into a more upright position and spoke clearly and happily.

"Take the next turn to the left and go up two blocks. As I told you, it's a corner house—the white one with a deep gallery—the prettiest house in Crowley. And it has the prettiest yard. And listen, did you know? I've got two of the cutest kids. I want you to see them. They'll be asleep now, of course, but you can go into the nursery and look at them."

"I'd like to. Boys or girls? How old are they?" Fleex asked, for the sake of saying something.

"One of each—Prosper and Anne Marie. Seven and four. We lost our first baby—that is, Lavinia had a miscarriage a few months after we were married. Of course, it was a dreadful disappointment at the time. But I don't think Lavinia grieves over it any more. Anyway, she never talks about it. And I don't—I've got so much else."

You've got so much else! I'll say you have! A wonderful wife, two cute kids, the prettiest house in Crowley. But can you keep them? Have you got enough life left in you after what I've done to you? I've coveted everything you've got, I tried to steal Lavinia from you, I wanted to father her children. But I wouldn't have killed you to do it. I went away and left you a clear field. And now that I've come back—Sainte Marie, Mère de Dieu. . . .

The unspoken words were choking him. But Claude was speaking again, with happiness in his voice.

"We're home, Fleex."

It was true. Fleex had been too distraught to notice when the faithful old horse stopped, of its own accord, beside a great granite block at the edge of the sidewalk, opposite a gate that stood open to disclose a flower-bordered path leading to a gracious gallery. This house was not in darkness. The porch light was on, the window shades raised to show the cheerful glow of lamps inside. Everything about it bespoke prosperity, ease, comfort, love. . . .

This time, Fleex did not fling the helpless figure across his shoulders, but cradled it in his arms, as he bore it over the flower-bordered path and up the gallery steps toward the lighted door, which opened at his approach. Evidently, Lavinia had been listening for footsteps, waiting to receive her husband. Now she stood, framed in the entrance, lovely and expectant, her white dress luminous, her golden hair crowning her with its radiance. Her sudden cry of horror pierced Fleex's heart with a sharper thrust than any knife could have given. Then, soothing and silencing her, came Claude's quick, kind words.

"Don't be frightened, darling. There's been an accident, but everything's all right now. Fleex was there to bring me home."

CHAPTER XXXII

There were no more screams, there was not even a delaying question. Swiftly, calmly, Lavinia led the way upstairs to a pleasant chamber where a coal fire glowed on the hearth and the lamps were softly shaded. She whipped back a flowered counterpane and fluffy blankets from a wide four-poster, and Fleex laid his burden down between spotless sheets, under a snowy canopy of dotted muslin. Claude looked up and smiled.

"That's what I wanted, to be in my own bed," he said. "My, but it feels good—as good as it looks! I'll be all right now. But, honey, maybe you'd better see if you can get hold of a doctor. Fleex'll stay with me while you telephone."

She bent over to kiss him and he lifted his uninjured arm and patted her shoulder. Then she sped down the stairs and they could hear her turning the crank that rang the telephone bell and speaking rapidly into the transmitter. Claude turned his head to look at Fleex.

"We've got three doctors in town now. One of them, Hadley, is away on his vacation. But she ought to be able to get hold of Morris or Cartier. Anyhow, as I keep telling you, I'm all right now."

His gaze wandered around the room, resting contentedly first on one object in it and then on another. Afterward, he looked back at Fleex.

"It's nice, isn't it?" he asked, and there was the same pride in his voice as when he had spoken to Fleex about his home in the course of their terrible ride.

"Yes, fine. I don't wonder you wanted to get here."

"And Lavinia, she's—she's—well, as I told you, she's wonderful. Not that you needed me to say so. You knew it, too."

"Yes, I've always known it."

"I'm sorry my good luck was your bad luck, Fleex."

"I'm not. This is the way it ought to have been. I mean, that it ought to be."

"I hope you really feel that way."

Claude closed his eyes, apparently satisfied that no more needed to be said, and undisturbed because Lavinia did not return more promptly, bringing a report from the doctor. With growing anxiety, Fleex listened as she continued to ring numbers and talk over the telephone. When at last she came upstairs again, he was aware of the concern underlying her calm report.

"Dr. Cartier's house doesn't answer. He's a bachelor and lives alone. Central is trying to locate him—he's probably out at a party somewhere. Dr. Morris is on a confinement case. Mrs. Morris helped me to reach him and I managed to talk with him briefly. But he says he can't leave his patient for at least another hour. She's having a very hard time. It's a matter of life and death."

Claude's eyes were closed. Fleex and Lavinia, standing face to face, looked into each other's. No words were needed to say that this was also a matter of life and death. Claude opened his eyes.

"Sit down, you two," he said. "I want to talk to you."

"Claude, please—I think you ought to save your strength. Wait until after the doctor's been here."

"I want to talk to you both *now*. We might not have such a good chance later on. The doctor might find a broken bone he wanted to set and give me something dopey. He might do that even before he started probing around, to ease the pain. Then I'd get muddleheaded. I couldn't talk so clear. Besides, we haven't got anything else to do, have we, while we wait for him?"

"No. I'd like to get your clothes off, change the bandages, make you more comfortable. But I think perhaps I'd better not move you."

"No, I expect you'd better not. I'm comfortable just like I am. But I want to talk to you—both of you. Pull up a couple of chairs, close to the bed. Only thing makes me uneasy is to have you keep on standing up."

It would do more harm than good to argue with him, they both realized that. They did as he asked.

"You remember Polydore Lasseigne, don't you, honey?"

"How could I forget him?"

"That's right, none of us could. Well, he and Fleex got into some kind of a no-account fight in New Orleans—all the fat pig's fault, of course."

"Yes, of course."

348

"But Fleex got the notion he'd really hurt Polydore—
hurt him bad, I mean. So he made a quick getaway.
Maybe it wasn't the most sensible thing to do, but it was
the most natural thing to do. You see that too, don't you?"

"Yes."

"Tobe Bennet came to the mill this afternoon and told
me about it. He asked me if I wouldn't see if I could find
Fleex's hideaway and get him to give himself up—thought
it might save a lot of trouble if I could. I don't know as
it's necessary to tell you all the whys and wherefores. . . ."

"No, it isn't."

"And I thought I knew where to look for Fleex."

"In our old cabin?"

"Yes. But Fleex didn't think it might be me coming to
look for him. He thought it was a posse. He thought
someone fired."

"I never—" Fleex began hotly. Claude held up his uninjured hand.

"Just a minute. I said I wanted to talk to you both and I
do. But right now, I'm talking to Lavinia. . . . You know
how it is, honey, there's crackling sounds in the woods
sometimes."

"Yes, I know."

"So Fleex fired, too—in self-defense. Do you understand?"

"Yes."

"You're sure?"

"I'm sure."

"You heard what I said to Lavinia, Fleex. Now I want
you to tell me that you understand, too."

"If you think I'm going to lie about what I did to you,
just to save my own worthless hide—"

"What are you talking about? Your hide isn't in any
danger of needing to be saved. But what you did to me
was an accident. And the accident happened just like I
said it did. You thought you were being attacked and you
fired in self-defense. If Lavinia can understand what I've
said, I should think you could. I'm getting kind of tired, I
don't feel like talking much more. I wish—"

"Fleex, tell him you understand. That's what he wants."

Again, Fleex and Lavinia looked steadily at each other
and again, no words were needed between them. This
time, however, it was not the significance of words already
spoken that was so clear to them, it was the meaning of
words which had not been uttered, which could not be uttered: *that's all he wants. That's all you can do for him*

now, to make up for what's already happened. That's the last thing he's ever going to ask of you.

"I guess I understand," Fleex said slowly.

"Fine! Now everything really *is* all right." Claude closed his eyes again. His breathing was becoming more labored and, though he did not seem to be suffering greatly, he was obviously growing weaker. Lavinia rose.

"I'm going to try Dr. Morris again. That baby must be born by this time."

Fleex rose, too, and followed her though the door. When they were in the hall, he spoke softly, in French.

"While you're at the telephone, hadn't you better try for a priest, too?"

"Yes, of course. Thanks, Fleex. I wouldn't have thought of it if you hadn't reminded me."

"What about the children? I don't need to tell you he thinks a lot of them. He talked to me about them, while we were driving in. Wouldn't he want—"

For the first time, Lavinia, instead of giving an immediate answer, pondered for a few moments. "No," she said eventually. "I think if he'd wanted to see them, he'd have asked for them. I mean, of course he wants to see them, but he doesn't want them to see him, all covered with blood that way. I think he knows if they were waked up, out of a peaceful sleep, and taken into his room—well, it might be a terrible shock to them, a shock they wouldn't get over. I think it's better for them. . . ."

She did not finish her sentence and, once again, the unspoken words were clear. She thought it was better for them to remember him as they had seen him at suppertime, when the little family had been together, well and happy and united. "You're right, of course," he said, and then added, "couldn't I do the telephoning this time? That way, you wouldn't have to be out of the room. Just tell me the numbers."

He came back to find Lavinia sitting quietly by Claude's bed and Claude apparently sleeping. The report he brought was encouraging: the baby had been born, things had gone better at the end, Dr. Morris could leave his confinement case very shortly and be at the Villacs' house in less than an hour. Father Van Alfen was starting for the house right away.

"I'll go back downstairs. Then I can let them in when they come. Unless there's something I can do for you here?"

"No, there isn't anything."

He hesitated. "Do you know how to get everything ready for Father Van Alfen, Lavinia?"

"We have some candles in the house that have been blessed and Holy Water, of course. Claude's always been very particular about that. And he's told me how everything is done when—at times like this. I've never actually done it or seen it done."

"Then perhaps I could help. I helped my father when my mother was dying."

It was the first intimation on the part of either that Claude might be dying. Deftly, Fleex laid on a little table the clean white cloth Lavinia brought him, took the crucifix from the wall and set it between two lighted candles together with the branch of dried palm that had been tacked above it, put the Holy Water into place. Then he hesitated again.

"There should be another clean white cloth across his chest. Wouldn't you like to put that there yourself?"

"No, I'd like you to do that, too. I think Claude would want you to."

Claude opened his eyes again as Fleex bent over him, and whispered something Lavinia did not hear. Then he seemed to lapse into unconsciousness.

"I'll go down now and meet Father at the door with another lighted candle. Then I'll come back upstairs with him. But I won't stay."

"I'd like to have you."

"If Claude rouses enough to confess and receive Communion, I couldn't anyway, you know. Besides, I think I should watch for the doctor."

"All right."

He was back again, almost immediately, with the priest and, after one glance at his cousin, left the room. But, as Father Van Alfen approached the bedside, Claude stirred slightly and spoke in a whisper. The priest signaled to Lavinia and she went out into the hall. But it was only a matter of minutes before he summoned her to return and asked if she would not care to kneel; he was already beginning his preparations to administer Extreme Unction. When he had finished anointing the dying man, he gently inquired whether it would be any comfort to have him remain longer. Without rising, Lavinia shook her head, and he quietly took his departure. On the stair landing, he met Dr. Morris, who was on his way up. Neither tried to detain the other. The priest had done all he could, the physician was hoping it was not too late for him to do anything. Fleex accompanied Father Van Alfen to his buggy and, as they went down the garden walk, the priest, who had not failed to observe his escort's disordered dress and ill-concealed agitation, slackened his pace to permit seemingly casual conversation.

"I am glad I arrived in time to hear Claude confess and give him Holy Communion. Everything was beautifully prepared for me. I had not expected to find such perfect order. Mrs. Villac has been scrupulous about keeping all her prenuptial promises; but she has never shown any leanings toward Catholicism herself."

"No, I'd hardly think she would."

"Perhaps you were responsible for the preparations?"

"I helped."

"I should have guessed that, knowing your family background. I am sure nothing connected with the Faith was neglected in your upbringing."

"I was baptized, of course. My mother taught me my prayers and lived long enough to see me make my First Holy Communion. I won't say it was also my last—but you must have heard that I'm the black sheep of the flock."

"No, Felix, I have not. I have heard your brother Clement, who used to be one of my altar boys, speak of you with the greatest affection; also, your sister Mezalee, who is an ornament to her Order."

"Yes, she's the saint of the family and Clement's the support. I'm the sinner."

"It's never too late to repent of sin, my son. . . . Perhaps you would care to come and see me tomorrow. We could have a talk. It need not be a formal confession if you are not ready for that."

"It's very kind of you, Father. I appreciate your interest. But I don't expect to be here tomorrow."

"Ah, well—there are understanding priests everywhere. Don't forget that. And God be with you wherever you're going."

Father Van Alfen raised his hand in blessing and got into his buggy, respectfully assisted by his colored driver. Fleex turned away and, with quickened footsteps, returned to the front hall. Surely the physician, who had arrived so tardily, would have finished examining Claude by now and have something to report, almost any minute now. But the wait seemed interminable, though it was actually only a short time before Dr. Morris, his face furrowed with fatigue, came down the stairs and stopped beside him.

"It's all over," he said gravely. "The poor fellow's drowned in his own blood."

"*Drowned* in his own blood!"

"Yes. The wounds on the shoulder and thigh didn't amount to anything—he could have recovered from those all right. It was the one in his chest that killed him. An internal hemorrhage gradually filled his lungs. From what you told me, over the telephone, I gather he was brought some distance in a buggy after the accident. If it had only been possible to bring him on a stretcher and save all that jolting—"

"It would have been. I could have left him and gone for help. He suggested it himself. But it would have taken a long while and, meantime, he would have had to stay alone and he wanted to get home to his wife. I thought the sooner he did—"

"You acted for what you thought was the best, of course. Well, it's a sad business. I'll get word to Toler, so you needn't worry about that."

"Is it all right for me to go upstairs again? I'd like to say good-by to him if I could. And—and to his wife—I mean, his widow. But if you think I shouldn't—"

"No, I think you should. As a matter of fact, Mrs. Villac asked me to tell you she hoped you would. It might not be a bad plan for you to stay with her until her parents or someone else can get here. I'd stay myself, but I still don't feel quite easy about that confinement case I've just left. Mrs. Villac seems perfectly calm now, but you never can tell what a woman's next reaction will be under these circumstances. I don't like leaving her alone in the house with a dead man and two small children."

"She didn't say she wanted me to stay, did she?"

"No, just that she hoped you'd come to say good-by. The other was my idea. After all, you're an old friend and a relative by marriage, aren't you?"

"Yes. But I think Lavinia's idea is a better one. . . . Could you let the two families know right away, as well as the undertaker?"

"Yes, of course . . . but wouldn't you rather notify the Villacs yourself?"

"I'd rather you did, if you don't mind."

"No, I don't mind."

"Then she won't be alone long. Good night, Doctor."

"Good night."

He turned and seemed about to ask a question, then apparently changed his mind and made a statement instead. "Of course, I'll have to report this accident to the authorities. So far, I'm rather in the dark as to exactly what happened." He paused, as if giving Fleex the opportunity of making an answer; like the priest, he had not failed to observe the extraordinary clothing and strange manner of Claude Villac's cousin; but, as no reply was forthcoming, he went on, "I'm sure you'll give me all the information you can. But it can wait until morning."

"It might as well, mightn't it? Morning's almost here."

"Yes. Well, good night again."

When Fleex re-entered the bedchamber, Lavinia was standing by a window just inside the door. All her radiance was gone, but in its place was a new quietude and a new dignity, an acceptance of tragedy which, far from crushing her, had given her greater stature than ever before. She had never seemed so beautiful.

She did not move or speak as he walked over to the bed and looked down at his cousin. The soiled garments and bloody bandages had been removed and the dead man was simply clad in clean white garments. He looked perfectly at peace. Fleex made the sign of the cross and knelt beside the bed, bowing his head. Then he came back to the place where Lavinia was standing.

"I loved him better than anyone in the world except you. Now I've killed him and ruined your life. This is the end for me," he said quietly.

"I know."

"I told you that once before. That time, I didn't mean it. This time I do."

"I know."

"That kind lie—it won't be necessary."

"I know," she said the third time.

On the threshold of her husband's death chamber, they stood looking at each other, as powerless to escape the aftermath of the catastrophe which had engulfed them as they had been powerless to express their love and longing when they had stood, many years before, looking at each other on either side of a garden gate. Then Fleex turned and walked slowly down the stairs and out of the house. Lavinia closed the door and went nearer to the window. Dawn was just breaking. There were streaks of rosy light above the trees, but beneath them, everything was still in semidarkness. She could see Fleex as he went down the garden walk. After that, he was swallowed up in the shadows. But she continued to stand motionless by the window, as if she were watching for the desperate act she would not see and listening for the shot she would not hear.

354

PART SEVEN

Lavinia, and Brent

November, 1905—September, 1910

CHAPTER XXXIII

As Brent Winslow sat waiting for Lavinia to come downstairs, he glanced around her pleasant living room, realizing that, even after all those years, it did not seem really familiar to him. His daughter and her husband and children had always been encouraged to visit at the farm and they had done so with faithful regularity; it had not occurred to him until now that perhaps they would have preferred to come a little less often, and to have more of the family visits in their home. His habits had become increasingly those of a student and a recluse and Mary had adapted herself to his way of living, apparently finding all the release she needed in her flowers. To be sure, she sometimes went into town without him, when there were necessary errands to do that lay outside the province of Jim Garland or a hired man, or when she thought she could be of help to Lavinia, but these occasions were rare. Jim Garland liked to do the grocery shopping, just as he liked to do anything that brought him into contact with other people; his natural geniality had increased, rather than diminished, with age. Mary still made all her own clothes; she was unconcerned with fleeting fashions, and the materials she bought all lasted a long while; consequently, her personal requirements were few and far between. Her daughter did not need her very often, either; the children were healthy, the servants willing and faithful and Lavinia herself extremely capable and self-sufficient. It had not occurred to Mary, any more than it had to Brent, that it might have been a good plan to drop in frequently, merely for the sake of keeping somewhat closer their relationship with their only child.

Lavinia's living room bore very little resemblance to the

cluttered one at the farm, for, eventually, she had won her point and had done away with the parlor altogether, throwing two rooms into one; but, in spite of its size, it was comfortable and homelike, for she had discarded the formality of the "company room," as well as the parlor itself. The chairs were all of the variety currently described as "easy," and were so placed to invite companionship; built-in bookcases flanked the chimney piece, where a cheerful little fire always burned brightly in cool weather; current magazines were neatly arranged in rows on the table which stood in one corner and the baby grand piano stood in another. Shallow glass vases, containing early camellias, were scattered around amidst family photographs in silver frames, and several pleasing pictures hung on the walls. Although it was not yet quite dark, two softly shaded lamps had already been lighted, adding their glow to that of the fire. The whole effect was tasteful, warm and intimate.

"It was Jonathan Fant who first gave Lavinia ideas about making a room look like this," Brent said to himself. "Way back in '86, before we left Illinois. Then, when I built her a house for a wedding present, he tried again. He didn't succeed at the time, but after a while, Lavinia talked Claude into letting her make a change." The thought lessened Brent's enjoyment of the evidences of culture and comfort with which he sat surrounded. "That gentleman tramp was putting ideas into her head even then—all sorts of ideas about fixing up a house and getting a fancy education, and going off to a big city, instead of staying quietly at home. He put ideas into Sally's head, too, of course—a different sort. Poor Sally! She thought she was getting romance and all she got was heartbreak. The same as Lavinia would have had, if she'd married that evildoer Fleex. Well, we can't be thankful enough that didn't happen, anyway. And Jonathan didn't do Lavinia any real harm, even if he did make her restless. What's more, he didn't get anywhere with Mary." With returning contentment, Brent thought of his own home, so inferior to this one in all its outer attributes, but essentially so exactly what he wanted. He thought of Mary, so single-hearted and loyal, and of the way she had submerged her life in his. "If it hadn't been for Jonathan Fant, Lavinia would have been more like her mother," Brent now reflected grudgingly. "Not but what she made Claude a good wife, I've got to say that for her. She's a good mother and a good housekeeper, too, and a credit to the neighborhood. Just the same, she's always been restless, inside. She's liable to be more so now. I've got to find out what's on her mind, I've got to nip any wild ideas she might have while they're still in the bud and try to give her one that's worth while."

It was for this purpose that Brent had ridden into town and that he now sat waiting, with growing impatience, for his daughter to appear. He could not imagine what was keeping her so long. Callie had greeted him at the door on his arrival and had said that Miss Lavinia would be right down. That was half an hour ago. Then Callie had come back with the children and they had both been very polite to their grandfather, doing credit to their upbringing; but presently they had scampered off to play in the back yard. Brent had a feeling they were relieved when they were free to go, after having done and said everything they had been taught they should, to show him proper respect. Perhaps they were afraid he would talk to them about their dead father and were, instinctively, on their guard against this. At all events, they had not wanted to linger with him, out of affection. Yes, he was beginning to think he and Mary had made a mistake in not coming here more frequently and informally. Not just because of the children, either. Because of Lavinia. It would be harder to talk to her now than it would have been if they had been closer together all these years. She had never told him her troubles, she had never confided in him about anything. She had had secrets from him even when she was a young girl. That horrible cabin in the swamp, for instance. . . .

He had become so absorbed in thought that he did not hear Lavinia when she finally came into the room, and he looked up with a start to see that she was standing close beside him. He was appalled by her appearance. On the day of Claude's funeral, she had been veiled at the time, both in the church and at the cemetery; now he saw that the fresh color, which had been one of her greatest attractions, was completely gone. In her white face, which had lost its soft outlines, as well as its rosiness, her eyes seemed preternaturally large and there were black circles underneath them. Her hair was brushed straight back from her bow and it was without sheen. She had on a plain black dress, unrelieved by even a touch of white at the throat and wrists; it fitted her closely and in it she no longer looked slender; she looked emaciated. Before he had sufficiently recovered from the shock of seeing her like this, she spoke to him, and her voice had changed, too.

He had heard it once or twice long before, when it had seemed to him hard for a young's girl's, but it had never been hard like this.

"You wanted to see me?" she asked, and it seemed to him she was suggesting that it was abnormal for a father to visit his newly widowed daughter, instead of the most natural thing in the world.

"Yes, dear," he answered, with a conscious effort to make his own speech gentle. It had never been his habit to use terms of endearment, even in speaking to Mary, except in their most intimate moments. Neither had it been his habit to fondle his daughter, since her baby days. Now he wanted to put his arms around her, urging her to lay her head on his shoulder and have a good cry, after which she would feel better. But though he had managed to call her dear, he did not dare attempt the caress. Certainly Lavinia's manner did not encourage it; and though undoubtedly it *would* help her if she could have a good cry, he had never seen a woman who appeared less likely to shed healing tears. "I've been concerned about you, of course," he ended lamely.

"There's no reason why you should have been. I'm perfectly well."

It was on the tip of his tongue to say that she did not either look or act perfectly well, that, on the contrary, she looked and acted very far from it. Just in time, he stopped himself from doing so.

"I'm relieved to hear it," he said, trying to put some heartiness into his voice. "Your mother and I have been rather worried. You haven't telephoned, as usual, and every time we've called you, Callie or Verna has said that you couldn't speak to us just then."

"There wasn't anything I wanted to say. There's nothing I want to say now."

"Then perhaps you'll let me talk to you. Because there are quite a number of things I want to say."

"All right. I'll listen."

She certainly was not making things any easier for him. He drew a chair nearer to the one in which she had seated herself and sat down, too.

"First of all, of course, I want to tell you that your mother and I stand ready to help you in any way we possibly can through this hard period. We gathered you wanted to be alone, at first. In fact, your mother says you told her so the—the day of the funeral. And then, when we couldn't reach you by telephone . . . but it's over a week now since—since the tragedy."

"Which tragedy?"

"Why—Claude's death, of course."

"I just wanted to be sure. Perhaps you've forgotten that the day after Fleex found out he'd killed Claude, he killed himself. Also, that the day after Claude's ceremonious funeral in the Crowley cemetery, Clement helped his father bury Fleex, whom he adored, in the little graveyard back of the orange grove. Of course, as a suicide, Fleex was a logical victim of bell, book and candle. I understand there was even some question raised as to whether he could be laid to rest beside his mother and his little brothers and sister, and that Phares Primeaux defied anyone to stop it. Hitherto, he's insisted that family graveyard was all consecrated ground; now he swears part of it isn't. I don't blame him. What did the Church expect him to do? Fling his eldest son's body into the swamp?"

"Lavinia, don't—don't talk this way. Of course, that's all very sad, too—very tragic for Fleex's family. I don't blame them for feeling bitter. But we shouldn't let our sympathy for them make us bitter, too. And we shouldn't speak of Fleex's death and—and burial in the same breath with Claude's. After all, Fleex went out of our lives years ago and—"

"He never went out of my life. When you love a man the way I loved Fleex, he doesn't go out of your life just because you don't see him."

"But, my dear, you did dismiss him from your mind—very sensibly, very bravely. I know you went through a hard time when he ran off to sea, just as you thought he was on the point of asking you to marry him. I know that, for a while, you kept hoping against hope that he'd come back. But he didn't and, very wisely, you listened to reason from your elders. Finally, you realized it was Claude who really deserved your affection and you returned his. You married him, you were his faithful and devoted wife for ten years. You never saw Fleex again until he came staggering up to your door, covered with blood."

"I'm afraid you don't know quite as much as you think you do. I never dismissed Fleex from my mind for more than a few hours at a time. I did try to, because that was what everyone told me I ought to do. After all, I was only seventeen, and I was not only terribly hurt, I was terribly confused. But I tried to reason things out, as well as I could, and it was natural for me to suppose that older people—people who were fond of me—knew better than I did. They certainly kept telling me so. And Claude never let go for an instant. If I hadn't gone to Lacombe with him that first time. . . . But perhaps you've noticed, once in a while I don't reason, I only feel. I guess I'm not the only one. And often it's a good thing, because it's a great release, and we all need release sometimes. But that night, it wasn't a good thing. I did forget about Fleex for a few hours and nothing worse could have happened to me. The next day, when I remembered again, I hoped I'd find some way to back out of my pledge to Claude and still not hurt him too much. You're right about one thing—he did deserve my affection, he did have it—affection and respect. But affection and respect aren't the same as love."

"They're better, Lavinia—better than the kind of love you're talking about. That isn't really love. It's—" Brent paused, embarrassed; men did not customarily speak of such things to their daughters, seldom to their wives—at least, not the kind of man he was, not the kind of men he knew. "Its primitive instinct, a short flare-up—"

"I'm surprised that you don't get really biblical and say concupiscence. The primitive instinct was what got the better of me on *Toussaint* at Lacombe. *That* was the short flare-up. The stage was all set for it. And there was one other flare-up, New Year's eve, the night Claude's mother died, after she'd given us a very strong potion which she believed would insure conception. Well, it did—or something did. Anyway, I conceived about that time. But it didn't insure birth. Among other things you're remembering, perhaps you remember I miscarried, just a few months after I was married."

"Yes, Lavinia, I do remember. But surely—"

"The way I loved Fleex was the way Mother loves you," Lavinia went, on interrupting him. Her words were not coming coldly and slowly any more, as they had at first; they were hot and hasty. "She loved you enough to marry you when you were poor and too proud to let her family make things any easier for her. She suffered and slaved and never complained. She loved you enough to leave her home and her people and strike out with you to an unknown wilderness. She's loved you enough to stand by you, year after year, while you've shut yourself up with your work, too full of it to think whether there was anything else she might like to be doing or not. I won't try to say much about the way Fleex loved me. But I think I've

360

got a right to say he didn't ask as much of me as you've asked of Mother."

"Lavinia, how can you be so unjust? I've never looked at another woman, I've been as steadfast as she has. And Fleex—"

"Yes, Fleex did look at other women, when primitive instinct, as you call it, got the better of him; but that didn't have anything to do with the way he looked at me. He did run away, when he thought he didn't have anything to offer me. He didn't want me to slave and suffer or even to go without, though I was willing and eager to do it, if I could only be with him. But as soon as he did have something to offer me, he came back."

"What are you talking about?"

"He came back," Lavinia said, speaking deliberately and scornfully now. "That was something else you didn't know. You thought he didn't. You thought I never saw him again until ten days ago. You're wrong. I saw him ten days after I married Claude. He had a good job on a banana boat, he planned to take me to Central America for my honeymoon. He'd heard a rumor that he was going to inherit the Labadies' *maisonette*—we don't know even yet whether that was true or not because they've lived on and on. But anyway, he was sure of enough to support me, to make me comfortable, to provide for me. He came and found me at the *maisonette*—in the *cabinet*. It was when Claude's mother died and he'd gone back to Crowley right after the funeral at Lacombe. I stayed over in New Orleans to collect the things I'd left there in the autumn. I'd taken off my engagement ring because I was handling dusty books and papers and my wedding ring had slipped off. It was too loose. I was so sleepy I hadn't even bothered to pick it up. I was still asleep when Fleex came and found me and took me in his arms and told me we could get married right away. There was nothing to show him that I was married already. And he'd never dreamed I wouldn't wait for him. He couldn't instantly grasp the fact that I hadn't, and even when he did, he couldn't accept it —instantly. I never saw him from that night until the night he killed Claude. But before he left me—"

Brent tried to speak and found that he could not. His throat was dry, his lips failed to form words. Involuntarily, he glanced down at Lavinia's hands, which had lain loosely in her lap when she began to talk and which were now tightly clenched. He noticed, for the first time, that they were ringless. She had put the rings on again, after that terrible, tardy visit from Fleex, and she had worn them as Claude's wife ever since. But now that Fleex and Claude were both dead, she never intended to wear them again.

"I've done the best I could," Lavinia was saying, speaking more slowly again. "I think I made Claude happy—well, I know I did. He couldn't have pretended to be happy, not for ten years. But, as far as I'm concerned, the marriage was a sham from the night that Fleex came back to me and took me in his arms. Now I'm through with shams. I'm going away from here and I'm never coming back. I'm going to do something real and be something real. I don't know yet what, but something."

"Lavinia, you can't go away! Why, you'd break your mother's heart if you did that! You'd—you'd break mine."

"You and Mother didn't mind breaking my heart. I don't see why I should mind breaking yours. Anyway, as I just said, what I want now is reality. I'm going to have it."

"You can have something real and be something real without deserting your home and uprooting your children."

With a precipitancy which suggested that they must have been lurking somewhere in the front hall, awaiting a signal to enter, and that they had seized upon the word "children" as such a sign, Prosper and Anne Marie came running into the living room. Prosper made straight for Lavinia's chair. More hesitantly, Anne Marie approached Brent and looked up at him with a cherubic smile. He lifted her into his lap and she nestled close to him, her plump little person adjusting itself easily to his angular frame, her golden head resting confidently on his breast. Now that her mother was in the room, too, she did not feel so shy with her grandfather.

"It's too dark to play outside any more," Prosper announced. "Aren't you going to read to us, Mama?"

"Not until after supper. You and Anne Marie shouldn't come rushing in like this, Prosper, when I have company. You know that."

"Yes, but I didn't know Grandpa Winslow was company. I thought he was family."

"He is family, but he's company, too. He's talking to me and he doesn't want to be interrupted."

"I don't mind," Brent, who was greatly enjoying the presence of Anne Marie on his knees, said quickly. "If they'd like to stay here while I'm talking to you, I'd be glad to have them."

362

"Perhaps you would, but I wouldn't."

Brent looked across at his grandson, to find that the little boy's magnificent dark eyes, usually so full of mischievous sparkle, were resting on him thoughtfully. What an extraordinarily handsome child he was—and so sturdy, so well built! Brent wondered why he had not been more conscious of this before. "I'd especially like to have Prosper hear what I started to say when I told you you could have and do something real right here in Crowley, Lavinia," he persisted. "Prosper, I want your mother to manage the Monrovia Mill. I mean I want her to take care of it, the way your father did, until you're old enough to do it, for your mother and your sister and yourself."

"Oh, Mama, you will, won't you?" the child exclaimed eagerly.

"Prosper, you don't know what you're talking about. Your grandfather's only joking. I couldn't run a mill."

"Yes you could. There's nothing you can't do, Mama." He looked at her with loving pride, throwing his arms around her neck and kissing her. She did not return the caress.

"I just said, you don't know what you're talking about. Women don't run mills. Take your sister out to Callie and stay with her until I call you. Get down, Anne Marie."

Lavinia spoke with a sternness which admitted of no argument. Brent realized that, on top of rousing her anger, he had now incurred her resentment by interfering with her orders. He had made a bad matter even worse by acting on one of his rare impulses; he should have told her what was on his mind, slowly and cautiously, when they were by themselves, instead of breaking it to her abruptly, in the children's presence. Obediently, but with obvious reluctance, Anne Marie slid off his lap and put her hand in her brother's. Prosper looked back once, when they reached the door, as if he were not satisfied with the situation and hoped that his mother would relent. But she gave him no answering glance and the children departed without verbal protest on their part or further comment on their mother's. Though thoroughly discouraged by the unfortunate turn things had taken, Brent attempted to go on where he had left off.

"I came here on purpose to talk to you about the mill, Lavinia," he said. "I wanted to offer you my sympathy and my help first, of course. But after that, I wanted to talk to you about this idea I've had."

363

"You must be crazier than I thought. There isn't a mill in Louisiana that would accept a woman for its manager."

"Yes, there is. The Monrovia would accept you. It wants you. The directors asked me to tell you so. They're convinced you'd protect its interests better than anyone else they could select, in Claude's place. After all, you're virtually its owner. Didn't you realize that?"

For the first time that evening, she was not ready with her retort. Yes, of course, she should have realized that, she told herself more quickly than she could say so aloud. Her grandfather had promoted the building of the Monrovia and had held a controlling interest in it from the beginning. He had been steadily buying up additional shares of stock, and he had been gradually putting everything he owned in the beginning, and everything he had acquired since, in either Claude's name or hers. Now, everything Claude had owned belonged to her and the children. She had not thought of that, since his death, because there had been so many other things to think of—things that seemed to her infinitely more important, infinitely more pressing. But she would soon have to think of it now. Her obligation to Claude might be over; her obligation to their children was greater than ever, now that he was dead.

"I suppose I must have, vaguely," she said at last, conscious of the inadequacy of her answer.

"It isn't like you, Lavinia, to be vague about anything. You're the owner of a very important piece of property, and its value is going to keep on increasing all the time. You can't neglect it."

"I can sell it," she said swiftly.

"Yes, you can sell it. But can you be sure of getting full value for it? Particularly, if you sell it in a hurry, because you want to leave town? Prospective buyers almost automatically take advantage of such a reason. That would make it a sacrifice sale to begin with, which wouldn't be fair to the children. And many people don't realize yet, as well as you and I do, the tremendous potentialities of a world market for our rice. We've hardly begun to tap that market yet."

"I don't see why you think I realize all this. As a matter of fact, I hadn't thought of it."

"You must think of it. Not just because of what it's worth in dollars and cents, either. Because of what it's worth in other ways. If you sell it, you must be sure you really want to. You've been trying to tell me, in your bitterness and grief, that you've been living a lie for ten years. You haven't been doing anything of the sort. You've been living courageously—righteously. I don't mind using biblical language. That's what you've been—a prudent and virtuous woman, the kind Solomon described. What's more, you've become a power in the community —a power of progress and good. You've sacrificed your personal happiness to do it. You sent away the man you could have had for a lover, even if you couldn't have him for a husband. If you'd kept him, then you *would* have been living a lie. And you couldn't have done and been everything else you've done and been. Even if you'd never been found out, you'd have been constantly on guard, constantly furtive; it would have told on you. And, of course, sooner or later, you would have been found out. Perhaps there wouldn't have been any great public scandal. But you'd have destroyed or at least undermined Claude's faith in you and, little by little, other people's faith in you, too. Eventually, your children would have known, too, and the knowledge would have done them great harm. You realized all this, down deep in your heart, so you made a great sacrifice. I understand that now. I'm sorry I didn't understand it before. I—I ask your forgiveness for my blindness —my bad judgment. You did love Fleex the way your mother loved and still loves me. And he didn't ask any more of you than I have of her—maybe less. Different things, that's all. I should have encouraged you to be patient and tolerant and trustful, to hold fast to the belief that he'd come back to you. I'll have to live the rest of my life remembering that you'd have been a happier woman if I had."

Brent Winslow had never spoken in this way to his daughter before—at such length, with such tenderness. Now he rose and, coming over to her chair, put his arm around her shoulders.

"So I hope you won't think I'm guilty of another mistake of judgment when I ask you not to make your sacrifice futile. You couldn't make it entirely futile, of course. Part of it—probably most of it—would still be worth while. But if you don't go on with Claude's work, you'll fail him for the first time. You've got a torch to carry for him and you haven't any right to lay it down. Besides, you're needed here, Lavinia. You're wanted. Is there any other place where you're needed and wanted? Wouldn't you feel a great lack of what you've had for so long, and can go on having in greater and greater measure here, than if you went among strangers? Could you be sure of giving your children such a goodly heritage?"

Again she did not answer immediately. But she did not draw away from him, as he had been afraid she might when he put his arm around her shoulders.

"I wouldn't have any idea how to run a rice mill," she said at last.

"Wouldn't you? You've got wonderful executive ability, Lavinia."

"That isn't saying I know anything about rice."

"That isn't saying you know anything about rice!" he repeated. For the first time in the course of their whole dreadful talk, he smiled, and though there was no answering smile, neither was there a scornful disclaimer. "You probably know as much about rice as any woman in Louisiana, if not more," he said. "You grew up on a rice farm. You were out weeding a rice field that was full of snakes when you were only nine years old. You shared the discovery that the rice flowers open briefly at noon with your mother and me. You saw my first attempts at cross-pollination with the help of bees. You've followed my experiments in selection ever since. You've watched the march of progress in machinery and irrigation."

"Yes. But breeding and harvesting rice aren't the same as milling it."

"Granted. But haven't you gone down to the mill every now and then, too? Didn't Claude encourage you to come?"

"He liked to have me. I didn't go very often. That was his work—his success. I felt I ought to keep my hands off it."

"But didn't he talk to you about his work, his success, in all those years from the time when he was just a sample boy to the time when he and you practically owned the Monrovia?"

"Well, yes he did—occasionally."

"Then you must have learned something. And you could learn a great deal more, easily and quickly. It's never been hard for you to learn anything you wanted to, Lavinia. And this is your work now—your chance for success. By-and-by, it'll be your son's. It should be your son's. Don't sell his birthright for a mess of red pottage."

There was a long silence. It was broken by the children's voices, coming to them from across the hall again —voices that Callie was trying to hush, but which, nevertheless, made themselves heard, not unpleasantly, but somewhat demandingly. Lavinia rose, though not abruptly, as if to seem she was trying to disengage herself from her father's embrace. Quite the contrary; as soon as she was on her feet, she slipped her arm through his.

"They're getting hungry. It's past their suppertime," she said. "Would you care to stay and eat rice—and perhaps a few other things—with Prosper and Anne Marie and me? You could telephone Mother you wouldn't be home until a little later, couldn't you?"

It was when he was preparing to leave, considerably later, that Lavinia said something Brent had not dared to hope she would say.

"You haven't told me anything about your experiments in a long while," she reminded him. "Do you feel you're making any real progress toward that ideal variety you've been searching for all these years?"

He smiled. "Yes, I do," he said. "And I will talk to you about it the next time I come in for supper. I may be even crazier than you thought, but you and I are going to be partners. I'll grow the rice for farmers to sell you for milling and I believe it will make us both famous."

CHAPTER XXXIV

The offices of rough rice, clean rice and bookkeeping were crudely housed in the Monrovia Mill, as in all others. They were quartered in one large room on the ground floor, for though there had been some discussion, when the plant was built, of having them upstairs, Jim Garland had not forgotten "Curley" Duson's warning: "Unless you want to scare a Cajun away, don't get him too far from outdoors."

The rough rice office was equipped with shelves for samples and a long table with a trough along the edge; on this table was a "beaded" hardwood rubbing board and an emery rubbing stone. At the clean rice side of the room were more shelves along the wall, which were used for sample boxes; there was also another trough-edged table. Here, the trough was usually overflowing; unless someone reminded the sample boy to empty it, the milled grain was scattered over the floor. This department was further supplied with a roll-top desk, a swivel chair and a typewriter for the assistant manager, and several chairs with cowhide seats and adjacent spittoons were placed at strategic points for the convenience of customers. The bookkeeper sat on a tall stool at a slant-top desk, behind a wooden railing with a swinging gate. The board walls were uniformly painted bright blue, the same color as the sample boxes.

In only one respect did the Monrovia differ from most other mills: it boasted a small cubiform office which could be shut off from the noisy, cavernous room housing the three departments, though, as a matter of fact, its door usually stood wide open. Jim Garland, who had his own ideas about rice mills, as on most other subjects, had insisted on this office, in much the same way and for much the same reasons that his daughter and granddaughter had insisted on entrance halls in their houses: a sales manager, Garland said, had a right to some privacy if and when he wanted it. The other promoters of the mill had not shared or even understood his viewpoint, but, after all, he was underwriting the project to a very large degree and they made no objection to his whim. The result was that, when Claude became the sales manager of the Monrovia, he had enjoyed a privilege almost unique in the locality—that of having his own small sanctum—and Lavinia had inherited it. It was Claude's sandy-haired, hatched-faced assistant Henry Blanchard, who afterward became hers, that sat in the swivel chair at the roll-top desk in the clean rice department, and that dealt firsthand with the employees of the mill, the farmers and salesmen as they came in, before they got to the "big boss." Not that Claude had remained aloof, or that Lavinia did so now; both had too much business sense, as well as too much natural geniality, to pursue such a course; but, if a representative from Anheuser-Busch appeared on the scene, Blanchard did not permit a conference with him to be interrupted by a farmer who was discontented with the toll milling system. The man from Anheuser-Busch might well have come with an offer to "buy the output" of all the "mill run" brewer's rice produced that season. The farmer would only want to complain that, under the toll milling system, he took all the risk and the miller none. His grievance might be just, but it would not help to balance the books, much less to show a profit at the end of the season.

It did not take much intuition to deal with such obvious cases as these; but Henry had tried to develop a sixth sense in dealing with others that were more baffling. Sometimes he succeeded and sometimes he did not. For instance, there was the time that, walking along the porch of the rough rice warehouse on his daily tour, Henry heard the unmistakable grunting of pigs. He remembered having seen three half-grown hogs rooting around the mill several days earlier and wondered idly to whom they belonged, without giving the matter much further thought. Now he called one of the men and asked for an explanation. After some questioning, he wrung a reluctant admission from the man that the pigs belonged to Tom Schaefer, who lived on the farther side of the depot, but that they had been "removed" from these premises and confined in a makeshift pen under the porch. Two of the mill hands had conceived the bright idea of doing this and fattening the pigs on the overflow from the bran spout, preparatory to a private *boucherie* at the expense of both their owner and the big boss. Henry accomplished the release of the pigs and their return to Tom Schaefer with a stern warning to the culprits and without recourse to Lavinia. But in other instances, he had not been so successful in shielding her —for example, in the case of Achille Fournerat. . . .

Achille was a well-known farmer in the Mowata section and a good customer. He had always boasted, "Me, I sell my rice to M'sieu Claude. Nobody else. Now I sell it to M'iz Claude." On the basis of this boast, which he made good, he felt it was his unquestionable privilege to do business direct with the big boss. But one day Henry had tried to block his path to the private office, knowing that Achille had no rice to sell that day. Since Achille knew that he knew, it seemed safe to say, "M'iz Claude is terribly busy. Why don't you let me help you this one time?"

Achille appeared to debate the question within himself. "Well, I guess it's all right for you to sell me some bran," he said finally.

"I'm sorry, Achille," Henry told him. "We haven't any bran today. We won't have any until next week."

The farmer frowned. *"Mais,* M'sieu Blanchard, I always sell my rice here, me! Nobody else. Now my poor pigs they starve! And you say you don't got no bran for me!"

Henry knew that, once lost, it would be hard to regain the confidence of a man like this. But what would be the use of calling Lavinia? She could only repeat what Henry had already said himself: that they had no bran that day. And then Achille would hold it against her. It was far better that he, Henry, the hired help, should get the blame. So he had tried to placate Achille.

"I've got a friend at the Columbia and I know they have some bran," he said. "Just go over there and tell them I sent you. They'll fix you up."

"Non!" Achille spoke the word with such finality that Henry knew it was useless to insist. But his curiosity was aroused and, as the farmer stalked away, he called after him, "Hey, Achille, you mean you're going to let your pigs starve after all? Why don't you want to go to the Columbia?"

Achille continued to march toward the door. When he had almost reached it, he paused and, turning his head, muttered contemptuously, *"Ils sont tous les Américains là bas!"*

It was fortunate that, at just this moment, Lavinia came out of the private office with a telegraph blank in her hand. "Why, Achille," she said swiftly, "are you going off without seeing me? Come right back here and tell me what I can do for you."

In no time at all the matter had been patched up: it was all too true that they did not have any bran at the Monrovia that day, but she knew where to get it. She would get it herself, immediately, and then she would sell it to Achille; he would buy it from *her*. Well, yes, that would be all right, Achille agree, after another silent debate with himself. He would do his other errands and then he would come back and get his bran. He was obviously trying to be not only reasonable, but generous, for he added, "An' don't tell me you *Américaine* you'self, M'iz Claude. You married a good Cajun, the best. You children growin' up good Cajuns. Tha's different!"

Lavinia watched him out of sight before she permitted her pleasant smile to widen into a delighted grin, and chuckled instead of bursting into the hearty laugh in which she would have indulged had there not been possible talebearers within hearing. "Hurry right over to the Columbia, Henry, for that bran," she said, still chuckling. "And, while you're out, you might take this telegram to the depot. It's in answer to one I had this morning from Bancroft, that old fussbudget in San Francisco. He wired me, 'TWO WEEVILS IN YOUR LAST SHIPMENT, ONE ALIVE AND ONE DEAD STOP WHAT SHALL I DO?' I'm wiring back, 'KILL THE OTHER WEEVIL AND SEND CHECK.' " . . .

Well, she had turned his failure to deal singlehanded with Achille into a joke and Henry was grateful to her. He was also glad to see that she seemed to be taking the problems of the mill more in her stride than she had at first. It was a reflection of her more generally cheerful outlook on life. Still, he was chagrined at his own ineptitude whenever there was an instance of it like this, and he also wished there were some way in which he could stop Brent Winslow from taking up so much of Lavinia's time. Henry knew it was Brent who had persuaded Lavinia to become the manager of the mill and that one of his strongest arguments had been that they would form a father and daughter partnership; but the assistant manager felt that the daughter was now contributing more to this partnership than the father. There was nothing to show that these long, frequent conferences were fruitful, as far as she was concerned; and, though Lavinia was a strong, healthy woman, Henry had the feeling that her father's visits, when the latter was tired and discouraged, often left her tired and discouraged, too. The visits nearly always took place the latter part of the afternoon, and Lavinia's working days, like those of everyone else at the mill, began at seven. By the time Brent Winslow came in, she had decoded the telegrams—delivered as they came in by the railroad agent, who was the only telegraph operator—and had dealt with the mail, dictating some of the letters to Henry, but typing others herself from her own notes, for she had somehow found time, after Claude's death, to take a course in stenography. After she had finished with the most urgent correspondence, she had given her instructions as to which lots of rice were to be milled that day. She had consulted with her rough rice buyer concerning the current market, in order to guide him as to quality, quantity and price for buying. She had issued the shipping orders for the day, ordering an empty boxcar from the same agent who had delivered the telegrams. She had frequently received a representative from a rice mill supply company who, after paying her his respects, had asked permission to check the mill; and, if it were noon before he had finished his tour of inspection with the miller, noting what repair parts were needed, she had invited him to have dinner with her, and had continued this friendly discussion herself. Such hospitality was the rule rather than the exception; but whether she had guests or not, she went home for dinner with the children. On her return, a little after one, she surveyed the entire premises, going to the boiler room and the engine room in the mill proper, and to both the clean rice and the rough rice warehouses. In the course of this survey, she carefully observed whether all was well with operative procedure, made suggestions or

371

gave orders as indicated, and "fraternized" with the mill help, in a way that never lacked dignity or authority, for all its friendliness; and finally, she made out her sample list, evaluating each lot.

With the inevitable interruptions which took place, all this represented a full day's work and Henry was reluctant to see her assume her father's burdens as well as her own. It was therefore with a feeling of genuine concern for his employer that he watched Brent Winslow cross the floor of the clean rice department, one afternoon in early September and, after a few brief words of greeting here and there, enter the cubicle. It had not only been a normally busy day; it had been a day when everything had gone wrong: at seven-thirty the machinery had not yet started up and the shipping crew was idle, lolling on the hand trucks and gossiping. Against her better judgment, Lavinia had kept on a first-floor attendant with a weakness for drink. She could easily have replaced him, for his duties did not require specialized skill. But he had a wife and four small children, so for a long time his transgressions had been forgiven. Now his backsliding had been costly: trying to work while half drunk, he had forgotten to lubricate a main shaft bearing, the bearing had burned out, and the mill was, perforce, idle until the engineer could effect repairs. This had hardly been done when a sack of rice slipped from the top of a stack, injuring a man who stood near by. After he had been given first aid, he had to be taken home for more expert medical attention; and when Henry returned from this errand, he found Lavinia visibly upset over a complaint that a shipment had not been "up to sample"; the buyer was demanding a rebate of fifty cents on the dollar.

"I didn't know there was anything wrong with that shipment," she said. "What do you think, Henry?"

"Might have been too much broken," he admitted. "But not anywhere nearly as much as Harris is claiming," he hastened to add.

"Would you think we might allow him ten cents on the dollar perhaps?"

"Yes, that would be plenty."

"All right. I'll send him a telegram."

She could afford to take the loss in dollars and cents; Henry knew she was not worried about that. The mill was making a steady profit; Lavinia was already very well to do, and she would soon be a really wealthy woman in her own right, quite aside from the substantial inheritance which would someday be hers. But her pride was touched; it was a matter of principle with her that every shipment should be as near specified grade as it was humanly possible to make it. Coming on top of the machinery's disruption and the injury to the workman, the telegram of complaint had seemed like the last straw. And now, here was Brent Winslow with a tale of woe to pour into his daugher's ears. There had been a bad storm the day before and Henry knew exactly what Winslow had come to say: that, in spite of all his careful selections of head and stool, all his patient experimentation with crossbreeding, he had failed to breed in the necessary strength of straw and neck, so that his rice would stand up under a heavy crop when there was wind and rain. Now he had come to talk to his daughter about this fresh disappointment.

The door of the cubicle closed behind him, and though Henry had formed a pretty good idea what course the ensuing conversation would take, some details of it escaped his intuition. Lavinia looked up with a smile from the papers on her desk and drew the extra chair which her father habitually used closer to it. He slumped rather than sat down in it and looked at her without speaking, dejection written in every line of his face and figure.

"I know," she said, trying not to show that she was herself dispirited. "It's terribly hard luck. I know you thought you were going to succeed this time."

"I did. I'd selected the finest heads and stools just before harvesting the field crop last year and the new plants showed greater vitality, not just of germ—of root system and growth, too. There was considerable extra productiveness and a much larger proportion of crystal grain than ever before. And still the fields were flat as a pancake this morning. I don't mean that the crop's a total loss—a good part of it can be retrieved. But as far as my experiments go, it's a failure. Success is just another mirage like those we see so often on the prairie in dry weather."

"No, it isn't. You're getting nearer and nearer complete success all the time."

"What makes you say that? You don't really think so. I haven't even had partial success yet and I've been trying for almost twenty years."

"Yes, I do think so. Yes, you have had. You've succeeded in producing a crop that's practically crystalline. That was your first objective—to get rid of chalk and shad. You've done that now. You can't do everything at once. Perhaps, another year—"

373

"That's what your mother keeps telling me."

"Well, you're not going to admit that your womenfolk have more sense and more stamina than you have, are you?"

Her tone was one of gentle raillery. Lavinia no longer argued with her father, as she had when she was a rebellious schoolgirl, given to disputing his remarks sharply or hotly. Maturity had brought with it a mellowness which she had lacked in her youth, and which tempered the determination she had retained. She smiled again as she asked her question, and there was no sting in it. But Brent did not smile in return.

"As you know, when we introduced Shinriki Japan, I thought that it would stand up under its grain," he went on. "It produced wonderfully on the newer lands that were free from grasses and red rice. But it was a slow grower and it was a short-straw, and both of those characteristics were against it when the land got worn and grassy, even if it was free from red rice. And it lacked uniformity of grain. It wasn't standardized, it was made up of hybrids. You've told me over and over again that, when it came to milling, no two lots were alike."

"Yes, I have. But you've stopped planting Shinriki. You've been experimenting for some time now with those selections you secured from that crop grown by Captain Harrison, near Mermentau."

"Yes, and what have I got? All sorts of outcroppings and variations."

"You're got the crystal grain."

"And along with it weak straw and weak neck."

"You've still got the crystal grain. And it's due to your efforts that the last crop showed so much more general vitality than ever before. It seems to me that when we founded this partnership of ours, your main arguments were that I ought to remember what I had, instead of what I'd failed to get, and that, because I'd succeeded along certain limited lines, I could succeed along more extended ones."

Her tone was still one of gentle raillery and she still smiled. If the smile was a little sad, a little weary, at least there was no bitterness in it, and she looked steadily and calmly at her father while she was speaking. This time, meeting her gaze, he accepted its challenge and managed to smile in return.

"You're right, those were my arguments," he said. "And you're also right to keep reminding me I have got the

374

crystal grain, I have made some general progress. But I get discouraged more easily than I used to when I was younger. It's done me good to talk to you, Lavinia. I'll go back and have another look at the fields. Perhaps they're not in such bad shape as I thought. And perhaps, as you say, another year—"

He rose slowly and stood beside her chair, looking down at her with loving pride tardily mingled with concern. "You put in long days, Lavinia," he said. "You must get very tired. Isn't it about time you went home?"

"I'm going presently. I still have a few odds and ends to clean up here. Father . . . I've been toying with a new idea lately and I've been meaning to speak to you about it, but there always seem to be so many things that are more important. Sit down again for a moment, will you? Or were you in a hurry to get home and have a look at the rice?"

"No, I'm not in any particular hurry. What's the idea?"

"Have you ever thought of naming your rice?"

"What do you mean, naming my rice?"

"Well, it's always seemed to me so impersonal to speak about a variety of rice just by the name of the country it first came from. It's undergone all sorts of changes since then, anyway. But—well, take the case of Scotch oatmeal. It never had any real vogue in the United States until the manufacturers started calling it Quaker Oats. Then it began to sell like wildfire."

"I think I see what you mean," Brent said slowly. "But I don't know that you could create a demand for a certain kind of rice, the way you can for a certain kind of oatmeal, just by giving it some special name."

"I don't see why not—if it was a special kind of rice. Oatmeal isn't the only product that's been promoted that way. Cologne water seems to smell a lot better when it's called Maria Farina or 4711. And think of the Gold Dust Twins and Spotless Town! And then, all the lovely names of Mother's camellias: Eleanor of Fair Oaks, Regina dei Gianti and Souvenir de Bahaud–Litou. No one calls those camellia japonicas any more, in general conversation, merely because the first varieties came to us through a missionary in Japan!"

"No, you're right again," Brent said, still slowly. "So you think that, if—I mean, when—I get my ideal variety, we might give it some appealing name?"

"That's it."

"Well, it's something to think about. I will think about

it. But I'm going home now—if I don't, you won't, either, and it's high time you did."

"You wouldn't like to have supper with me?"

"Thanks, not tonight. I do want to have another look at that rice."

He bent over her, giving her one of his infrequent caresses. Then he went out of the cubicle, closing the door after him. As he walked across the bare floor of the clean rice department, Henry Blanchard, who was still at his roll-top desk, looked up and nodded. Brent Winslow nodded and said good night in return, but he spoke as if his mind were on something else, and he did not stop until he had reached the farther side of the office. Then he picked up one of the little blue samples boxes and stood looking from the shelf where these were ranged to the blue walls above them, before he disappeared from Henry's line of vision.

When Lavinia reached home, she found Jonathan Fant in the living room playing games with the children. His presence there did not surprise her for, in the last few months, he had become an increasingly frequent visitor. At the time of the dual tragedy involving Claude and Fleex, both Callie and Verna had taken time off from their tumultuous mourning outcries to utter sinister predictions: when there were two deaths in the same general circle, there was always a third. Lavinia had heard them and had silenced them sharply; had there been any deaths in the family after Mrs. Villac's? No, the servants sniffed, but that was only *one;* it was when there were two that a third was sure to follow; they would pray to the Lord, but they were afraid it would not do much good; that was the way He unsparingly acted. Well, if they were determined to talk such nonsense, they had better not do it in front of the children or where she could hear them, Lavinia told them, and they knew better than to disregard her orders. Nevertheless, when Sally died, a few months later, their attitude was triumphant rather than somber. Hadn't they warned their Missus right along that she had better be prepared to grieve again?

As a matter of fact, Lavinia did not grieve very deeply for her aunt, and perhaps one of the saddest circumstances surrounding Sally's death was that nobody else did, either. She had deeply hurt her father by making him feel superfluous in his own house, as soon as she was married, and he had never felt the same toward her afterward; besides, he had long since ceased to think of Illinois as home, and had never entered into the life at St. Martinville; all his interests were now divided between those which were bound up with the Winslows on their farm, and those which he shared with the other members of his family and his business associates and poker-playing cronies in Crowley. Sally's estrangement from her husband had not come as quickly or been as complete as that from her father; nevertheless, her lack of intelligence and tact had doomed her marriage almost from the beginning. She was pretty without being charming, sensual without being provocative, talkative without being arresting; even if Jonathan had not been in love with her sister, instead of with her, when he married her, she could never have held him long. To do him justice, he had tried to be a good husband, in as far as it lay within his character to try to do anything which required prolonged effort; but the more tearful, the more voluble, the more importunate she became, the less he desired her; she drove him away from her by her very insistence on holding him, just as she had caused the initial attraction he felt toward her to cool, because she had so persistently thrown herself at his head. There was never a formal separation between them, but they were less and less in the same house, and—without so much reason for her detachment as her father—she had never entered into the life at St. Martinville, either. Jonathan had shown surprisingly good sense in the way he handled his modest patrimony and he was, by no means, a poor man; nearly all his investments had brought him in good returns, one of them—a lumbering project with headquarters at Jeanerette —surprisingly good ones. He could afford to let Sally stay at luxury hotels and she enjoyed doing so, drifting aimlessly from New Orleans to Chicago or New York and back again, going to the theater, buying clothes for which she had no particular use and eating more confectionery than was good for either her health or her figure. She grew very fat and her obesity finally became a contributing cause to her death. Her sons had both been sent to the Citadel, in Charleston, as soon as they were old enough for boarding school, and they made friends with whom they spent a large part of their vacations; they were headed for the University of Virginia, where their father had gone, as soon as they were old enough. They came home for their mother's funeral, respectfully and correctly; but they had already become outsiders to the family circle; they were Carolinians, elegant as to dress, suave as to manner, smooth as to speech; it was possible to associate them, in a vague way, with St. Martinville, but it was quite impossible to do so, either with the farm in Illinois or one in southwest Louisiana. They returned to their school as soon as the services were over.

Very shortly thereafter, Jonathan severed his connection with the Illinois farms, to his further financial profit. Jim Garland was perfectly willing that he should accept a good offer he had received for them; the old man never intended to go back there now, and he conceded that Jonathan had made an excellent deal. They divided the proceeds of the sale without disagreement and parted without acrimony, but with the mutually satisfactory knowledge that there was now no reason why they should continue any sort of an association; and Jonathan had long realized that Mary did not intend to see him, if she could possibly help it. Lavinia, however, had never done anything of the sort; and when it was obvious that Sally was dying, she had gone straight to St. Martinville, and had been kindness and efficiency personified, throughout the last few days of her aunt's life and in the days immediately following her death. Moreover, Lavinia had always been glad to make Jonathan welcome at her own house; and though Claude's cordiality had been tempered by a latent distrust, which he admitted to himself was unreasonable, he had been careful not to let this show. After Claude died, Jonathan did not call any more frequently than he had been doing for years —until Sally died, too. Then he became a more and more constant visitor.

When Lavinia came home late after her conference with her father and found Jonathan in the living room, playing games with the children, she realized that they had just reached a very exciting point in their play; so she nodded and smiled and, after saying she would go and freshen up a little, disappeared to do so. There was never any question, nowadays, as to whether Jonathan would stay to supper or not; it was understood that of course he would. If there were time after he put in his appearance, or if he telephoned beforehand to say he was coming, which he seldom did, Verna prepared at least one of his favorite dishes for him, without prompting. He was a liberal tipper, and his manner with the servants, while inviting no liberties on their part and offering none on his, was easy, jocular and understanding. They liked him immensely.

Lavinia had observed, with admiration, the so-called *robes d'intérieur,* or tea gowns, which the mothers of her classmates at Sophie Newcomb often wore in the evening, when dinner was only an informal occasion. Mlle Haydee did not affect them; in her opinion, they were too much on the order of a *robe-de-chambre,* though she always changed for the evening, it was into something as rigid of line as what she had worn all day. Until after Claude's death, Lavinia had never worn them, either; her evening hours had been as active as her daytime hours, and it was neither suitable nor convenient to trail around the house in a long dress. Now, her mourning precluded social diversions and her day's work was over when she returned from the mill. Verna took entire charge of supper, Callie helped Anne Marie, who was rapidly becoming self-sufficient, with her bath, and Prosper scorned assistance and had even been persuaded to hang his clothes up neatly, on the condition that he should be allowed to do it by himself. Lavinia still read aloud to them, heard their prayers and sang to them and she intended to keep up these practices indefinitely; but they did not preclude the wearing of the type of clothes, designed especially for hours of ease, which she had so long secretly admired. She went to the mill, trimly clad in tailored black; but when she came home, she shed everything she had worn, took a second bath liberally sprinkled with lavender water, and put on only fresh linen undergarments beneath her flowing *robe d'intérieur.* For a time, this had been all black, too; but presently it had been relieved by folds of white and now it was usually all white. She had some on order that were pearl gray and violet, besides more white ones; they were made for her by Madame Sophie, in New Orleans, and though Sophie knew, as well as Lavinia, that it was too soon for her patron to be wearing half mourning, even in the privacy of her own home, she wisely did not say so.

The game was over when Lavinia came downstairs in snowy, floating chiffon, belted in around her slim waist with white grosgrain ribbon, and Prosper came dashing out to meet her, telling her that he had won and that she smelled good. Then they all went in to supper, which was delicious, and which they ate unhurriedly, by shaded candlelight. Anne Marie was going to kindergarten now and wanted to talk about the bird's nest she was making out of clay and the pictures she was drawing with crayons; she was encouraged to do so. Prosper was beginning to take an interest in baseball, so that was another favorite topic of conversation. On the other hand, he loathed his music lessons and did not wish to discuss them, except in protest.

Jonathan never seemed to find the children's chatter tiresome; like their mother, he listened to it with apparent interest and made all the properly enthusiastic rejoinders. Quite as often as not, he was also the one who did the reading aloud after supper, and the children found him almost as acceptable as their mother for this. When she went upstairs with them, Jonathan sat down at the piano and played. He still played beautifully, better than Lavinia did even now, and sometimes they played duets. She had once suggested to Prosper that, if he would only practice as faithfully, someday he might play as well as Uncle Jonathan. He had scoffed at the suggestion and it had not been repeated. This was partly because, seeing that he had hurt her feelings, Prosper had said that maybe he might like to play something else, not a piano—a violin, for instance; and then he saw a strange expression come on his mother's face, as if he had hurt her, before she turned away. So he knew a violin was not the answer, either. . . .

Tonight, when Lavinia came downstairs, Jonathan was still at the piano, and he went on playing, after half rising to acknowledge her presence, and looking around to smile at her. She sat down in an easy chair, near at hand, and listened to him with enjoyment. These evenings with Jonathan Fant were bringing her an increasing sense of contentment, greater than she derived from any other companionship. In fact, she had very little other companionship that counted in the least, at the moment. She took the children regularly to church, for she had never tried to evade her promise that they should be brought up as Catholics and, if anything, she tried to keep it all the more faithfully now that their father was dead. Because they were too young to go alone, she remained at church with them, but she felt no more drawn to Catholicism herself than she ever had, nor did she make an attempt to go to the Presbyterian church of her own nominal allegiance, as she had when Claude could take Prosper and Anne Marie to St. Michael's. Therefore, the usual round of Altar Society meetings or gatherings of the Ladies' Aid, which would have been natural under a different set of circumstances, were lacking in her case; and she would have caused criticism if she had taken part in secular meetings, whether civic or social, so soon after her husband's death. When Mass was over, she drove out to the farm, spending the rest of the day with her family and Claude's on alternate Sundays. During the week, she was at the mill all day and every day, and she came home healthily tired, eager to see her children, but indifferent to casual visits. At first, her craving for solitude had been so obvious and so natural, not only because she had lost her husband, but because of the horrible way she had lost him, that the neighbors understood and respected it. Now, those who had not fallen out of the habit of going to her house were waiting for her to give the first indication that she would like to have them visit her again. Thus far, she had given no such indication.

She found it pleasant to look at Jonathan, no less than to listen to him, as he sat there playing. His hair had grown quite gray, but that was becoming to him; in fact, it gave him an added air of distinction. Lavinia had never given much thought to the difference in their ages, in considering their association, and she did not do so now. There was nothing except the gray hair, which she admired, to call her attention to it, for, otherwise, he had changed remarkably little. He had kept his graceful figure and, if the lines in his face had deepened somewhat, they had not spread; they had always added to the attraction of both his mouth and his eyes when he smiled, and they did so still. As his music trailed off into chords and then into silence, and he swung around on the piano stool to face Lavinia, without rising from it, she realized she had never seen him when he looked more beguiling.

"A penny for your thoughts," he said idly.

"I don't want to make you vain. But I suppose there's no other reason why I shouldn't tell you. I was thinking how much I enjoy having you here, how good looking you are and how ageless you seem."

He laughed. "Could any man help feeling flattered by such a statement? Shall I tell you what I've been thinking, all the evening?"

"Yes, if you want to."

"I've been thinking how much you look like your mother when she was your age, or thereabouts. The resemblance is quite uncanny—quite upsetting. Except that, of course, you've never been an overworked drudge, and that you've learned how to dress, besides having the money to do it with."

"Mother was beautiful, even if she was an overworked drudge, and she's still beautiful, even if she's never learned how to dress."

"Yes, but you're just that much more beautiful because you haven't been the former and have learned the latter."

"Don't talk to me about flattery! All the same, I've got to admit that what you're saying isn't exactly displeasing to me."

"It wasn't meant to be. And I might add that I enjoy being here with you quite as much as you can possibly enjoy having me."

"I had an idea you did. After all, it's a far piece to St. Martinville. I didn't think you'd take the trouble to make the trip if you didn't find it more or less rewarding."

He laughed again. "I want to ask you another question, Lavinia. The answer might be worth more than a penny this time."

"Well, the mill's doing all right, but we can always use more money. What the question?"

"Do you invariably think of me as an uncle?"

"Why, no! I never did—that is, not primarily. You and I were friends before you ever saw Aunt Sally, long before you married her—from the moment we looked at that old geography book together, remember?"

"Yes, I remember. . . . And you've kept on feeling friendly toward me ever since?"

Lavinia considered. "Well, perhaps not every moment. I realized, in a dim way, by the time I was in my early teens, that you and Aunt Sally weren't very happy together and I wondered if it wasn't partly your fault. It was, of course. But perhaps I haven't blamed you for that as much as I should have. I realized, before I was much older, that it was partly her fault, too, and by that time I was fonder of you than I was of her. So I made excuses for you."

"Always?"

Again Lavinia considered. "Nearly always, I think. There was only one time—"

"Yes?"

"It was just before we left Monroe to come to Crowley. I thought you'd made Mother unhappy and I resented it. But I didn't understand what it was all about and she wouldn't tell me. However, I noticed that she never acted the same to you after that. She doesn't to this day."

"You're right, she doesn't. And you're right, I did make her unhappy. I'll tell you why: I told her I wasn't in love with Sally, I was in love with her."

If Jonathan had expected an outcry, he would have been surprised, for Lavinia looked at him for a moment or so before she spoke to him, and because, when she did speak, this was calmly, too. However, since she was acting

382

more or less as he had thought she would, he was prepared for it.

"I see," Lavinia said. "Well, that made things very awkward all around, didn't it? I wonder if Father ever guessed?"

"I think he was vaguely uncomfortable about me and I know he never really liked me. But I don't think he put his finger on the reason."

"I see," Lavinia said again. "Well, that would explain Mother's behavior toward you, too. I think you upset her more than you realized. I don't mean that she was angrier than you realized. I think you altered her general outlook and I think you stirred her a little. I'm almost sure, for instance, that if it hadn't been for the ideas of education you gave her, I wouldn't have been sent away to school. I've thought that for a long time. Now I also think that, if she hadn't been more attracted to you than she wanted to admit—more than she thought was right—she wouldn't have been afraid to go on seeing you. She'd have laughed off your declaration of love and that would have been the end of the whole thing."

"Perhaps. But she'd have been perfectly safe. I really did try to make Sally a good husband, for quite a long while. And eventually I fell in love with someone else, so I wasn't interested in the way your mother felt any longer. I had a much tougher problem on my hands. I fell in love with you."

"I see," Lavinia said for the third time.

"Is that all you're going to say? Aren't you even going to laugh off my declaration? Didn't you ever guess?"

"I'll answer your questions one at a time. It isn't all I'm going to say, but I've got to hear a little more before I know just what I want to say. I'm certainly not going to laugh off your declaration though. And I think I'm rather like Father, for once, however much I may look like Mother. I was 'vaguely uncomfortable' about you that spring in New Orleans, from the time you compared the *cabinet* to a 'safe room' you'd seen in an old house, somewhere in Virginia. You said that night you were afraid the Labadies wouldn't think your interest was 'entirely architectural or entirely avuncular' if you went up to see the *cabinet*. And of course I knew, in an indefinite sort of a way, that they wouldn't. So I would have stopped feeling like your real niece then, even if I had felt that way before —which, as I said, I didn't."

"But you didn't feel afraid of me?"

383

"No. Perhaps I should have. Did you want very much to seduce me?"

"Yes, very much."

"It probably wouldn't have been too hard," Lavinia said thoughtfully. "I was so inexperienced and so unhappy and so fond of you that you might very easily have persuaded me that you were unhappy, too, but that you would forget all your troubles if you found I cared enough for you to trust myself to your tenderness. And I believe you would have been tender—at first. Until I wasn't frightened any more. And I believe you'd have told me that I needed love as much you did and that, presently, I'd stop being unhappy, and be grateful to you for giving it to me."

"You did need love as much as I did. But I couldn't be sure you'd be grateful to me for giving it to you. I thought you might be sorry. Because I wasn't sure it was my love you wanted."

"It wasn't, of course. I would have been sorry, after a while. But not right away. I think you could have made love to me all that spring. Not at the *maisonette*. M. Clisson always went out to give his lessons, but Mlle Haydee gave most of hers at home. We could have had a little secret place somewhere else though. It might have been rather sweet."

"When you talk like that, Lavinia, it makes me wish I had seduced you."

"Then I must stop talking like that. And you must stop saying things that encourage me to do so."

It was a positive statement, but there was no severity in the way she made it. She was still smiling, and when he leaned forward and took her hand, she did not attempt to withdraw it.

"What we must do," he said, "is to stop talking about what happened—or rather, what didn't happen—years ago. We must begin to talk about what we're going to do now. Would you consider taking me for a lover, Lavinia?"

"You know I wouldn't. I'm not inexperienced or unhappy any more. You couldn't seduce me now. I'd be taking *you*, as you've just said—not the other way around. Respectable widows with small children don't indulge in sordid pastimes like that."

"I thought you'd say something of the sort. But occasionally respectable widows with small children remarry, and I'd much rather be your husband than your lover anyway. It's perfectly possible now—there's not an atom of blood relationship between us. Will you marry me, Lavinia?"

For the first time, he had really surprised her. While she sat looking at him, in utter amazement, without making an immediate move or answer, he took advantage of her silence and immobility and went rapidly on.

"I really do think I could make you happy, Lavinia. I don't think there'd be any regrets this time, on either side. We've known each other for a good many years and we've always been fond of each other. Our tastes are very congenial. Neither of us would interfere with the pattern of the other's life. Three's no reason why you should go on with your work at the mill, as far as I'm concerned; I can support you and I think you'd enjoy St. Martinville; you've lots of friends there. On the other hand, if you feel you ought to carry on, for Prosper's sake, I wouldn't try to prevent you; I'd be perfectly willing to come and live here. Your children like me and I like them. I think they'd accept me, without any protest, as a stepfather. And my sons are almost grown up—almost grown away. You must have seen that for yourself when they came home. They'd never be a complication. My dear, I'm very much in earnest. I never loved you as much as I do this minute. I know I'm not worthy of you, but I'd do my best, my very best, to make you a good husband."

"Oh, Jonathan, don't! Please—please stop!"

She withdrew her hand and, rising hurriedly, crossed the room and stood with her back to him. He was almost sure she was crying, which was wholly unlike her; and he longed to go to her, to ask her forgiveness if he had said anything, involuntarily and unconsciously, to distress her. But his instinct told him that he must give her time to recover from a proposal which had obviously been more of a shock to her than he had dreamed it would be. It was true that she had never thought of him as an uncle; but she had not thought of him as a husband, either. When, at last, she turned, he saw that he was right about one thing: she had been crying. But she was not offended. She came back to him and put her hands on his shoulders.

"Everything you've said is true," she told him. "We are fond of each other, we do have congenial tastes, we could fit into the pattern of each other's lives. I think, this time, you would be a good husband. And the children wouldn't protest; they'd be pleased. But there's one great drawback, one reason why it wouldn't work. I don't care as much as you do—that is, in the same way you do. I couldn't marry you unless I did."

"Why not, Lavinia? If I understood, if I wanted you to marry me anyway?"

"Because I've done that once already. Lots of people make a mistake once. But if they have any sense at all, they don't make the same mistake twice."

"Lavinia, you know I don't want to say anything that would seem to disparage Claude. Just the same——"

"It wouldn't have mattered who it was, if it hadn't been Fleex."

"Fleex!"

"Yes. Fleex Primeaux was the only man I ever loved, the only one I ever shall love. I loved him with all my heart and soul and now there's no love left to give to any other man."

"You can't say that, Lavinia. You're not thirty yet. You don't know how long life will seem to you without love."

"Yes I can. Yes I do. But it's something I can't help. If anyone could have made me change my mind, it might have been you. And do you know why? Because I've always thought you and Fleex were something alike inside, that sometimes you even looked like each other. I told Mother that once, years ago, and she was very indignant. She said you were a cultured gentleman and that Fleex was just an ignorant Cajun. You see she stood up for you even if she wouldn't see you. And of course she was right —about the ignorance and the culture, I mean. But that didn't make any difference."

"In as far as your love for Fleex was concerned. I can see that. But there might be a difference in other conditions that would affect your willingness to marry again eventually."

"There might *have been*. For instance, if Fleex had never come back and if Claude had died in some natural way—from illness or as the result of an accident or even if he had been killed by some total stranger . . . perhaps, after a long while . . . yes, I think under those conditions. But, Jonathan, Fleex did come back; he came back twice. The first time was just after Mother Anne died and I'd had an awful experience with all the gruesome details of laying out the dead and holding a wake and preparing for a burial. I'd attended two widely separated funeral services for a woman I was very fond of and ridden hours and hours on a dirty local train. I'd sat up all one night beside a corpse and I'd shared a room with five other girls the next night—three of us to a bed. When I finally got back to New Orleans, I was completely exhausted, physically and emotionally. Fleex found me asleep in my bedroom and waked me up by making violent love to me. The second time he came back, he killed my husband. I'm not blaming him for what happened. He didn't know, the first time, that Mother Anne had just died and he didn't know I was married—he meant to marry me himself. He didn't know, the second time, it was Claude who was trying to find him—he thought he was shooting in self-defense. But just the same. . . . And then, he killed himself! Jonathan, don't you understand that in my memories death and love and horror are all so intermingled that I can't disassociate one from the other any more? Don't you understand why I've deliberately tried to stifle all the kind of feeling for a man that would make a normal happy marriage possible?"

"I can understand why you'd try to. I'm not sure you've succeeded. I still think that in time—"

"It's nearly three years now since Fleex killed Claude. Don't you believe that, if I hadn't succeeded, I'd know it by now?"

Jonathan made no immediate answer and Lavinia knew it was because he could not honestly say no and because he was still reluctant to say yes.

"I'm sorry, Jonathan," she went on swiftly. "I'm terribly sorry. If I'd dreamed you were serious, that you really wanted to marry me, I never would have let things go so far. But I honestly thought all there was between us was just—well, a very wonderful friendship, different from other friendships, better than others, perhaps with more awareness that you're a man and I'm a woman. But nevertheless. . . . I haven't anything else left to give you, Jonathan."

Her hands were still resting on his shoulders, but now she bowed her head. He knew that she was weeping again and he knew, too, that nothing he could say or do would make her change her mind. He put his arms around her and lowered his head to touch hers.

"It's all right, darling," he said. "If that's all you have left to give, you can't help it. I'm thankful that you'll give me that much."

CHAPTER XXXV

It was a beautiful day, warm even for September, and Lavinia found it hard to keep her thoughts focused on the service. She would have liked to sleep late Sunday mornings, since she was at the mill by seven every other day in the week, and then to take her time doing the little personal, feminine tasks for which office hours gave her no opportunity on other days. But the latest Mass was at nine-fifteen, so she did her best to shake off her somnolence; her children were still too young, in her opinion, to go to church unattended, though many other children, much younger, did so. They also went without as many preliminaries as Lavinia considered necessary: not only were both her children bathed; their nails and ears were inspected, Anne Marie's curls were brushed and combed, Prosper's shock of black hair smoothed into place. Then came hair ribbons, fresh frilly muslin and a silk sash for Anne Marie, a shirt with a stiff collar and a spotless serge suit for Prosper. All this took time to maneuver and, in Prosper's case, sometimes a struggle.

Lavinia sat in a pew near the front, between the two, who were, in general, well behaved, but whose good spirits sometimes got the better of them. She tried hard to fight against the pleasant lassitude which the warm air, drifting in through the open windows, seemed to intensify; she also tried hard to listen to the sermon, which bore no relation to either the Epistle or the Gospel or, indeed, to anything which might logically hold her attention. It dwelt on the reasons why parents should send their children to parochial, rather than to public, schools, and her children were already in a parochial school—indeed, Prosper had been there for nearly five years now and, in the meanwhile, Lavinia had listened to an average of four sermons a year urging such attendance. Moreover, this particular sermon, like most of its predecessors, had been delivered by a visiting priest who spoke English with a very strong accent of indeterminate origin, and it went on and on. Glancing surreptitiously at her watch, Lavinia saw that it had already lasted twenty minutes. Anne Marie had begun to fidget and Lavinia drew her closer, encouraging slumber and wishing that it were proper for her to take refuge in oblivion, also. Prosper was playing cat's cradle with small pieces of string. Lavinia shook her head, but as Prosper pretended not to see, she decided against making an issue of it, especially as the priest, having exhausted several aspects of his subject, had now embarked on still another and seemed likely to continue for ten minutes more at least.

Once the sermon was over, the service did not seem long, for nothing could rob the Mass of its beauty between the recitation of the Creed and the last Gospel. Ursin, Phares and Pauline were all waiting near the church steps to greet Lavinia and the children when they came out, and Clement, who had already gone to unhitch her buggy for her, lingered to chat a few minutes when he came back with it. This was the Sunday for visiting the Winslows, not the Villac-Primeaux', so the chat did not last long. But all three men took time to tell Lavinia that she would find the best stand of rice she had ever seen when she reached her father's farm.

"An' not nothin' goin' happen to it this year, no," Phares added reassuringly. "Brent is fixin' to start cuttin' tomorrow, him, an' he bound to be finish' with it biffo' the weather changes, or either I'm a po' judge, me. I guarantee you, yes, that ol' blowtorch sun got to be good fo' 'nother two weeks, at leas', an' with them binders we got now, us, a hundred acres gets done mo' quicker'n we used to could do twenty acres with reap hooks, like when Brent first came on the prairie."

"I hope you're right about the weather, *Oncle.*"

"Of course, he's right. How often have you known him to make a mistake?"

"Not often, Clement. But you know how it is—if you have one disappointment after another, all for the same reason, you get the feeling you're never going to have good luck in that particular direction. I'm afraid that's the way Father feels. And when he worries, Mother and I do, too."

"He ain't goin' have no kind of disappoint this here time, him," Phares said confidently. "Not no kind at all, no. Well, we got to be movin' on. . . . Nex' Sunday you comin' to us fo' true, Lavinia, yes?"

"Yes, for true."

They parted with mutual and sincere expressions of good will; there was genuine affection between Lavinia and the members of her husband's family; and, as a matter of fact, Prosper and Anne Marie would have enjoyed the Sundays they spent at the Primeaux-Villac farm more than they did those they spent at the Winslow farm, had it not been for Jim Garland's horses—or rather the horses he permitted them to call theirs, but which they rode only when they went visiting. Brent and Mary Winslow adored their grandchildren, but did not know how to give them the same rough-and-tumble good time as did their great-grandfather or their Cajun relatives. After their unexciting welcome had been bolstered up with milk and cookies—or perhaps milk and hard gingerbread, cut in fancy shapes—they bolted outdoors, to be seen no more, until they were called in for the invariably excellent dinner. And at dinner, conversation lagged, as far as they were concerned. Again they wanted to be out and off.

Lavinia's pleasant feeling of languor continued as they left the church and took the Parish Road out of Crowley. The children were chatting happily with each other, asking few questions, and she felt no compulsion either to amuse or instruct them; but somehow, her lassitude became tinged with nostalgia. She had been just about Prosper's age, she reflected, glancing at him fondly, when she had first gone over this road; and in the twenty-odd years that had elapsed since then, the face of the countryside had changed completely. There were fewer trees—the wide stretches of woodland which had formerly bordered the bayous had nearly all disappeared. On the other hand, there were many more acres under cultivation, many more fences, many more drainage ditches. While the old Indian trading post, where Bazinet had established his blacksmith shop, once marked the only sign of human habitation between a straggling village and a one-room cabin on the prairie, several neat farmhouses with adequate outbuildings were now scattered over the landscape, and the fields that surrounded these were well supplied with irrigation canals. Even more farms would have been individually owned, Lavinia knew, if her father had not steadily increased his holdings. He now owned a whole section—six hundred and forty acres—and nearly half of this was planted to rice. They would see only a small part of the vast acreage on their way to the house, because much of it was on the farther side of this and the garden, beyond the orange grove, the watermelon patch and the orchard; but, as they left the Parish Road and turned into the lane which had been given Brent's name, and which was bordered on one side by the Weller Canal and on the other by the West Field, Lavinia shook off her lethargy and spoke with pride.

"Prosper, look at that rice! Can you see any difference between that and the rice in Mr. Lowry's field, that we just passed?"

Prosper turned away from his sister and surveyed the scene with a gravity that was rare for him. "Yes," he said thoughtfully. "I don't see any red rice in it. Or any indigo weeds. And it's taller."

"Good! Anything else?"

His gaze became more searching. "It looks more even, too," he said at length.

"That's right. It hasn't any straight heads."

"I'd forgotten what they were called. But I remember now."

"I'll tell your grandfather at dinner how much you noticed. He'll be very pleased—just as I am. Get down and open the gate into the *passage* for me, will you?"

As a schoolgirl, Lavinia had given this name to the large, open square, bordered by the Weller Canal, the experimental garden and the two enclosures at right angles to each other, the first containing the stables, feed pens, warehouses, sheds and other outbuildings, the second the Winslow and Garland homes, Mary's flower garden and the vegetable garden. In local parlance, an enclosure like the latter was always designated as "the yard" and so was any similar space. On most farms no confusion resulted and no harm was done. But Mary's flower garden had so quickly achieved sizable dimensions, as well as outstanding importance because of its beauty, that it required protection; and, since it was impossible to teach any of the hired hands, or many of the visitors, to discontinue calling it anything but "the yard," it became necessary, for practical purposes, to find some other way of identifying the well-fenced area which was primarily intended as a place through which vehicles could pass or where they could be hitched, but which was also used as a grazing ground. One or two horses and a few cows were generally pastured there to keep the grass down, and these animals were always more closely associated with the family and its needs than those on the range. Lavinia's children felt a special affection for them, just as she had. Prosper and Anne Marie were also proud of the *passage* itself, and of the fact that their mother had thought up a good name for it. Indeed, up to now, no one else had succeeded in making a mere yard seem so impressive, through setting it apart from other yards by giving it a name of its own and keeping it green and shady and pleasant.

Prosper jumped down with alacrity to open the gate from the lane, and then ran over to pat the cows, which were peacefully chewing their cuds under a big oak tree, before he returned to help his mother hitch the buggy. Mary was standing at the garden gate, waiting to welcome them, and they all went into the house together. Brent rose from his measuring board and, as Lavinia had predicted, showed great pleasure at the news that Prosper had been so observant about the rice. He continued to talk to the boy about it while Mary and Lavinia put dinner on the table. In spite of their prosperity, the Winslows had retained their simple way of living and, on Sunday, had no outside help. The meal progressed in its customary quiet way and, as usual, the children rushed out the minute dinner was over. Brent went back to his measuring board and Lavinia helped Mary clear away the dishes. It was while they were doing these that they realized how dark it had suddenly become. Even though the days were already noticeably shorter than in midsummer, the kitchen was still normally flooded with sunshine until late afternoon on a bright day. The departure from this seasonal pattern was so exceptional that Mary commented on it as she reached up to the shelf where the lamps were kept and lighted the one which she took down.

"Perhaps you'd better carry this in to your father," she said, handing it to Lavinia and taking down a second lamp for the kitchen. Then, as she glanced at the clock, she added, "Why, it's only half-past three! I thought it must be later, that we'd sat talking longer than we realized. And we were just saying that we couldn't remember a more beautiful September day."

"It isn't beautiful any more." Lavinia went to the door and was almost immediately caught up in a gust of wind. "I must get the children back to the house," she said hurriedly, over her shoulder. "It's much cooler and I'm afraid we're in for a storm."

She ran into the yard, calling to Prosper and Anne Marie as she went. The swirling dust choked her and she coughed hard, trying to clear her throat and call more loudly. Her grandfather heard her and appeared at the entrance of his house, cupping his mouth in his hands and shouting to her reassuringly: the children were with him and he would keep them until the storm was over. But it was coming on fast. She had better get under shelter before she was soaked to the skin. He had hardly finished his admonition when the rain began to fall, not with refreshing lightness, but with destructive force. A flash of lightning zigzagged in a fiery path from the zenith of the black sky to the dark horizon, and the thunderclap that followed instantly thereafter was deafening. Lavinia turned and started back toward the kitchen, bowing her head and fighting her way along. She had gone only a few steps when a door slammed and, to her amazement, she realized that her father was coming toward her.

"I'm all right!" she cried. "I'll get there in a minute. Please go back, Father!"

"Go back! I'm going *on*—on to see what happens to my rice this time!"

He had pushed past her and, despite the hard going, was out of the yard before she could stop him and heading through the *passage* and the experimental garden toward the West Field beyond. Then, in a flash, it came over her that she must not try to stop him, that he was right; he had to see what was happening this time. Neither high winds nor pelting rain nor thunderbolts should keep him from his fields. If the rice were beaten down again, he was a beaten man. But if it were not! . . . He could not wait to find out whether this sudden, violent storm meant another defeat or ultimate victory.

Almost in the same moment that she understood this, Lavinia understood that she must not let him forge his way out to the field alone She must go with him over this last hard mile; it was her fight, as well as his, their joint battle. Again she bowed her head and struggled forward, thrusting her way, as he had, between the strands of barbed wire and reaching his side just as he came to the field.

While the storm was at its height, Lavinia did not try to look at her father. Buffeted by the wind, blinded by the rain, it was all she could do to maintain her footing and to glimpse, intermittently, the drenched field. But when the fury of the elements slackened and she could stand securely and see before her, she turned toward him and reached for his hand. He seemed unaware both of her glance and of her touch. His eyes were fixed on the rice. Despite the wind and the downpour, its golden heads still rose, erect and triumphant, above the strong straw and firm necks which supported them.

His gaze continued steady; there was disbelief in it, then wonderment, then joy; but it remained unwavering. It was his mouth which betrayed the emotion he could not control. His lips were quivering, and his long silence was not wholly one of volition; it was physically impossible for him to speak. Lavinia, who was also deeply moved, and whose eyes had misted, though her lips did not tremble, made no effort to hasten any expression of the feeling which was obviously too deep for utterance. This was a supreme moment in her father's life; probably only those in which he had received his bride and taken his newborn child in his arms could have been comparably rewarding. And for those, there had been no seemingly endless wait, no blind search, no desperate struggle. His beloved had returned his love in the same measure and with the same spontaneity that he had given it; their child had been the undelayed result of this happy and natural union. But for years he had known the bitterness of that hope deferred which maketh the heart sick; now, at last, he had found what, to him, was the tree of life. . . .

With patience and understanding, his daughter waited until he became aware of her touch and her gaze. The rainfall had ceased entirely, the thunder rumbled and the lightning flashed only in the distance, the dark clouds were shredding away, and the wind had died down to a gentle breeze when he at last drew a deep breath and spoke without faltering.

"I must go in and tell your mother."

"Yes, of course."

"Won't you come with me?"

"No, I'd like to stay here a little longer, if you don't mind. Besides, I think it would be better for you and her to be alone when you tell her. After all, she's had a share in your victory."

"You've had a share in it, too."

"A very small one, compared to hers."

He hesitated, tardily conscious of her drenched condition, though still unconcerned about his own. "You're wet through, Lavinia. You ought to get into some dry clothes."

"The sun will dry me off in no time. It'll be shining in full force any minute now. Look! There's a rainbow!"

"So there is! If we were superstitious, we'd think it was an omen!"

"Well, let's pretend we are. What's the harm?"

"None. Of course, there often is a rainbow, after a hard storm, but that's neither here nor there." He hesitated again. "Do you remember telling me that I ought to give my rice a name, the day I came to the mill so utterly discouraged, about a year ago?"

"Yes, have you thought of one?"

394

"I had my first inkling that same day, when I looked at the blue walls and sample boxes as I went out. But I couldn't seem to connect their color with anything that had much meaning—much symbolism. Now it's come to me. We've got what we thought was impossible after all, haven't we?"

"Indeed we have."

"All right. I'm going to tell your mother we have her blue camellia."

"Oh, Father, that's great! A great name for a great discovery!"

"You don't think it matters because we've found it in my garden, instead of hers, do you?"

"No, she'd rather have it that way. Do go quickly, Father, and tell her."

He needed no further urging. He was smiling now, thinking not only of his beautiful strong rice, but of the surprise and pleasure the name he had given it would bring to his wife. Lavinia watched him hurrying in the direction of the house and smiled, too. She had no wish to go with him. The presence of a third person, even their daughter, would be an intrusion on this meeting between husband and wife and on their subsequent communion. Besides, to Lavinia, solitude had become more welcome than companionship. There was no one with whom she wanted to share this moment.

She unpinned her hair and shook it down over her shoulders, so that it might dry more quickly; it hung about her like a bright veil, as golden as the fields which were now shining in the sun. Then she wrung out the wet garments which clung to her as if they had been sculptured; thus revealed, her figure took on not only a statuesque grace, but a feminine loveliness of line which she would have hidden at the mere suspicion of an admiring gaze. Any normal man, seeing her as she stood there, would have felt a sudden quickening of the senses. But she herself was oblivious of her beauty; the beauty of her surroundings absorbed her completely.

The rainbow was fading slowly, but the clouds massed on the horizon retained much of its radiance, and this radiance was reflected on the earth. Gradually, the clouds drifted away, too, leaving the sky as completely clear as it had been that morning—as clear and as blue as the imagined color of that mythical flower which was to be a symbol of their success. Blue Camellia! The name, like its significance, was perfect.

395

Yet it was not of her father's success or of the name that was to herald it to the world that Lavinia began to think as she stood alone, her gaze on the golden fields. These in themselves had become a symbol—a symbol of plenty with which to feed a hungry and needy world, a symbol of fellowship with all those people, hitherto alien to her, who were dedicated to the same great task as the one which she now saw clearly as her life's work. Henceforth, she would put into this work not only all the earnestness, all the intelligence, all the effort of which she was capable, as she had from the beginning; she would also put into it all the love which, in another direction, had gone unrequited, and for which she now saw a fulfillment greater than she had then envisioned. Her father's triumph had released her from the past. She would not withdraw from the world any longer. She would seek out her fellow workers, not only those who lived near by, but those on the other side of the globe, who labored on terraces and in paddies. She would learn what she could from them and teach them what she could in return. She would take the children with her and visit all those countries in South America which were still only names on a map and statistics in a book; she would go to Japan and to Java. These travels would bear no relation to those she had so desperately contemplated in the first days of her widowhood, when her one thought had been of flight, of escape. These would be undertaken in search of knowledge which she would share with those she found in the course of her happy wanderings, and then bring back with her to enrich the place which was her home. And she would be able to accomplish all this because at last there would be abundance instead of emptiness in her heart. . . .

She never knew how long she stood alone, pondering, with an ever-increasing sense of peace and compensation. But she was suddenly aware, for the first time since she could remember, of the longing and the need for prayer —a prayer which would be, at one and the same time, a petition and a thanksgiving. In the fading light, she sank to her knees and bowed her head. She needed no bell to let her know that, for her, this was the hour of the Angelus.

NOTE

The greater part of the work on BLUE CAMELLIA was done at Compensation, the place acquired in Crowley on purpose to give me a writing center at the scene of my story. I was the happy possessor of the house and grounds comprising this pleasant property for ten years, but sold it under the mistaken impression that my work in Southwestern Louisiana was practically done, so the book was finished in nearby Lafayette, where I was fortunately able to secure a pied-a-terre. Work on the book was also done at Beauregard House in New Orleans; The Oxbow at Newbury, Vermont; Pine Grove Farm, North Haverhill, New Hampshire; London, England; Paris, France and the S.S. EXETER of the American Export Lines while en route from New York City to Jerusalem.

REFERENCES

Files of the Crowley SIGNAL—1886 through 1910, inclusive.

The SIGNAL Annual—1908.

Golden Anniversary Number Crowley SIGNAL;—1889 through 1949.

Louisiana Historical Quarterly—October, 1944.

History of Crowley, Louisiana by Velma Lea Hair. (Reprinted from above.)

SADLER'S EXCELSIOR GEOGRAPHY published by William H. Sadler, New York, 1875.

THROUGH STORYLAND TO SUNSET SEAS by H. S. Kneedler, published by the A. H. Pugh Printing Co., Cincinnati, 1896.

LAND OF PLENTY published by Farm Equipment Institute, Chicago, 1950.

HARVEST TRIUMPHANT The Story of Massey-Harris by Merrill Denison, published by Dodd, Mead & Company, New York, 1949.

THE PRODUCTION AND MARKETING OF RICE by John Norman Efferson, published by Simmons Press, New Orleans.

THE AMERICAN CAMELLIA YEARBOOK—1946 and 1947, edited by R. J. Wilmot, published by the American Camellia Society, Gainesville, Florida.

A CAROLINA RICE PLANTATION OF THE FIFTIES by Herbert Ravenel Sass, published by William Morrow and Company, New York, 1936.

A WOMAN RICE PLANTER by Patience Pennington, published by The Macmillan Company, New York, 1913.

COME HOME A Romance of the Louisiana Rice-Lands by Stella G. S. Perry, published by Frederick A. Stokes Company, 1923.

HISTORIC NEW ORLEANS, weekly feature on CATHOLIC ACTION OF THE SOUTH by Roger Baudier.

LOUISIANA CREOLE DIALECT by James F. Broussard, published by Louisiana State University Press, 1942.

LOUISIANA FRENCH FOLK SONGS by Irene Therese Whitford, published by Louisiana State University Press, 1939.

LES ACADIENS LOUISIANAIS ET LEUR PARLER *publie par* Jay K. Ditchy, Professeur a l'Universite Tulane, L'INSTITUT FRANCAIS DE WASHINGTON, Published by The Johns Hopkins Press.

LES DANSES RONDES. Louisiana French Folk Songs collected, arranged and edited by Marie del Norte Theriot and Catherine

Brookshire Blanchet. R. E. Blanchet, Distributor, Abbeville, La., 1955.

In addition to these newspapers, magazines, pamphlets and books, which I have consulted personally, John Hall Jacobs, Chief Librarian of the New Orleans Public Library has consulted and caused to be consulted others in my behalf and has kindly given me the benefit of his findings.

The Branch Bearers

BY Glen Petrie

ONE OF THE BEST HISTORICAL ROMANCES SINCE THE FRENCH LIEUTENANT'S WOMAN!

Ten years had elapsed since Chalmers had seen the beautiful Clementina. In the London fog as they met again, his loving feelings flamed again. Nothing would stand in the way of their passionate love affair—even her revelation of a shady romantic past. Until one day, he learned of the mysterious deaths of each of her former lovers—and shuddered at the thought he might be next....

THE BRANCH BEARERS A HAUNTING VICTORIAN LOVE STORY

POCKET BOOKS

▼ AT YOUR BOOKSTORE OR MAIL THE COUPON BELOW ▼

P103/4